TANGLED TIES

A NOVEL

SHOSHANA SCHWARTZ

SAPIR PRESS
JERUSALEM / NEW YORK

Originally published in serial form in *Mishpacha* magazine, 2011.

FELDHEIM PUBLISHERS
POB 43163 / Jerusalem, Israel

208 Airport Executive Park
Nanuet, NY 10954

www.feldheim.com

10 9 8 7 6 5 4 3 2 1

Printed in Israel

For Grandpa

כל עצמותי תאמרנה...
(תהלים לה:י)

Acknowledgments

BESIDES THE OBVIOUS *siyata diShamaya* I was blessed with when writing this book, there are many people whose help was invaluable:

Batya Ruddell, my incredibly essential writing partner and dear friend, who went over every chapter, sometimes several times, until it was well past "good enough."

Deena Nataf of Feldheim Publishers Jerusalem, who took a serialized story and turned it into a work that flows as a novel should. And to the rest of the Feldheim staff, among them: Bracha Steinberg (design), Rebecca Aber (typesetting), and Michael Silverstein (cover and graphics), whose workmanship is apparent on every page and who pulled together to meet tight deadlines without compromising on professionalism.

My sister, Dr. Marcie Strasser, who helped me understand countless medical details and checked over my work for accuracy from ER through discharge.

Toby Gershbaum, who dipped into her storehouse of *chochmas hachaim* to help keep my story true to life.

Naama Schechter, whose insights on enmeshed families helped me shape the overall structure of the family.

Miriam Lewitan and Susan Reuben, for their clever (and amusing) advice from *shadchanim* who've been there.

Michoel Guttman, for sharing his technical knowledge of wiring and renovations.

Ephraim Siegel, from Hatzolah Flatbush, for providing me with the details of emergency procedures.

A special thank you to Bassi Gruen, my editor at *Mishpacha* magazine. Working with a professional of Bassi's caliber has been, and continues to be, an experience I will always treasure.

Most of all, thanks to my husband, Sender, who not only encouraged me chapter by chapter but also took over at home (in more ways than one!) so that I could... focus.

TANGLED TIES

1

TOVA SAT AT THE kitchen table and watched her oldest son alternately rub his chin and push string beans from one side of his plate to the other. "What's the matter, Shimon?"

"The matter with what?" Shimon asked, bringing his eyes back into focus.

"You've barely eaten. A thin slice of meatloaf, a few forkfuls of potatoes—that's not dinner, it's barely even a snack."

"Sorry, Mommy, I'm just not very hungry." He pushed his plate away and slumped forward, arms crossed and elbows on the table. "Can you tell me again exactly what the *shadchan* said?"

Tova smiled. "She said that at this point, Ilana is perfectly comfortable with you calling her directly."

Shimon's Adam's apple rose up and plunged back down. "But what if I'm not comfortable doing that?"

"Well, why shouldn't you be? You've met her five times already."

"I don't know, exactly. It's just sort of a big leap. You know, till now we went through Mrs. Krieger, and it was working just fine that way. I don't see why we need to change." His eyes were open wide, his brow furrowed slightly.

Tova studied Shimon. His light brown hair brought out the blue in his eyes, and the particular expression he was wearing, a sweet mixture of innocence and shyness, made her want to hold him close and hand him an ice cream cone. "I guess she feels ready to move on. That's a good sign, isn't it?"

"I suppose."

"Shimon, you said this has potential."

"It... it does."

"So what's wrong?"

"Nothing's wrong." Shimon grabbed his napkin and twisted the ends into tight little points. "It's just too fast. I'm not comfortable talking to her on the phone yet."

"Well, can you talk to her in person? Do you have what to say to each other when you meet?"

"Yes." The answer was definite, no wishy-washiness there.

"So what's the difference?"

A small shrug of the shoulders was his answer.

"Look, I don't think you need to read into this so much. She obviously enjoys your company and wants to see if this will work out. It's just a matter of not needing a go-between to plan your meetings. That doesn't mean she's ready to get engaged."

"I know, but shouldn't she wait until *I* decide not to go through the *shadchan*?"

"*Tatteleh*, how complicated do you think the phone call will be, anyway?"

Shimon released his elbows and drummed his fingers on the table.

"You'll call, ask how she's doing, make up a time, and *fertig*. It's just being practical."

At the word *practical*, his shoulders relaxed a bit. "That's exactly what you said when you met her, remember? You said from the way she dressed you could tell she was practical and refined."

"Yes, and sweet, just like we heard." Tova sometimes felt as if she did nothing but research, especially now that both of her *bachurim* were in *shidduchim*. She didn't mind checking out families, but getting into the nitty-gritty was a bit overwhelming. Some girls were *ehrlich*, some were outgoing, but it seemed that every single one was a "fine, *frum* girl." Yet she had a good feeling about Ilana. "Don't you need to be getting back to yeshivah now?"

"Yes, my *chavrusa* is very punctual. Practical, you know." His boyish smile drove the worry out of his eyes.

"It's pretty hot out tonight. Take a cold drink with you."

"Okay." He went to the refrigerator. "Dr. Pepper?"

"It's for Brachie," Tova explained. "I want everything to be perfect for her when she comes home."

"Like it was for me after my year in Eretz Yisrael," Shimon remembered.

Tova smiled to herself. Shimon's stint in Eretz Yisrael had amounted to exactly one *zman*. He said the learning was better for him in his local yeshivah in New York, but she and Avner were pretty sure Shimon chose it because it was the most appropriate place close to home—and with no dorm. And so what? It was healthy for a boy to be close to his parents, and Tova loved having him home. Personally, she didn't understand the need for any of the children to go away until they were married. But Avner felt strongly that a year away was important.

"Learn well."

Tova tidied up the kitchen and made her way upstairs. She poked her head into Meir's room before she remembered that he was at a friend's house. Then she continued on to Brachie's room. She stood in the doorway and looked around. Cute knick-knacks, flowery bedspread, glued-together puzzles with photos of waterfalls and sunsets decorating pale pink walls—a room both young and feminine. Tova wondered how the post-seminary Brachie would differ from the high school girl who'd left nine months ago. Their phone conversations were not particularly deep, but she could hear Brachie practically floating through the phone line. Tova had a feeling it would take Brachie more time to get grounded than it had taken the boys.

One thing was certain; for Brachie, *shidduchim* were not even on the horizon.

Even before the bus started moving, Brachie stared out the window, willing herself to sear every last detail into her brain. Rena dropped down into the seat next to her, careful not to disturb the middle-aged woman sitting directly across, who was saying Tehillim.

"This is kind of depressing," Brachie said, not taking her eyes off the sun-bleached stones.

"Endings are always hard," Rena agreed, staring over her friend's shoulder.

"I'm not going to let it end."

"What do you mean?"

"I'm not going to let it end—the year, the *kedushah* of Eretz Yisrael, the focus on what life's really all about." Brachie turned to Rena. "We may be getting on a plane tomorrow, but I'm not going to land. This high is going to stay with me forever."

Rena smiled and sat back in her seat. "And how will you accomplish what hundreds, make that thousands, of girls before you haven't?"

"Oh, some of them have. I don't know how, exactly, but I plan on staying away from bad influences."

The Tehillim was lowered a half-inch, then raised again.

"Like what?"

"Like college, for one thing."

Rena shook her head. "Come on, Brachie. No one expects you to go to a regular college. There are some really good *frum* programs out there. Day classes, evening classes, you name it. You can get a degree and stay all pure and holy. It's not a contradiction, you know."

The bus lurched to the right, and Brachie leaned hard into the window. "I know, but who needs a degree?"

"Um, Brachie, didn't you tell me just yesterday that your mother *insists* you get a degree?"

"Yeah, and she didn't mean regular college, either. She was looking into some places with separate programs. But three or four years of school? No way! I thought about it, and I'm going to become a *sheitel macher*. It's perfect! I really want to end up in Lakewood, and I hear that besides babysitting, that's about the only thing you can do without commuting."

"That's not true. My sister lives in Lakewood, and she says you just have to think out of the box. And anyway, who says you'll marry someone who wants to learn in Lakewood?"

"Whatever." Brachie flapped her right hand. "*Sheitels* is something I can do anywhere, right?"

"Yeah. But why *sheitels*?"

"Because it's the fastest."

Rena burst out laughing. "You're going to choose a career based on what's fastest? You don't even like to play with your own hair! You always clip it up in a half-pony."

Brachie tossed her head, tight brown ringlets cascading just past her shoulder.

"Sorry, Brachie. I'm not laughing at you. You just surprised me," Rena explained.

Brachie folded her hands primly on her lap.

"Honestly, I apologize. You'll be great at whatever you do."

A small smile crept up Brachie's cheeks. "You think so?"

"For sure. But do you really think your mother will go for it?"

"I don't see any reason why not."

Rena hiked her purse up higher onto her shoulder. "And I don't see what the big rush is. It's not like you're engaged and need to start making money immediately."

"Think of it this way. A three-month course is perfect. I can start dating right away, and by the time I've finished the course and can start earning money, I could be engaged already!"

"But who says—"

A short stop halted all conversation. The woman across from Rena grabbed the pole for support. A shopping bag at her feet tipped over, and apples spilled out in every direction. Rena jumped up and chased after them before they could roll to the stairs. She smiled as she put them back into the woman's bag while Brachie crouched down under her seat and fished out two more.

"Thank you, girls," the woman said in English. "That was very kind."

"You're welcome," Brachie answered for both of them. "Glad we could help."

The woman closed her Tehillim and slipped it into a large, beige canvas bag with lots of buckles. "Did I hear you say you were leaving?"

"Yes, we are. In..." Brachie checked her watch, "less than twenty-four hours." She locked eyes with Rena.

"Don't take it so hard," the woman said. "You'll be back before you know it."

"Amen," Rena whispered.

Brachie's eyes were drawn back to the window. The Old City walls beckoned her. Multifaceted, multihued, burned and bullet-ridden and holy. When *would* she be back?

"Zelda Fogel. I'm from New York, visiting my children and grandchildren." She turned to Brachie. "And where are you from?"

It was hard for Brachie to turn her eyes away from the view

that the window of the bus afforded. "New York."

"Boro Park?"

"No, Flatbush. P and 32nd," Brachie added, before Mrs. Fogel could ask.

"P and 32nd," she mused, studying Brachie's face. "Let me guess. You're a Lehrfeld."

Brachie's eyes widened.

Mrs. Fogel laughed. "I know your mother. You look a bit like her." She turned to the girl directly in front of her. "And you? I don't believe I caught your name."

"Rena Kaplan. From Denver."

"Denver. Sorry, not familiar territory."

The bus rounded the corner and pulled up to the last stop, and Brachie craned her neck to see the Kosel through the window.

"It was nice meeting you two," Mrs. Fogel said as she clutched her bags and pulled herself to her feet. "Perhaps we'll be doing business together before long."

Brachie stood and smiled. "Oh, will you let me do your *sheitel* once I learn how?

"My *sheitel*?" Mrs. Fogel laughed, a high-pitched, tinkling sound. "No, my dear, I'm a *shadchan*."

Tova smoothed out the tablecloth, making sure the stripes were perfectly parallel to the fully opened table.

"Too bad I didn't bring my measuring tape," Aidel said. "Then you'd be absolutely sure the stripes were even on both sides."

It took only a second for Tova to realize that her mother was teasing her. She smiled. "I just want everything to be perfect for Brachie's homecoming."

"It will be beautiful, as always, and she'll be pleased. Some people spoil their children rotten. You spoil yours sweet."

Her mother smiled in her special way, and Tova felt a familiar comfort wrap itself around her shoulders. She walked to the kitchen and came back holding a stack of matching napkins. "What time should Avner come pick you up?"

"Pick us up? Tovaleh, I told you we're not coming for dinner."

"But I don't understand. Avner will bring you and Tatty, so Tatty doesn't have to walk. Brachie will be so happy to see both of you."

"Feh! First she needs to see her parents, not her grandparents. We'd just be in the way."

"But—"

"Don't you remember when Shimon came home? He just needed his mama, needed you to fuss over him and give him all your attention."

Tova began folding the napkins into perfect triangles. "Of course I remember."

"He gave me a peck on the cheek and then ignored me and Tatty."

"He didn't mean—"

Aidel waved her hands. "He did nothing wrong, you don't have to excuse him. He just needed his mama." She raised one eyebrow and threw Tova a sly grin. "Still does, doesn't he?" Tova made no comment, and Aidel continued, "Brachie is a lot like Shimon. She'll want some pampering."

"I'm looking forward." Tova stood still, a smile lighting up her face.

"Enjoy, Tovaleh. Ask Brachie to put me on her long list of phone calls."

Tova hid a frown. There was no talking to her mother once she'd made up her mind. "At least let Avner drive you home, he should be back from *maariv* any minute."

"*Sheifeleh*," Aidel chuckled, "my legs work just fine. I walked here, and I'm walking back. There's a wonderful summer-evening breeze."

Tova escorted her mother to the front door. "I'll send someone by for the rugelach, if you're still planning to make them."

"I am, and I'll bring them over myself, early enough so you
can make some fancy-shmancy arrangement." With a nod and a
smile, Aidel was gone.

Shimon paced the living room, checking his watch every time
his polished shoes brushed the edge of the carpet. "It's seven
o'clock already," he announced.

"Six fifty-eight," Meir corrected him.

Shimon didn't react. He'd reached the other end of the carpet and checked his watch again. "Mommy, can you call Tatty
and find out when they'll be back?"

"Mommy just called ten minutes ago," Meir answered for her.

"Maybe just find out if they're almost here," Shimon pleaded,
turning his back on Meir.

"Why are you so nervous?" Meir asked Shimon.

Shimon threw a desperate look at Tova.

"I think I hear a car. Meir, is that them?"

Meir stepped over to the window. "It is them!" He flew to
the front door and threw it open.

Brachie was already halfway up the front steps. After a hurried hello to Meir, she flung herself at her mother.

Tova wrapped her arms around Brachie and held tight. A
burst of emotion shot outward from her heart, and tiny tears
tickled her eyes. Words poured forth without thought—words
of welcome, of happiness, of love. She couldn't let go. After some
time—Tova could not say how long—Brachie stepped back and
they studied each other.

Brachie's face had filled out, her clear, pale skin tanned and
dotted with freckles. Her hazel eyes glowed, revealing none of
the exhaustion she must be feeling.

For the briefest second, Tova felt self-conscious under Brachie's scrutiny. Did Brachie notice that she had also put on a few pounds? Her *sheitel*, bobbed and just this side of blonde, had not changed, but her once-smooth skin had developed a few new creases. She moved past the thought quickly; she only wanted to focus on Brachie being home. She clutched her daughter's arm and steered her inside, leaving Meir and Avner to bring in the luggage.

Brachie tried to look everywhere at once, drinking in both the familiarity and the strangeness of home. She studied everything in sight and then without warning bounded up the stairs.

Tova followed and found Brachie standing in her room, nearly spinning in circles.

"Mommy!" she squealed. "It's perfect!"

Tova leaned against the doorframe. "I'm glad you like it."

"I *love* the way you kept everything exactly where it was before." She opened the closet door. "It's like I never left! I'm going to start unpacking. Can you ask Meir to bring up my suitcases?"

"First eat something," Tova said.

"I'm not hungry, Mommy."

"Of course you are," Tova smiled. "I made steak and mashed potatoes."

"Wow! Thanks, Mommy. I'll be right down."

Tova's hand caressed the banister on her way down the stairs. It felt so... *right* to have Brachie home. And with *bein hazmanim* right around the corner, Yoni would be home from Lakewood, too. A pleasant tingle ran down her spine.

When she reached the kitchen, she was greeted by a head of dirty blonde hair hovering inside the refrigerator.

"What are you looking for?" Tova asked.

"Mustard," Meir answered.

"Second shelf, right side, behind the watermelon." She paused. "Why mustard?"

"Yoni says *bachurim* eat it with everything. I want to try it with steak."

Bachurim eat mustard on everything? Yoni had picked up all sorts of strange ideas in yeshivah, and since Pesach, Meir had been spouting Yoni-isms as if they were *Torah l'Moshe miSinai*.

Meir found the mustard, Tova handed him a saltshaker, and he disappeared into the dining room. She followed, carrying a bowl of mashed potatoes. Two more trips, and everything was ready. Shimon was already seated, but his feet tapped the floor while he continuously checked his watch.

Tova sat down next to Avner. Their eyes met, a silent, comfortable exchange. They were only waiting for Brachie.

After several minutes, Meir said, "What's with Brachie? Why isn't she coming down?"

Tova pursed her lips. Her question exactly. They were all waiting for her, the guest of honor. It wasn't every day a girl came home from a year away in seminary! She smoothed out a wrinkle in the tablecloth and moved the saltshaker an inch closer to Avner.

Avner gave her a gentle smile and sat back in his chair, hands folded in front of him. He opened his mouth to speak but closed it as Brachie entered.

She flounced into the dining room, a cordless phone pressed to her face. "I can't believe you got a job teaching there, that school is *so* hard to get into." She sat down next to Tova, oblivious to the faces around her.

Tova stared, unsure how to react. Dinnertime had always been family time. Not exactly quiet, but together.

"Brachie, can you please pass the salt?" Avner said.

Brachie paused mid-sentence and looked around her. "Oh. I have to go, we're eating dinner. Call you back later, 'kay?" A giggle, then, "'Bye." She looked around for the salt. "It's right in front of you, Tatty."

"Uh, so it is. Thank you." He sprinkled a tiny amount over his meat.

"Did you bring me something?" Meir asked.

"Of course," Brachie said.

"She'll show you *after* dinner," Tova said. "How was your flight, was it crowded?"

"Totally. Me and Rena were stuck between a young mother with a sleeping baby on one side, and a snoring older woman on the other." She sipped her Dr. Pepper. "Poor Rena! She has a three-hour layover till her connecting flight."

"What's Rena doing next year?" Tova asked.

"Probably Sarah Schneirer. Unless she gets married first, that is."

Tova saw Shimon turn and stare at Brachie. Marriage seemed to be the only topic that could hold his interest at the moment. During the rest of the meal, his eyes came in and out of focus as Brachie caught up on family and neighborhood news. Of course, Tova and Brachie spoke every day on the phone, but it just wasn't the same as being together.

Tova encouraged everyone to eat, but she herself barely touched the food; her heart was full and she had little appetite. She would have liked to linger a bit more, but Shimon kept checking his watch, his face questioning his mother. At exactly seven forty-five, he jumped up and raced up the stairs, mumbling, "I have to run."

Brachie followed him with her eyes as she collected the plates. She turned to Avner. "Tatty, what's with Shimon? He's so jumpy."

"I'll clean up here soon," Tova said. "Do you want to give Meir his present now?"

"Sure. Anyway, I want to unpack, so if you can bring up the suitcases, Meir, I'll look for your present."

Meir ran to the living room, and Brachie and her parents climbed the stairs ahead of him. When they reached her room Brachie said, "Um, Mommy, I'm sorry, I have lots of laundry."

Tova laughed. "I'll be happy to do it for you."

"Brachie," Avner said, surprised, "you were away for the whole year. Didn't you learn how to do laundry?"

"Oh, no, we had laundry service. Once a week, they would come and pick up our laundry, and it came back clean and folded."

Avner stared.

"And ironed."

"I see." Avner cleared his throat. "Well, Brachie, I'm sure now that you're home you'll learn to do laundry, and iron, and..."

Now it was Brachie's turn to stare. Avner looked at her, then at Tova. Apparently, neither one of them shared his thoughts. He gave a mental shrug. If Brachie didn't want to do laundry, and Tova was happy to do it, he certainly wasn't going to mix in. It just seemed strange to him that after a year away, things would slide back to exactly how they were before Brachie left.

Meir came huffing into the room wheeling a large black duffle. "What's in here, rocks?"

"It has wheels," Brachie said.

"I couldn't exactly wheel it up the stairs." He paused for breath. "How did you get that thing off the conveyor belt?"

"Tatty took it off for me. Bring up the other one, please. Your present's not in here."

"How do you know? They're exactly the same."

"The markings are different. Look." She pointed to a patch of duct tape near the side handle. "This one is a smiley face. Yours is in the heart."

Meir rolled his eyes and went to get the other duffle bag.

"I brought something for each of you, too."

"You didn't have to do that," Tova said.

"But I wanted to! To show you how much I missed you, and to thank you for such an amazing year. I shopped for *days* till I found just the right thing."

Avner hid a smile. It was his money she had spent! But he knew what Tova would say: It was the thought, and the effort, that counted.

Meir's voice was heard grunting up the stairs.

"I better go help him," Avner said.

The two of them returned, Meir giving the duffle a last kick through the door. "This one's even worse."

Brachie sat down and pulled open the zipper. A jumble of clothing, shoes, and plastic bags stuffed with unidentifiable objects tumbled out. "I didn't have time to really pack properly," she said. "I just threw everything in. *Baruch Hashem*, it all fit after I gave away some stuff." She started pulling things out of the bag and tossing them to the floor, scattering them about on the carpet. "I also threw out lots of my old shoes. I never did so much walking in my whole life."

If these were the shoes that she kept, Avner wondered how many pairs she'd actually taken along to begin with. "What kinds of things did you give away?"

"Shampoo, soap, toothpaste, Ziplocs, Q-tips, that sort of thing. I had tons left over."

Avner thought back to when he'd seen this process in reverse, nearly ten months ago. He knew she'd taken along a stash of toiletries, but surely not enough to last so long and have so much left over that she could give some away. "Didn't you use any? I seem to remember your packing a lot of that up."

"Of course I used it. And when I ran out, Mommy sent me more."

"Mommy sent more?" Avner raised an eyebrow at Tova. "How?"

"Oh, there's always someone going," Tova said.

"Wouldn't it be easier to just buy whatever she needed over there?"

"I couldn't always get the brands that I needed. And I didn't always have time to shop, either."

"Besides," Tova added, "I sent Brachie other things, too."

"Such as?"

"Chocolate chip cookies, blueberry muffins, Dr. Pepper... all her favorites."

Brachie sat back down on the floor, eyes far away. "Mommy's packages were awesome. I got one almost every week. I'd be sitting there, in my dorm room, schmoozing with my friends about life, getting married—you know, the important things—and we'd be munching on a box of Mommy's famous brownies."

Mother and daughter exchanged a warm smile.

Avner wasn't sure if he should be amused or concerned. If going away for the year was meant to make Brachie less dependent and more mature, how did sending her weekly care packages promote that? And how could he have been so completely unaware of this?

Meir was pulling at a wire, trying to find out what electronic device was attached to the hidden end inside the duffle bag.

"Wait, don't pull that too hard. It's my MP3 player." Brachie leaned forward and reached deep into the bag, finally pulling out a slightly crushed package that was once neatly wrapped and tied with a blue bow.

"Thanks," Meir said, peeling off the paper. He shook it, then pulled apart a layer of tape, flipped open the box and pulled out a can. He peered at the English writing and squinted. "I don't get it."

"It's air from Israel."

Meir looked at the can again. "Huh?"

Brachie smiled, her eyes drifting off again to somewhere else. "Air from Israel. From Eretz Yisrael. It's holy air!"

"Holy air? Uh..."

"It sounds like there are more things in the box," Avner said, keeping a straight face. *Holy air?*

"Oh, right." Meir poked his fingers into the box and took out another can, this one with Hebrew writing. "Israeli Coca-Cola?"

"Right. You drink the soda then keep the can."

Meir's face fell.

"There's one more thing inside."

Slowly, almost reluctantly, Avner thought, Meir reached his fingers inside the box again. He pulled out a photo key chain.

"It's Kever Rachel," Brachie explained. "Only it doesn't really look like that anymore. The whole outside is built up into a big complex for security."

Meir clutched the key chain and dropped his hand beside him.

"How about a Thank you," Tova prompted.

"Thanks," Meir said flatly. He collected his presents, mumbled something about homework, and left the room.

"Do you think he liked them?" Brachie asked hopefully.

"I'm sure he appreciates that you thought of him," Avner said.

The answer seemed good enough for Brachie, who seemed still to be floating in the airplane above the clouds.

"And here's something for you, Tatty. Sorry I couldn't wrap it."

It was a *shtender* made of olive wood with sketches of the Old City skyline and his name at the top. "Thank you," he smiled. "This will be perfect for those long, hot summer Shabbos afternoons so I can learn at home."

"I'm glad you like it. And this is for you, Mommy."

Tova fingered a slim box with silver paper and opened it. Under a sheet of tissue paper lay a stiff plastic apron with a picture of the Old City walls and emblazoned with the words

"Yerushalmi Balebuste." Tova's mouth twitched and she looked at Avner.

"Just what you needed!" he cried. "Didn't you mention that the lace on your every-day apron is coming apart?"

"Yes, I did say that," Tova managed. Then she smiled widely and kissed Brachie's cheek. "Thank you so much, Brachie, it's perfect!"

Brachie's face shone. "I knew you'd love it. Reminds me of Yerushalayim."

The Yerushalayim theme was not lost on Avner.

"I have something for Shimon, too. Guess I'll give it to him tomorrow. Oh, and I also have Yoni's present. When's he coming home?"

"He has an out Shabbos next week."

"I guess I'll store it, somewhere or other." She opened and closed the desk drawers. As she slid the top drawer back into place, something caught her attention. "What's this, Mommy?"

"That's the brochure from Parnes."

"Parnes?"

"You know, the school that offers the programs I told you about."

Brachie scanned the brochure, a crease denting her forehead. "I don't remember talking about this."

Tova laughed. "You were probably too busy shopping for presents. Have a look, you'll see that I circled the good ones."

Brachie looked more carefully and found notations all along the margins, with two topics circled in red pen. "I don't understand."

"What's not to understand? You're going to Parnes, and you'll get a degree."

Brachie's shoulders sagged, her lower lip quivered. She looked like she wanted to say something, but no words came out.

"What kind of degree?" Avner asked for both of them.

Tova turned to him. "Well, she has a choice, of course. Either medical billing and coding or graphic design."

Avner snuck a peek at Brachie. Her freckles were becoming more prominent, and she hadn't yet found her voice. "Those sound, uh, interesting. When would Brachie need to submit her application?"

"No need," Tova said with triumph. "She's already registered."

Brachie's mouth dropped open. "Medical billing?" she managed after a long pause. "I never even heard of it."

"Medical billing and coding. You haven't heard of it because it's not something all the *frum* girls are doing—yet. Now that this program opened up, you'll have first crack at the jobs. It's a great field."

"A great field for what?"

"For earning a decent living. Think about it, there are dozens of *frum* doctors' offices within two miles of here."

Brachie sucked in a breath. "You want me to work in an *office*?"

"Of course, *sheifeleh*, that's where the money is."

"But I can't work in an office!" Brachie cried.

Tova tilted her head to the side, her brow sinking down slightly. "Brachie, we talked about this on the phone, remember? You said you didn't want to go to a full-time program. You didn't want special ed, or PT or OT or any of those fields, you didn't want computer programming or accounting or business. So what's left?"

"Mommy!" Shimon's voice called from down the hall. "Where's my tie?"

Cupping Brachie's chin in her hand, Tova said, "Brachie, Shimon needs my help. You're tired, and now is not the best time to discuss this. Why don't you just make me a pile of laundry, and leave the rest of the unpacking for tomorrow."

Avner moved aside as Tova hurried out the door. He saw the

tears welling up in Brachie's eyes, and his stomach dropped. He ran a hand along his salt-and-pepper beard and up through his jet-black hair.

Brachie plopped down on her bed. Elbows resting on her knees, she raised her eyes to her father and whined, "Tatty, I don't want to work in an office!"

That much seemed pretty obvious. What was less clear to him is how this situation arose in the first place. From Tova's perspective, she and Brachie had discussed this on the phone, with the conclusion that Brachie would get a degree in a field other than the many she'd objected to. Presumably, Tova had done careful research—Avner would not have expected otherwise—and settled on these two choices as the most suitable for Brachie.

But obviously something had been lost over the phone line. Brachie clearly did not have a desk job in mind. Had they discussed the details and Brachie had been too involved in preparing to leave, too oblivious to focus on mundane details such as career choices?

He needed more information before he could discuss it further with Brachie. But, as Tova said, now was just not the time. Shimon didn't need only tie-finding and, in all likelihood, tie-straightening and hat brushing; he needed moral support. A sixth date! For the briefest moment, Avner allowed himself to consider the possibility of Shimon standing under the *chuppah*. Before his thoughts carried him too far, though, he pulled himself back to the present and cleared his throat.

"Don't worry, no one's forcing you to do anything. I see you're upset, and this is something we'll talk about more."

Brachie's eyes looked hopeful.

"I don't even know what medical coding is," Avner added. "But Mommy's right, and this is, uh, not the best time."

"Okay, Tatty. Really, I'm so tired, I can't even think straight."

She pointed to the smiley duffle and covered a yawn. "I'm going to leave all this for tomorrow."

"I'm sure that's fine. Have a good night." He hung back and let his eyes linger on his only daughter's face. "Welcome home, sweetheart. It's good to have you back."

As he finished speaking, the phone rang.

Brachie jumped up off the bed with a sudden burst of energy. "Hello? Chava Miriam! I was *just* about to call you! Yeah, I got in a little while ago…"

Avner chuckled to himself as he walked down the hall to Shimon's room. Unsurprisingly, Tova was there, giving a final pull on Shimon's tie.

"You really think I should wear this one, Mommy? Not the stripes?"

"Yes, it's just a bit more subtle."

"But maybe subtle is not good. Maybe she's looking for more… I don't know, bold?"

"Subtle is better than bold." She turned to Avner. "Right, Tatty?" Without waiting for an answer, she stepped back and looked Shimon over. "You're pulled together. That's more important than bold or subtle, anyway."

Shimon smoothed out imaginary wrinkles from his jacket and pulled himself to his full five-foot eleven inches. "Okay, I'm ready. I think."

Tova laid a hand on his cheek. "It should be with *hatzlachah*."

His answer was a small, scared smile and a nod of his head.

"Come, Shimon. Let's get the car keys." Avner led him downstairs to the foyer. The keys sat in a tiny basket on a small shelf in the front closet.

"Thanks, Tatty. Do I look okay?" he asked one more time.

"You look great. Remember, just relax and be yourself."

Another scared smile, and Shimon was off.

Avner's features dimmed. Why was Shimon so concerned

with how he looked? What about pride, or confidence, in his good qualities? His dedication to learning, his gentleness, his consideration for others, his loyalty. And Ilana—was he looking past her *aidelkeit* to see what made her tick?

"What do you think?" Tova asked.

He hadn't realized she'd followed them down. "I think he's really nervous."

"Yes, I agree."

"In fact," he said, thinking as he spoke, "I think he's more nervous now than he was at the beginning."

"Could be. It's a good sign, no? It means he's seriously thinking about marrying her."

"Maybe. But he looks like he did when he was six and I taught him how to ride a bike. Like he's not quite sure he wants to be there, and he feels like he's about to fall off."

"It's just jitters. Everyone goes through it."

"I don't know, Tova, it doesn't look like jitters, it's more like panic."

"Well, we'll see what happens when he comes home. I'm going to clean up from dinner, put Meir to sleep, and make sure Brachie doesn't forget to call Bubby and Zeidy."

Avner had a date of his own—with his Gemara. His evening was off schedule because of Brachie's arrival, and he'd learn at home this evening instead of in shul. But he also needed to talk to his wife. "Uh, I wanted to hear a little more about Parnes. When you finish upstairs, would you mind joining me in the dining room?"

"I'd be happy to. It's nice to have you home one evening."

Avner settled himself at the dining room table and immersed himself in *Maseches Berachos*. As he learned, he jotted down a few notes. As a tutor in Yeshivas Torah v'Yirah, he had a long-ingrained habit of using what he learned for the benefit of his students. After some time, he closed his Gemara and transferred his attention to his end-of-year summaries.

He was deep in thought when Tova entered holding a steaming cup. "I made you some tea. I'll be right back." She went out and came back with a plate of her mother's rugelach, then came back a third time with another steaming cup for herself.

Her bustling gave Avner a few welcome minutes to consider his opening; after twenty-six years of marriage, he was still reluctant to engage in conflict. "So," he began, his tone light, "what's this Parnes program?"

"Oh, I thought you must've read the brochure. You want me to go get it?" She began to push away from the table.

"No, no," Avner said quickly. "Just tell me a little about it."

Tova settled back down. "Parnes opened just a few years ago. They ran a program for girls to become administrators. The girls loved it, and most of them found good jobs. The program was so popular, they decided to expand and give girls more choices about what to train in."

"And Brachie said she was interested in medical billing?"

"Oh, you know Brachie. She's flexible, she'll do fine."

"I'm sure she will. But this is a very important decision. It's going to affect the rest of her life."

Tova smiled. "That's why I gave her two choices."

Avner shifted in his seat. "Two choices aren't an awful lot."

"Avner, you just said that this is a very important decision. Brachie's simply too young to decide by herself. She'll make a mistake and choose something ridiculous that doesn't bring in any money, or that she'll end up hating after a few years. That's what parents are for, to help their children be successful in life, no?"

"Well, yes, to help them. Of course. But her tastes need to be taken into consideration."

"Her head is up in the clouds, and she has no idea what she wants or what's good for her. When she settles down, she'll see that this is the only sensible solution. The only *practical* solution." Tova tapped her right index finger on the table.

Avner recognized the gesture, something his wife did when she was feeling irritated. He hesitated. Was this worth taking a stand on? Brachie really was flexible, or perhaps persuadable would be more accurate—if the right person was doing the persuading. Tova wouldn't actually force Brachie into a career she hated.

Would she?

"How about this," Avner suggested. "Tomorrow, you tell Brachie more about the program, and about the two options you suggested, and then we'll talk about it some more?"

"Yes, that's exactly what I plan to do." She stood. "Can I get you anything else? You didn't touch your tea."

"No, thank you, I'm fine. I'm going to —"

Shimon appeared out of nowhere.

"You startled me," Tova said. "I didn't hear you come in."

"How'd it go?" Avner asked, but from the way Shimon looked, the question was completely unnecessary.

2

SHIMON'S EYES SHONE.

"It was nice. Really nice." He sat down next to Tova. "The talk really flowed this time. Ilana seemed really comfortable, and I was much more comfortable, too." He stopped.

"Go on," Avner encouraged.

"I don't know, exactly. It was like... like I didn't have to think three times about everything I was saying. I could just say it."

"What did you talk about?" Tova asked.

"Lots of things. First I was telling her about Brachie coming home, and then we got to talking about being away from home. I told her about when I was away in yeshivah, and about coming back, about learning here."

"And she told you all about her year in seminary?"

"Yeah. She got a lot out of her year, but she didn't like being so far away from home. I *really* understood, you know?"

Avner smiled. That was one thing Shimon was sure to understand.

"She still has a *kesher* with lots of her friends from seminary, and she even keeps in touch with some of her *rebbeim*."

"So she's someone who forms and holds on to solid relationships," Avner clarified.

"Right, that's exactly what I'm trying to say."

They were silent for a moment, then Shimon continued, "Did you know that her family runs a *gemach*?"

"Yes," Tova said. "A job-search *gemach*."

"Right. Ilana is also involved. She learned how to use the database, and she even learned how to talk to people looking for work. She's not shy, exactly, but she is kind of quiet. I mean, she has this way about her, like every word she says is thought-out but soft spoken. She said she had to push herself to be able to ask the right questions, but she felt strongly about being a part of the family project. Isn't that special?"

Avner and Tova exchanged a quick look. For Shimon, that was a long speech. And to hear such praise flowing from his lips, with that delighted look on his face, was encouraging.

"I think," Shimon said slowly, "she'll make someone a great wife."

"Someone?" Avner asked.

"Yes." His eyes drifted up to the ceiling, a half-smile playing on his lips.

"Are you saying that she'll make *you* a great wife?" Avner pressed.

Shimon's eyes snapped downwards, his shoulders drew in. Avner could practically see him land with a thud.

"Uh, I didn't say that. I just... I don't know."

"You don't know," Avner said, drawing out his words.

Shimon rubbed his chin and straightened his *kippah*.

Avner was careful to keep his tone light. "So what do you think is missing? What do you need to know?"

"I'm not sure." He looked from his father to his mother and quickly added, "But I'm willing to go out again, maybe I'll see next time."

Avner probed a bit more. "And what kinds of things do you think you'll see next time?"

Shimon rubbed his chin again, then let his hand drop. "I think... I think I'll know it when I see it."

Avner's instincts told him that something else was going on here, something that he couldn't quite pinpoint. And he was left wondering how many "next times" there would be. It was time for Tova to put in a call to the *shadchan*.

Aidel placed the last of the dishes in the cupboard and surveyed the small kitchen. The sinks were empty, the floor swept. The beige Formica counters, showing signs of age, were clear except for a set of pale green ceramic canisters that added a touch of color to the otherwise faded area. Aidel draped the dishtowel on a small rod inside a bottom cupboard and pushed the three chairs snug against the round table.

She removed a package of ground meat from the freezer and pondered whether to make meatballs or stuffed cabbage. Stuffed cabbage, she decided, placing the package in the sink.

Yerucham entered the kitchen. "I guess you missed your early-morning walk today, because of all that rain."

"Yes, but now it's cleared up. I'm just going to run out to the store for some onions, and when I come back we can go out for our walk together."

"Let's go now, and then on the way home you can pick up the onions."

"Fine, I can do it that way, too."

"Just give me ten minutes. I want to finish balancing my checkbook."

Aidel smiled. In ten minutes, she could go to the store and be back. But if Yerucham wanted her to wait, she'd wait. "No problem," she said. "I'll get a head start on dinner."

"Dinner? Already? What are we having?"

"Stuffed cabbage."

"Stuffed cabbage!" His eyes gleamed. "Uh, now that's something worth going to the store for."

"Yes. Brachie's coming."

Yerucham's face contracted in mock consternation. "Oh, so Brachie gets stuffed cabbage, and I get broiled chicken."

Aidel knew he was joking, but she was temporarily at a loss for words. Of course, she didn't mind to *patchke* for Yerucham, but stuffed cabbage only tastes right with a lot of salt, which wasn't good for him. But she couldn't say so without letting on how much his diet factored into her food preparations. He'd insist that there could be nothing wrong with eating regular, normal foods.

"She called yesterday," Aidel said, steering the topic away from food.

"Oh, so she did call in the end? What did she have to say for herself?"

"We spoke for all of sixty seconds. We kept being interrupted by beeps—call waiting. Half the neighborhood must have been trying to reach her! I was surprised she managed to call me at all, until I pictured Tova standing over her: 'Nu, did you call Bubby yet? Call Bubby. Did you call yet?'"

Yerucham chuckled. "Tova likes to be on top of things."

"She sure does. You've got to hand it to her, she has a real eye for detail. You should have heard her plan Brachie's homecoming. The only thing she couldn't swing was to have Yoni home."

Yerucham stared. "She wanted him to miss yeshivah?"

"Well, I'm not sure what she was trying to arrange, exactly, but I suppose Avner put his foot down on that one."

"Good for him. All this coddling is okay for Brachie, but Tova should leave the boys alone."

"Yerucham, she doesn't always realize that she's coddling. In her view, she's just taking care of them."

He crossed his arms. "Then I'll explain the difference to her the next time I talk to her."

"I don't think wanting Yoni home was coddling him, she just wanted all her birds in the nest."

Yerucham's hand sliced the air as he spoke. "Boys need to be independent. She needs to let go a little, to let them grow up a bit."

Aidel couldn't disagree. Tova did tend to go overboard sometimes. But since introspection was not Tova's forté, telling her wasn't likely to help much. Besides, she'd learned early on in the game that telling married children what to do was unproductive, at best. Well, Tova and the rest of the family would figure it all out, sooner or later.

"Ten minutes is all I need," Yerucham said, pulling Aidel out of her thoughts. He brought his checkbook and some papers to the table, then sat down. "Aidel, where's my pen?"

Aidel brought him a blue pen from a drawer in the kitchen and then went to see if she had everything she needed for tonight's dinner. She made a mental note to pick up another can of tomato paste, tied on an apron, and began pulling apart cabbage leaves industriously.

"Aidel," Yerucham called from the dining room, "could you come here a minute?"

Aidel rinsed and dried her hands, then stepped into the dining room.

"What are these two checks?" he asked, holding out the checkbook. "Numbers 4081 and 4087."

"Just a second, I need my glasses." She walked back to the kitchen and pulled a small eyeglass case from the same drawer where she'd gotten the pen a few minutes earlier. She sat down next to Yerucham, perched the glasses on the end of her nose, and peered at the check register.

"Look," he said, pulling the checkbook back toward himself,

"this one's for forty-three dollars and sixty-nine cents."

"Forty-three sixty-nine, let's see." She reached out for the checkbook.

Yerucham let her hold it for a few seconds then pulled it back to himself. "What's it for?"

"I didn't get a good look at it. Let me see what it says."

Yerucham passed the checkbook to her.

"Uh," Aidel said as she read what was written there. "It says 'Diamond.' It's for groceries."

"Diamond means groceries? In what store? There's no store called Diamond."

"Mr. Knopferman officially changed the name of his store to Diamond's. He told me he had too many problems with the bank, like checks with the name spelled wrong or written in a foreign language."

Yerucham looked stricken. "He changed the name?"

"Officially, yes. But don't worry, he said he'll still be known to his old-time customers as Knopferman's."

Eyebrows drawn, Yerucham muttered, "His father never would have done such a thing."

"A tzaddik if there ever was one," Aidel commented. "But times have changed, Yerucham, and if it saves him money and heartache, it's just a name, after all."

He grunted.

"What about the other check?" Aidel asked.

Yerucham took the checkbook out of Aidel's hands and flipped to the right page. "This one, 4087, for seventy-two dollars. The writing is completely illegible, Aidel."

"May I see that?" She held out her hand. "I think it says 'safer goat.'"

"Safer goat? What kind of business is that? Please, Aidel, when you write a check, you have to mark down what it's for. I keep telling you that."

Aidel peered at the writing. "One second, I think it says 'safety gate.'" She took off her glasses and held the checkbook at arm's length. Then she laughed. "I got it. It says *sefer Torah.*"

"*Sefer Torah*? What did you mean by that?"

"You wrote this check, not me," she smiled. "You remember, Morrison made a collection to buy a *sefer Torah* in memory of his father?"

"Oh." He grinned. "I must have been in a hurry when I made out the check. It was right before davening, now that I'm thinking about it. Well, never mind. I'm done here. You ready to go?"

"Sure. I'll just put away the cabbage." She went to the kitchen while Yerucham put away his papers. Cabbage in the refrigerator, glasses in the drawer, a quick wipe-down of the counter. Aidel took off her apron and hung it in the closet.

And as she closed the closet door, the room suddenly began to spin.

Avner turned right and circled the block for the third time, his head turning from side to side as if watching a ping-pong match. Just before the corner, an ATV signaled and Avner hit the brakes. He parked, clutched his briefcase and set the alarm. His watch told him that he had time to spare. Really, between the one-way streets, morning congestion, and parking, it would have been just as fast to walk. Tova was always trying to get him to exercise, and his daily drive to work was regularly under discussion. Perhaps he would start walking when the new school year began. Or a few weeks after that, when the weather turned mild. For now, he was comfortable with his routine.

He reached the yeshivah, a large edifice with four stories in the main building and two wings running out to the sides. He stopped in the office. "Morning, Mrs. Strauss."

"Good morning, Rabbi Lehrfeld. This is for you." She slid a manila folder to the corner of her desk.

"Thank you." He placed his briefcase on a chair and tried to open it, but the left-hand button was stuck. As he fiddled with it, he heard Rabbi Newman's voice from behind his office door. It was atypically harsh—and loud.

"...I understand your position, but this is completely unacceptable."

Automatically, Avner looked up at Mrs. Strauss. Her eyes ran away from his, and she threw open her bottom desk drawer and began to rummage around inside.

Avner hesitated only for a moment. He grabbed his briefcase and snatched up the envelope. "Briefcase is stuck," he said awkwardly. "Guess I'll deal with it later. Have a good day."

Mrs. Strauss nodded.

"...doesn't make it okay... last minute..."

The words followed him as he walked away. Who had Rabbi Newman been speaking with? And what catastrophe would prompt their normally unruffled principal to raise his voice? Avner's sense of privacy prevailed over his curiosity, and he did not look behind him to see if anyone was exiting the principal's office.

Avner climbed a flight of stairs, passed the library on his left, and unlocked his own little room. Automatically, he flipped on the air conditioner thinking, as he always did, that as much as he liked this room and its proximity to the library, he wished it had a window.

The bell rang, and Avner heard the corridor grow quiet. Students would be settling into their seats, *rebbis* would be clearing their throats, and three boys would be quietly slipping out of their classroom to meet with him.

The door opened.

"Good morning, Yosef, hello Levi."

"Hi."

"Good morning."

"Where's Sruly?"

"Didn't come in," Levi answered.

"He was out yesterday, too," Yosef said.

"Oh. Well, I'll call him later on and see if he's feeling okay. Maybe you can give him a call as well. Meanwhile, I'm looking forward to seeing those pictures you drew."

The boys sat down and pulled papers out of their folders.

Avner smiled at his students and sat across from them. "I see you're both ready. Who's first?"

"I am," they said at the same time, then giggled.

"You can go first," Levi offered.

Avner threw Levi a wink. "Okay, Reb Yosef, let's see those *bigdei kehunah*."

Yosef slid his paper over.

Avner scrutinized the drawing. It was done in pencil, but it was obvious that these were no quick sketches. Each garment was drawn with care and precision, lacking no detail, down to the bells on the bottom of the *me'il*. The *efod* swooped down majestically, and the kohen's face was shaded, the fire from the *mizbe'ach* illuminating his features from the side. This wasn't a homework assignment; it was a work of art.

"Is it good?"

It wasn't good. It was magnificent, a drawing he'd like to include in his future lessons, to distribute to all *rebbis* who taught this subject, to enlarge and hang up as a poster in this room.

"I can see that you put a lot into this drawing. I want to go over the details with you. But first let's see Levi's."

Levi's face was pinched. Frowning, he pushed his paper over.

Avner understood Levi's reluctance. Compared to Yosef, these pictures were not only plain but babyish. And yet, though there was nothing artistic about the drawing, it portrayed the same attention to detail.

Two weeks ago, neither of these boys had been able to piece together more than a few disjointed sentences about how these garments looked. But here was proof that they both grasped not only the basics but also every aspect.

"Boys, I'm really impressed. You understood exactly how the *efod* looks. Here, Levi, look at these bells, I can almost hear them ring as he walks! And here, Yosef, see the way the *ketones* falls gracefully, stopping just by his ankles. I can practically hear the murmur of the crowds after the *avodah* on Yom Kippur."

Levi glowed. Yosef smiled, but a question hung in his eyes: was his drawing no different from Levi's?

"Would you mind if I kept these for a few days? I am so pleased with these drawings, I want to make a copy to keep for myself."

The boys agreed, and they moved on to other matters. When the period ended, Avner said, "Yosef, just a second."

Levi shrugged and left.

"Looking at your drawing is like stepping back in time and actually seeing the *bigdei kehunah*. I'd like your permission to give this to Rabbi Newman. I'm sure he'll want to give copies to the *rebbis* who teach this."

Yosef's skin paled and his eyes grew wide. "But it's just homework. It's not good enough for other people."

"On the contrary. It's the best illustration I've ever seen on the subject."

Color creeping up his cheeks, Yosef said faintly, "Thanks."

"Just sign your name, the way artists do. You have a real talent, you know."

Yosef floated out of the room.

Avner smiled at his retreating figure. It never ceased to amaze him how a boy who could not score over forty on a test could shine in so many other ways. A child with this level of understanding and expression should not be graded based on his ability to answer a multiple-choice test. Unfortunately, he didn't know if the *rebbi* would agree.

It was a crusade of his, trying to get educators to see the whole child and not the number of red marks on an exam. Some of the *rebbis* understood, some agreed, and some were downright hostile. But sixteen years in this room had taught him that every child has strengths, and it was his job to find them and bring them out.

A surge of energy pulsed out to his fingertips, and he stood, bringing himself up to his full height. This drawing was Yosef's report card.

And his own, too.

After two classes, Avner made himself a cup of coffee in the teachers' room, then went downstairs to the principal's office. He knocked, and a quick "come in" followed.

"Avner," Rabbi Gedaliah Newman greeted him, "I was just thinking about you!"

"Good thoughts, I hope," Avner smiled.

"Of course. In fact, I need your help with something."

Avner paused. Being intimately familiar with the flow of operation in the school, Avner couldn't imagine what kind of help might be needed at this point and came up with only two possibilities: either Gedaliah wanted him to officially take on more responsibilities next year, or it related to whatever discussion—or argument—had taken place here earlier. The former meant pressure; the latter, conflict. Neither one appealed to him, and he felt his shoulders tense.

"I'll be glad to help," he said. "A new student for me?"

"In June?"

Avner shrugged.

"No, not that kind of help." His eyes narrowed almost imperceptibly as he studied Avner, then his face softened. "Have a seat, Avner."

Tova held the cordless in her hand without moving. By now, she knew Mirel Krieger's number by heart. What was she going to say?

Shimon wasn't ready to talk about getting engaged. But he *was* interested in seeing Ilana again, ostensibly to get to know her better so that he could make a decision.

Enough dillydallying. "Good morning, Mirel. It's Tova Lehrfeld."

"Tova, I'm so glad you called. I just spoke to Perel Moskowitz. She sounded quite confident about the direction this *shidduch* is taking and asked me to give you a ring." She chuckled. "I told her I'd give you a call, and we'd save the ring for Ilana."

It was lucky for Tova that Mirel kept talking, since she was, uncharacteristically, quite speechless.

"They have only the nicest things to say about your Shimon. Ilana is such a special girl, so *aidel*, so honest, and she really *understands* Shimon. She said—these were her exact words—she never met a more *mentschlich bachur* in her life. Her *exact words*."

Tova fumbled for an intelligent reply. "Uh, thank you. That's lovely. I see she really does, uh, understand Shimon."

"Perfectly. They are made for each other. I have over forty *shidduchim* to my credit, *baruch Hashem*, and I can tell you that not every couple is so well matched both on paper and in person. Ilana's ready, so just tell me, when do you want to make the *l'chaim*?"

"The *l'chaim*?" Tova managed.

"The Moskowitzes asked for a few days' notice. One of Perel's sisters makes professional miniatures, and she needs time to make enough. They're expecting a pretty big crowd."

Her head swimming, Tova said nothing.

"They're not looking to do anything ostentatious," she added quickly. "But they have a very large family, as you know, and they want it to look right."

This conversation had to be stopped, and fast. Tova gripped the phone in one hand and held onto the countertop with the other. "Perel, miniatures sound lovely. I, uh, just don't think..." She cleared her throat and forced herself to breathe. "Shimon really likes Ilana, he's just not ready to get engaged yet."

Mirel's drawn-out "Oh" was loaded with meaning, but Tova was too overcome to attempt an interpretation. "Listen," she said, keeping her voice steady, "I'm sure he just needs one more meeting. He had only the nicest things to say after last night, and he just needs to be sure."

"One more date? I suppose... Forgive me, I'm just a little surprised. From what the Moskowitzes said, it sounded like things were pretty settled between them. I guess Ilana misunderstood some of his comments. I'll have to talk to them again and clarify—"

"I don't think that's necessary," Tova said, feeling herself on firmer ground. "It sounds like Ilana has made up her mind, and Shimon will, too. I'm sorry about the misunderstanding. Maybe you can just prepare Ilana, so she's not surprised when Shimon calls her."

"Yes, I'll do that."

They hung up, the phone line a few degrees cooler than it had been a few minutes ago.

Aidel grabbed the closet handle as a wave of dizziness swept over her. She squeezed her eyes tight, trying to block out the sight of her entire world spinning in circles around her head.

It didn't help. Even with her eyes closed, she felt the floor beneath her moving, and her legs threatened to buckle. She sucked in a breath. Her free hand flapped wildly and knocked over a glass that sat on the counter. It fell to the floor and shattered.

Yerucham called out from the other room, "Aidel, what was that?"

Instinctively, Aidel opened her eyes. She saw the cabinets in front of her, perfectly vertical, blessedly stationery. Her feet felt firm on the floor.

She let go of the handle and placed her hands on the counter. The dizziness had passed. She took a clean glass and poured herself some water.

"What happened?" Yerucham asked, coming into the kitchen.

"Sorry to have alarmed you. I knocked over a glass by mistake. Don't worry, I'll clean it up. Are you ready to go?"

"Yes, I'm ready whenever you are."

"Just give me a minute to clean this up." Aidel finished her water, then swept up the broken glass. As she bent over, she wondered what had come over her. She was feeling completely fine.

3

SIDDUR IN HAND, BRACHIE stood in the living room, swaying.

"Brachie," her mother called from the kitchen, "your breakfast is ready."

She barely noticed. *"T'ka b'shofar gadol..."*

"Brachie, breakfast is on the table."

"V'l'Yerushalayim ircha..." Oh, how she missed Yerushalayim!

Out of the corner of her eye, Brachie saw her mother appear in the doorway. She pressed her nose inside the *siddur*. Her first *shemoneh esreh* back in *chutz la'Aretz*—how could she be torn away for *food*? Didn't her mother understand?

"Modim..." A pang of regret. She should be thankful that her mother took such good care of her! *Thank You Hashem for my wonderful parents, for my incredible year in sem, for my coming home safely!*

When she finished davening—down to the *shir shel yom* and not a moment before—Brachie closed her *siddur* and made her way to the kitchen.

Tova was there, leaning against the countertop, arms folded. She smiled at her daughter's entrance. "Sorry I interrupted. I didn't realize you were still davening." She looked Brachie up and down and chuckled.

"What's so funny, Mommy?"

"You're all dressed, hair neatly pulled back, and look at your feet."

Brachie looked down at her pink elephant slippers and giggled. "I couldn't find my shoes. They must be under all that mess, somewhere." She looked at the table where an onion bagel with cream cheese and tomato, a mushroom omelet, and a glass of orange juice awaited her. "Mommy, that looks awesome. Thanks!"

Tova's face lit up. "You're very welcome. Go wash, I imagine you haven't had a bagel since before you left."

"Actually," Brachie said, filling a washing cup, "there's a great little bagel shop in Geulah."

"Really?"

"Sure," she said after she took a bite. "You can get practically anything in Israel."

Tova poured from the coffee machine into a mug, and the scent of coffee filled the kitchen. She tore open a packet of NutraSweet, added some milk, and set it on the other side of the table.

"Mmm, coffee, too, thanks!" She reached across the table.

"Since when do you drink coffee?"

"I don't know," she shrugged, "they served it at breakfast." She sipped from the coffee and saw her mother's lips turn upward. "Oh, is this yours?"

"It was," Tova smiled, "but you keep that one and I'll make myself another."

While her mother refilled the coffee machine, Brachie sipped her coffee, but it was her surroundings that she drank in. She'd heard people use the word "cozy" to describe kitchens, but until now she'd never understood the term. Wood-grain cabinets formed an L-shape, with ivory countertops running the length underneath. Hand towels, neatly folded, sat by either sink in front of copper washing cups. The frying pan and some assorted utensils stood out; the kitchen was usually clean by the time Brachie made her appearance downstairs.

"So," Tova said as she sat down with another mug, "did you decide which course you want to take yet?"

Brachie sputtered and dropped her bagel. She picked the tomato up off her plate where it fell and shoved it back into the cream cheese, then snatched her napkin and wiped off her hands.

"So have you given it any thought?" Tova asked.

Brachie stole a glance at the clock which told her that her father was long gone. Her neck prickled and her palms began to sweat. "Um, not exactly. I mean, I was so tired last night, I didn't think about much except getting some sleep. And today all I did so far was get dressed and daven."

Tova nodded. "Of course, you were too tired to think about anything!"

Like air escaping from a tire, Brachie blew out a breath she didn't know she'd been holding.

"But you know how these things work."

Actually, Brachie had no clue. Her mother had always handled these things for her. She squirmed in her seat.

"The best courses fill up first, and then you'll be locked out."

Brachie sighed.

"It's like the electives you had this year," Tova said. "You had one or two courses that you got to choose. Didn't the best ones fill up first?"

"I don't remember. I think they all sounded good, and I just signed up for whatever my roommates took."

"Well, I'm sure the most popular classes filled up quickly. That's the way it goes. These two programs I told you about are the best ones in today's market."

"What are they again?"

"Medical billing and coding, and graphic design."

"Oh, right, graphic design. That's *for sure* not for me. My friend's sister does that, and she hates it. But what's medical billing?"

"Every medical procedure has a code for identification," Tova explained. "You enter the codes, and then you bill the patient or insurance company based on the code."

"So what's so good about it?" Brachie asked, rubbing her eyes. She was good with numbers, but this sounded boring.

"Once you get a degree, you start out working in a medical office."

Brachie stiffened.

"The pay is good, even for someone just starting out. There are so many *heimish* doctors' offices around, and they would certainly want to have a *frum* girl working for them. You'd have your pick of jobs!"

A *heimish* office? What happened to keeping away from *any* kind of office? Wasn't that something she'd promised herself? Brachie chased a mushroom around the plate. "I don't know. I mean, I was kind of thinking of doing something else entirely."

"Like what?"

"Like, um, maybe, *sheitels*."

"*Sheitels?* Brachie, being a *sheitel macher* is not so easy. You stand on your feet for hours, and you have to deal with some very difficult customers."

Brachie waved her hands, wishing away uncomfortable possibilities. "I'm not worried about that. I can take breaks whenever I want. I mean, I'll be setting my own hours. And I can always turn a customer away if we don't get along." She took a breath and continued, "And, like, it's *important*. A Jewish woman should always look put together. She's a princess, and her head covering is her crown!" She closed her eyes and was transported to Rebbetzin Berlinger's weekly class.

Her mother interrupted her reverie. "After you're married, you can wear your *sheitel* to work and look put together. It doesn't mean you have to make a *parnassah* out of it."

A heaviness settled on Brachie's shoulders. Her mother always understood her. What had happened all of a sudden? Why couldn't she see that office work was so... mundane? "I don't know, Mommy. It just doesn't sound like something I want to do."

"Well, I think you'll get used to the idea. We already discussed the importance of getting a degree. If you don't get a degree, how do you expect to support a family?"

"Right. That's why doing *sheitels* is perfect. It's a degree I can start using right away."

"It's not a degree, it's a license." The words were clipped.

Brachie stirred her coffee.

"There's a difference." Tova's voice returned to normal. "It can take a very long time to get a good name, and that's only if you deserve one—if you're very good. What would you do in the meantime?"

"Hashem will help."

"*Sheifeleh*, the *Aibishter* always helps. But you have to have a plan—a realistic plan."

"Of course I have a plan." What, did her mother think she was totally unrealistic?

Tova raised her eyebrows. "What's your plan?"

Brachie thought it was obvious, but she obliged Tova. "Since I'm going to marry a learning boy, Tatty will support us."

Tova's hand froze as she brought the mug to her lips. Slowly, she placed the mug back on the table and repeated, "Tatty will support you."

"Right," Brachie said complacently, "so at the end of the day it doesn't really matter what my degree is in."

Tova stared, and her lips narrowed to half their size. She opened her mouth to speak, then closed it again.

Brachie watched, confused.

"Did you already discuss this with Tatty?"

"Not exactly. But, I mean, isn't that what happens?"

Tova's expression changed again. The lines around her mouth deepened, then her shoulders relaxed and her lips turned up at the corners. "Even if Tatty helps out, that doesn't mean a house in Boro Park and cleaning help."

Brachie heard the words, but she wasn't so focused on the details. Tatty had always taken care of her; even after she was married, he and Mommy would make sure she had what she needed, somehow or other.

Tova drummed a finger on the table. "Imagine yourself eight years down the road. You're married, a bunch of little kids, some in school, some at home."

Brachie closed her eyes and let herself be swept up in the pleasant dream.

"Even if you can get by doing *sheitels*, you're going to want nice things. A house, a car, fine clothing..."

A smile stretched her face wide.

"Tatty can't provide all that, *sheifeleh*. With the *Aibishter's* help, you'll never go hungry, never lack the basics. But you can't really expect Tatty to supply you with all the comforts you're used to, can you?"

A crease puckered Brachie's forehead, and she opened her eyes.

"Maybe you can get by doing *sheitels*, but you'll want a more reliable source of income. And who says you'll be good at *sheitels*—good enough to really make it? Plus, it means giving up one of the bedrooms, hair all over the house..."

Brachie's mouth formed a little O.

"But with a real degree," Tova continued, "even your start-ing salary is good, and it only goes up from there."

Brachie folded her arms. Why was money so important? She was prepared to live in a small house, and do without those nice things, if it meant that she could support her husband and stay home with her children.

"And then," Tova continued, "when you have enough expe-rience, you can do it at home."

Home? "How long would that take?"

Tova smiled. "I don't think there's an exact time span. It would depend on how long it took you to get really good. But it could fit right into your life. By the time you'd want to stay home with children, you could be making your own hours at home."

Home. This medical billing thing was starting to sound interesting.

"And you have to know yourself. Once you cut a *sheitel*, you can't undo it. There's no room for mistakes, no second chances. Would you really be able to cut a two-thousand-dollar wig knowing that?"

Brachie felt as if a caterpillar were crawling up her esopha-gus. She was never great at making decisions, fearful of making the wrong one. How could she have missed this point? "I never thought of that," she said, her voice a near whisper.

"Come, eat. Your omelet is getting cold."

Automatically, Brachie picked up her fork and speared a mushroom. She could taste her mother's love in each bite.

She sat back in her chair and sipped her orange juice. With Mommy taking care of her again, life was just so much... simpler. A warm feeling washed over her. It was so good to be home!

Tova transferred the broom to her left hand and picked up the ringing phone in her right. "Hello?"

"Hi, Ma."

"Yoni! How are you, *tatteleh*?" She lodged the phone between her ear and shoulder and continued her tour of the kitchen.

"*Baruch Hashem*, good. How's Brachie?"

"Wonderful. Haven't you spoken to her yet?"

"There was no point in calling yesterday, I'll call her later. Ma, I only have a minute now. I just wanted to talk to you about something."

"Yes?"

"So, you know I told you I have an out Shabbos next week, and—"

"Yes, I'm looking forward to having all of you home."

"Yeah. So, Ma, it's like this. I can come home again in another two weeks, but I was invited to Reb Dovid's for a meal next Shabbos, so I need to stay in the dorm."

Tova stood in place and gripped the broom. "Who's Reb Dovid?"

"He's a great guy. All the *bachurim* want to be close to him, but I have a good *kesher* with him. I eat by him often on in Shabbosos."

"Yoni, your sister is home after being away for a year. Reb Dovid can wait another two weeks."

"I'd really like to come home, Ma, it's just that Reb Dovid's brother and sister-in-law will be there, and she knows somebody for me. She just wants to meet me first."

Tova's grip intensified, her white knuckles jutting out. "You mean she already told you about someone?" she asked, trying to keep her voice from rising. "Without calling me first?"

"No," Yoni said quickly. "She didn't give me any information, no name or anything, she just said that she might know someone, and before she calls you, she wants to meet me to see if it's *shayach*."

Tova released her grip and rested the broom against the wall. "Yoni, you're twenty-two. What's the hurry? Shimon's not even married yet."

"You and Tatty agreed that I don't have to wait for Shimon. And I'm not in a hurry, it's just that this sounds right. Reb Dovid is... well, he knows me, and he's a great guy, and I want to give it a shot. Okay?"

Tova sighed. "I'll talk it over with Tatty." She grabbed the broom and attacked the corners.

"So, what kind of help do you need?" Avner asked.

The intercom beeped, and Mrs. Strauss's voice could be heard through the speakerphone. "Rabbi Newman, Mr. Tenenbaum is on line three for you."

Gedaliah Newman pressed a button. "Ask him to call back in an hour." He turned to Avner. "The story is like this—"

"I'm sorry, Rabbi, he says it's urgent."

The principal sighed and picked up the phone. "Rabbi Newman speaking... Yes, I am aware of that... No, I can't see how..." A long pause followed. "Mr. Tenenbaum, the person you really need to speak to is the chairman of the board ... Yes, I know, but he's the one who can best help you... Good-bye." He pressed a button on his phone. "Mrs. Strauss, please hold all calls."

This exchange gave Avner ample time to try to assess his long-time colleague's mood. He seemed calm, as usual; Gedaliah was generally unflappable. His suit, off-black with fine pinstripes, sat squarely on his five-foot ten frame, with only the slightest hint of middle-age spread keeping it from dropping in a straight line. Gold-rimmed glasses gave him an air of dignity.

"Sorry," Gedaliah said. "It seems that Rebbi Oberlander is leaving."

Avner did not believe he'd heard correctly. "Did you say Rebbi Oberlander is leaving?"

"Yes. He informed me this morning."

"But that's impossible!" Avner blurted out. "Rebbi Oberlander has been here for years, even longer than I have. His leaving will be a major blow to the yeshivah!"

A small pause, then, "Yes."

He didn't need to elaborate. The two shared a friendship borne of mutual respect, shared goals, and constant interaction. Avner's official position was tutor, but Gedaliah relied on him to help with decisions on textbook purchases, class division, even curriculum development.

But he had nothing to do with the hiring of staff, so why was Gedaliah bringing this to him? Was he looking for moral support? He knew there were teachers who would be flattered at sharing the principal's confidence in these situations, but Avner felt like he was about to be sucked into a wind tunnel. He crossed one leg over the other, laced his fingers, and placed his hands on top of his knees, gripping them. "What are the chances of finding a *rebbi* with even half his experience at this time of year?"

"What do you think?" Gedaliah smiled. "Every *rebbi* with experience has long ago signed a contract for next year."

"Didn't Rebbi Oberlander have a contract as well?"

"Of course. But we both know that the contract is really to protect the employee, not the employer."

"I'm sure he has a good reason," Avner offered.

"He thinks so. But that doesn't solve our problem."

There it was again, that jolt of anxiety. He sensed that it wasn't only moral support Gedaliah wanted. "So, what are you going to do? Put an ad in the paper, *seeking seventh-grade rebbi*? You'll get dozens of fresh faces, but unless someone's just moved to town, you probably won't find anyone with much experience." He uncrossed his legs. "This is seventh grade, we're talking about. It doesn't just take teaching experience. It's a tough age, a transitional age. You have to be sharp. And both friendly and firm, and understanding. And—"

He stopped short, realizing that he had no need to explain

the job to Gedaliah. He was only a tutor, after all. Sure, he subbed often, in all the grades, but that didn't make him an expert on classroom management. Gedaliah had been out of the classroom for many years, but he was still a master *mechanech*.

"Go on," Gedaliah encouraged. "You were just warming up."

"Sorry, I was just thinking out loud. I see that it's a big problem. But this might be an idea. What if you do put an ad in the paper, but not for a seventh-grade *rebbi* position. Take someone less experienced and put him in one of the easier grades, like second grade."

"Don't let the second-grade *rebbis* hear you say that!"

Avner smiled. "Never. Take the new *rebbi* for second grade, and push one of those *rebbis* up to seventh."

"It's a bit of a jump," Gedaliah said. "They're both wonderful *rebbis*, but I'm not sure either one of them is up for dealing with teenagers."

"So you may have to juggle a bit more. Maybe Rebbi Fast could move up to fifth grade, and then Rebbi Borenstein could move up to seventh."

"I can see at least four reasons why that wouldn't work, though it is something to think about. But I'm not ready to move in that direction yet."

Avner's eyes widened. "Do you have another idea?"

"Oh, yes," Gedaliah said. His voice was peculiar, and something told Avner that he wasn't going to like what came next.

Avner sat back.

Gedaliah waited.

"So," Avner finally said, "who's the new *rebbi*?"

"I'll tell you about him. He's intelligent, articulate, thought-out, and well liked."

Avner ran a hand through his beard.

"Not so curious, I see. Well, I'll just go on, then. He has many years in the teaching field and has earned a rather impressive reputation."

Avner gave a tight smile. "How's his discipline?"

"The boys hang on his every word, so he doesn't have to play the bad guy too often."

"Maybe that report is exaggerated."

"I've seen him in action, and he's tops."

Avner was not enjoying this. If Gedaliah was describing him, he was certainly stretching things. And if he was describing someone else, why not just come out and say who? Avner inhaled and braced himself. "Sounds great. Anyone I know?"

Gedaliah leaned forward. "You know very well who I mean. It's time to take the plunge, Avner."

Avner felt his pulse quicken. "I'm not a teacher, never was. I'm just a tutor."

"You sub all the time, in all the grades."

"Subbing isn't teaching."

Gedaliah barked a short laugh. "No, it's much harder. You don't just fill in, Avner, you actually teach, and the boys learn. They *enjoy* learning with you. You are highly skilled, no matter what you call yourself. You are a first-rate educator."

Avner's cheeks grew warm. "I have no formal training."

"Many of our *rebbis* don't. How many training programs were there ten or fifteen years ago? Your degree is sixteen years on the job! You have an uncanny ability to find a boy's strengths, to make *him* see his own strengths."

"If you feel that way, then you agree that I'm making a difference doing what I do."

"Yes!" he rapped the desk with his knuckles. "But imagine how much more of a difference you can make when you're working with twenty-five boys at a time, instead of two or three."

Avner shook his head. "I appreciate your confidence, Gedaliah, but I'm happy with my position." He thought of his little room, the close connection he shared with his boys.

"You can keep your position in the afternoon. This is a morning *rebbi* job. Please, just think about it. Go home and talk it over with your wife."

"Rabbi Newman," he addressed him formally, "there's really nothing to think about. I'm simply not qualified to be a classroom teacher." He stood. "I'm truly sorry to disappoint you."

Gedaliah stared at him, then came around the desk. "Avner, it's June. There is no way I'm going to find a teacher of your caliber who hasn't already signed a contract elsewhere."

Avner swallowed hard.

Gedaliah laid a hand on his shoulder. "Please, Avner. The school needs you. Think about it."

"I—"

"Just think about it."

4

"WHAT A MESS," BRACHIE complained. She was sitting on the only bare patch of carpet in her room. "I can't even tell what's clean and what's dirty."

"After sitting in those duffles for so long," Tova said, "everything's dirty. Just put it all in the wash."

"But I have nothing to wear to Bubby and Zeidy's!"

"What you're wearing now is fine, just find some decent shoes."

Brachie looked at her feet. "What's wrong with my shoes?"

"There's a hole by the big toe!"

"Oh. But these are so comfortable for walking. I think I wore them every day for the last two weeks. I would never have survived without them."

"You mean you actually went out in those shoes?"

"I had no choice. I wasn't going to spend my last two weeks shoe shopping."

"But that's not your only pair of shoes!"

"In Yerushalayim you do tons of walking, so you need walking shoes. I *love* to walk. Nowhere is too far, every step a mitzvah." She could see the streets of Meah Shearim, the jux-taposition of very old and very new vying for center stage. She could practically hear the traffic light ticking at Kikar Shabbos, counting down the seconds until the little green man would tell her it was safe to cross.

"I'm glad you walked a lot, it's good exercise. But you can't go out in shoes with a hole."

Brachie shrugged. "I just didn't think it was a big deal."

"You yourself said yesterday that a Jewish woman always has to look put together."

"Oh, yeah. I guess I hadn't thought about shoes. Well, thanks, Mommy. I'll ditch them. But I don't know how I'll find anything in this mess." She threw some shirts across the room.

"Here, I'll help you." Tova leaned over and started sorting things into piles.

"Come sit in the chair," Brachie offered. She tried to pull it away from the desk, but it was wedged in by a mountain of—something. She grabbed the whole pile and heaved, clearing a small area.

Tova sat down, and the two made a huge pile of laundry. "Take this out, then we'll see what else we can do."

Brachie stood, brushed off her skirt, and wrapped her arms around as much of the pile as she could.

"Go get a laundry basket," Tova said.

Tova made piles of notebooks while Brachie made four trips to the laundry room in the basement.

"I can't do any more," Brachie declared and plopped down where the laundry had been. "I'll finish later."

Tova frowned. "I'd like to vacuum in here."

"There's no way I can finish today, anyway. I need a shower, and I told Bubby I'd be there around five."

Tova looked at her watch. "Five? It's a fifteen-minute walk. You won't have time to shower first."

Brachie stared. "I'm not walking."

"You're not?" Tova looked out the window. "It's a beautiful afternoon. Why not?"

"It's too far," Brachie said, stating what was, to her, obvious.

"But we always walk to Bubby and Zeidy's, all of us."

"That's just because you don't drive."

Tova waved her words away. "I don't drive because I never got around to getting a license. Besides, who needs a car in Brooklyn? But that's not the point. Their apartment is close enough even for Bubby and Zeidy to walk here. And you just told me how you love to walk!"

"That's in Yerushalayim, where every step is a mitzvah. Here it's just... Brooklyn. What's so special about that? Besides, I'm totally jet-lagged, and you just told me I can't wear my walking shoes."

"I see." She paused. "Well, waiting for a bus can also take time."

"Mommy, I'm taking a car service."

Tova cocked her head to the side. "A car service?"

"Yeah. In sem we took cabs everywhere."

"I can understand that you're too tired today to walk, but why not a bus?"

Brachie's eyes opened wide. "A *bus*? Do you know what kind of gross advertisements can be on public transportation?"

Tova pursed her lips. "I know that Brooklyn buses lack the *kedushah* of Israeli buses, but they get you where you need to go."

"But—"

"You don't have to look at the ads! You can keep your eyes closed, once you're sitting down. Or you can bring along a Tehillim, if that makes you feel like you're back in Yerushalayim."

Brachie pouted.

"Hello?" A voice called from downstairs.

"It's Tatty!" Brachie jumped up and raced down the stairs. "Hi, Tatty. Can you please drive me over to Bubby and Zeidy's?"

"Hello, Avner," Tova smiled as she walked down the stairs. "You're home early today."

"If Tatty drives me, I can still shower and then I don't need to take a bus or a car service."

"Brachie, let Tatty be. He just came home."

"It's okay, Tova," Avner said, not looking at either one of them. "I'll drive you. Is a half hour okay?"

"Perfect!" Brachie gushed. "Thank you so much!" She bounded up the stairs.

A short while later, a freshly showered Brachie climbed into her father's car and went to her grandparents' house.

"Bubby!" Brachie threw her arms around Aidel and held on tight. "How are you? It's so good to see you!" She let go, her eyes darting all around. "You look amazing! Oh, it smells so good in here. Ha! I see you have that picture of me at the Kosel hanging on the refrigerator! Oh, I miss Yerushalayim! And my friends, too! How are you, Bubby?"

Aidel smiled as Brachie's words tumbled over each other. "It's wonderful to see you, we've missed your special spark. I'm so glad you came! There must be a dozen people you're anxious to see."

"I missed you so much, Bubby! Wow, I can't believe I'm back."

"I suppose you're jet-lagged. It's a long flight, no?"

"Yeah, and I'm way off time-wise. Where's Zeidy?"

"He went to a *shiur*. He'll be back soon, and then we'll have dinner."

"You made stuffed cabbage, right?" She sniffed the air. "I love you, Bubby, thanks for making my favorite."

"I love you too, *sheifeleh*, and you're very welcome. Now, I want you to tell me about your favorite class. I seem to remember that it was Rebbetzin Berlanger's yes?"

"Berlinger. Her classes were *really* special. We did a different topic every week..." She launched, breathless, into a long rapture about Rebbetzin Berlinger's *shiurim*.

Brachie barely stopped for breath until Yerucham walked in. After a warm greeting, she slapped her hand to her forehead. "Oh, no! I forgot your presents!"

"You didn't have to bring us anything," Aidel said with a smile.

"But I found the most *perfect* gift for you, Bubby. It's an apron. I won't tell you what it looks like, because I don't want to spoil the surprise. I'll just say that it's the same exact one that I bought for Mommy. And for you, Zeidy—"

"Don't spoil it for me," he said. "You'll have to come back here a different time, that's all."

"I'd love to. Or maybe I can give it to you on Shabbos, since it's something you wear..."

"No more hints," he admonished. His voice was stern but his eyes smiled.

"Okay. Anyway, I think we learned that you can't give presents on Shabbos. I'll have to look it up in my notes."

"Sounds like you learned something in Eretz Yisrael, then," Yerucham said.

"She'll tell us more about it while we eat," Aidel said.

The kitchen table was already set. Aidel served everyone a bowl of vegetable soup. "I'll get you some salt, Brachie. I know how teenagers like everything to be over-salted, not like us old folks who prefer to taste the food."

Brachie grinned.

Aidel opened the cupboard, and lifted her hand to reach inside. But her arm stopped with a jerk and fell back to her side.

Brachie waited. Aidel didn't move.

"Bubby, what happened?"

"Aidel, are you okay?"

Her back to them, Aidel gave no answer.

Avner chewed silently.

Tova stirred. "Avner, you're awfully quiet today. What's bothering you?"

He swallowed. "The seventh-grade *rebbi* is leaving."

"And...?"

"Rabbi Newman wants me to take over for him."

Tova's eyes lit up. "You're going to become a *rebbi*! That's wonderful! I—" She stopped short. "You're not happy about it?"

Avner put his fork down. It hit his plate with a loud clink. "I'm good with my boys. I'm making a difference."

"Wouldn't you make a bigger difference in a classroom?"

Avner grunted. "That's what Rabbi Newman said. I'm good at what I do, and I don't see the point in switching jobs."

"It's not switching jobs, it's a promotion."

"Why, because one has a more impressive sounding title?"

Tova looked down at her plate.

"Rabbi Newman would have to spend at least a year coaching me and also hire a new tutor, as green as they come. Why train two people, when he can just hire a new *rebbi* and train one person?"

"If Rabbi Newman didn't think you'd be a good *rebbi*, he wouldn't make this offer."

"This isn't the first time he's offered me a teaching position."

"But maybe it's time to take him up on it."

Avner was silent.

"Just think, you'd be a regular teacher, you'd get a raise..."

"Do we need the money?" Avner interrupted.

"No," she admitted. "But Shimon's probably getting engaged, and that means new expenses. And Yoni and Brachie are not far behind, and I just thought—"

"I turned him down."

Tova blinked "You did?"

"Yes. I'm going to remain a tutor."

Their eyes met.

Avner looked away first. He made a *berachah acharonah* and left the table.

After Tova cleaned up, Avner returned to the table with a *sefer*. Before he had a chance to open it, he heard the front door open and quick steps across the living room.

"Hi, Tatty!"

"Hello, Brachie. How are Bubby and Zeidy?"

"Terrific, they haven't changed a bit! Bubby thinks she pulled a muscle in her arm, but she looks fine. One of these forever-young Bubbys, you know?"

Avner smiled. "How'd you get home?"

"Bubby walked me. She said I shouldn't bother you to pick me up."

"That was kind of her. I wouldn't have minded, though."

"Zeidy also said the walk wouldn't hurt me, and no one argues with Zeidy. Bubby made stuffed cabbage!" She slipped into a chair.

"So you had a nice time and got some attention along with great food."

"Yeah." Brachie rested her head on her hand. "I didn't realize how much I missed them. I missed you and Mommy tons. I thought about you every single day. Sometimes, when it was real quiet—you know, that special kind of quiet that happens all of a sudden in Yerushalayim, when the sun is shining and a gentle breeze is blowing, and there's no sound anywhere except some leaves blowing across the parking lot—I'd feel so... connected to Eretz Yisrael. And I'd think that I never want to leave, or that I'll go back there one day to live. But then that quiet, comfortable feeling made me think of home, of being close to everyone I love, and I'd realize that I could never live so far away."

Avner stroked Brachie's arm. "Never is a big word. I seem to remember one little girl who said she'd never go away to seminary."

"That's different. I really was a little girl when I said that. When I grew up, I realized I wanted that experience even more than I wanted to stay home."

"You matured, and developed a different viewpoint. "

Brachie nodded.

"And when you mature more, your viewpoint can change again."

Brachie's nose wrinkled. "I'm eighteen, Tatty, how much more growing up do you think I still have to do?"

It was a question Avner had been asking himself since he'd picked her up from the airport. He assumed that once she was past the excitement of coming home, he'd begin to see some changes, somewhere, and he'd been looking forward to getting to know the new Brachie. But besides an infatuation with Yerushalayim, had anything really changed? Perhaps it was time to find out.

"Have you given any more thought to what kind of course you'd like to take?"

"Lots. Mommy says that medical billing and coding is the best idea."

"I heard you say you wanted to be a *sheitel macher*."

"Yeah, I thought that'd be a good idea. But Mommy thinks medical billing is better. The starting salary is much higher, and once I get good at it, I can work from home."

Avner tread carefully. "And what do *you* think?"

Brachie paused. "I suppose Mommy knows best. She looked into it, and she says I'll get into this field before everyone else, so I'm sure to have a good income."

Avner felt a pulse beat hard in his stomach. "Does it sound

interesting to you? Something you can see yourself doing for years?"

"Yeah, sure." She smoothed a spot on the tablecloth.

"Sitting in front of a computer screen with papers, typing in numbers?"

Brachie's eyes grew worried. "I guess so. But I'll also be talking to clients, dealing with insurance companies, talking to doctors... and I'll have a real degree." She stopped and bit her lip.

His thoughts flew back to Gedaliah's office. He'd told the principal that without a degree, he was less qualified. How could he encourage Brachie to pursue a career without a degree? That piece of paper could mean a lot to her in the future, and would give her the confidence to proclaim herself as an expert, to demand a higher salary.

As the silence between them stretched, he looked at his daughter. Brachie really didn't know what she wanted, nor what it would be like to be out of school or to become an active part of the workforce. She lacked life experience to weigh the options and make a mature decision. As much as he wanted her to make an informed decision, he understood that delving further would only create conflict between her and Tova—and likely between himself and Tova as well.

He exhaled and smiled. "I'm sure you'll make the right decision. I have confidence in you."

Brachie returned a shaky smile. The phone rang, and she jumped up with her usual energy. Cordless in hand, she climbed the stairs.

He sat before his unopened *sefer* pondering the day's events. It was interesting how he and Brachie were both grappling with career issues. No, he was *not* grappling with career issues. He was offered a job and turned it down. Brachie was the one who had to make a decision—and that decision seemed to have already been made for her.

He had just opened the *sefer* when Tova entered and sat across from him. Avner could smell another serious conversation brewing. He sighed as the book closed on itself.

"I wanted to discuss Yoni a little more."

At least it wasn't about his job. "About next Shabbos?"

"Really, the bigger question is about *shidduchim*. Yoni thinks he's ready to get married."

"So he's told me."

"Well, what do you think?"

He turned the question back to Tova. "What do *you* think?"

"He's awfully young."

"True. But he's also pretty mature."

"Mature?" Tova squinted at Avner. "What makes you say that?"

"He knows what he wants—"

"So he's decisive. That doesn't mean he's mature!"

"Well, he *is* decisive. But I meant that he knows what he wants in life. He wants to learn, and he wants to have some kind of *parnassah* plan up his sleeve for later, and he wants to raise a family of *yere'ei Shamayim*."

"Clichés."

Avner smiled. "You know, some people go to Lakewood because it looks good on a résumé. And some people go because that's the kind of learning, the kind of environment they want. Yoni is sincere, he's real. And he means what he says."

"But—"

The phone rang. Avner was prepared to ignore it, but Tova began to look for it.

"Only the base is ringing. Brachie must have taken it upstairs."

"That's right, I saw her take it."

Tova threw up her hands. "It'll stop ringing by then. Why doesn't she pick up?"

"They'll call back, it doesn't matter."

"I'll put it on speaker," Tova said.

Avner shrugged.

Tova pressed the button. "Hello?"

"May I speak with Tova, please?" The voice resounded clearly through the phone.

"Speaking."

"This is Zelda Fogel. You know, we were on the yeshivah's tea committee together last year."

"Yes, of course. You arranged the entertainment. I was so impressed at the way you spoke at that first meeting."

"How sweet of you," Zelda said.

Avner opened his *sefer* and flipped to the page he wanted.

"But that can't be why you're calling," Tova said. "The tea is in December. Is there another committee forming?"

"No," Zelda laughed, and the sound was like wind chimes magnified by amplifiers.

Avner was wondering when Tova would stop and locate the cordless. His *sefer* had been calling to him for what seemed like hours. He looked at Tova, who shrugged and pointed to the phone. Instead of waiting it out, Avner picked up his *sefer* and began to walk toward the kitchen.

"I don't know if you're aware of this," Zelda said, "but I'm also a *shadchan.*"

Avner stopped short.

"Uh, no, I had no idea," Tova said. She turned to Avner and motioned frantically for him to get the cordless from upstairs.

Avner smiled at her motions and made an about-face, heading for the stairs instead.

"It's so thoughtful of you to call," Tova said. "We were just discussing *shidduchim,* in fact."

"Were you? That's wonderful! She's so sweet, she'll make a darling wife."

Avner paused again. Did Mrs. Fogel have a girl in mind for Shimon?

Tova seemed just as perplexed. "Uh, which child is this for? Do you want to tell me some more about her?"

The wind chimes tinkled some more. "No, no, my dear. I know you have two boys in *shidduchim*. But I'm calling with someone for Brachie."

Avner's breath caught. Brachie? The idea was so foreign to him that he couldn't even form a coherent thought connected to it. Instead, his mind latched on to the first part of what she'd said. *Two* boys in *shidduchim*? He quickened his pace, exceedingly aware that regardless of which child it concerned, this conversation should not be taking place at this volume. If Meir overheard, it would engender a slew of unnecessary questions and spark interesting discussions with his friends.

Avner reached the foot of the stairs and turned. There was Brachie, sitting on the third step with the cordless in her hand, her eyes bursting with excitement.

5

YERUCHAM SAT AT THE head of the table, an unopened *sefer* pushed off to the side. He was rubbing his right thumb and forefinger together, a familiar gesture that showed Aidel exactly where his mind was.

She paused only for a second. "I see you're finished here already. Perfect! I'm ready for our walk."

Yerucham sat up straight and cleared his throat. "Let's skip the walk today."

"What? And miss out on all that brilliant sunshine?" Aidel tugged the dining room curtain open, and a bright patch of sunshine spilled onto the floor.

His voice was firm, but his fingers kept moving. "That's the problem, it's much too sunny. It'll be too hot for walking."

"Who's afraid of a little heat? We'll take a shorter walk, if you like, and we'll pass by the rabbi's house. He said he wanted to show you that new *sefer*, remember?"

Yerucham's fingers grew still.

"And when we get home, I'll make you a nice glass of ice cold lemonade, just the way you like it. I picked up some fresh lemons yesterday on my way home."

"Fresh lemons?" His hand hovered over the table, then dropped to his side. "Okay. Let me get my hat." He stood, ambled over to the front closet, and reached for his gray straw hat. He began to close the closet door.

"One second," Aidel stopped him. "I'll get my sun hat, too." Yerucham stepped back and Aidel reached for her wide-brimmed straw hat, sitting up on the shelf. Thankfully, her arms were working just fine, unlike yesterday when for some strange reason she had trouble reaching for the salt. But the hat was just out of reach. "It's too far back. Would you mind getting it for me?"

Yerucham nodded, reached up, and handed Aidel her hat.

"Thank you," Aidel smiled. She perched the hat atop her short blonde *sheitel*. "Now I just need my sunglasses." She fished through a large brown purse that hung from a hook inside the closet and pushed an oversized pair of brown sunglasses onto the bridge of her nose. "I'm ready."

Aidel went first, and Yerucham closed the door behind them. The stairs creaked as they descended from their second-story apartment. They stepped outside the main door and Yerucham secured all three locks, then slipped the key ring into his left front pants pocket.

"We'll stay in the shade of these gorgeous sycamores," Aidel said. "See, out of the sunshine, there's a nice breath of air."

"So there is," Yerucham agreed.

Contentment flowed through her veins. Lifting Yerucham's spirits, coaxing him away from his dark thoughts, made her feel like a bird flitting between the trees, and the passage of years made no dent in her pleasure.

She breathed in the summer air, redolent with blossoming hydrangea and peonies and honeysuckle. Once they reached the end of their cul-de-sac, the flower beds bordering the properties grew smaller, but the gentle sway of the towering sycamores blanketed them with shade.

As they strolled down the avenue, Aidel watched Yerucham out of the corner of her eye. His brittle, snow-white hair, deeply lined face, and slow gait often led people to believe that he was in his eighties, not his early seventies. And her lithe form, quick step, and vibrant eyes at times made them wonder if she wasn't his doting daughter instead of his wife of many years. Then again, most people didn't know that while she'd been born after the war's end, he'd become the family patriarch at the tender age of eight.

A sudden gust of wind surprised them. Aidel grabbed her hat just before it flew off, but Yerucham's took flight and tumbled into the grass to their right.

Yerucham reached out for it, but his hands caught only air. Aidel chased the hat and snatched it up before it could go any further. She inspected the crown, brushed off the brim, and handed it back to Yerucham. "None the worse for wear."

He accepted it with a sheepish grin and a dignified nod. "Thank you."

Yerucham settled the hat back on his head and resumed walking. Soon his stride slowed.

"I'm getting a little tired," Aidel said. "There's a nice bench up there on the next block. Would you mind stopping for a few minutes?"

Yerucham agreed, and they made their way to the bench. Yerucham eased himself down.

Aidel joined him. "That's much better. Now I can look at those incredible impatiens across the street."

Yerucham was silent, contemplative. His thumb and forefinger took up their earlier dance. Suddenly, his shoulders tightened and his voice grew thick. "It's in four weeks."

The non sequitur did not throw Aidel; she'd been awaiting

this exchange for several days already. Over the past week, she'd seen the change come over him, especially in his eyes. They were steely, those two sky blue eyes, but as spring gave way to summer, they were weighted down like the heavy air preceding a summer storm.

"Did you mark the date?" Yerucham asked.

"Of course."

"And their names? In Yiddish?"

"Yes, of course. I wrote their names in Yiddish." If this were about any other topic, she would add that she dotted the *ayins* and crossed the *tavs*. But this subject was sacrosanct, and she focused wholly on saying the words her husband needed to hear.

"And my father, *zecher tzaddik liverachah*, you wrote *Halevi* by my father? You didn't forget *Halevi*?"

"I remembered to write *Halevi*. I couldn't forget something as important as that, could I? Not when you have such a beautiful voice."

"And my brothers and sisters? You remembered their names? Their full names?"

"Yes. And *Halevi* by the boys' names as well."

His shoulders straightened a half inch, his fingers relaxed.

"Now," Aidel said, taking him a step further, "if you want to head over to the rabbi's house, he has that *sefer* you wanted to look at. Maybe you'll find a nice *vort* for the *yahrzeit seudah*."

"Yes, I would like that." He pulled himself up off the bench. "If you're up to it, that is."

The rabbi's house was only another four blocks. "Oh, I think I can manage the walk," she smiled.

Rabbi Hess was in his study and seemed quite pleased to receive his guests. The rebbetzin served Yerucham a glass of cold lemonade, and to Aidel she gave a glass of water. Leaving a plate of *kichel*, she apologized for running out, but she was just on her way to visit Mrs. Abramowitz in the hospital.

Aidel assured her that they were in good hands, while secretly wondering if the lemonade was made from powder.

"It's wonderful to see you. Please, make a *berachah*," Rabbi Hess said.

Yerucham passed on the *kichel* and reached for the lemonade. After one sip, Aidel could see on his face that it was not homemade. She didn't begrudge the rebbetzin her homemade *kichel*, but only *she* knew how to make lemonade the way Yerucham liked it.

The men exchanged pleasantries, and Aidel shared the news that Brachie had just come home from seminary. The rabbi remembered Yerucham's interest in the new *sefer* and offered to lend it to him. Yerucham's eyes lit up, and he thanked the rabbi aloud while Aidel thanked him many more times in her heart.

They stood, ready to leave. The rabbi walked them to the door and down the six stairs to the stone path that cut through the small lawn.

Aidel followed a step behind. As the rabbi bid them goodbye, she felt her leg grow suddenly heavy, and the next thing she knew, grass poked into her eyes as she lay sprawled out, face down, on the rabbi's lawn.

Tova closed the oven door and sniffed the air. Today, Meir would come home to freshly baked peanut butter cookies. Amidst Shimon's dating and Brachie's homecoming, Tova felt he could use something to make him feel special. She set the timer and made her way down to the laundry room, and was greeted by a satisfying buzz as the drier finished a load.

She enjoyed cooking and baking, slipping into her kitchen the way some people slip into the driver's seat of a car. But the laundry room was her haven. She loved the swish of the rinse cycle, the hum of the dryer, the hiss of the iron. The rhythm of her hands folding the still-warm clothing made her feel like an orchestra conductor, creating a symphony, bringing harmony to her being, her home, her family.

Tova reached into the drier, plucked out a pair of Meir's pants, ran her hand down the legs, and neatly folded them. A shirt, a pair of socks, another pair of pants—one garment at a time, Tova smoothed and folded.

Upstairs, she knew that Shimon was standing next to his closet, deciding which white shirt to wear. Soon, he'd be asking her how he looked, and she'd have an opportunity to talk to him about Ilana. She'd ask him questions to which she already knew the answers—one of Avner's tricks that she'd picked up over the years—such as did he and Ilana have a good time together, did he feel torn when it was time to end the date, did he think about her after the date and look forward to seeing her again. Once he started talking, it would be easier for him to decide if they shared common goals and *hashkafos*, if she had good *middos*.

If that checked out, then all Shimon needed was a nudge. It was natural to get cold feet before making such a momentous decision, and she wanted to remind him that he really did want to get married, to embark on a new stage of life with a carefully chosen partner who would help him carve out—and meet—new life goals. Shimon's uncertainty revolved around one question: Was Ilana that carefully chosen partner?

Tova had a strong hunch that she was. And so, apparently, did Ilana. It was a tribute to Shimon's modesty, his *finekeit*, that he was still uncertain. If he knew that Ilana was sure, he'd be ready.

Or so Tova thought. She was prepared to tell Shimon that Ilana was just waiting for him to say the word. Avner, though, thought otherwise. He suspected that if Shimon knew that Ilana was ready to get engaged, he would feel pressured and it would have the opposite effect. And so Tova had agreed not to reveal Ilana's true sentiments. Instead, she would bolster his courage and answer any questions he may have.

It was hard for Tova to swallow her instincts, but she couldn't overrule Avner. She'd been brought up with the deeply ingrained notion that Tatty's word was law. Besides, Avner was so easygoing about so many things that when he did feel strongly about something, she found herself automatically agreeing—outwardly, at least. And eventually, she came around to seeing that Avner usually knew what he was talking about.

Tova paired the last two socks and carried the loaded basket to Shimon's room. She knocked on the door.

"Come in." Shimon was inspecting his cuff links, making sure they were perfectly straight.

"Is that a new tie?" Tova asked, putting the basket down on Yoni's bed.

"It's borrowed," Shimon mumbled.

"Borrowed?" He might have said it was stolen and she would not have been more surprised. Did he actually tell someone that he was dating? Her spirits soared. He really *was* ready to get engaged, or he would never have shared this information with anyone outside the family.

"From Nechemiah."

"Your *chavrusa*?"

"Yeah. He said he wore it the night he got engaged."

Was he trying to tell her something? Tova almost asked, before she remembered Avner's admonition: No pressure. No *hints* of pressure. She swallowed. "It will look nice with your suit. Where are you going today?"

"I thought we'd go to Central Park. It's not too hot, and there are some nice spots where we can sit and have some quiet." He turned and faced Tova. "I'm hoping to have a serious talk with Ilana."

Now, if that wasn't an invitation... *Forgive me, Avner.* "A serious talk about what?"

He spoke quietly. "There are some things I need to know."

"Such as?"

"Where she would want to live, and how she feels about working once she has children."

These were the big questions. "Shimon, are you ready to get engaged to Ilana?" the question ran out of her mouth before she realized she was saying the words.

Shimon folded back into himself. "I, uh, didn't say that. I just... I just want to know, in theory, how she feels. So that I can think about it, and see if it fits with what I want."

Tova was unsure of how to respond. She should have listened to Avner and said nothing! It was too late now to take back her words. Well, it was all for the best. Wasn't it?

The kitchen timer sounded, and a second later the phone rang. Tova hesitated. It was difficult for her to ignore the phone. Maybe it was the *shadchan* calling; maybe something happened and they needed to change the time. And anyway she had to take the cookies out of the oven.

Shimon gave a shy smile. "I'll be down soon, Mommy. I'm going to brush my hat."

"Okay," Tova agreed. Should she pursue the conversation? What would Avner do? Tova walked down the stairs to the kitchen, picked up the phone, and grabbed a pair of oven mitts. "Hello?"

"Mrs. Lehrfeld?"

"Speaking."

"This is Rabbi Hess. First let me assure you that everything is fine, and everyone is okay."

Tova threw the oven mitts onto the counter and grabbed the back of a chair. "What happened?"

"I repeat, everyone is fine."

Tova's heart pounded. "Rabbi Hess, that is the same introduction I got when Yoni broke his leg nearly ten years ago.

Please, tell me what happened!"

"Well, I'm standing here with your parents. They were in my house for a few minutes. On the way out, your mother seems to have fallen down."

"*Oy vey, Ribbono shel Oilam!* Is she okay?"

"She looks perfectly fine. But I'm concerned, and I think she should go to the hospital."

Tova's thoughts resembled a basket of unfolded laundry: a confusing jumble of colors that needed sorting out. As she tried to think coherently, she heard several voices at once over the phone line.

Two seconds later, her mother was talking; she must have taken the phone from the rabbi. "Tova, I'm fine. I don't know why everyone is making such a fuss. I just caught my foot on something."

"But you fell down, Aidel. Maybe you broke something!" That was her father in the background.

Tova heard what was likely her mother's palm cupping the receiver, then a loud but muffled, "I didn't break anything. But Tatty is nearly hysterical, and the rabbi is ready to call Hatzolah. Is Avner home?"

"No. He should be home in a few minutes, though. What—"

"Good. Please have him come pick us up. I am *not* going anywhere in an ambulance." She gave Tova the rabbi's address.

"Okay, Ma, I'll send him right away. But maybe—"

Yerucham started to speak again, Aidel didn't let him finish, and Rabbi Hess was trying to get a word in.

"Tova, I can't hear a word you're saying. Please send Avner with the car, and you'll see for yourself that this whole situation is ridiculous."

The line went dead. Tova stared in disbelief at the phone in her hand, which she only now noticed was trembling. Her mother had fallen? She simply couldn't imagine such a thing.

Her mother walked more than most people in their twenties and thirties and was as surefooted as a woman half her age.

The front door opened, and Tova flew to Avner. Quickly, she told him about the phone call she'd received. Without another word, Avner marched straight back out the door and into the car. Tova followed.

"I'll be right back," Avner said. "You can stay here."

"No, no, I want to come." She opened the passenger side door.

"Won't Meir be home any minute?"

Tova waved his words away. "We'll be right back. He can let himself in."

Avner's eyebrows arched high into his forehead. "Does he have a key?"

"I didn't lock it. Let's just go. Please!"

Avner said nothing as he started the engine. They arrived at the rabbi's house in less than four minutes. Tova had the car door open almost before Avner came to a full stop. She rang the bell and waited impatiently until they were let in.

Rushing past Rabbi Hess, Tova cried, "Ma!" and ran straight to her.

Aidel sprang to her feet. "There you are!" she turned to Yerucham. "Okay, we can go now."

Tova turned to her father and was taken aback. His aged face was ashen, his back hunched over as if his shoulders could not bear the weight of his head. Tova thought that of the two, it was her father who seemed to be more in need of medical attention.

Aidel followed Tova's eyes and stopped. "Oy, Yerucham, you look awful. Come on, let's get you home, and I'll make you a nice cup of tea. Or that lemonade I promised you."

"I don't need tea, Aidel," he said in a small voice. "It's you who needs help."

"Feh! I'm fine. Do I look sick to you?" She turned to her host.

"Rabbi Hess, thank you very much for your concern. As you can see, we're in good hands now."

Rabbi Hess saw the four of them into Avner's car and said a reluctant good-bye. As they drove, there was an unspoken agreement to hold off on all conversation until they'd reached home. It was equally obvious that the home they were going to was Tova and Avner's.

As they turned the corner from the avenue, their way was blocked by emergency vehicles.

The silence in the car grew thick. Three of the four occupants gasped.

But Tova's mind was so full of concern for her parents that it took her a few seconds to realize that a fire engine was parked right in front of her house—and a fireman was walking down her front steps.

TOVA'S HAND FLEW TO her mouth. Where was Meir?

It was Sunday, and the many people milling about blocked her view. After Avner jumped out of the car, she stayed glued to her seat, eyes frantically scanning the thinning crowd. Not finding Meir, she searched for Avner.

There he was, talking to Shimon. Shimon! In all the excitement, she'd forgotten that she'd left him at home, getting ready for his date. Tova dashed out of the car, leaving her parents behind. "Where's Meir?" she panted.

"He's inside," Shimon said.

"Inside!" Her voice was shrill.

"There's no fire," Avner explained quickly. "It was just smoke. He's opening the windows to air out the house."

Tova grabbed Shimon's arm and glared at him. "Can you please explain what's going on?"

"Uh, well, there was lots of smoke coming from downstairs."

"And?" Tova prodded.

"I went to the Feingolds and called the fire department."

"Just like that? That can't be the whole story!" Tova's heart was still pounding, and she thought her legs were going to give out. To steady herself, she closed her eyes. When she opened them, a tall man in a black suit with yellow markings was approaching, holding his hat in his hands.

"Well, folks," he greeted them, "you sure know how to make a barbeque."

Avner and Shimon exchanged confused looks while Tova just stared.

"I'm the fire chief, and ma'am, there was enough smoke comin' outta your house to been seen a block away."

She looked around at the collection of fire trucks and firemen. There must have been, to warrant such a response.

"The smoke came from the kitchen, inside the oven. Were you cookin' somethin'?"

Had she been cooking something? The minutes before she'd gotten that phone call from Rabbi Hess seemed like a blur. She suddenly slapped her hand to her forehead. "The cookies! I baked Meir some peanut butter cookies."

The fireman laughed, a loud, guttural laugh that drew the attention of everyone in a ten-foot radius, making her instantly aware of the presence of half the neighborhood. "Ma'am, are you sayin' that pile of ash in the oven started out as peanut butter cookies? Lemme guess, the tray was lined with paper, am I right?" He laughed again, louder than before. "Hey, Johnny, c'mere, you gotta hear this."

"No, please," Tova begged, "I don't—"

"Those were cookies," he called out, well before Johnny was within normal hearing range. "Peanut butter cookies!" He drew out the words peanut butter, as if to imply that if they had been sugar cookies, the situation would not have been so amusing.

Johnny seemed to think so as well. "Peanut butter cookies?!" He added his laughter to the fire chief's.

Tova had never been so conscious of so many pairs of eyes on her at once. She turned to Avner. "The timer went off, I remember now, but before I took them out of the oven, Rabbi Hess called saying—"

"We'll discuss it later," Avner broke in, warning her with her eyes not to say any more in front of Shimon.

"I can't believe a few trays of burned cookies could make that much smoke!" Her words were strangled.

"Here it is, chief." Yet another fireman joined their circle. He was holding what might once have been a baking tray. Tova looked away, flooded with humiliation. Did he have to parade the tray all over the lawn, in full view of the one or two neighbors who might not have already heard that she, Tova Lehrfeld, nearly burned her house down while baking peanut butter cookies?

The fire chief squeezed out a few remaining chuckles. "You'll have to forgive us, ma'am. We get lotsa calls." His voice turned serious. His face was sober, his eyes steel. "Lotsa calls. Most of 'em don't have happy endings like this."

Avner nodded. "We understand."

"You people have a fire extinguisher hiding in that kitchen somewhere?"

"No."

"Maybe it's time you get one." He looked from one to the next. "It's safe to go inside, but don't you forget to count your blessings." He nodded and walked away.

Tova dabbed at her eyes. He was right, of course. Still, she knew this story would quickly make its rounds. She grasped for a detail to latch on to. "Shimon, when did Meir get home?"

"Everything happened so fast, I'm not sure exactly what happened when."

"I know what that's like," Tova said, feeling like she was staring out the window of a speeding train. "Oy vey, Bubby and

Zeidy are still sitting in the car! Go to them, Shimon, tell them everything's fine. They must be so worried!"

Shimon ran to the car.

Avner nodded. "We need to hear the whole story about your mother." He peered at Tova and rubbed his beard. "And you need to sit down and have a drink."

Once Tova assured herself that Meir was okay and everyone else was settled in the living room, Tova looked around and chewed her lip. "Go get some drinks," she told Shimon absently.

Shimon looked at his watch, nodded, and left the room. He came back with a bottle of Dr. Pepper and some plastic cups. "Here, Mommy. I have to—"

"Dr. Pepper?" Tova interrupted him. "What kind of a drink is that to serve Bubby and Zeidy? Go get something normal, like water, or lemonade."

Shimon's eyes darted to his father.

"Shimon," Avner said, "don't you have to leave soon?"

"Uh..."

"Oy, Shimon, I'm so sorry. I'm so *farblunget* I forgot all about your date."

All eyes were on Shimon. He blushed.

Aidel stood. "This is ridiculous. *You*," she pointed crisply at Shimon, "go get ready. *You*," she pointed at Tova, "go wash your face and take a good, few deep breaths. *I* am going to bring out some drinks." Her voice softened almost imperceptibly. "Yerucham, just stay put, and I'll make you a glass of lemonade." She marched into the kitchen, carrying the bottle of Dr. Pepper.

Shimon escaped, and Tova did as her mother bade her. By the time she returned to the living room, a pitcher of lemonade sat on the coffee table, everyone held a glass in one hand, and the atmosphere had lightened considerably.

"Here, *sheifeleh*," Aidel said, thrusting a cold glass into Tova's hand. "Drink."

Tova made a *berachah* and sipped, allowing the icy sweetness to bring her back to herself. "Ma," she said with a calmness she was just beginning to feel, "can you please tell us what happened?"

Aidel put her hands out as she spoke. "Nothing happened! I had just come down the stairs, and my foot must have caught on something. A rock, maybe. That's all there is to it! I didn't hurt myself, I fell onto the soft grass." She chuckled. "Nothing was wounded except my pride. And maybe my hat."

Shimon appeared holding the car keys.

"Good luck," Aidel said.

He looked at Tova and brushed imaginary lint off his arm. "My jacket smells like smoke."

"That's wonderful," Aidel said with a big smile. "At least you'll have something to talk about."

Shimon grinned, said good-bye, and left.

Aidel turned to Yerucham. "Are you feeling better now? You're still pale."

"Ach, I'm fine." He waved his hand, then let it fall to his side. The creases on his face seemed to have deepened.

Tova looked at Yerucham. Besides his color, his unusual quiet unnerved her. She glanced at Avner.

His eyes smiled back at her, then he turned to Aidel. "Bubby looks fine to me. But to make everyone happy, perhaps you could see a doctor anyway."

"Yes!" Yerucham said with a sudden vehemence. "That's right, Aidel. Go see Dr. Sassoon."

Tova thought that her mother would agree just to erase that pinched look on her father's face.

"Avner, thank you for your concern. I can't imagine why I need a doctor."

"Tova, get the doctor's number for us, please. We're going to call and make an appointment." Suddenly, Yerucham was taking charge, once more sure of himself.

Tova stood and brought her phone book. She picked up the cordless and waited.

Aidel sighed. "Okay, fine. We'll make an appointment, if it will make you happy. But not tomorrow."

"Not tomorrow," Yerucham said. "Today."

Aidel put her glass down. "I can't today," she said with her own unique blend of firmness and gentleness that Tova always tried to imitate. "I already defrosted the ground meat and grated the onions. I'm making a big pot of meatballs for the *yahrzeit seudah*."

Pushing aside another flicker of guilt for having forgotten the *yahrzeit*, Tova studied her father. He looked torn—and vulnerable.

Yerucham cleared his throat, hesitated, then nodded. "Tuesday, then."

"If you make it early enough, maybe Avner can drive you."

"I am perfectly capable of walking there," Aidel said with her usual self-assurance and good cheer.

Meir came in from outside.

"I thought you were upstairs clearing the smoke," Tova said.

"I was. Then I went out to talk to the firemen."

Avner smiled. "What did they say?"

"They said that people should never be embarrassed to call the fire department."

Embarrassed. Humiliation zigzagged through Tova's chest once more. What would people think?

After the doctor's appointment was secured for Tuesday, Tova sat down next to her mother. "Please stay for dinner."

"Tova, will you stop trying to baby me? I told you, there is nothing wrong with me."

Tova's eyebrows arched. "Ma, I didn't mean it like that at all. It's just so nice to have you and Tatty here. How often do we get to spend a Sunday afternoon together like this?"

Aidel glanced at Yerucham and Meir, then looked deeply into Tova's eyes and her own softened. "You're right, Tovaleh. Brachie's been away for so long, and Meir's home for a change. It's so nice to be here with you today." She smiled and Tova felt as if she were a little girl in her mother's warm embrace. "I guess my meatballs can wait a little longer."

A sudden longing welled up in Tova's heart and she wished, for a moment, that she could always be surrounded by her family: her parents, her husband, and her children. She wanted to hold on to this moment, to keep her parents just the way they were and within arm's reach, to keep her children with her at home, to not let things change—ever.

The intensity of the feeling surprised her and was replaced by a swift, sudden awareness that nothing lasts forever. And without understanding why, she tasted fear.

TOVA SAT ON THE couch, quietly saying Tehillim.

A key turned in the lock, and Avner stepped through the front door and past the foyer.

Tova looked up and smiled. "Hello, Avner."

"Hello, look who I met up with."

Shimon followed on Avner's heels. "We ended up at the same *minyan*."

Tova sat up straight. "Shimon, you were gone the entire afternoon! How was your date? You must have had a nice time, to be out so long."

Avner put his hat in the closet. Shimon kept his on.

"Are you going back out again somewhere now, Shimon?" Tova asked.

Shimon's face was blank.

"Don't you want to take off your hat, or do you still need it?"

"My hat?" He felt his head with his hand and seemed surprised that he was still wearing it. "No, I'm not going anywhere, I'll put it away." He made no move to do so.

Tova chuckled, and Avner lifted Shimon's hat up off his head and carried it to the closet.

Shimon sat down. "I had a really good time. We walked through Central Park, found lots of cool, shady places."

"And...?"

"I like her, Mommy. She's... nice.

Tova peered at Shimon. After seven dates, was that all he could say about her?

Apparently, Avner was wondering the same thing. "What's nice?" he asked.

"You know, nice. Caring."

Avner sat down and laid a hand on Shimon's shoulder. "What makes you say that?"

"I, uh, just get that impression."

"Can you think of something she said, or maybe something she did, that gave you that impression?"

Now Tova looked at Avner. Shimon said "nice" meant "caring." Agreed, it wasn't poetry, but if he got an impression, he got an impression. Why press him for details that he clearly hadn't noticed, or thought important?

After a strained silence, Shimon said, "Maybe this is what you mean. I bought some drinks and we sat down on a bench. We were in the middle of a conversation about Flatbush, and I knocked over my Sprite." He shrugged. "It didn't spill on me or anything, and once I stopped feeling stupid about it, it was no big deal. Soon after, when we were getting up to walk around more, Ilana bent down to pick up her purse, and she noticed that some Sprite had spilled on the bench. So she took a tissue out of her purse and wiped the drops away."

Tova thought the story showed that Ilana would make a good housekeeper, but she didn't see how that made her caring.

"I was kind of embarrassed. I mean, maybe she thought I was a slob. I guess I looked uncomfortable, because she explained to me that she didn't want someone else to come along and accidentally sit in the Sprite."

Not the most eloquent example of caring, or compassion and consideration, perhaps, but it was enough for Shimon—and for Tova.

Avner, though, pursued his questioning. "Okay, so you felt that showed caring. Do you feel it showed anything else?"

Tova didn't understand why Avner was putting their son through this. Shimon and Ilana's *hashkafos* were similar, their backgrounds as well. If he liked her, enjoyed her company, and was comfortable, that was saying a lot. Why break it down into the nitty-gritty? If you dig deep enough, you'll always find something that's not perfect.

"Um..." Shimon crossed his legs and sat back with his hands wrapped around his knees. Then he unlaced his hands and crossed his legs the other way. "I think it shows she... she pays attention to details. Yeah, that's right. Most people wouldn't think of wiping up some spilled soda. Or they wouldn't have some tissues to wipe it with. She notices things, thinks about them." He seemed to warm to the idea. "And another example. When she put her cell phone away, she didn't just toss it into her purse. She unzipped and zipped two zippers so that it would go back into the pocket it came from. And, I remember now, when we got out of the car, she checked to make sure the door was locked."

Avner nodded.

"So," Tova said, before Avner could ask any more questions, "what's the next step?"

Shimon folded his arms and took a deep breath. "I've made up my mind," he said. "I'm ready to get engaged."

Tova hit the "off" button and threw the cordless down on her dresser, eyes aglow. "That's it," she said, "it's all arranged. We're going over to the Moskowitzes at nine o'clock."

Avner smiled weakly in response.

"Oh, Avner, this is so exciting! I can't believe it's really happening! The way Shimon was dragging his feet, I was sure this *shidduch* would never go anywhere. And now, we're meeting Ilana's parents! I don't know how I'm going to keep this a secret until Wednesday." She threw open the closet door and began flipping through hangers.

"Wednesday?" Avner asked. "Today's Sunday. They can get engaged and we can have the *l'chaim* tomorrow night."

"No, it can't be tomorrow." She pulled out a black skirt, made a face, and put it back.

A blizzard of thoughts whirled through Avner's head. Even after he'd agonized and finally come to this decision, Shimon was still procrastinating? "I'm a little concerned about that."

"Oh, I know, it's silly, but that's what they want."

They? "Ilana also wants to wait until Wednesday?"

"Ilana?" She fingered a blue suit. "No, no. Her parents."

Avner was more confused than ever. "I don't understand."

Tova turned around to face Avner. "Perel Moskowitz's sister is making miniatures for the *l'chaim*. Since there won't be a *vort*, they want the *l'chaim* to be a little fancier. They asked for some time."

"And you agreed?"

One hand on her hip, Tova said, "Avner, there are going to be many things we'll need to compromise on. It's important to them, and I knew about it already."

"You did?"

Tova's brow furrowed, and Avner instinctively backed down. Whatever Tova had arranged, it was already done. But he was privately incredulous that two people's futures could be put on hold for a few platters of cookies. Shimon was anxious to begin with. How was he supposed to sit in the *beis midrash* and learn with this hanging over his head? A formal engagement would remove that layer of pressure called uncertainty.

Despite her concerns to the contrary, Tova found something suitable to wear to meet the *mechutanim*. Avner's anxiety made it hard for him to be as enthusiastic as the occasion called for, but Tova's grace was enough for both of them. They made preliminary arrangements, and Avner went home with a headache.

Avner walked into school the next day with more than a twinge of unrest which was pushed aside by a mountain of paperwork. He did not work with students the entire morning; instead, he tied up several loose ends. With a satisfying feeling of closure, he placed a file on a corner of the table and stretched.

The bell rang, signaling recess. Avner made his way to the teachers' room. His time was structured differently than the standard classroom *rebbi*'s, and he had the freedom to make himself a cup of coffee anytime he wasn't sitting with a group of boys. But he enjoyed being with the others. Besides providing a stark contrast to his own quiet niche, he felt he gained from listening to the give and take, and he often went away with a new appreciation for how dedicated these men were. They truly cared about their students, enough to use this precious "free" time to share resources or ask advice. Avner thought that Gedaliah had helped shape that atmosphere. Years ago, when a different principal ran the school, the mood in the room had a subtle negative flavor, almost an us-against-them attitude. It was Gedaliah who brought in optimism and purpose. Looking around the room now, Avner felt that this was the secret to the principal's success. Yes, he had many good *rebbis* under him; it was the way he had influenced them that had turned a mediocre school into a great one.

Avner's presence in the teachers' room also gave him opportunities to informally speak to a *rebbi* about a student. He'd been hoping to catch Shmuel Cantor, the eighth-grade *rebbi*, in order to convince him that Pinny Bloom deserved an award. This

nore open-minded than some of the others,
ping that Pinny's improvement in *derech eretz*
al recognition.

onors seemed to be the topic under discussion,
't there. In fact, only Kalman and Yitzchak and
were in attendance, and Avner surmised that
the others were also busy with paperwork. He made himself a
coffee and sat down. In the absence of the usual banter, his mind
wandered to Shimon's upcoming engagement.

Avner knew that boys tended not to have a long list of qualities they were looking for in a girl, and Shimon was no exception.
Though he had never put it down on paper, Avner suspected
that Shimon's list might read like a help wanted ad: "Seeking
pretty girl with fine *middos* to like me, take good care of me, and
make a loving mother."

Shimon was not a deep thinker, and expecting him to read
into every action and comment was completely unrealistic.
Still, he felt that Shimon was pushing himself into something
he didn't truly want or feel ready for. It was as if he had a sore
shoulder, and was popping two aspirin to numb the pain despite
not knowing the cause. Once the discomfort subsided, things
would take care of themselves—or so Shimon thought.

The *shidduch* process had been typically gradual, one date
leading to the next, but his ultimate decision seemed like a leap
off a cliff. Sure, everyone has doubts and has to take that leap
sooner or later. Yet Shimon's feet were leaving terra firma with
a one-two-three-go without first being securely anchored in the
ground.

Avner swirled his coffee around the cup. He watched white
wisps of foam dance, subtly changing shape as they closed in
on each other. Shimon, Ilana, Tova, a *chasunah*, a new life. Tutor,
teacher. Dilemmas, decisions. He held his cup firmly between
his hands and closed his eyes.

From across the near-empty room, Kalman's voice broke into his churning thoughts. "So, Avner. I hear you're going to be the new seventh-grade *rebbi*."

All eyes turned to Avner. His tongue felt like a sponge.

"I didn't hear that," Yitzchak said, interrupting his conversation with Chaim. "Mazel tov!"

"I only heard this morning," Kalman said.

Avner looked away from Kalman, who had a track record of alienating at least one student every year. Avner invariably ended up with that student.

"One second," Yitzchak said, "what happened to Oberlander?"

"Old news," Chaim said. "He took a job as assistant principal over at Chochmas Moshe."

"Well, I'm happy for you, Avner," Yitzchak said. "It's about time you moved out of that little room of yours."

Avner's neck prickled.

"Yeah," Kalman agreed. "You're too good to babysit a few boys who just can't fit in to a regular classroom."

Is that what they thought of him—a glorified babysitter? He had to find a way to end this conversation.

"Who's going to replace you?" Chaim asked.

Do it. Now. "Actually, I'm not being replaced."

"You're not?"

Kalman took a step closer. "You mean Rabbi Newman is finally giving an axe to the remedial program?"

Avner had never heard Kalman speak so plainly before. Each word stabbed him. He had a sudden urge to snap back, to say that it was teachers like Kalman who ruined a boy's chance of success. The impulse was powerful rather than lasting. When the conversation was over they would part ways, but tomorrow they would all have to face each other again.

Forcing his shoulders to relax, Avner kept his tone light. "I think there must be some kind of misunderstanding. I'm not going to be the seventh-grade *rebbi*."

"So who—"

"I'm still the tutor. That's all."

Kalman's face contorted into a half grimace.

"My work is important." Avner nodded at the others and left, making straight for his room. He was surprised to find that he was still holding his coffee. He dropped into a chair and took a sip. It was cold and bitter, but Avner had no inclination to return to the teachers' room for another. He would drink it as it was.

He got through the rest of the school day without any other difficult conversations. He avoided Gedaliah and slipped out of the building as soon as his last period ended.

"This one's pretty." Brachie pulled out a beige suit.

"I like the style," Tova said, "but beige is so impractical."

"Oh, okay." She suddenly hugged the suit and squealed, "Ooh! I just can't believe he's really getting engaged!"

"Shhh!" Tova hissed.

"Oh, Mommy, it's just *so* exciting! I have to tell *someone*. You got to tell the uncles!"

Tova smiled. "As soon as it's official, you can call all your friends."

Brachie hung up the suit as Tova pulled out another. "What about this one?"

"But do you think it would also be good for a date?"

Tova stopped and looked at her daughter. "Brachie, who said anything about a date? You've been away all year, and you need something presentable for the *l'chaim*."

"I just thought—"

"Hello there!" a voice boomed from behind.

Brachie and Tova spun around at precisely the same moment, making them look like a dancing duo.

"Shaindy, how nice to see you," Tova said, wondering how

much she'd overheard. If Shaindy Ungar heard that they were making a *l'chaim*, the whole neighborhood would know within the hour.

Shaindy shifted her glance to Brachie. "And you too, I'm glad to see you're back. You didn't gain too much weight, I see." She leaned in close to Tova. "I see you're *shopping*."

Tova put on her most politic smile. "Yes," she said, covering one side of her mouth with her hand. "If there's anything to report, you'll be the *first* to know." Without waiting for a reply, she grabbed Brachie's hand and led the way to the other side of the department.

"Brachie, this is not the place to talk about any type of..." she looked around before whispering, "dating."

"So when *can* we talk about it?"

Tova sighed. Why was Brachie in such a rush? "Let's deal with shopping now. Tonight, or tomorrow, we can sit down with Tatty and discuss *shidduchim*. Okay?"

"How about after dinner? Please?"

Tova considered. Avner would probably be spending the day doing paperwork, as he always did at the end of the school year. With no students to teach, he'd have an easy day and would be happy to discuss this. "Sure, Brachie, tonight after dinner."

At dinner, Avner knew he was being unusually quiet but had no heart to make light conversation. The mood in the house was buoyant and no one seemed to notice his preoccupation.

When Meir left the table, Brachie pounced. "Tatty, can we talk about *shidduchim* now? Mommy said it'd be a good time."

Inwardly, Avner cringed. He was still bothered by the exchange in the teachers' room; and yet that was a light spring rain compared to the torrent of anxiety he was feeling over Shimon's imminent engagement. He'd tried so hard to get through to Shimon, to get him to evaluate for himself if he was really ready to get married—and if Ilana was the girl he wanted to get married to. The effort was like trying to go fishing without a rod or a net.

And now Brachie wanted to open up the same topic! He didn't relish the thought of yet another such conversation. On the other hand, maybe right now, while all his worries about Shimon were uppermost in his mind, was the best time to talk to Brachie about dating, to make sure she saw it as a means to an end.

He dove in. "What would you like to talk about?"

Not unexpectedly, Brachie answered, "I'm ready to start dating."

A quick glance at Tova told him that he had her blessing to speak openly.

"What makes you think so?"

"I'm ready to get married."

"Mm-hmm. And why do you want to get married?"

Brachie blinked. "Because... I'm ready to start a family."

"Are you?"

"Of course! I love children, and I'm the best babysitter on the block, everyone says so. In sem, the *eim bayis* always asked me to babysit."

"And you're very patient," Tova added, smiling

"So you like children, you're good with them, you're patient. But why do you want to start a family?"

Brachie's smile faded. "Everyone wants to get married, Tatty. I don't understand what you're asking."

From the look on her face, neither, apparently, did Tova. "Avner, I don't see—"

"Just bear with me. Please," he added.

A half-smile settled on Tova's face.

"What are your goals? What do you hope to gain by getting married?"

"I want to marry a *ben Torah*. I want to marry someone who will sit and learn and..." Her eyes met his, and her voice faded. She closed her eyes. When she reopened them, Brachie answered in a different voice, "Torah is important to me, Tatty. I want to make it happen, to make learning happen. I want to have a house like ours, where children are loved and taken care of and accepted. Some of my friends don't have that. Some go to the right schools, but, I don't know, something's missing. I want my family to be happy, to care about each other—and to care about doing the mitzvos." She blushed. "I sound like Rebbetzin Berlinger. Sorry."

A tiny seedling of hope beginning to unfurl in Avner's chest. Some of that *hashkafah* she was spouting sat on her like a hat two sizes too big. But some of it had begun to sink in past the surface, and he thought he was getting a glimpse of what could develop more fully.

If they pushed off dating, it would probably serve to keep her in the role of little girl. If they allowed it in theory, Brachie would have to face certain truths, to mature in some ways.

Still, Avner hesitated. This conversation had Tova's tacit approval, but she didn't know what he was about to suggest. He made a quick decision. "I have an idea," he said before he could change his mind.

Brachie's nod was eager, Tova's wary.

Avner cleared his throat. "If someone has a specific suggestion for Brachie, we can investigate and see if it's worth pursuing."

Brachie clapped her hands and jumped up.

"But as far as contacting *shadchanim*, let's wait another few months. This way, we're not completely closing the door on her *bashert* if he comes knocking, and at the same time we're not actively pursuing anything until we feel Brachie's a bit more ready."

"I'm so happy!" Brachie gushed. "Oh, I just have to call Rena!" She was up the stairs before either one of them could react.

"Well," Avner said, looking at Tova, "what do *you* think?"

"I don't think she heard anything past the 'we can investigate' part."

"I know," he chuckled. "At this point, wait and see is best for her."

"I agree. I'd like her to start school, get at least a year behind her before she gets married. Besides, she still has a lot of growing up to do. She sounds like she hasn't left seminary yet—all those lofty ideals."

Avner was pleased with those "lofty ideals" and hoped that she'd hold on to them, internalize them. He hoped, too, that Rebbetzin Berlinger and the other teachers had spoken about marriage, not just about dating. He didn't yet know how much groundwork they'd laid, but he planned to make sure the foundations were there, even if it meant asking tough questions and making Brachie—and Tova—uncomfortable. This was Brachie's future they were talking about.

Avner tried to exhale the accumulated tension that had settled in his chest. *Shidduchim* were pushing at him from every angle, and he was more than relieved to have come to a resolution. Now he could learn something, and then concentrate only on Shimon.

"Where are we going?" Yoni asked, following Meir out of the house.

"To the cleaners, to get the suits," Meir answered.

"I know that," Yoni said with a smile, "I meant which cleaners?"

"Smith's. Mommy says you can rely on them to have your clothes ready when they say they will. Tatty dropped them off on Monday."

Yoni nodded.

"Personally, I don't see why they needed cleaning at all. They were cleaned last week, and mine still looks fine. Tatty doesn't clean his every week. Do you?"

"No. I spot clean with a damp rag."

"Right, like Mommy does for me."

"I can show you how to do it, if you want to learn to take care of it yourself."

Meir raised one eyebrow but said nothing.

"We need to look our best. These are Shimon's future in-laws we're meeting, and we need to make a good impression."

"I can make just as good an impression in a suit that was spot cleaned."

Yoni chuckled. "What can I say, if it makes Mommy happy, it makes Mommy happy. You see she's pretty nervous." And if their mother was nervous, Yoni thought, Shimon must feel like he has ants crawling down his shirt.

"Yeah, why is everyone so nervous, anyway?" Meir asked. "The *l'chaim* is not even in our house. There's nothing to organize, nothing to fuss over."

That, Yoni knew, was part of the problem. The bustle of making a *l'chaim* at home would have lessened their mother's anxiety and given her something to do with her hands. "Getting engaged is a big change. And change," Yoni dropped an arm onto Meir's shoulder, "makes people nervous."

"But Shimon's getting married, not Mommy. So I don't get it."

Yoni let his arm fall. "Even when I get a new *chavrusa* I'm a little nervous."

"But getting married is a *simchah*, right?"

"Sure, but everything new takes us time to adjust. Even *simchahs*."

"Well I don't see what's such a big change for Mommy. Shimon's in yeshivah anyway. He's hardly home." He looked sideways at Yoni. "And you're *never* home."

Yoni's smile was distracted. His place was in yeshivah. It wasn't *home*, but it was where he hung his hat, so to speak, where he very much felt he needed to be, where he was growing the most. Of course, he had to come home for Shimon's *l'chaim*, but he would have preferred to come home in the evening instead of missing an entire day.

But his mother insisted that he be home early, and the *mashgiach* gave him his blessings. So here he was, spending the greater part of the day with Meir, enjoying himself yet feeling torn.

"...nine."

"Sorry, I spaced out there for a minute. What did you say?"

"I said, why'd you come home so early? Tatty said the *l'chaim* isn't till at least nine."

"To see you, of course." He threw Meir a playful punch.

"No, really."

"Yes, really. And to spend a little time with Brachie. I was supposed to come home for Shabbos—"

"You're not coming home for Shabbos?"

"Not this week, no."

Meir stopped in his tracks and crossed his arms.

"Easy, little bro', I'll be home in another two weeks instead, okay?"

Meir resumed walking without answering.

"It's better this way, really. If I came home this week, it would be all about Shimon. This way, we get to hang out today, and then in two weeks we'll have the whole Shabbos to schmooze."

"If you say so."

The two entered the dry cleaners. Meir handed over the ticket, and Yoni accepted the clean suits.

"So tell me," Meir said when they were outside again, "what's this *l'chaim* gonna be like?"

"You've been to one before."

"Yeah, but not at my own brother's. What am I supposed to do? I'll get introduced to the Moskowitzes, and then what?"

"You don't have to do anything, but if you want to, you can greet aunts and uncles and whoever, help them find Mommy and Tatty, steer them to the food, make the introductions. It'll give you something to do besides eat cake."

"Ha! Mommy said I shouldn't eat up all the cake."

"You won't eat it all up. You'll just sample everything so you can report on what's good."

Meir chuckled.

"Making other people comfortable is a great way to become comfortable yourself."

Meir nodded sagely. Yoni smiled, acutely aware of the influence he had over his little brother.

"So how does the day work? What's the schedule?

Yoni grinned. "It's not an exact schedule, but basically, Shimon is going to take Ilana out. They'll go someplace where they can talk, and then he'll ask her to marry him."

"Why does he have to ask if he already knows the answer?"

"Because..." Yoni stopped. He desperately wanted to come up with a witty comeback, but his mind was blank. Really, he couldn't even come up with a non-witty comeback. Why *did* he have to propose if they both knew the answer?

Fortunately, Meir wasn't stuck on that detail. "Okay," he continued, "so he asks and she says yes. Then what?"

"Then they call home to say they got engaged."

"Why do they have to call? Aren't they coming back together?"

"Sure, but this way everyone knows that they're really engaged and we can start the phone calls, even before they get back."

"Don't Mommy and Tatty want to meet Ilana first?"

"They already did."

"They did? Mommy didn't say anything about that."

"Yeah. And our parents met with her parents, too. There are some things they needed to talk about, before there could be an engagement."

"Like what?"

Yoni shifted the suits from his right hand to his left. "I don't know. I'm not engaged, so I really don't know what it's like."

Meir looked sideways at Yoni. "Have you started going out?"

Yoni hesitated before answering. "No."

"Do you want to get married too?"

"Yes, I do." Up ahead, Yoni saw their house.

"I mean, soon?"

"I don't know, Meir. There are just some things in this world that we don't have control over."

"What do you mean? You get to decide if you want to get married or not, don't you?"

"Sure, but it's Hashem Who sends you the right person, at the right time."

"How do you know when it's the right time?"

They had reached the house, and Yoni stopped to look at Meir. "That, little bro', is a very good question."

Avner put his briefcase in the front closet. "Hi, Meir. Where's Mommy?"

"In the kitchen, trying to get Shimon to eat."

"Please go tell her that I'm home."

"Mommy, Tatty's home!" Meir yelled through the living room.

"Thank you, Meir," Avner said with a wry grin.

"Oh, Avner," Tova came bustling in. "Shimon is terribly jumpy. Can you please talk to him?"

"Sure." He followed Tova into the kitchen, where Shimon bounded out of his chair, nearly knocking it over. One look told him that Shimon was well past jumpy; overwrought or hysterical would be a better description. "Hi, Shimon."

Shimon's eyes bounced around the room, not landing anywhere in particular. "Hi, Tatty."

"Has it been this bad all day?" He motioned to Shimon's chair and slid into the one opposite.

"Yes, he's been like this all day," Tova answered for him. "He hasn't eaten a thing!"

Avner's eyes didn't leave Shimon. "What's going on?"

Shimon rubbed his chin, then tilted his chair back on two legs.

"Put your chair down," Tova admonished. "You're going to fall over."

Avner cast a sidelong glance at Tova. If she'd been hovering over Shimon like this all day, it was no wonder he was in such a state. "Tova, could I trouble you for a glass of iced tea?"

"No trouble at all," she smiled, and put up the kettle.

"It's perfectly natural to be nervous," Avner said quietly. "This is a big step. Do you—"

Meir's head popped into the kitchen. "Bubby and Zeidy are here!"

"They are?" Tova asked, clearly surprised.

"Yeah. Bubby said they were out walking and on the way they wanted to see Yoni. But he's in the shower, and—"

Aidel entered, followed by Yerucham. "Hello, everyone. Now, I know you must be very busy, talking and being nervous before the big moment. We won't be getting in your way, we just stopped in for a moment on the way to the doctor."

"You're never in the way," Tova said. She pulled out a chair for her father. "Come, Tatty, have a seat. I was just making some iced tea for Avner. I'll make you some, too."

"Thank you," Yerucham said, sitting between Avner and Shimon.

Aidel and Yerucham often popped in unannounced for a brief visit, though less often as the children grew older. They were pleasant and never overstayed their welcome, and Aidel's lightheartedness always brightened up a room. Now, though, Avner was concerned that the wrong question could cause Shimon to fall apart completely. He was pondering how to steer the conversation away from Shimon's upcoming date, when Yoni's entrance made it unnecessary.

"Hello, Bubby," Yoni smiled widely. "Hello, Zeidy."

"There you are," Aidel said. "Did you grow again, or is it my imagination?"

"I'm twenty-two, Bubby. I doubt I'm still growing. It must be my shoes," Yoni laughed.

More likely his self-confidence, Avner mused. Shimon was actually taller than Yoni, but unless the two were standing shoulder to shoulder, no one would think so.

"You look healthy, Yoni, that's what counts," Aidel said.

"And how are you feeling, Zeidy?"

"*Baruch Hashem*," Yerucham nodded.

"Did you get that *sefer* you wanted from Rabbi Hess?"

"Yes, I got it."

"How sweet of you to remember," Aidel said.

Yoni's smile faded as he peered at her. Something was wrong—but what? "Bubby, what did you say?"

"I said it's sweet of you to remember."

Yoni stared. "Tatty!" he said suddenly, not taking his eyes off his grandmother. "Tatty, look at Bubby!"

Yerucham grabbed the table.

"Yoni, what's gotten into you?" Aidel said.

"You see, Tatty? Bubby's face is all wrong. Only one side of it is moving."

Avner leaned forward, his features turned to stone. "Yes, I do see."

"There's nothing wrong with me," Aidel protested. "Can you all stop fussing? I'm on my way to the doctor, we'll ask him if there'sh anything shtrange."

Yerucham froze. Tova gasped.

No one spoke. With each word, Aidel's speech had become more and more slurred.

"There's no time for the doctor," Yoni said with authority. "I'm calling Hatzolah."

"What—"

"I think Bubby's having a stroke."

8

NO ONE MOVED, NO one dared breathe.

Tova's hands were clasped in front of her; her eyes wide with fright.

Yoni's voice reverberated through the kitchen as he spoke to the Hatzolah dispatcher. When he hung up, everyone seemed to move at once.

Tova rushed over to Aidel and eased her into a chair.

"Shimon, go outside and wait for the ambulance," Avner barked.

Shimon fled.

"How are you feeling?" Tova asked.

"Feeling ffff... fine," Aidel said.

Tova shuddered.

"Tova," Avner said, "please go get Doctor Sassoon's phone number. We'll need it."

A sob escaped Tova's lips as she ran from the room.

Sirens pierced the air.

"Don't you worry, Bubby, we're going to get this all figured out." Yoni smiled. "I once rode in an ambulance. Keep your eyes open, you'll enjoy the ride."

Aidel smiled back. But only the left side of her mouth curled upward, and there was a tinge of fear in her eyes.

Shouts assailed them from the living room.

"What's Hatzolah doing here?"

"Go through there!"

"Meir, stay here!"

Yoni looked up just as a man wearing a yellow vest entered the kitchen. As the man threw off his bicycle helmet, Yoni said, "Well, Bubby, today's your lucky day. You remember Chezky Hirsch? From your shul."

"Yesh," Aidel said.

"Why were we called here today?" Chezky asked as he sat next to Aidel.

Avner nodded at Yoni.

"I think my grandmother is having a stroke."

Chezky didn't take his eyes off Aidel's face. "What makes you say that?"

"Only one side of her face is moving."

"Mrs. Lewin, do you know what day today is?"

"Wendshday."

"Right. Mrs. Lewin, I'm going to put this mask on you. It's just oxygen. You can breathe normally." His hands worked as he spoke. "There you go." He pressed a button on his walkie-talkie. "I need a bus. Advise hospital stroke center." He clipped the walkie-talkie onto his belt. "I'm going to ask you some more questions, Mrs. Lewin. Does anything hurt?"

"No."

"You have any health problems? Are you taking any medication?"

"No."

Tova was back, holding her address book and the cordless. "I—" She stopped short. "Ma can't breathe?"

"She's breathing fine," Yoni said. "It's probably standard procedure."

"Should I call Dr. Sassoon?" Her voice shook.

"Not yet," Avner said, "maybe just take care of Zeidy."

Tova's head whipped around to look at Yerucham, then back to Aidel. She hesitated, bit her lip, and went to sit by her father.

A second Hatzolah member entered the kitchen.

"Hi, Moish. Evaluating for a possible stoke."

"You called a bus?" Moish asked.

"On its way."

Tova looked at Avner. "A bus?"

"An ambulance," Yoni explained.

Chezky took hold of Aidel's hands. "Can you squeeze my hands?"

Aidel did as he asked.

"Good." He let go. "Right hand weakness. Moish, you writing?"

"Yes."

"Slurred speech, right facial droop. Do vital signs."

Moishe laid two fingers on Aidel's wrist.

"When did this start?" Chezky asked.

"Nothing'sh wrong," Aidel insisted.

Moish wrapped a blood pressure cuff around her arm.

"Have you been having headaches lately?"

"No."

"Vision problems?"

"No."

Chezky shined a light into Aidels eyes. "Dizziness?"

Aidel didn't answer.

"Has there been another episode of slurred speech?"

"No," Yerucham croaked.

"Anyone notice anything different lately?"

They all looked at each other.

"Muscle weakness? Falls?"

"Yes!" Yerucham, Avner, and Tova answered.

"When?"

"A few days ago," Tova said.

"The day of the fire," Avner said. "Sunday."

"And her arm!" Yerucham cried. "She had some kind of trouble with her arm the day Brachie came for dinner."

More sirens filled the air.

"Has she gotten any medical attention since she fell? Was she hurt? Did she hit her head?"

"She didn't hit her head," Tova said. "My mother said she was fine and didn't want to go to the hospital. She was just on her way to the doctor."

The sirens grew loud and then were silenced. Two paramedics burst into the kitchen.

"One of you can stay with her," Moish said to the family, "and the others should wait in another room please. Oh, and bring a scarf or something for her to wear instead of her *sheitel*."

"I'll stay," Tova said immediately.

"Will you be going with her in the ambulance?"

"Yes."

Yoni's head whipped around toward Avner.

Avner met his gaze, then seemed to come to a decision. He looked at Yerucham and said, "Okay. Zeidy, I'll follow the ambulance in my car, you can come with me. Yoni, get a scarf, then stay here and handle Meir. And Shimon. And whatever else needs handling, I'm sure you'll figure it all out."

While he spoke, Aidel was shaking her head. "No amblansh. I can go by car."

Yoni eyed Chezky, as if asking his permission.

Chezky nodded.

Yoni pulled out a chair and sat directly in front of Aidel. He spoke softly. "Please, do this for Zeidy, okay? He needs to know that you're being taken care of."

"Tatty can drive ush."

"Bubby, if you won't go in the ambulance, I think Chezky here may try to take you on the handlebars of his bike."

Aidel gave another eerie half-smile and turned to look at Yerucham. He sat with his hands clasped and his head down. "Okay," she said. "But if I'm not home in time for dinner, please make sure Zeidy eats."

Yoni smiled. She sounded like her mouth was stuffed with stale crackers, but her intent was quite clear. "Leave it to me." He left the kitchen.

"What's going on?" Meir pounced on Yoni as soon as his nose appeared in the living room. "How's Bubby?"

"One sec." Yoni ran up the stairs and came back, breathless, holding one of his mother's scarves. "She's going to the hospital now. Tatty will drive Zeidy there."

As if on cue, Avner led Yerucham through the living room and straight outside.

"What happened?" Meir insisted.

"Is it... a stroke?" Shimon's voice was low and he was scrunched deep into the couch cushions.

"I think so. We'll know more after they run some tests."

Meir began to cry.

"Hey," Yoni said, putting his arm around Meir, "don't panic. People can fully recover from a stroke."

"They can?" The question came from Shimon.

"Sure."

Shimon leaned forward. "How do you know?"

"One summer in camp, one of the staff was a Hatzolah guy. He was into everyone knowing this kind of stuff."

Meir wiped away a tear. "So Bubby's not... she's gonna be okay?"

"Like I said, we'll know more after they run some tests."

The three boys watched in silence as Aidel was carried on a stretcher. Tova followed, wringing her hands and keeping as close to her mother as she could.

Yoni thrust the scarf at Tova. "*Hatzlachah*," he whispered, not knowing what else to say.

Tova mumbled a good-bye.

Yoni dropped into an easy chair and forced himself to breathe deeply as he replayed the last few minutes over in his mind. Now that it was quiet, he felt like he'd had twelve cups of coffee.

Another deep breath. "Okay, Meir, let's get a move on. First thing we do is say some Tehillim."

"That's what we've been doing," Meir said.

"While you were being important and useful," Shimon muttered.

Inwardly, Yoni winced. He usually tried not to upstage his older brother, but this situation had called for focus and action, not social niceties. "I think saying Tehillim is just as important and useful as whatever I was doing," he said simply. "Next, we have to make a list of who needs to be called, starting with Dr. Sassoon. We need Mommy's phone book, paper, and a pen."

"I'll get it," Meir said, heading toward the kitchen.

"Her address book's in there somewhere, too. Look around." He turned to Shimon. "I think we should call the uncles, no? They should know what's going on with Bubby."

"Yeah. Though they can't actually do anything except worry, since they're all out of town."

"True," Yoni agreed.

"But I guess that's not our decision to make."

"Yeah, you're right. I'll tell them what we know so far, and they can figure out what they want to do."

"I'll make a list," Meir said, coming back also with the cordless. "Then we can check off who we get through to, and write down cell numbers if we need to."

"Great idea," Yoni said.

Meir got to work.

"Yoni."

Yoni looked at Shimon. "Yes?"

"What should I do?"

"About what?"

"About... Ilana."

Yoni didn't understand the question. "What do you mean?"

"Well, I'm obviously not getting engaged tonight. Should I call her directly, or should I call the *shadchan*?"

"Who arranged the date, you or the *shadchan*?"

"I did."

"So why not give her a quick call and explain what happened? I'm sure she'll understand."

"I just, uh, I don't think I can. I mean, I'm not comfortable doing that."

Yoni adjusted his glasses to cover his confusion. Shimon was comfortable asking Ilana to marry him, but not comfortable enough to tell her that his grandmother was on the way to the hospital and they'd need to push their engagement off? "So, you're thinking of asking the *shadchan* to call her?"

"Maybe, but I've never spoken to her. Mommy's the one who always speaks to her. It's a little strange for me to call her, no?"

"In this situation, yes."

"So maybe I can wait till later, after we get some news, and then Mommy can call instead. Or Tatty, if Mommy's not up to it."

"Later? Shimon, I know you're really worked up right now. Hey, we all are. But, they're going to start setting up for the *l'chaim* soon. You have to call now!"

Shimon sighed. "Yeah, I guess so." He dragged himself to the phone and pushed the buttons almost apologetically as he plodded into the kitchen. He soon returned, face flushed.

"How'd it go?"

"I don't know. Okay, I guess."

"What did you say?"

"I told her that Bubby went to the hospital just now, and that Mommy and Tatty went with her, and that it was off."

Something about the way Shimon said "it was off" caught his attention. "Did you tell her you'd call her later?"

"No." He rubbed his face. "It doesn't really matter, anyway."

Yoni's pulse quickened. He began to wish that he'd taken Zeidy to the hospital and his father had stayed home. "Why doesn't it matter?"

"I've been thinking. Maybe the timing of this whole thing is really *bashert*, and this was all a mistake. Yoni, I don't know if I want to marry Ilana."

Yoni was sure he'd heard wrong. "Um, Shimon, what did you say?"

Shimon blushed. "I said I don't know if I want to marry Ilana."

Yoni leaned forward. "Did you just decide that now?"

"I don't know, exactly. When I called her, I realized that I was relieved that we wouldn't be getting engaged. And I started thinking that maybe I'm relieved because I don't really want to marry her, I was just feeling pressured to get engaged."

"Hold on. Shimon, we're all under a lot of strain. This is a crazy time to think about a major life decision like this. Did you say anything to Ilana?"

"No, I just told her our date was off."

"Okay. Don't say anything to anyone about this. You, too," he said, turning to Meir. "We're going to wait until we hear what's going on with Bubby, and no one is going to even mention Ilana until Mommy or Tatty asks."

"Well, they're gonna ask," Meir said. "Sooner or later someone is going to remember about the *l'chaim*, and make sure we called Ilana's family."

"He's right," Shimon said. "I can't avoid the subject."

"Okay," Yoni conceded. "We won't avoid the subject, but whoever speaks to them will just say that Shimon called Ilana, and everything's on hold. Agreed?"

"Agreed," Meir said easily.

Shimon's response was slower in coming. "Agreed."

"And that means no stewing on it, either," Yoni said, wagging a finger at Shimon. "Just push it out of your mind until we've all had a chance to calm down and think clearly."

"Easier said than done," Shimon muttered.

"True. Shimon, I can't even imagine what you must be feeling now. I've never dealt with anything like this before. I've never even gone out! I'm just being practical." He looked seriously at Shimon. "Really, I'm sorry I can't be more help."

"Shouldn't we be making those calls?" Meir asked before Shimon could say anything.

Yoni switched gears. "Yes. First the doctor. Here, throw me the phone."

9

FROM INSIDE THE AMBULANCE, the siren didn't seem loud. Tova didn't notice the bumpy ride, but when they turned the corner, she nearly fell over. Aidel put her left arm out to steady Tova.

"I'm fine, Ma," Tova said. She turned her head away so Aidel wouldn't see the tears which sprang once more to her eyes. She surreptitiously wiped them away and then faced her mother again, taking hold of her hand. "I think we're almost there." *Please, Hashem, please make my mother okay.*

Aidel smiled in what was probably meant as a gesture of encouragement, but it had the opposite effect on Tova. Seeing only the left side of her face move was haunting. Her mother *had* to be okay. Tova pressed Aidel's hand tighter and nodded. *Please, Hashem...*

The ambulance pulled to a stop. The doors were thrown open and hands grabbed the stretcher. Tova hurried to follow as Aidel was wheeled into the emergency room. They paused in the hallway and were met by two doctors and three nurses. The paramedics spoke to one of the nurses and handed her some papers.

One woman stepped forward. "Hi there, I'm Dr. Berg. I'm going to ask you a few questions, okay?"

"Of course," Tova said.

"I'm sorry," Dr. Berg said, "I was talking to Aidel. Are you her daughter?"

"Yes. I'm Tova. I—"

"Okay, Tova, that's great. I'm gonna ask you to take one step back so that we can ask your mom some questions, okay?"

"Uh—"

"Thanks. Aidel, is it okay if I ask you some questions?"

"Yesh, fine."

"What month is it?"

"June."

"Good. Can you tell me how old you are?"

"Shikshty-five."

"Okay, good." Dr. Berg took hold of Aidel's hands. "Can you squeeze my hands? Very good." She let go. "Now I'm going to shine a light at your eyes."

While they talked, Aidel was connected to a blood pressure cuff, an oxygen monitor, and other devices Tova didn't recognize. Tova didn't understand why they were wasting time with the same tests they'd done only minutes before at her house. She said nothing, but the effort of keeping quiet while under so much pressure made her feel like a rubber ball being pumped past maximum capacity.

One of the nurses addressed Tova. "We're closing this curtain around your mother, and we need you to step outside."

"No!" The word burst from her before she could stop it. "My mother needs me."

"We understand. It's just that your mother needs a little privacy now, and she'll be more comfortable if you step outside."

Tova began to sweat. "But I... I need to be with her—"

"We'll take good care of her. I promise."

A hand landed on Tova's shoulder and guided her backwards, away from the curtain they were drawing around Aidel. The hand disappeared inside the newly created cubicle, and Tova was left alone to stare at the apricot-colored fabric.

I should be with her. I shouldn't have let them pull me away.

She stood, a statue amidst the bustle of activity that made up the emergency department. Another nurse approached her and said, not unkindly, "We have some chairs. I'm sure you'll be more comfortable."

"Thank you." Tova didn't budge.

"Over there," the nurse pointed.

Tova tore her eyes away from the curtain. "I have to stay here, to be close to her."

"I'm sorry, it's just that you're standing in a high-traffic area, and you can get hurt if someone moves in a hurry."

Tova crossed her arms. "That's my mother in there. I'm not going anywhere."

"If they decide to move your mother out of there real quick, you'll be stopping her from getting where she needs to go. For your mother's sake, I'm asking you to please have a seat."

The heat in the room seemed suddenly unbearable.

"Hey, you okay?" She laid a hand on Tova's arm. "You look real pale."

"I'm fine!" Tova nearly shouted. "I... I'll just go sit down, like you said." She felt the nurse's eyes on her back as she plodded over to the chairs. Once seated, she closed her eyes.

"I think you should drink this." The nurse stood in front of her with a cup of water.

"Thank you so much." She nodded, a dismissal.

The nurse nodded back but didn't move.

Tova let out a breath. She whispered a *berachah* and took a sip. "Really, I'm fine, thank you."

"If you start to feel faint, tell someone. You can't help anyone if you pass out." She walked away.

Tova ran a hand over her eyes. When Yoni had broken his leg all those years ago, Avner had been by her side. Now, she felt like she'd been plunked down all alone in the desert.

Where was Avner? She so badly wanted his support right now. Most likely, he was in the waiting room providing much-needed support to her father. She could only imagine what her father was going through in the torturous minutes that were creeping by.

The curtain opened, and Tova ran to Aidel. "Ma, I'm right here."

The gurney began to move, and Dr. Berg nodded at Tova. "We're taking her for a CT scan."

"What is it? Did she have a stroke? Is she going to be okay?" The questions came tumbling out in one breath.

"We'll know more after the CT scan."

Tova walked alongside. "Can I come with her?"

"You can ride along in the elevator and stay with her while she's waiting for the test, but you can't be inside during the procedure."

"What are you doing a CT scan of?"

"The brain."

They exited the emergency room and walked through several corridors until they entered an elevator. They got out on the third floor and headed for radiology.

Another waiting room, another bout of fear and anxiety. Tova whispered Tehillim while she paced the corridor. Her nerves settled a bit, and she sat down once more. Then the pressure began to build again.

She wanted to tell Avner where they were, but she couldn't take the chance on not being there when the scan was finished. Besides, what if...

Tova didn't allow herself to continue the thought.

A door opened, and a white coat emerged. "You can come in now."

Tova stood by Aidel's side. "Here, Ma, let me fix your *tichel* for you."

"I'll do it." She raised her left hand to her head and held it there, suspended in the air. Her face contorted into a one-sided grimace. "Smthngsh wrong ff mhand."

The muscles in Tova's back contracted in a spasm. She ignored the pain and fixed the *tichel*.

"We're wheeling you back to emergency, Mrs. Lewin. The doctor will meet you there."

Corridors, elevators, white coats—it was all a blur. They brought Aidel into a curtained-off cubicle. Dr. Berg was there in an instant.

"Aidel, I'm going to tell you and your family about the test results now, okay?"

Aidel nodded.

Dr. Berg addressed Tova. "We're going to have to make some decisions. Are you the one helping Aidel do that?"

Tova's voice shook. "My husband and father are outside. Can someone call them in?"

"Certainly."

Tova steeled herself. No matter what, she would stay calm.

Avner and Yerucham entered the cubicle. Tova's knees felt weak, and she choked back a relieved sob.

Dr. Berg wasted no more time. "Is this everyone?"

"Yes."

"Okay, then. Aidel, the CT scan showed that you've had a stroke."

Tova squeezed her eyes shut tight.

"Let me explain more about what's happened. There's a blood clot lodged in your brain that's preventing oxygen from getting to all your brain cells. That's why the right side of your body is not working properly right now."

Tova's eyes were locked on the doctor. She could not—would not—look at Yerucham.

"Imagine you wrapped a rubber band around your pinkie. Within seconds, your pinkie would start to turn colors, because the blood in your finger isn't being exchanged with clean, oxygenated blood. If you don't remove the rubber band, your finger will become permanently damaged. This kind of stroke works the same way. The clot prevents oxygen from reaching the brain."

Tova tried to speak, but only a thin squeak came out.

Avner spoke up. "And then what happens?"

"Quickly—very quickly—brain cells begin to die."

"Thanks so much for coming with me," Brachie said.

Chava Miriam walked beside Brachie. "I was happy to, it was lots of fun. How often do I get to pick out a bouquet of flowers? For a *kallah*, no less!"

"Shhh!" Brachie put her finger to her lips. "It's still unofficial, no one's allowed to know."

"Sorry," Chava Miriam whispered.

"When I get engaged," Brachie said, "there won't be any of this official-not official stuff."

"I know what you mean. But you don't always have a choice. My brother did the same thing. He got engaged but we couldn't tell anyone till a week later."

"A week! I'd go crazy."

"Yeah, it was hard to keep it secret for so long," Chava Miriam said, "but my sister-in-law is from out of town, and—well, it was complicated. What's your brother waiting for?"

"Oh, who knows? They don't tell me everything. But I do wish I could see Ilana's face when the flowers get delivered to her door!"

"Me too. Well, here's my corner," Chava Miriam said. "Call me later, when it's official."

"I will." Brachie waved good-bye and walked another two blocks to her house. She flung the door open and called out, "Hi, I'm home! I bought the flowers, they're totally gorgeous!"

Shimon, Yoni, and Meir all looked up at Brachie, then looked at each other.

"So," Brachie said, "what were you all busy with while I was running such an important errand?"

"The good news," Dr. Berg said, clipboard in hand, "is that you've had what's called an ischemic stroke. This kind of stroke is easier to treat than the other kind."

Yerucham, who had been silent and withdrawn until now, pounced on her words. "How do you treat it? Can she be completely cured?"

"When we talk about strokes, we don't talk about 'cure' but 'recovery.' Our goal is to get the blood flowing as fast as possible to reduce the amount of brain damage, and then to rehabilitate whichever functions may have been reduced."

This was too much for Tova. But as she began to drown in a wave of desperation, she saw her father's face crumple, his shoulders slump. She forced herself to stand up straight, blinking away the tears that had snuck, against her will, into the corners of her eyes.

"We need to make a pretty quick decision," Dr. Berg said, "because time is working against us."

"What do you mean?" Tova asked. "She's already had the... stroke." The word was painful to hear, torturous to say.

"There's a certain drug that can break down the blood clot. It's called tPA. But to maximize its effectiveness, tPA has to be administered within three hours of the stroke. The stroke occurred some time before..." she flipped over a page and swept her finger down toward the middle, "two fifty-seven this afternoon. That's when Hatzolah was called."

Three sleeves were instantly pushed up to check the time. "It's just after five," Yerucham said.

"That gives us nearly an hour to make a decision," Tova added.

"No," Avner said. "We don't know when Ma actually suffered the stroke. Yoni called Hatzolah at two fifty-seven. But that was only after he noticed that her face looked lopsided. It could have happened before."

"It could be," Yerucham said, "but she looked fine when we left the house. Or maybe it had started before and I just didn't notice."

"What were you doing before you left?" Avner asked. "Were you together?"

"Not until it was time to go. By the front closet, she said something about seeing Yoni. She made a joke and we both laughed."

"And her face seemed okay?"

"Yes, I'm fairly certain. But, doctor, what about her fall?"

"That was on Sunday," Avner said. "And her arm was acting strange. That was, let's see, the day after Brachie came home. Exactly a week ago."

"You mean the stroke could've happened last week?" Tova felt like she was being pressed in on all sides.

"We don't know anything 100 percent for certain," Dr. Berg said. "But in all likelihood, the prior episodes were TIAs, or what's commonly known as mini-strokes. They're more a warning sign that someone is going to have a full-fledged stroke. TIAs aren't counted in the three-hour window. Still, the faster we give tPA, the more effective it is." She looked directly at Aidel. "That's why time is critical. I need to ask you some more questions to see if you're a good candidate for tPA. Have you had recent surgery?"

"They already asked us that," Tova said.

"I may repeat some of the questions they've already asked. I have to go through a checklist to make absolutely certain she's allowed to receive this medication. Then I'll explain the risks, and you'll have to make a decision."

Tova nodded.

"Have you had recent surgery?"

"No," Aidel said.

"Have you suffered a head trauma of any kind in the last three months?"

"No."

"Aidel," Yerucham said, "you did fall, how do you know you didn't hit your head?"

Dr. Berg looked at Yerucham. "Were you there when she fell?"

"Yes."

"Don be shilly, Ruchm. I tribd nfell onda grass, I'm qui certn I didn hi my head."

"Aidel," Dr. Berg said, "you're speech is becoming more difficult to understand. Just to move things a little faster, I'm going to ask your family the rest of the questions, and then you'll have to make a decision, okay?" Turning to the others, she went quickly through the list in front of her.

Between the three of them, the questions were easily answered. When the last one was checked off, the doctor turned to Aidel. "Okay, Aidel, so far, so good. You're eligible for tPA. Now you need to hear the risks. The most common risk is bleeding."

"Bleeding?" Tova repeated, her voice catching.

"Yes. Statistics vary, but between three and seven percent of people who get tPA experience bleeding in the brain." She paused. "Bleeding in the brain is very dangerous. In fact, it can be fatal."

Tova swallowed hard. "And what if my mother doesn't get

this treatment? Can she recover?"

"Yes. Many people do recover from strokes, some partially, some completely. It depends on the location of the clot, the extent of the damage, the age and overall health of the patient, and other factors. Recovery is generally a slow process requiring rehabilitation."

A slow process. "And steady?" Tova asked.

"Again, that depends on the patient."

"And this tPA works quickly? If there are no complications, then my mother can walk out of here none the worse for wear?"

Dr. Berg shook her head. "That's a bit unrealistic. If the tPA successfully dissolves the clot and there are no unwanted complications, then we hope that rehabilitation does happen, slow and steady, and that the patient regains complete function. But it's not a miracle drug that magically restores full function and erases all damage. In general, there is still a period of rehabilitation that follows a stroke."

Tova frowned. She kept waiting to hear that this drug would provide a complete cure.

"I'm sorry," Dr. Berg said. "There are no guarantees."

"What do you suggest we do?" Avner asked.

"You understand that this decision has to be made by Aidel."

"Yes," Tova said, looking at her mother, "but what do you recommend?"

"For a stroke such as this, with moderate symptoms that don't quickly resolve, tPA is generally recommended, though, as I said, there can be serious side effects." She looked at each of them in turn. "I urge you to discuss this among yourselves for a few minutes."

Avner was blunt. "If this was your mother, what would you do?"

Dr. Berg hesitated. "Well, one can never discount the side effects. Bleeding in the brain can be fatal, and..."

Avner's eyes held the doctor's.

Dr. Berg sighed. "If it were my mother, I... I'd give her the tPA." She looked at her watch. "I'll step out for a few minutes, then I'd like to hear your decision."

"Thank you," Avner said as she slipped outside the curtain.

Yerucham inched over to Aidel and gripped the bedrail.

Aidel attempted a smile.

Tova took a step away from Aidel and muttered to Avner, "What do you think we should do?"

"It's your mother's decision."

"But how can she? She's not up to this."

"It's her muscles that aren't working, Tova. Her mind is clear. We can advise her, but the choice is hers."

"Well if you had to decide, what would you say?" Tova asked.

Avner didn't answer.

"Don't you have an opinion?"

"Actually, I do." He stopped.

"Well?" Tova demanded.

"I'm a little hesitant to share it with you. What if your mother decides something different? Or your father disagrees?"

"Then maybe we can convince her." She crossed her arms over her chest. "Or him."

"I'm not sure I want to. This is a major decision, Tova."

"I *know* it's a major decision," she hissed. "That's why I want to hear your opinion!"

Avner took a deep breath. "I think she should get the clot buster."

Tova tapped her right index finger on her left arm. "Why?"

"The percentages are good. And Dr. Berg recommends it as the best course of action."

"But it's not a sure thing."

Avner's eyes opened wide. "Tova, nothing is a sure thing.

Everything is in Hashem's hands."

Tova rubbed her eyes. "I know that. Of course I know that. It's just that... well, if she'll anyway have to do some kind of rehab, maybe she's better off without a dangerous drug."

"On the other hand, while the doctor said it's no miracle drug, it can dissolve the clot and she can move straight into rehab."

"Oh, this is impossible!" Tova cried. "How can we possibly make such a decision?" She chewed her lip while she stared at her parents. No words passed between them, but a full conversation seemed to be taking place in their eyes.

"We're going to do it," Yerucham said suddenly. "We're doing this treatment."

"Tatty, what, just like that? Dr. Berg said we should talk about it! There are risks. What if—"

"We all heard the doctor," Yerucham grimaced. "This is the best chance we've got."

Tova edged forward until she stood by Aidel's side. She reached out and grabbed Aidel's right hand. It was warm—and unresponsive. "Ma, is this what you want to do?"

Silence reigned in the little cubicle.

Outside the curtain, a gurney *squeaked*, a monitor beeped.

Time was passing, their window was closing. Soon the doctor would ask for their decision.

"Ma?"

Aidel didn't take her eyes off Yerucham. "Yesh."

"HERE WE GO," DR. Berg said.

Everyone's lips moved in silent prayer as the needle went into the IV.

Instantly, Tova asked, "Can my mother get a room now?"

"It'll be at least an hour."

A chirp sounded from Dr. Berg's hip, and she looked down. "Sorry, urgent call."

Tova turned to the nurse. "Look, I know everyone's busy, but my mother will rest better where it's quiet. An hour's a long time."

"It has nothing to do with being busy. After administration of tPA, the patient shouldn't be moved for one hour."

"Oh," Tova said weakly.

"How will we know if the medication worked?" Yerucham asked.

"We'll rerun some tests to see if the clot's dissolved."

"When?"

"Starting tomorrow."

Tova studied Yerucham, trying to fathom the look in his eyes.

What was he thinking? How did it feel to see your wife of over forty years—your partner, your support, your confidant—lay helpless in a hospital emergency room, hooked up to wires and tubes?

"Temem nda wrr," Aidel said.

Tova swallowed hard. If it was this difficult to be a spectator, how must her mother be feeling? What kind of agony was she going through, to be perfectly lucid and yet not be able to communicate? Her throat felt suddenly tight. "Ma, why don't you just rest now, okay?"

Aidel closed her eyes.

Tova checked her watch. Was time their friend or their enemy?

"What's with you guys?" Brachie asked. "I ask a simple question, and you start looking at each other as if I just said it's snowing outside. All I want to know is where everything's holding. Shimon, what time are you picking up Ilana?"

"Uh, I was supposed to pick her up at eight, but—"

"Oh, there's plenty of time. Let me tell you about the flowers."

Shimon cracked his knuckles.

"There's something we need to tell you first," Yoni said.

Brachie plopped down on the sofa. "Let me guess. Your suits didn't come out nice and Mommy sent them for an emergency cleaning."

"Not exactly." He cleared his throat. "Brachie, Bubby was here, and she wasn't feeling so well."

"Don't tell me she's going to miss Shimon's *l'chaim*!"

Inwardly, Yoni groaned. "Listen, we were a little worried, so we called Hatzolah."

"Hatzolah!" Brachie jumped up. "What happened? Is she okay? What's wrong?"

"We think Bubby had a stroke."

Brachie burst out crying.

Yoni wished he had the words to comfort her. He'd come home, at his mother's insistence, to spend the day with his family before Shimon's *l'chaim*. Well, the *l'chaim* was off—for how long was another looming question—yet he was certainly spending time with his family.

Brachie buried her face in a couch pillow.

"Here." Meir thrust a box of tissues at her.

Brachie blew her nose.

"We're all shocked," Yoni soothed.

Brachie's hands flew to her mouth. "Shimon, did you call Ilana?"

"Uh, of course."

"Poor girl! She was planning on getting engaged tonight, and now she's not. That must be awful."

Shimon's eyes begged Yoni to say something.

But all he could think of saying was, "Yeah, awful."

Two men pushed Aidel through a door that said, "neurology."

Tova walked by Aidel's side. Yerucham and Avner followed behind.

"Here we are, room 516."

"Careful," Tova pleaded, "watch the doorway."

With practiced ease they rolled the gurney through the doorway. In a few minutes, Aidel was settled in her hospital bed and a nurse was introducing herself.

"Hi, I'm Sue. How're you feeling, Aidel?"

"I think my mother needs to rest now," Tova said. "It's been a very difficult day for her."

"It sure has, Mrs..."

"Lehrfeld."

"I need to take your mom's blood pressure, and—"

"Again? They just took it, right before we got here."

"Right. I'm just going to take it again, and then your mom can get some rest. I need you to step outside for a minute, okay? Thanks."

"Come on, Tova," Avner said.

Tova chewed her lip as she followed Avner and Yerucham. "I don't see why they have to keep throwing me out. How much privacy does a person need to have their blood pressure checked?"

"She'll be okay, Tova, it's only for a few minutes. Anyway, we need to talk, figure out who's staying with Ma and who should go home."

"I'm staying," Tova said immediately.

"*I'm* staying," Yerucham said. "My place is by Mommy's side."

Avner looked from Yerucham to Tova. He sensed the tug-of-war that was taking place between them. The victor would be rewarded with an uncomfortable chair, sleepless nights, feelings of frustration and helplessness. And yet the loser would fare worse, with the added burden of doubt and uncertainty gnawing away at his—or her—heart.

Worry weighed on Avner like a lead apron—and not only about Aidel. Yerucham depended on Aidel for everything, both physically and emotionally. His need to be near her was apparent. But for the next few days, at least, Aidel's companion needed to be someone who could see to her needs, or even anticipate them; someone who could make inquiries, ensure proper care, and perhaps make some vital decisions. Could Yerucham do that?

There was another point to consider as well. If Yerucham stayed with Aidel, she would probably try to take care of *him*, not the other way around. Her inability to do so would frustrate them both.

Tova was a much better choice. She would be zealous—

overzealous—on her mother's behalf. She was a nurturer, someone who would pour out a glass of juice before the recipient realized he or she was thirsty. But if she stayed in the hospital, who would take care of Yerucham?

Avner looked from one to the other. Jaws set, arms crossed, neither one looked ready to back down. As his thoughts raced, his lips stayed firmly shut. He could make suggestions, but these two were going to have to work it out for themselves.

Yerucham shot the opening salvo. "Tova, you have children to take care of, whereas I'm free to stay. I can learn here just as well as in shul."

"I'm sure I can juggle the back and forth," Tova insisted.

"But why is it necessary? You can take care of everything at home, and come when you can, without needing to juggle anything, or anyone."

"Tatty, you can't possibly stay here twenty-four hours a day."

"And why not?" Yerucham growled.

"Because you need your rest. You know you get sick when you don't sleep properly. And then how will you be able to help Ma?"

"I just don't want to be away from Mommy," Yerucham said, his voice suddenly sounding small.

"I know, Tatty, I understand." She laid a hand on his arm and looked deep into his eyes. "What if you stay here most of the day, and you'll come to my house when you need to rest? That way I can give you proper meals as well."

Yerucham cocked his head.

"Then," Tova continued, "I'll sleep here at night. You'll stay by us. Okay, Tatty?"

Avner cleared his throat. "Tova, you can't possibly stay every night."

"Why not?"

"You also have to sleep sometime."

"You think I'll be able to sleep at home, knowing my mother's all alone?"

"Who said anything about being alone? There are other options besides the two of you."

"Who?" Tova said. "My brothers live out of town. And you know how hard it is for them to get away."

Yerucham sighed.

"The boys are in yeshivah, Meir's too young, and I'm working," Avner said. "That leaves Brachie."

Tova stared. "Brachie? You think Brachie can spend the night here?"

"Yes, I do."

"Avner, Brachie's head is in the clouds. I can't imagine she'd be any use here. And you know how teenagers are, they stay up late schmoozing with their friends, then sleep late the next morning!"

"Brachie is eighteen," Avner said softly, "and it won't hurt her to be on the giving end."

Tova shook her head. "And what would she do in case... in case of emergency?"

"I'm going to make a little prediction. When Brachie is given more responsibility, she'll rise to the occasion."

Tova raised an eyebrow.

"And either way, she's going to have to pitch in. If you're here, someone has to be doing all the things you usually do. Or at least help you do it."

"But Brachie?"

"Yes," Avner said, "Brachie."

"I'm hungry," Meir said, watching Shimon pace back and forth across the kitchen.

Yoni opened the refrigerator and stared. "There's nothing here."

Brachie shook her head. "You guys never know how to look. You have to move things around." She nudged Yoni aside. "He's right, there's nothing here."

"Hey," Yoni said, "you can whip up something for us."

"Very funny. You know I can't cook."

"I just thought maybe you actually learned something in Israel," Yoni quipped.

"I learned loads, thank you very much. Cooking wasn't one of the subjects." She closed the refrigerator. "Too bad we don't have a sandwich maker. I actually do know how to make grilled cheese."

"See? You did learn something."

"Can you two cut it out?" Meir said. "I'm hungry and there's nothing to eat."

"Sorry," Yoni said with a smile. "I forgot how much fun it is to tease Brachie."

Brachie laughed. "I missed you, too."

"Let's just order pizza," Meir said.

Brachie's face fell. "How can we have pizza when Bubby's in the hospital?"

"Yeah, and everything's up in the air," Shimon said, rubbing his chin.

Yoni felt for Shimon; his was a double worry. "You have any cash, Shimon?"

Shimon pulled out his wallet. "Not much. I have Tatty's credit card, though."

"We can't use it without his permission, and I don't want to bother him on his cell phone right now."

"I'll make tuna," Yoni said. "Brachie, you cut up some cucumbers. First you wash them, then you take a knife—"

"I think I can figure out the rest," Brachie said.

"Listen," Yoni said as he rifled through drawers, "I think we should make up a bed for Zeidy. Anyone know where the can opener is? Oh, never mind, I found it."

"Is Zeidy coming here?" Meir asked.

"I imagine so. There's no way Mommy will let him go home alone."

Meir scrunched his nose. "Since when does Zeidy need Mommy's permission for anything?"

Yoni smiled. "I just meant that Mommy will convince him to stay here."

"Are you going back to yeshivah tomorrow?" Meir asked.

"I don't know yet." He turned to Shimon. "There are too many things up in the air right now."

"Well, Zeidy can sleep in my bed," Meir said. "How long can it be for, anyway?"

His words were met with silence. That was the question they all wanted answered.

Avner slipped inside the front door and heard Brachie's voice.

"Really, Shimon, can't you pace somewhere else? Or go learn with Yoni and Meir, or say some Tehillim, like me. You're distracting me."

"Sorry."

Avner stepped into the living room, Tova right behind.

Brachie jumped up. "Tatty! Mommy!"

Yoni and Meir came running.

"Hello everyone," Avner said.

Tova sank into the easy chair and closed her eyes.

"Mommy, can I get you something?" Brachie asked.

"No, thank you. Let Tatty talk first."

Avner updated them, adding that they'd know more tomorrow.

"Where's Zeidy?" Meir asked.

"With Bubby. He'll be sleeping here."

"We made up my bed for him," Meir said.

Avner smiled. "I'm pleased to hear it."

"I'm going back to the hospital soon," Tova said. "But first, you must all be starving." She pushed herself up out of the chair.

"Actually, we ate," Yoni said.

Tova stopped short. "You did? What did you eat?"

"Tuna."

Tova looked wide-eyed at her children. "Who made tuna?"

"I did. And Brachie cut up vegetables."

Tova's lips parted, but no sound came out.

"Excellent," Avner said. "Then Meir can go straight to bed. I'll write you a note about homework."

"No homework, Tatty. Tomorrow's my last day, remember?"

Oy. "Actually, I forgot. I don't get summer vacation like regular teachers. When does camp start?"

"In a week."

Tova rubbed her eyes. "It's a good thing we decided on day camp for the first half. We couldn't possibly get him ready for sleep-away. Still, what will Meir do all week?"

For the briefest moment, Avner's stomach tightened. Then he created a mental folder called "Meir, vacation" and slipped it into the filing cabinet he'd been using all week to compartmentalize the various surprises thrown at him. "We'll deal with that later."

"Fine. I'll make you something to eat."

"I don't—"

"My father needs to eat, anyway, Avner, and you need a nice, filling meal." She plodded into the kitchen.

"When can we visit Bubby?" Brachie asked.

"Let's see how she's doing tomorrow."

"Tatty, can I go back to yeshivah in the morning?" Yoni asked.

Avner looked at Shimon. "I can't tell you how soon you'll need to come home again."

Shimon paled.

"It's just a bus ride away," Yoni said. "Unless Mommy needs my help."

"I can help," Meir said.

"Me, too," Brachie said, chin in the air.

"I knew I could count on you," Avner said with a smile.

"Kitchen's that way," Yoni pointed, smirking.

"Very funny," Brachie retorted.

"Okay, kids. We have to get moving. Meir, to bed. Yoni, you have an early bus tomorrow. Brachie, please stay off the phone. You can use your time to wash the dishes."

Brachie's face darkened and she lumbered into the kitchen. Meir and Yoni headed upstairs. Shimon began to follow.

"Just a minute, Shimon."

He couldn't be sure from the back, but Avner thought he saw Shimon's shoulders slump.

"Yes, Tatty?"

"Have a seat. What did you tell Ilana?"

"That Bubby was on her way to the hospital and we couldn't meet. Uh, that we couldn't meet tonight."

"Mm-hmm." A long pause, then, "What did she say?"

"What could she say? She wished Bubby a *refuah sheleimah* and asked me to keep her informed."

"And have you?"

Shimon's fingers drummed on the coffee table. "Tatty, you have better things to be thinking about now."

Avner's eyes bore into Shimon.

"I mean, it's just a *l'chaim*. A party, no big deal. It can wait till things settle down."

"The party is no big deal, Shimon." He drew his face closer and dropped his voice. "The engagement is."

Tiny beads of sweat broke out on Shimon's forehead. "How can we get engaged when we have no clue how long Bubby's going to be in the hospital?"

"We do need to see that Bubby is stable first. But assuming she is, how much longer do you want to wait?"

"I... I don't know."

"No. I see that you don't. I think the real question is, how much longer do you want to make Ilana wait?" Avner's eyes searched Shimon's. "Or perhaps that isn't the question at all."

Shimon looked away.

"Whatever it is you're not telling me, well, perhaps now would be a good time to tell me."

"You and Mommy have so much to worry about already," Shimon muttered.

"Fathers have broad shoulders."

Shimon cracked his knuckles.

"Do you remember what you did the summer when you were thirteen?"

"Same thing I did every summer. Went to day camp."

Avner nodded. "While all the other boys your age went to sleep-away camp. Because you weren't ready to go away from home. You needed more time, more... nurturing. You were always a sensitive kid, Shimon, there's nothing wrong with that. That's why Mommy and I didn't push you, even though the yeshivah felt strongly about it. And the following year, you felt you could handle half a summer away."

Shimon's brow furrowed. "I never went to sleep-away camp."

"Right. You decided the night before that you just couldn't do it."

A flush spread across Shimon's face. "So you're saying that I'm a chicken."

"Not at all. I'm saying that you don't always listen to yourself. Camp wasn't right for you. But because you felt pressured to go, you made yourself believe you were ready."

"I thought pushing yourself was a good thing. You know, you psych yourself up, give yourself a little push, and just do it."

Avner chose his words carefully. "That works when you're ready to believe in yourself, when you're ready to let your feelings of 'I can do this' take over, and carry you where you really want to go. But when it takes you somewhere that you *don't* want to go, but only say you want to go because it's what everyone else is doing..." He stopped. This was getting too convoluted. "Shimon, let me just ask you straight out. Do you want to get married?"

Shimon chewed his lip. Then he crossed his legs and cleared his throat. "Uh, yeah, I guess I do. I mean, yes." He uncrossed his legs. "It's just..."

"Yes?"

"Well, it's just... I think maybe Ilana's not the right girl for me."

Tova marched through the living room. "I'm done in the kitchen. Really, Avner, why'd you send Brachie in there? It took me twice as long. I'm going to pack myself some things, I'll be down in a few minutes." She was gone.

Brachie appeared, her skirt dark with water. She said nothing as she passed through, lips pressed firmly together.

Shimon turned worried eyes on Avner.

"No, Mommy didn't hear. We'll spare her this discussion until she's less frantic about Bubby. Now, you were saying. You think maybe Ilana's not the right girl."

"Really, Tatty, maybe this should wait—"

"No," Avner snapped. "No more waiting. It's one thing to torture yourself. It's another thing to torture a young lady who's waiting for you to ask her to marry you. *Expecting* you to ask her."

"I'm sorry," Shimon breathed.

Avner's jaw seesawed. He was not the one who was owed an apology. He opened his mouth to say so, when he saw that Shimon's eyes were wet. Avner forced his shoulders to relax.

"What changed since Sunday?"

"I, uh, gave it a lot of thought, and well, it's like you just said. I'm sensitive."

"And?"

"I don't think Ilana is sensitive enough for me."

"Hold on. When we talked about this last week, you said that was one of the things you *liked* about her, that she's sensitive. Remember the Sprite? It spilled, and she cleaned it up."

"I said it showed she was caring. It was a nice, caring thing to do—for *other* people. But she didn't stop to think about how *I'd* feel about it, whether or not *I'd* be embarrassed. Same thing with the cell phone."

"The cell phone?"

"Yeah. Remember I said she opened and closed two zippers to put her cell phone back in her purse, instead of just tossing it in?"

Where was Shimon going with this? "Yes, I remember."

"Well, maybe she shouldn't have answered her phone in the first place. I mean, isn't that *in*sensitive?"

"Who called her?"

"Her father. We'd been out a long time, and he wanted to make sure she was okay."

"You think she shouldn't have picked up for her father?"

"I don't know, isn't it rude to pick up the phone when you're with someone? If the phone was off, like it should have been, she wouldn't have known it was him, and the whole thing never would have come up."

Tova charged into the room. She had changed her clothes and thrown on a *tichel*, and was holding a bag. "Okay, Avner, if you don't mind taking this, I have a thermos for Ma."

"Sure," he said automatically as Tova hustled away, but he barely heard her. Shimon seemed completely unaware of his own motivations, allowing his fears to mask his other emotions and cloud his thinking. Avner felt like he was trapped in a maze, making wrong turns and hitting dead ends. What could he say to help Shimon see himself more objectively?

Tova was back. "Okay, I'm ready."

Avner didn't move. His heart, already laden, was becoming bloated with concern for an ever-widening circle of people. He wished he could separate it all out, tackle one crisis at a time, and then move on. But there wasn't only one stone thrown into his lake, creating independent ripples in ever-expanding circles. There were a handful of rocks tossed in at once, a collage of intersecting arcs creating unpredictable patterns.

"Avner?"

Avner forced his eyes from Shimon's face. "Sorry. Let's go, then."

Tova hustled outside.

Avner followed. He held the doorknob and whispered, "Shimon, don't go to sleep, I want to talk to you."

"Sleep?" Shimon said with a tortured smile. "I haven't slept in days."

11

YERUCHAM WAS SILENT DURING the drive home. Avner didn't even attempt to engage him in conversation; they were both drained, physically and emotionally. After serving Yerucham the food Tova had left them, he showed him where he'd be sleeping. Avner was pleased to see that there were clean sheets on Meir's bed. And fresh towels! Which one of the children had thought of that?

Avner checked on Meir, who was sprawled out on the floor next to Yoni's bed, then went back downstairs to find Shimon wearing out the living room carpet.

"What did you think about while I was gone?" Avner asked without preamble.

Shimon turned and froze, looking like a deer caught in the headlights.

"Shimon," Avner continued, "you're torturing yourself for nothing. Whatever it is, you'll feel better after you get it over with." A pause. "Do you need more time? Is that it?"

"No, not exactly."

"So what, exactly?"

Shimon took a deep breath and blurted, "I want to call it off."

Avner nodded, surprised only that Shimon was finally facing up to reality and saying the words. "Is that what you're so nervous about? You feel you're being forced to go through with this when it's not what you want?"

"Yes," Shimon exhaled. "That's it exactly. I don't want to marry Ilana. It's just that things have come this far, and it's not fair to back out."

Avner studied his son. When Shimon said the word "yes," he'd straightened up as though an invisible monster leaped off his back. "Shimon, I'm not sure what made you suddenly realize this..."

"I'm not sure, either." Shimon stretched his limbs for the first time in days. Or perhaps weeks.

Avner waited for Shimon to say more. When he didn't, Avner continued, "Marrying someone because it's not 'fair' to back out is not fair, either." *Or wise*, he added silently. "If you two are not suited for each other, it's much better to end it now, not later."

Shimon nodded.

It was nice to see Shimon finally stop looking like a hunted animal, but Avner had a niggling feeling about this conversation, as if he was writing a note to his son's teacher saying, "Please excuse Shimon from getting engaged. He simply wasn't thinking."

His gut told him that Shimon believed what he was saying, that Ilana wasn't the right girl for him. But that was only what lay on the surface. If Shimon would dig deeper, he'd see that this had less to do with marrying Ilana than with his readiness to get married, period.

For a fleeting moment, Avner thought of convincing Shimon to go through with it. But coercion would do more harm than good. At this point, all he could do was rubber stamp Shimon's decision and help everyone through the next few days. Even without this new kink in their lives, Tova would need his full support. While he could see a silver lining in this latest cloud that had melded into the recent storm—not having to deal with a *l'chaim*, new *mechutanim*, an overly nervous *chasan*, or planning a wedding—she would see it as another downpour in the thunderstorm. Avner would have to be her umbrella. And as soon as he could, Avner would have to give some serious thought as to how he could help Shimon build himself into a self-assured, independent adult.

"So what do I do now, Tatty?" Shimon asked, drawing Avner out of his reverie.

Avner pulled his shoulder blades together in a vain attempt to work out the knot that had settled there. "Now, you go to sleep."

"And what about Ilana?"

Avner turned the question around. "What do you think?"

"Me? I don't know. What's done in these cases?"

What's done? Avner wanted to shout. *What's done?* This isn't "done." Breaking off with a girl you were supposed to get engaged to the night before isn't "done," and there's no protocol for it, like there is for buying a gold watch.

Avner let these thoughts speed through his head, then steadied himself. "Shimon, if your positions were reversed, what would you want?"

"I guess I'd want some sort of explanation."

"From who?"

"From you and Mommy."

"And where would we get this explanation from?"

"I guess from the *shadchan*." He rubbed his chin. "So we have to explain it to her. What are you going to tell her?"

Again, Avner threw the question back to Shimon. "What do you think I should tell her?"

"Uh, tell her I just don't think it's *shayach*. Tell her I liked

Ilana a lot, and think she's a great girl, but that she's just, uh, not for me."

Half of Avner's lip curled up. "If it was you, after seven dates and the expectation that you were about to get engaged, would that satisfy you?"

Shimon colored. "No. But what can you say?"

Avner waited.

"I never even spoke to the *shadchan*." He scratched his arm. "How am I supposed to know what to say?"

"Shimon, what would *you* want to hear?"

Shimon's voice was flat. "I'd want to know that I didn't do anything to make it happen. That it wasn't my fault, that I'm not a reject." He crossed his arms. "But this is going to make me look like an idiot! I go out seven times, I'm ready to get engaged, and at the last minute..."

"Yes?"

Shimon's arms fell to his sides. "And at the last minute, I realize that... I really don't know what I want."

The light of dawn peeked in from behind the curtains.

"Temperature time," a nurse chirped. She held a thermometer out to Aidel, who slipped it under her tongue.

Tova was generally cheerful and appreciated the trait in others, but the nurse's perky smile was not a welcome sight at—she squinted at her watch—"A quarter to six?" She rubbed her shoulder, which sported an indentation from the metal arm of the chair where she'd slept—if the fitful rest she'd managed could be called sleep. She pulled herself fully upright and turned to Aidel. "Good morning, Ma! How are you feeling?"

"Grmdg."

"Just one second, I'll bring you *negel vasser*."

The thermometer bobbed up and down as she nodded.

"Here you go." Tova brought a cup and bowl. "Just hold out

your hands, I'll pour the water."

Aidel held her left hand over the bowl. Her right hand moved but lay on top of the blanket. "Cndmn, hpm pn."

"That's all right, Ma, I'll hold it for you." Tova smiled and washed Aidel's hands. She took the bowl and headed toward the bathroom.

"There we go," the nurse said as she removed the thermometer. "Now blood pressure."

"Thank you," Aidel said. "Take my left arm, pleash. My right one doeshn't sheem to be working."

Tova spun around, sloshing water onto the floor. "Ma!"

"Good morning, Tovaleh," Aidel said.

The room seemed suddenly full of light. "Ma, your speech! It's back!"

Aidel laughed. "Sho it ish."

Tova paused, then ran to the bathroom to dump the water. "How are you feeling?"

"I'm fine, shame ash yeshterday."

"Are you hungry? Can I get you something to eat?"

"Hold on there," the nurse said, "you'll need to talk to the doctor about eating first."

"But—" Tova began.

"That's fine," Aidel interrupted. "Right now, I'd like a shiddur sho I can daven."

Tova dived into her bag. "Here you go. You want me to find the place for you?"

Aidel's eyes twinkled. "I think the shiddur's shmall enough to manage one-handed if you tell me how thish elevator worksh."

"Elevator? Oh, the bed!" Tova laughed.

"You just press the button on that little remote," the nurse said. "You want me to do it for you?"

"Thank you, I can manage." Aidel raised the head of the bed.

"You can go back to sleep now till the doctors make their רום

morning rounds," the nurse said.

"Thank you, mish..."

"Kim," the nurse said.

"Thank you, Kim. Maybe I'll take a nap later if I'm tired."

Kim smiled. "You ring if you need anything, okay? The red button over there." She bustled out.

Aidel propped the siddur on her lap. Struggling with the pages, she said, "Tova, maybe jusht find me the firsht page, then I'll be able do it myshelf."

"Here, Ma."

Aidel looked inside, and her brow contracted with mock disapproval. "Really, Tova, do you think I didn't already shay *Modeh Ani*?" A huge grin spread from her lips to her ears. "It's wonderful to be alive, to be able to speak normally."

"Oh, Ma! This is incredible!" Tova's heart beat fast. Both sides of Aidel's mouth seemed to pull upwards as she smiled, but her speech was thick, and every *s* sounded like a heavy *shhh*. Did Aidel hear how she sounded?

Tova turned the page and sat down, watching Aidel daven.

Suddenly, Tova was a young girl, sitting on the couch in her flannel nightgown and slippers. She had woken up earlier than usual, while the sun's reaching fingers had only begun to silently creep across the wall, and sought out her mother. She found her in the living room, davening. Tova had sat down on the sofa and watched.

Aidel was standing still, her hands clutching a siddur to her chest. Her eyes were closed, face pointed upwards. A serene smile rested on her face while tears glistened on her cheeks.

Tova sat, mesmerized. Was her mother happy or sad? How could one cry and smile at the same time? She remembered the moment, remembered how the juxtaposition of those two conflicting emotions had puzzled her for so long.

And now, looking at Aidel, adult comprehension overlay the

childhood memory. Tova could almost touch the wellsprings of gratitude that bubbled up from her heart's innermost chambers, while trepidation's dark form lay in waiting. She thrust her fears aside and gave herself over to the joy of the moment.

"Tovaleh."

"Yes, Ma?"

"Today's Thurshday, isn't it?"

"Yes."

"What happened with Shimon's *l'chaim*?"

A loud knock sounded on the door. Brachie groaned and turned over.

"Please be downstairs in five minutes," Avner said.

Brachie stretched and looked at the clock: six twenty-five. What on earth? Her eyes fluttered closed.

"Brachie!"

She bolted upright. "I'm up!"

"It's a quarter to seven. Get dressed and get downstairs. Now."

She jumped out of bed. A few minutes later she was standing in the kitchen, rubbing her eyes.

"Sorry to wake you." Avner turned to Meir. "Tell Brachie what you need for lunch. Zeidy and I are catching an early *minyan* so I can bring him to the hospital before work."

"Will Mommy be home later?" Meir asked.

"Probably. If not, Brachie will. Enjoy your last day of school." Meir smiled. "I will."

"Brachie, you're in charge. Yoni's gone, Shimon's leaving soon. Please make Meir lunch, and be sure he eats breakfast. Zeidy needs breakfast, too, so have it waiting by the time we're back. You can work on dinner later."

Brachie paled. "Dinner? I don't know—"

"Whatever you don't know," he smiled, "now's the time to

learn, figure it out as you go. Mommy has my phone, but only for emergencies, okay?"

Brachie swallowed. "I—"

"Good. If Mommy calls, tell her we'll be there before eight." He flew out of the kitchen.

"I'd like tuna," Meir said.

Brachie glared at him.

"Uh, please. With tomato. And some cucumber slices, and a container of dressing. And cookies, and a bag of chips, and ketchup."

"Is that all?"

"Oh, and a juice box."

Brachie rolled her eyes. "Meir, how about something simple, like peanut butter?"

"We're not allowed peanut butter."

"What kind of crazy rule is that? It's easy, you just take bread and a knife and smear. I can even put jelly on it if you like."

"A kid in my class is allergic. Can I have scrambled eggs for breakfast? You can make enough for Tatty and Zeidy, too."

"One thing at a time." Brachie opened the tuna, dumped it into a bowl, and plopped in some mayonnaise.

"Why does it look like that?" Meir asked as she smeared the tuna on bread.

"Dunno," Brachie shrugged.

"It looks... oily."

"Don't worry. Gimme a tomato." Brachie finished putting Meir's lunch together and handed it to him.

"What about breakfast?"

Brachie stomped over to the cabinet. "Here." She banged a bowl down on the table, followed by a box of corn flakes.

"You're gonna give Zeidy corn flakes?"

"I'll make more tuna."

"Maybe first try to figure out how come it's so oily."

"Yeah," Brachie sighed. "I'll try."

"So," Tova was telling Aidel as Avner walked into the hospital room, "I told Yanky and Hershel that everything was under control and they shouldn't come now. Oh, good morning, Avner."

"Good morning." He smiled at both of them.

"Anyway," Tova continued, "they'll be here for the *yahrzeit seudah*, and you know how impossible it is for them to get away, especially together. Yanky's going to call this morning, Herschel later on."

"Sorry to interrupt," Avner said, "but I have to run or I'll be late for work. You ready?"

She walked with Avner out the door but stopped just outside. "I'm not leaving."

Avner put his hands on his hips. "What happened to taking turns with your father?"

"I can't go until I hear what the doctor has to say. We don't even know if my mother's allowed to eat." Her brow wrinkled. "Did you eat anything?"

"Not yet," Avner admitted, "but Brachie made me a sandwich."

Tova's hand flew to her mouth. "Brachie?"

Avner grinned. "Yes. I left her in charge. But don't worry, I'm told she cut up a whole cucumber by herself last night."

"Don't make fun," Tova wagged a finger but couldn't quite hide a smile.

"*Chas v'shalom*. I'm thrilled she's finally learning her way around the kitchen."

"Well, if my mother keeps this up, we'll both be back home in no time. Then she won't need to."

"Maybe she should anyway," Avner said, growing serious.

Tova blinked. "What are you talking about?"

"Never mind, I have to get going. You have my cell phone, so if there's anything urgent call the yeshivah. Otherwise, I'll call you. And here, take some money and buy yourself something to eat." He raced down the corridor.

Tova returned to her seat.

Yerucham looked at her. "Mommy says you didn't get much sleep."

"How did you know, Ma? I thought you were fast asleep."

"I was," Aidel smiled, "except when I wasn't. Why don't you go home? Tatty can bubbysit."

A man in blue hospital scrubs and a white coat entered. "Good morning, Aidel. I'm Dr. Lawrence. I'd like to see how you're doing this morning."

"What a coincidence," Aidel quipped, "so would I."

"Do I need to leave again?" Tova crossed her arms.

"Too bad you didn't bring roller skates with all this going in and out," Aidel said.

Dr. Lawrence chuckled, "You're fine where you are, Mrs..."

"Lehrfeld."

He nodded. "Aidel, please lift your right arm..."

After a brief examination, the doctor said, "We'll start you on liquids. The dietician will be by soon, and the PT, OT, and speech therapist also."

"Oh, and I thought I'd go swimming today."

Dr. Lawrence laughed.

"Doctor, since I'm so much better, can I go home today? My grandson is waiting to get engaged."

Tova smiled. Aidel was outdoing herself this morning. Then Tova looked at her mother's face and realized that this time, she wasn't joking.

"We still have to run some tests."

"So let's run them quickly. My speech is back to normal and I can see the therapists at home."

"According to your chart, there is a vast improvement in

your speech. However, I don't believe it's back to normal." He smoothed out an imagined crease in his white coat.

"Feh. There's nothing wrong with my speech."

The doctor turned to Yerucham. "Are you her husband?"

"Yes."

"Would you say her speech is normal for her?"

He threw Aidel an apologetic look. "No. But can't she get speech therapy at home?"

"Let's first make sure the blood clot isn't going to cause another stroke."

Aidel sighed. "I'm sorry, Yerucham."

"We do what the doctor says. I know you're not comfortable—"

"I'm not worried about my comfort, I feel terrible I'm causing so much trouble."

"Aidel—"

Doctor Lawrence cleared his throat. "I'll be back later. If you need me, I'm on duty all morning."

"Nice fellow," Aidel said as he left, "even if he looks nineteen."

Yerucham smiled. "Why don't you rest now?"

"Good idea," Tova seconded.

"You, too," Yerucham told Tova.

Aidel drifted off quickly, but sleep eluded Tova. What were the kids doing now? When would they reschedule the *l'chaim*? She must have dozed off at some point, since she was awakened by the rattle of a breakfast tray. Aidel's jello didn't look particularly appetizing, but it reminded Tova that she hadn't eaten since lunchtime yesterday.

She went to the cafeteria and bought coffee and a shrink-wrapped Danish with a decent *hechsher*. She returned just after Joy, the physical therapist, appeared.

Aidel's bed was lowered, and she sat up without too much assistance.

"How's your leg feeling?" Joy asked.

"Fine."

"Well, we're going to try to stand."

"We?" Aidel grinned. "I suppose you mean me."

Joy returned the smile. "Put one hand there, and lean on me like this... that's right. Just watch the IV."

Tova held her breath.

"On three, try to stand. One, two, three."

Aidel heaved herself up. If Joy hadn't held on tight, she would have fallen straight to the floor.

"Great job. Back onto the bed now." Joy eased Aidel down.

Aidel fixed wide eyes on Joy. "I can't stand," she whispered and glanced at Yerucham before her gaze dropped to the floor. "I can't stand."

"You didn't this time," Joy said evenly, "but we're going to try again."

"My leg..." Her voice trailed off.

"It's okay, Aidel," Yerucham said. "She'll help you."

"Here we go, on the count of three," Joy said.

"Wait. Please!"

Tova dug her nails into her palms. That raspy voice did not sound like her mother. Aidel's brow creased, and Tova tried to fathom her mother's expression. Was it frustration? Pain? Determination?

"Are you ready now?" Joy asked.

Aidel turned anxious eyes on her. "I'm very tired now. Perhaps you can come back tomorrow."

Joy shifted her weight from one leg to the other. "I really think we should try again now, okay?"

"My mother says she's tired," Tova said a bit too loudly. "Please, she's done enough for today."

Yerucham nodded.

Joy looked from Tova to Yerucham, then to Aidel. "Okay. Let

me just help you back into bed."

"Thank you," Tova said.

"I'll be back tomorrow."

With obvious difficulty, Aidel turned onto her side.

"Ma, do you need anything?" Tova asked.

Aidel pulled the sheet up over her ears.

Tova looked at Yerucham. The whole time Joy had been there, he'd been quiet, his chair just off to the side. Now, he seemed to have completely shut down, his features chiseled from stone.

Her father had always been a closed book. He was solid, dependable, ever-present. But closed. And yet, Tova had always sensed that under his stolid façade whirled a maelstrom of emotion. She had glimpsed it at random moments: the Shabbos morning when a little boy addressed him in a lisping Yiddish, and he'd reached out and grabbed his pudgy little hands; the spring day when he'd gotten caught in a sudden downpour and was inexplicably immobilized. And then there was the sacredness of the date he considered his family's collective *yahrzeit*. That, at least, made sense to her, even as a child.

Now, looking at Yerucham, Tova wished she understood him more.

Tova's hands shook. If Aidel could not resume her role as nurturer, she would shrivel up like a plucked rose left out in the sun. And Yerucham would wither as well. Tova could not—would not—let that happen. She would see to it that Aidel would walk.

No matter what.

12

BRACHIE TRIED TO WEDGE the phone between her ear and shoulder, the way her mother always did. It kept falling to the floor. "Sorry, Rena. Tell me again: I wait until the rice boils and then I turn it down, like, how low?"

"As low as you can, but don't let the flame go out."

Brachie turned the knob. "Got it. Thanks."

"Did your mother speak to my mother by any chance?"

"No, why would she speak to her?"

"You're right. Never mind. Um, how's your rice doing?"

"Just a sec, why would your mother call?"

Rena giggled. "Oh, Brachie, I'm not supposed to say anything."

"You already did, so don't leave me hanging!"

"Well... okay, but promise you won't tell."

"I won't!"

"I told my mother all about you, and I told her you'd be perfect for my cousin Mordechai."

Brachie squealed. "Really? You'd set me up with your cousin?"

"They checked you out already, and they liked everything they heard."

"I'm so excited!"

"Me, too. I can't understand why no one's called yet."

"Maybe they tried. Things have been totally crazy around here."

"Because of your grandmother?"

"Other things too. I'm not at liberty to say," she added with an air of self-importance.

"Don't tell me one of your brothers is getting engaged!"

"I didn't say that."

"Brachie, you can't do this to me!"

"Just tell me more about your cousin!"

Rena didn't have to be asked twice. "He's really nice, and..."

The bell rang. Avner snapped his briefcase closed and hurried to the main office. He called Tova, informing her that he was on his way. She was terse and only said that her mother was the same. As he hung up, he heard a familiar voice.

"Avner, if I didn't know better, I'd say you were avoiding me." Gedaliah stood outside his office.

Avner gripped his briefcase and stepped inside. "Just busy. End-of-year business, like that book order."

"I was waiting for you to get back to me about the teaching position."

He tried to smile. "I already gave you my decision."

"I asked you to think it over again. Did you?"

"Yes. I'm afraid my answer is still no."

"And what if I tell you that I still haven't found anyone? School's out tomorrow. Even if someone applies with a perfect résumé, I can't see him in action."

"I'm sorry, Gedaliah, I—"

"I know, you're making a difference. But look at the big picture. Without a good seventh-grade *rebbi*, upwards of thirty boys will suffer."

Avner felt his muscles go taut. Right now, he had enough suffering people in his immediate circle to think about. "Gedaliah, forgive me. My mother-in-law had a stroke yesterday. I'm on my way to the hospital."

Gedaliah immediately backed down, and Avner escaped. Though he tried to concentrate on the usual Brooklyn traffic, his mind kept wandering. Fumes snaked in through the air conditioning vent, assaulting his nostrils, as unwanted thoughts crawled down into his stomach.

He found Tova pacing outside Aidel's room. "Did something happen?" Avner immediately asked.

"No. Ma's sleeping."

Avner popped in to say hello to Yerucham, who only nodded. Tova said a quick good-bye and marched out of the room, leaving Avner to scramble behind.

They sat down in the car. "Tova, you're obviously upset. What happened?"

Tova's eyes remained fixed on the dashboard. Her breathing was shallow and she didn't blink; only her jaw moved.

The silence between them grew thick. Avner waited.

Finally, Tova blurted, "My mother can't walk." Deep, heaving sobs burst forth unchecked. The traumatic events of the past twenty-four hours coalesced into a lump of anguished shock.

Avner watched in helpless silence. Finally, he said, "This is only the beginning. Is she giving up so easily?"

"Giving up easily?" Tova cried. "It was a terrible shock!"

Avner fumbled for the right words. "Of course it was. For all of you."

"You should have seen her," Tova gulped. "She just... crumpled! And her face looked like someone had slapped her."

Avner waited until the sobs settled into sniffles. "She's tough, I'm sure she'll rally."

Tova squeezed her eyes shut. "I hope you're right."

"I'm sure I am."

Tova leaned back on the headrest. "I know I'm an adult, Avner. But... I need my mother to be okay." She turned moist eyes to him. "I need her."

"I understand." Avner wished he knew what else to say.

"Let's go home," Tova said, wiping away a lingering tear. "I need to see what Brachie's done to my kitchen."

Avner started the engine and drove.

Tova stared out the window. Abruptly, she said, "Shimon."

Avner stole a peek at his wife.

"We can't keep the Moskowitzes on hold so long. I've got to pull myself together and call them when we get home."

Avner's tongue stuck to the roof of his mouth.

"You know what, I'll call them right now. Does my voice sound okay?" She whipped out the phone and started to dial.

Avner slammed on the brakes and pulled over. "Tova, wait!" He lunged for the phone. It fell to the seat. "We need to talk." His thoughts danced to the beat of his racing heart. He yanked the steering wheel and put his foot on the gas. "Hold on, I'll take Ocean Parkway, it's fastest." He made a sharp right turn.

Tova tapped her foot on the floor of the car. "Avner..."

"At home, okay? I need to concentrate on driving."

"Since when?"

Her voice was shrill, and Avner realized that stalling was not an option.

"Fine, let me pull over again and I'll give you the whole story."

"What whole story? What are you keeping from me?" Her voice rose with each word.

"Let me just get off—"

"Avner, don't do this to me!"

It was all he could do to safely pull onto the service road. "There have been some... developments."

"Please, Avner, have *rachmanus*. Say it already."

He took a deep breath. "Shimon doesn't want to marry Ilana."

Tova's eyes nearly jumped out of their sockets. "He *what*?"

"He doesn't feel she's the right girl."

"And you just let him off the hook?"

"There's not much choice. If Shimon feels that way, there's no sense forcing him."

"He doesn't know what he feels! He's just nervous."

"I completely agree with you—he's nervous and doesn't know what he feels. In fact, that's really the problem."

"Well, I'll let him know how he feels!" Tova cried. "You should've done that already, instead of coddling him."

The irony of her accusation struck Avner in the ribcage. Coddling—yes, that was certainly part of the problem. "It's not just nerves. Until he was about to get engaged, he didn't realize that he's simply not ready to get married."

"Nonsense, of course he's ready. He's twenty-five years old!"

"He's afraid of commitment. Afraid of responsibility."

"He'll learn to handle both. Everyone does."

Avner shook his head.

"Let's go home." Tova's lips were pressed firmly together. "I have to make dinner."

"Hopefully, Brachie made dinner."

Tova rolled her eyes. "Yes, I can imagine what that will taste like."

Avner signaled and pulled into the stream of traffic. Sometimes, talking to Tova was an exercise in searching for the right key to unlock the door of her mind. Even before Avner had set the parking brake, she stormed out of the car. He hurried to stay close behind.

"Hello, Brachie."

"Mommy! You're home! Wait till you see what I cooked. How's Bubby?"

"The same. Where's Meir?"

Brachie's brow creased. "In his room. What do you mean 'the same?'"

"Still in bed. Call Meir. No, don't call him. Show me what's doing in the kitchen."

Clearly confused, Brachie led the way. Avner followed silently.

"I made little hamburgers and rice, and I also cut up a salad." She pointed to the counter. "It took time, but it looks nice, no?"

"Yes. Where are the hamburgers?"

"Staying warm in the oven." She took an oven mitt and slid out the bottom of a broiler pan. "Oh, they look a little... I don't know." She started to put them down on the counter.

"That's *milchig*," Tova snapped.

"Here, let me." Avner grabbed a towel and relieved Brachie of the tray. He approached the counter.

"You'll burn the countertop!" She threw down a trivet. "Here."

Avner lay the pan down, thinking that the hamburgers certainly did look "I don't know." He begged Tova with his eyes not to say anything to Brachie.

"Here's the rice." Brachie lifted the cover off a pot. "I called Rena in Denver for help."

"That was very resourceful of you," Avner said, injecting a lilting note into his voice.

Tova looked into the pot and frowned. "That's not rice. That's wild rice."

"Is there a difference?"

The frown deepened into a scowl. "How long did you cook it for?"

"Twenty minutes. I set the timer."

Avner laid his hand on Brachie's shoulder.

"Fine," Tova sighed. "Maybe it's salvageable."

Brachie's face fell. "I'm sorry, Mommy. I did my best."

"We're proud of you," Avner said. "Right, Mommy?"

"Yes," Tova said, her voice wooden. "Thank you, Brachie. I'll finish up."

"I'll wash the dishes after dinner," Brachie said with a puppy-dog look.

"That's a big help," Avner said quickly.

Tova marched out.

"Mommy's tense about Bubby," Avner soothed. "We appreciate your help."

Brachie returned a weak smile.

Avner caught up with Tova in their room as she rifled through some drawers. "Why don't you rest now?" he suggested.

"I need to change and then redo dinner. Will you take it to Tatty, maybe spend some time with him and Ma? I want to be here when Shimon comes home. I'll go back there later to sleep."

Avner had been ready to propose that dinner would suffice as is, and that Brachie could sleep at the hospital instead, but realized that neither of those was the page he wanted to turn to right now. "How about I drop Brachie off there with dinner?"

"That's a nice idea. She's good at cheering people up."

Avner raised an eyebrow but said no more about Brachie. He succeeded in convincing Tova to rest while he was gone and made sure to be present when Shimon came home.

Tova was waiting for him.

"Hi, Mommy. How's Bubby?"

"The same. Come to the kitchen please." Her eyes smoldered. "I want to talk to you."

Yerucham stood in the doorway. "It's good of you to come, Rabbi. I really appreciate it. Aidel will, too."

"My wife says she's going to stop in tomorrow sometime," Rabbi Hess said.

"Aidel will be so happy to see her," Yerucham said, aiming a worried glance behind him.

"She's not doing well?"

Yerucham sighed. "She's speaking much better, but since she realized she can't walk, she seems very low. If the nurse hadn't come in and made her eat, I think she'd still be laying there doing nothing."

"Depression is quite common after a stroke."

Yerucham blinked. "It is?"

"Certainly, Yerucham. I'd like to say hello. May I go in?"

"Yes, of course." Yerucham led the way. "Aidel, look who came to visit."

"Hello, Rabbi Hess. Thank you for coming." She glanced at the rolling night table beside her. "I'm sorry, I have nothing to offer you."

Rabbi Hess smiled. "And I'm sorry I have nothing to offer you, either, Mrs. Lewin. You'll have to stop in for a visit when you're back on your feet. Faigy will never forgive me for coming without at least bringing you a piece of *kichel*."

"I couldn't eat it anyway," Aidel said. "Tomorrow I'll be allowed to try solids. Probably soft solids, so please tell the rebbetzin not to waste her *kichel* on me."

"I'm sure she'll send some anyway, then both of you can enjoy it. And speaking of enjoying, I believe you left this in my house on your last visit."

Eyes bright, Yerucham reached for the proffered *sefer*.

A small smile softened Aidel's features. "It was very kind of you to remember."

"My pleasure. Now, Yerucham, how about we learn a little together? I'll just pull these chairs to that little desk over there."

Yerucham immediately agreed and they were soon huddled together over the small *sefer*. They only looked up when they heard footsteps.

"Dr. Sassoon!" Yerucham stood and greeted him.

The doctor put out his hand to both Yerucham and the rabbi. "I certainly didn't expect to meet you here at this hour." He turned to Aidel. "I'm so sorry I didn't stop in this morning. I was here, spoke to your doctor, and then had to run out for an emergency."

Rabbi Hess said a quick good-bye.

Yerucham turned to Dr. Sassoon. "But aren't *you* our doctor?"

"I meant Dr. Lawrence," Dr. Sassoon replied. "He's the one in charge during the hospital stay."

Yerucham's forehead contracted. "But you're still our doctor, right?"

Dr. Sassoon smiled at both of them. "Of course I am. I just don't have much say about what goes on around here. But don't worry, I read your chart and spoke to Dr. Lawrence earlier. You're in the best possible hands."

Yerucham nodded uncertainly.

"Mrs. Lewin, you're doing remarkably well."

"Doctor, if I were doing remarkably well, I'd be able to get up on my own two feet." She tried to keep her voice light but failed.

Yerucham sighed.

"A stroke is never a simple matter," Dr. Sassoon said, "but you've responded beautifully to the tPA. The clot is dissolving, and your speech is excellent."

"Dr. Lawrence said my speech is not normal."

"It hasn't completely returned to normal, but the fact that it's so much better is a very good sign."

"They brought me a speech therapist." She made a face. "I spent ten minutes trying to teach her how to say 'Yerucham,' and then we played word games."

"Who won?" Dr. Sassoon asked.

Aidel frowned. "I'm not some silly little girl who needs to play games, you know."

"Mrs. Lewin, try to work with the therapist. She's only try-ing to help you."

"Can't you see if they have someone else?"

"It's only temporary, while you're still here."

"He's right," Yerucham said. "Once we're home, we can find someone you like better."

"There you go."

"Doctor," Yerucham said, "my daughter Tova wants us to move in with her for a while. We think it's a good idea. Tova is home during the day, and my granddaughter Brachie is also around."

"I haven't seen Tova in years," Doctor Sassoon said. "I still think of her as a sweet little girl with bright green eyes. It's hard for me to picture her as a mother of grown children."

"She's a very dedicated mother," Aidel said.

Yerucham nodded.

"And a wonderful daughter," she added, her voice suddenly breaking.

Yerucham stared at his wife.

"Then I can't think of a better place for you to be while you get stronger," Dr. Sassoon said.

"But there are stairs," Yerucham explained. "Stairs to get into the house, and the bedrooms are upstairs, too."

Dr. Sassoon laced his fingers together. "There are ways of managing that. Have you spoken to the hospital social worker?"

Yerucham took a step back. "We don't need a social worker."

"You might find she can be a big help to you. She has a lot of experience in directing people to the right resources. I'm sure she can give you some ideas."

"Such as?" Yerucham asked.

"It will depend on how you're doing by the time you get there. If you're in a wheelchair—"

Aidel gasped.

"I'm not saying you will be! I said 'if.' You might need a wheelchair, just temporarily. Or maybe you'll have a walker by then."

Aidel closed her eyes.

"Mrs. Lewin, in order to get better, you have to go one step at a time. It's a process. You're an otherwise healthy woman." He looked hard at her. "You're strong. You can do this."

Yerucham and Aidel stared at the doctor, then at each other for a long moment.

"Well then," Aidel said, her mettle returning, "I'll just pretend that I'm in a hotel. Tova will do all the cooking, and I'll take a little vacation."

Yerucham smiled. "We'll figure out what to do about the stairs. I'll talk to Tova and Avner, they'll have ideas."

"And we'll enjoy spending time with the grandchildren."

Dr. Sassoon grinned. "That's the spirit. You talk it over, and then while you're at the rehab center, you can make the arrangements."

As one, Yerucham and Aidel turned to the doctor. It was Aidel who voiced the question. "Rehab center?"

Shimon followed Tova to the kitchen. He looked pathetically at Avner, who nodded slightly. *Yes, Mommy knows.*

They sat at the table, forming a triangle.

Tova tore into the conversation. "Shimon, I want to know what's going on. Tell me everything."

"Well, uh, it's like I told Tatty." He looked at Avner.

Avner folded his hands. He couldn't say anything without putting Tova on the defensive. The best he could do was damage control after this storm blew over.

"I want to hear it from you, not Tatty. What's all this about not wanting to marry Ilana?" Her voice was a distant rumble of thunder, insidiously creeping closer.

"I just don't think that she's the right girl for me." He ran his sleeve across his forehead.

"Is there something wrong with her?" Tova demanded.

"N-no," Shimon stammered.

"Did you hear something about her family?"

"No."

"Then explain to me why on earth you want to throw away

a perfectly good *shidduch*!"

Shimon's eyes darted back and forth. "I don't know, Mommy, I just don't think she understands me. It doesn't feel... right."

"Feel right? What kind of nonsense is that?"

He shrugged miserably. "I can't see myself marrying her."

"It's only nerves. Cold feet. Shimon, you went out with Ilana *seven* times. Seven! That's way more than most people in our circles. You never said anything negative about her, not a single word. She has good *middos*, you get along well, the families are similar, you want the same things. Am I right?"

"Well, yeah, I guess so. She's, uh, very nice and everything."

"That's exactly what I'm saying."

"I just think maybe she doesn't understand me."

A light flashed in Tova's eyes, and Avner was suddenly on guard.

"I see the problem." Her voice had leveled, but a lingering trill hung at the edges. "You look at Tatty and me, you look at Bubby and Zeidy, and you see solid marriages. And then you look at you and Ilana, and you say, why don't we have that? Shimon, you can't compare a marriage of twenty or thirty or forty years to an engaged couple. You're just starting out, so of course you don't have that level of connection."

Shimon nodded.

Avner clenched his jaw.

"Ilana's a fine girl. You'll see, *tatteleh,* after you're married for a while, you'll feel understood. And the longer you're married the better it'll get." She patted Shimon's hand. "Do you hear what I'm saying?"

He cracked his knuckles. "Yeah."

"On your last date—no, your last two dates. Didn't you feel comfortable with her?"

"Yes, I did."

"And you weren't just comfortable, remember? When you

came home, you were feeling great. You were singing her praises, you were nearly glowing!"

The hint of a smile brightened Shimon's features.

"Nothing changed, *tatteleh*, nothing. This is just a bad case of nerves. It's perfectly normal." She looked suddenly at Avner. "Right, Tatty? Isn't it normal to get nervous right before you get engaged?"

"Well, of course it's normal to be nervous—"

"You see? Instead of thinking that you want to forget the engagement, think of how nice it will be once you're actually engaged. When the pressure is off, you'll be able to relax again, go back to learning, and leave the rest to us."

Avner's thoughts ricocheted, and he was unable to catch one and condense it into coherent words.

Shimon rubbed his chin, deep in thought. "So you think I should go ahead and get engaged?"

Tova's smile was relaxed now, and she said with full confidence, "Yes, I do."

She was a locomotive running at full speed on a narrow track, while Avner was performing mental gymnastics, trying to find a way to contradict Tova without openly confronting her in front of Shimon. But this could go on no longer; he had to say something—and fast.

"Shimon, can you go upstairs for a few minutes please? Mommy and I need to discuss something."

Avner could almost hear the screech of brakes as Tova's engine ground to a halt. Her lips were tight, her eyes flashing yellow warning signals. As soon as Shimon left the room she exploded. "What do you think you're doing? I was finally getting somewhere."

"Yes, you were. But you were heading to the wrong station."

Tova's eyes blazed.

Avner's mind screamed at him to back off. Locking horns

with anyone was anathema to him; and the closer the relationship, the more loathsome a confrontation. He wanted to apologize, to erase that look on her face. He could picture himself racing out of the room, calling Shimon back saying, "Your mother's right, just get engaged!"

But another picture formed, as well. A picture of Shimon, sitting at this table, crying over a broken engagement. Or worse, a broken marriage.

"I'm sorry, Tova," he said, truly meaning it, "but this is a terrible mistake."

Her right finger beat a steady tattoo on the table. "The mistake here is that you are letting Shimon's nerves get in the way."

"No." It came out more forceful than he'd intended.

Tova laid her hand down flat.

"No," he repeated more softly. "The biggest mistake would be to let him get engaged when he's really not ready."

"No one is ever ready to get married, Avner. Everyone's nervous, everyone's inexperienced. The only way to do it is to just do it."

Avner blew out a long breath. He would not be able to change her mind. But instead of trying to reason with her, perhaps he could appeal to her emotions. "Let's say you're right. Let's say it's just cold feet."

Tova raised an eyebrow.

"If we push him into this, he'll always have doubts."

The second eyebrow joined the first.

"As soon as a problem crops up, even a small difficulty, he'll wonder if it's because he married the wrong girl. Sooner or later, they'll hit a bump in the road—every couple does. You want Shimon to go into a marriage because we pressured him?" He leaned in closer. "You think that just because he's our son and we told him this is a good match, he'll be able to overcome all obstacles and stay married, no matter what?"

Tova drew her hands onto her lap and looked down at them. When she looked up, there was doubt in her eyes. And worry. "Shully Klein's daughter just got divorced. They were married only five months."

Avner nodded. "It happens more and more, I don't know why. But we can't hide from reality. If we want Shimon to get married and stay married, he has to be sure."

"This is just too much." Tova dropped her head in her hands.

Avner paused, then, "I'll talk to the *shadchan*, okay? You have enough to deal with."

"Okay," she said, her voice shaking.

Avner took a big lungful of air. He hadn't actually convinced Tova of anything, but he wasn't looking to score a victory—just prevent a disaster. He had an urge to check that all his limbs were still intact. He had a funny sensation in his chest, like the achy nausea he'd felt once when he'd lost control of his car and came within inches of hitting a giant oak tree. Then, as now, he was uninjured but utterly dazed.

"Are you ready to call Shimon back now?"

Tova rubbed her eyes. "I'm exhausted beyond words, over-wrought, and not ready for anything. But the poor boy is probably pacing his feet off. Call him back."

Shimon didn't make eye contact with either parent upon his return. He stationed himself behind a chair, hands clasped behind his back.

"Have a seat," Avner said.

Shimon sat, his eyes not leaving the napkin holder in the center of the table.

"Mommy and I really haven't had a chance to talk about this until now. We wanted to make sure we both understood what you want. What you need."

Shimon snuck a peek at Tova.

"This is your decision," Avner continued. "Whatever you

decide, Mommy and I support you."

Tova nodded.

Shimon stared, as if waiting.

"If you need more time," Tova said, "that's fine."

Shimon's lips parted, his eyes welled up with tears.

"And if you want to call it off completely, that's fine too," Avner said.

Tova swallowed and nodded again. "Yes. If it's not *bashert*, it's a blessing you found that out now."

Shimon's eyes did not leave Tova's face. Tentatively, she patted his hand.

His whole body seemed to unwind at once. "Yes, a *berachah*," he stammered. "This is all wrong. I can't..." his voice trailed off.

"Tatty will speak with the *shadchan* and settle everything. Avner, do you think Shimon ought to speak to Ilana directly?"

"Absolutely. I think he should give her an explanation and apologize."

"Apologize? I... I can't do that. I... what would I say? I'm so embarrassed!"

"She probably will be, too," Avner said. "There is nothing comfortable about any of this. But it's something you have to do."

"I agree," inserted Tova. "She's going to be one very disappointed young lady."

The helpless look on Shimon's face would have been comical if it wasn't so desperate. Avner said as much to Tova after Shimon left them alone again.

"Yes," Tova agreed, the corners of her mouth turning down. "That'll be a very difficult phone call for him. For Ilana's sake, maybe you can help him find the appropriate words."

More hand-holding? Avner had been thinking—hoping— that facing Ilana would shake him up, make him realize that he had some work to do in order to be ready to marry, not just ready to date. Preparing for such a difficult conversation would force him to examine the issue from all sides—from *her* side.

On the other hand, Ilana deserved a proper apology; it would help bring her some closure. Avner and Tova had a responsibility to make sure Shimon said the words she needed to hear, even if it did mean a little more hand-holding.

"For her sake," Avner said, "maybe you're right. And speaking of phone calls, I guess I'd better speak to the *shadchan*."

"I'm sorry I'm throwing that on you. I feel I'm being neglectful."

"Neglectful! You? Tova, you're the most dedicated mother I know. And daughter." He looked into her eyes. "And wife."

A warm smile, slow to form but rich in meaning, spread across Tova's features.

"Mommy's sending chicken soup," Brachie said, leaning over the hospital bed. "She made *lokshen* and *kneidlach*. Plus soup chicken. That ought to be easy to chew."

"Thank you," Aidel said. "Tell Mommy not to fuss over me. The hospital provides kosher food. I can eat whatever I'm served."

With a quiet *krechz*, Yerucham shifted in his seat.

"I'm sure she'll send enough for you and Zeidy," Brachie said.

Aidel looked sideways at Yerucham. "Zeidy can eat at home with the rest of you."

"I'm staying here," he growled.

"Look at you," Aidel said. "How much more sitting in that chair can your back take?"

"Zeidy, please can I stay with Bubby over Shabbos? Please?"

"Now that's a wonderful idea," Aidel said.

Yerucham's jaw was set. "No. I don't want to be far away over Shabbos."

"But Zeidy, I was in Eretz Yisrael for a whole year, and I'd really love a chance to catch up with Bubby. Oh, please say yes!"

"Really, Yerucham, it would be such a treat for me. And I simply can't look at you hunched over in that chair another day!"

"Aidel, I—"

"If your back goes out, who's going to bring you hot water bottles? And arrange the pillows the way you like? You can't take the chance. I need you, Yerucham. You simply have to take a day off so that you can come back here and keep me company."

His face was stern, but a half smile teased itself onto his features. "Well... okay. If Tova allows it, Brachie can stay."

Brachie clapped her hands. "I'll call Tatty, I'll ask him to pick me up now, while it's still early. I need to go home and shower, then I'll be back."

Before Yerucham could say another word, Brachie pulled out Avner's cell phone. She punched in two numbers and stopped. Her index finger hovered over the buttons, her mind's eye lingered over her father's face. "Maybe... I'm better off taking a bus. I'm sure Tatty has better things to do on Erev Shabbos than pick me up." She grabbed her pocketbook. "I'll be back as soon as I can."

She didn't have to wait long for a bus. Brachie took a seat behind the rear door, called her parents to make sure it was okay to stay with Bubby over Shabbos, then stared out the window.

Chessed was ingrained in her; picking up a dropped object, giving up a seat for an older person—these were reflexive. And of course there was school *"chessed"*— two hours a week of "helping." But getting inside someone's head and trying to figure out what he needed? Unchartered territory. Helping within the family? A different planet. Brachie didn't know how to cook, had never done laundry, didn't know a dust cloth from a pincushion. What could she possibly contribute? Yet it was as if her mother's sudden absence caused a vacuum that she was drawn to fill. And what surprised her more than anything was that she was beginning to enjoy herself.

She was soon home, and in and out of the shower in record time. She dressed quickly, leaving her hair wet, and packed herself a small bag. She found Tova in the kitchen, rinsing out the sink.

Brachie kissed her mother's cheek. "Have a good Shabbos, Mommy."

"Good Shabbos, *sheifeleh*. I'm still not crazy about you staying there, but Tatty thinks it's a good idea. Are you sure you'll be all right?

"Of course I will."

"I packed you an extra piece of kugel."

"Thanks, Mommy."

The phone rang. "I'll get it," Tova said.

Brachie poured a handful of soup nuts into a plastic bag and added it to the shopping bag Tova had prepared. She scanned the kitchen, looking for something that would make Shabbos in the hospital a little nicer for her grandmother. She reached into a drawer and grabbed a towel embroidered with the words "*al netilas yadayim*" and added it to the bag.

Phone wedged between her ear and her shoulder, Tova said, "Masha Kaplan? I'm sorry, I... Oh, Rena's mother."

Holding the bag in one hand, Brachie reached for the phone with the other.

Tova shook her head. "Yes, of course I've heard all about Rena, she sounds like a lovely girl. Does she want to speak to Brachie?" She smiled at her daughter.

Brachie stood, waiting.

"Oh, you wanted to speak to me directly." She paused, her eyes fixed on Brachie. "Of course I'd like to hear."

14

"HERE YOU GO, ZEIDY," Meir said, leading Yerucham to a captain's chair.

"I don't want to sit at the end," Yerucham said.

"But you always sit there."

"Well, I don't want to sit there now. I'll sit there," he pointed, "next to Mommy."

"Okay, Zeidy, I'll move your *becher* there."

"And I don't want to make my own Kiddush," he growled, "so you can just take that *becher* away."

Meir's eyes were a pair of question marks.

"I'll do it," Shimon said.

Tova came in from the kitchen carrying twin salt cellars.

Avner began *"Askinu Seudasa"* in the tune his father-in-law favored.

Yerucham stopped him. "Thank you, Avner. Please do what you usually do."

Avner smiled uncertainly. "We always sing this tune when you come."

"Bubby's not here now to know the difference. So just go

ahead and pretend I'm not here."

Avner and Tova looked at each other, then Avner switched to his regular tune. Shimon joined in and poked Meir with his elbow to do the same.

Yerucham didn't sing, but he made no further comments. Instead, he pushed the food around his plate and sighed loudly and often. He asked for wine but didn't open the bottle. He asked for tea but it was too hot; when Tova added some water, it was too cold.

Shimon made Yerucham another tea which, inexplicably, was "just right." If Shimon was the one with whom Yerucham was the most comfortable, he would do his best to be helpful. Besides, every time he looked at his mother he felt a stab of guilt, and being busy with Yerucham kept his eyes off Tova.

Since that conversation with his parents, his thoughts and feelings had been rolled out, knotted together, and pulled apart again like the silly putty he'd played with as a child. After the initial shock and relief that his mother had accepted his decision, he was left with a void in the place where all his anxiety had previously collected. And for the first time in many weeks, he began to realize that he'd been so busy agonizing over whether or not Ilana would make him a good wife, he'd forgotten to be a good person—considerate, honest, direct. This whole situation was the result of his ridiculous insecurity, his severe nervousness, his absurd shyness. Why couldn't he be more like Yoni—confident, self-assured, outgoing, always knowing what to say? Why—

He stopped himself. This line of thought was not going to make things better. He needed to figure out how to manage these traits, not drown in them.

Still, there was no denying that he had toyed with Ilana's feelings. And with his mother's. The bad taste in his mouth that his behavior left him with made him want to *do* something.

"Shimon," Yerucham said, "please give me my hat for *bentching*."

Shimon obliged. "Zeidy, can I get you something else? Another glass of tea?"

"No. Thank you."

"Which *shacharis* do you want to go to tomorrow morning?"

"It doesn't matter. Wherever Tatty goes."

"You want to learn something with me?"

Yerucham grunted.

Shimon's eyes scanned the room, landing on a chair pushed slightly away from the table. He walked around and picked up a small *sefer* that sat hidden from view. "What's this?"

Yerucham looked up. "I was looking for that. Let me have it." He held the book with two hands. "Good."

Shimon hesitated. Was that a dismissal or an invitation?

"Nu, sit down." Yerucham opened the *sefer* and pointed. "Look at this."

The two were soon deep in discussion and remained that way for a long while.

When it was *minchah* time, Shimon got himself ready and waited by the front door.

"I walk slow," Yerucham said. "You can go ahead."

"That's okay, Zeidy, we have time. I'll walk with you." He matched his pace to Yerucham's. In front of the shul, Yerucham stopped short and looked up at his grandson, his lip curling into a half smile. "Thank you," he said.

Shimon looked back, a matching smile forming. "It was my pleasure."

Avner rubbed a fork with a dishtowel and slipped it into the drawer with the others. "And he's Rena's cousin? I suppose Rena is the one who thought of it."

"Yes," Tova said, dipping the Shabbos sponge into a bowl.

"I'm sure Brachie's already decided he's perfect for her."

Avner smiled. "Well, it sounds worth looking into, doesn't it?"

"I don't know, he's awfully young."

"Twenty-one isn't so young these days. Look, Yoni's only twenty-two."

Tova grimaced. "I don't think his starting *shidduchim* is a good idea, either, but no one seems to listen to me."

"Meanwhile nothing's come up for Yoni yet, so let's not cross that bridge until we come to it."

"Yoni is eating at this Reb Dovid's house for Shabbos, remember? He's probably sitting there right now with his brother and sister-in-law. I'm expecting a phone call right after Shabbos."

"So we'll talk about it if and when it comes up. We were discussing Brachie, not Yoni."

Tova placed another dish onto the drying rack. "There's so much going on right now. Brachie just got home from seminary, what's the rush?"

"We agreed that we wouldn't start calling *shadchanim*, but that we would consider suggestions."

"How on earth am I going to find the time to check this boy out?"

"I can do the checking. I have a lighter load in yeshivah now that it's summer vacation."

Tova shut the water and stared at Avner. "That's not how we did it with Shimon."

"That doesn't mean we can't do it this way now. Besides, this is a *bachur* we're checking out, not a girl."

Tova picked up a towel and dried her hands. "Fine, I'll leave it to you."

Avner blinked.

"I'm going upstairs to collapse. Good Shabbos. Oh, I forgot, I need to make my father a glass of tea."

"Shimon brought him one not long ago. I'll make sure

everything's settled down here, you just go to sleep."

Tova didn't argue, and Avner finished drying the dishes, wondering if Tova's quick surrender was a result of exhaustion, overload, or just plain practicality.

Tova tossed her slippers into the bag and zipped it closed. She grabbed the cordless and dialed. "Hi, Brachie, how was Shabbos? How's Bubby?"

"She's fine now, *baruch Hashem*."

"What do you mean, 'fine *now*'?"

"One sec, okay?"

"No, it is *not* okay. Tell me what you meant by that."

"Sorry, Mommy, I just went out into the hall so Bubby wouldn't hear. This afternoon Bubby got a little confused. She wasn't sure where she was. She kept asking if it was time to *bentch licht* yet, and where was her *leichter*."

Tova's palms began to sweat. "I knew I should have stayed with her!"

"It only lasted around ten minutes or so, and she's been fine since."

Tova snatched her bag. "I'm coming right away. I must speak with the doctor!"

"I spoke to him," Brachie said.

Tova stopped short. "You did?"

"Yeah. Last night I met a nice, *heimish* woman staying with her sister down the hall, and I asked her to stay with Bubby for a few minutes while I tracked down the doctor. He said that I should keep an eye on her, but that it's a pretty normal thing to happen after a stroke."

Tova dropped down onto her bed.

"Other than that, Bubby was fine. She really enjoyed your soup, and was able to chew the chicken and *kneidlach* with no problem."

Air filled her lungs. "Anything else happen over Shabbos?"

"Not really. Joy came by—you know, the physical therapist. She wanted Bubby to stand, but Bubby said she wouldn't do anything on Shabbos, so Joy left."

"I'm happy to hear that. They have to respect Bubby's wishes."

"I guess. But she's not going to get anywhere if she just lays in bed. I think Joy should have tried harder to convince Bubby. At the time I wasn't sure what to do, so I left it between them, but after I thought more about it, I'm not so sure that was the right thing."

"You did just fine, Brachie, you handled it very well. I'll be there soon. What should I bring Bubby?"

"I don't know, but bring the phone charger. I think the battery's almost finished on this thing."

Tova tossed the phone onto her bed. It did sound as if her mother was okay. On the other hand, she wouldn't be calm until she spoke to the doctor herself—and that would only be tomorrow. But at least she could hurry to the hospital and see her mother with her own two eyes. She picked up her bag and went down the stairs to find everyone in the kitchen. "I'm ready, Avner, I just need to make you a *melaveh malkah* first."

"Thanks," Avner said, "but I'll have something later."

"What about you, Tatty? A roll and some soup? Chicken and salad? Rice?"

"Not right now, thank you."

"But Tatty, I don't want you to get hungry while I'm away."

"Don't worry, Shimon can heat me up some soup later."

Tova raised her eyebrows at Shimon. He gave a small shrug and the hint of a smile.

"Can I have a pizza bagel?" Meir asked.

Yerucham said, "Tova, Avner, I need to talk to you."

"Meir," Avner said, "I'll put your pizza bagel in the oven and call you when it's ready."

Meir took the hint and left. Shimon hesitated, then began to follow Meir.

"Shimon, please pour me a glass of Mommy's lemonade."

Shimon changed course.

"I didn't want to say anything till after Shabbos," Yerucham began, "but Dr. Sassoon came by on Thursday."

Tova gripped the edge of the table.

"He said that when Mommy leaves the hospital, she's going to need to go to a rehab center."

Tova frowned. "That makes no sense. I can take much better care of her here, and she can get any therapy she needs. And—"

"I know, I know, it's not what any of us expected. But for the first few weeks, she'll be better off there."

Tova pressed her lips together.

Yerucham made a *berachah* and sipped his drink. "Thank you, Shimon. The question is, what happens after that? We agreed Mommy would come here. But what about the stairs?"

Avner ran a hand through his hair. "I hadn't thought of that."

"Neither did I," Tova said.

Quietly, Shimon moved toward the door.

"Shimon," Yerucham stopped him, "come here and sit down. I have an idea that involves you."

Shimon's brow puckered in confusion.

"*Bein hazmanim* starts soon. Bubby and I can move back home, and you, Shimon..."

Three pair of eyes focused intently on Yerucham.

"You can stay with us."

Voices washed over her. She hovered between the last lingering wisps of a dream and the familiar cadence of her parents' voices. Tova squinted up at the stark hospital lights, then sat upright.

"Good morning, Tovaleh," Aidel said.

She spied a hospital breakfast tray, along with an empty

container that had come from her own house. "What time is it?"

"Nine-thirty," Yerucham answered. "Avner said to let you sleep, everything's under control at home."

Tova frowned. A lot of help she'd been, sleeping the morning away. "Was the doctor here yet?"

"Dr. Lawrence was by very early, and Dr. Sassoon also came to visit."

Tova sprang up out of the chair. "What did he say?"

"Dr. Sassoon says hello," Aidel smiled.

"Dr. Lawrence said Mommy should be discharged either today or tomorrow. He's going to come by around two and let us know, and he wants to talk to us about where to go from here."

Tova bit her lip. Her parents had known since Thursday that Aidel would be going to rehab. If they had shared that information earlier, she could have already researched the options. "I'm going to find Dr. Lawrence."

"There's no need," Aidel said. "Tatty told you he's coming by later. He's waiting for some test results, and then I'm going to be discharged. Why do you need to chase after him?"

"Brachie said..."

"Don't you worry about what Brachie said. It's what the doctor says that counts."

Tova grabbed the phone. "Then I guess I'll get busy looking into rehab facilities."

It didn't take long. Fortunately—or unfortunately—it wasn't difficult to find people with family members who'd had strokes. A very few phone calls narrowed it down to two choices; location narrowed it down to one. She slipped into the hall to call Avner. "There's a place in Brooklyn that sounds like what Ma needs. Another advantage is that it's a *frum* place."

"You got good references?"

"Yes, families of people who've been there, plus I also spoke to some of the patients themselves."

"Sounds like you were thorough."

"Yes." She started to say good-bye, but Avner interrupted her.

"I made some phone calls of my own," he said. "This Mordechai sounds like a good match for Brachie."

Tova shook her head. "After one morning you're ready to let her go out with this boy?"

"Actually, I started last night. Motza'ei Shabbos can be a good time to catch people."

She leaned against the wall. "Go on."

"He's the oldest of eight, outgoing but not overly loud. Serious learner, budding *talmid chacham*, but not the type to snub someone in favor of a *sefer*."

"That sounds like a nice start."

"He's looking for a girl who is willing to work, someone who's not too shy, who would encourage his learning without being his *mashgiach*."

Tova nodded. "I guess we can look into him further."

"Well, I spoke to his *rosh yeshivah*, his roommate, and two other friends. I'm waiting for two more people to get back to me, but I have a feeling that by tomorrow we should be able to call back the *shadchan* with a yes."

Tova stood up straight and put her free hand out in front of her. "Hold on, Avner. Isn't that rather quick?"

"I don't see any reason to wait."

"Hmpf. I thought after this whole business with Shimon, you'd insist that things move more slowly."

"No. After this business with Shimon, I'm going to spend more time listening." A pause; then, "Maybe we both will."

Those words reverberated in her mind long after they hung up. Tova roamed the corridors, barely noticing her surroundings. Her stomach felt queasy, the way it had the day Brachie boarded the plane to Eretz Yisrael.

What did Avner mean, "more time listening"? She always made herself available for her children. She and Brachie could spend hours schmoozing!

She thought back to the conversation they'd had after Brachie's homecoming. Brachie had expressed interest in becoming a *sheitel macher*, and Tova had explained the drawbacks—that she was better off getting a degree. She explained that it was unrealistic to expect to be supported forever.

Tova traced a crack in the wall with her finger. She had explained, explained, explained... was that really the same as listening?

Don't be ridiculous. An eighteen-year-old girl needs to be guided.

Does she? And what kind of guidance does a girl this age need?

Her hand fell to her side and she resumed walking. Maybe it was Brachie—perhaps she simply needed more guidance than most girls her age. Shimon, too. Look what a mess he'd made of things! He needed *more* guidance, not less. Like his willingness—no, his eagerness—to move in with her parents. It was sweet, but it was just another example of how unrealistic he was. She was glad she'd nixed that idea as soon as she heard it.

Tova nearly walked into a door and looked up to get her bearings. She'd made a complete circle around the fifth floor and was back in front of Aidel's room. She meandered inside and sat down.

"You haven't eaten anything," Aidel said. "There's a container of melon waiting for you."

"I'm not hungry, Ma, thanks."

Aidel smiled. "I think Brachie cut it up. She'll want to hear how much you enjoyed it."

Tova found herself eating the melon.

"Yidel Blaustein is back," Yerucham told Aidel.

"Wonderful," Aidel said, "now you two can go back to your morning *chavrusa*."

Yerucham grinned. "Not while I'm here with you."

"Maybe he'd be willing to learn in the evenings?"

"Mmm. I can ask."

Tova studied Aidel. Even from the confines of a hospital bed, she had a way of nurturing, of taking care without taking over. Tova had always strived to be like her mother, and she knew she'd succeeded in creating a warm nest for her children. Still, there was something different. Something...

"Tovaleh," Aidel said, "Tatty's here with me. Why don't you go home. I'll call you with a report the second the doctor leaves."

"I'd rather stay. I'll feel better if I can speak to him myself."

"I know, but *I'll* feel better if you weren't stuck here with me all day.

Tova sighed. "Okay, Ma. If you really don't need me, I'll go." She did need to make another round of phone calls, and they were better made out of earshot. She needed to find a reliable contractor to prepare the house for her mother. They'd decided that the pantry would be turned into a small bedroom for Aidel, which meant shifting everything in the kitchen around and widening the doorway. The front door also had to be widened in order to accommodate a wheelchair, a ramp had to be put in... It was going to be a headache, and until the renovations were completed, the less Aidel heard about them, the better.

A surprise awaited Tova at home: a single place setting on the kitchen table, a sesame bagel in a paper bag, and a note from Brachie letting her know that tuna and cream cheese were in the fridge along with some sliced tomatoes and cucumbers. And p.s., she'd gone shopping with Chava Miriam.

Tova smiled at the note and looked around. The counters were bare, the sinks empty, the floor swept. A wet dishtowel lay crumpled near the milchig sink and the broom was left out, but otherwise the room was tidy. It looked as if Avner was right after all. Brachie was starting to learn her way around the kitchen.

Tova ran a hand along the counter, smiled, and then sighed.

Well, even though the kitchen was clean, there was other work to be done—laundry, straightening up, and dinner to think about. Or perhaps she should get started on those phone calls. Who did she know that had done renovations in the last few years?

She rested her hand on the phone, but something stopped her. The phone calls, the housework—suddenly it seemed like a burden. She'd been moving at full speed for a week; it was time to regroup. Tova made herself a cup of decaf, spread a generous amount of cream cheese on her bagel, and picked up a magazine.

Half a bagel and two pages later, she gave a satisfied smile. When was the last time she'd treated herself to a leisurely meal? It wasn't a question of whether or not she deserved pampering; she generally just didn't feel the need. Tova sipped her coffee and turned the page.

The phone rang, and she jumped out of her seat.

"Mrs. Lehrfeld? Hi, this is Na'ama Rubin. I met your son Yoni over Shabbos, and I was very impressed. I'd like to tell you about a girl I have in mind for him..."

Inwardly, Tova groaned. This was simply too much to handle right now. At this rate, she'd be getting a call tomorrow about a girl for Meir. "A girl for Yoni? Thank you. What did you say your name was?"

"Na'ama Rubin. My brother-in-law Dovid knows Yoni from yeshivah."

"Of course. Yes, I would like to hear about this girl."

"Her name is Penina Solomon. Comes from a solid family, very *heimish*. She's eighteen, just back from Eretz Yisrael. She's very intelligent..."

Tova whipped out a pen and paper. Na'ama was thorough, leaving her with few questions and many references.

"She sounds lovely, thank you," Tova said, trying to mean it. She knew she should be grateful for the call. Even when a suggestion was way off, Tova always appreciated being thought of. But now, gratitude was a tiny thread in a huge tapestry of people and events that dizzied her eyes and muddled her thinking.

"Mrs. Lehrfeld, I must tell you, Yoni is... well, he's exceptional."

"Oh?" Tova put her pen down and stood still.

Na'ama gave an embarrassed chuckle. "I'm sure you know this already, but I can't help saying it anyway. Yoni is considerate and put together. He really has his priorities straight. On Shabbos, he didn't go for a rest and then wait to see how the rest of the afternoon would pan out, he set up a time to learn with Dovid and woke himself up in time for it. When Dovid was delayed a few minutes by one of the kids, Yoni pulled out a book and started reading to another child. The kids absolutely adored him. I know he's pretty young, but he's very mature. I'd love to help him find the right girl; he deserves someone equally special."

Tova stared through the window and struggled to find her tongue. "Well, that's... that's very nice to hear. I'm so glad that he was a good guest."

Na'ama laughed. "You can say that again. He even helped clear the table. Very few *bachurim* think to do that. You've certainly done a wonderful job with his *chinuch*. Yoni is one of a kind."

Mature. One of a kind. Has his priorities straight. Mature! "Thank you, we're very proud of Yoni. And thanks for the suggestion, we'll look into Penina and get back to you as soon as we can."

Tova closed her eyes. Rehab facilities and contractors and a young man named Mordechai—for a moment, it all faded as she savored the words of this woman she'd never met.

"Was there something special you wanted to talk about," Avner began, "or are we just enjoying a pleasant walk?"

The moon was rising, the trees waving a regretful goodnight to the setting sun.

Tova led the way, turning right at the corner. They passed a public school where a handful of children ran around the open lot, making the most of the dwindling daylight. She stopped, her hand brushing the fence. "I'm getting old," she said unexpectedly.

"Compared to whom?" He pointed to the children with his chin.

"Even Meir is older than those kids." She sighed. "I've never felt like this before, Avner."

"Like what?"

Tova turned right again. "Do you know what I did today?"

"You hired a contractor and signed your mother into a rehab facility. You took care of—"

Tova waved his words away. "I made a to-do list."

Avner chuckled.

"Information I write down, but lists? I never need to-do lists, I keep it all in my head."

"And that's making you feel old? Life's gotten pretty busy lately. There's so much going on, there's no way you can remember everything."

"If I were ten years younger, I wouldn't need lists."

Avner grinned. "If you were ten years younger, you wouldn't have three kids in *shidduchim*." He grew serious. "Tova, this is a rough time for you, for all of us. It's hard to see your mother like this. It's not just a matter of juggling information, it's emotionally wrenching."

They walked in silence. After two more turns, a tear trickled down her cheek. "I'm just not sure what to do with all of this."

Avner nodded, looking thoughtful. "I know."

"Things are changing too fast. When did everyone grow up?" She stopped and faced him directly. "I'm scared, Avner. I've always tackled one thing at a time. Now I feel like... like I'm in over my head, drowning in a sea of change."

"Change is scary." He paused. "For me, too."

Tova tilted her head.

"It's much more comfortable, and safer, to be sitting inside the boat, steering with long-handled oars," Avner continued. "But even when you're treading water, longing for that dry, safe haven, you're not drowning, Tova."

She sniffled. "I'm not?"

"No. You're swimming."

15

BRACHIE EASED THE BROOM out of Tova's hands. "Please let me do this. You look exhausted."

"Thank you, *sheifeleh,* I'll just finish up and ask Tatty to drive me to the hospital."

"Mommy, let me sleep there tonight."

"Oh, I don't know."

"Let's ask Tatty what he thinks."

Avner entered with a big smile. "What he thinks about what?"

"I'd like to stay with Bubby tonight. I have nothing special to do tomorrow, anyway."

"Actually," he said, drawing out the word, "you do."

"I do?"

Avner threw Tova a smile. "That was the last reference on the phone. We're on."

"What are you talking about?" Brachie looked from one to the other.

"Mordechai. Rena's cousin. You're meeting him tomorrow night at eight-thirty."

The broom crashed to the floor. "I can't believe it!"
Avner chuckled.

"I can't either," Tova said. "Tomorrow, Avner? We're moving my mother tomorrow."

"It's fine. I'm taking Meir with me to yeshivah. When we come home, we'll take Bubby and her things to the new place. That gives us a good few hours to get her settled until we come back here and get ready."

"I didn't even show you what I bought yesterday!" Brachie flew out of the room.

Tova threw her hands up in the air. "I have workers coming tomorrow morning. How are we supposed to host Mordechai?"

Avner crossed his arms. "If Mordechai thinks less of us because of some dust—from construction done in order to accommodate your mother—he will *not* fit into this family."

It was that thought which kept her mouth closed as she watched Mr. Andrews work the next morning. He began early; he needed the whole day in order to take apart the old door and put in a new, wider one. The mess he made was beyond anything she'd anticipated.

She was about to look in on him again when he called her.

"Mrs. Lehrfeld, can you come here a minute?"

Tova came, bearing a glass of lemonade.

"Thanks. Here, I'd like you to see this."

"I know absolutely nothing about electricity, Mr. Andrews."

"You don't need a degree to understand this."

Tova followed his outstretched arm. A thin metal tube ran the length of the now-exposed doorway. "Yes?"

"There, up near the top, where the wires peek out to connect to the porch light."

The connection was black, as if it had been burned. Tova turned to Mr. Andrews with wide eyes. "What does that mean?"

"There was a short."

"Mr. Andrews, I appreciate you taking the time to show this to me. Please let me know when you've fixed it."

Mr. Andrews pushed his cap back. "I'm not qualified to fix it."

Tova stared. "You're a contractor."

"I do renovations. This needs a licensed electrician."

"Are you saying that I don't have a porch light?" How would Mordechai find their house tonight?

"That's correct. You also don't have a living room light. They're on the same circuit, and I had to shut the breaker off for that section of the house."

Tova's voice grew sharp. "I have a very important guest coming this evening and I simply cannot be without electricity in the living room. I need this fixed today."

"I understand, and believe me, I'll do my best to find someone. Let me make some calls."

"Thank you." Tova began to move away.

"You know, you people are really lucky."

Slowly, Tova turned to face him.

"That thing could have started a fire. You might even say it *should* have started a fire."

Tova closed her eyes. She saw the fire chief's face, heard his voice.

We get lotsa calls... Most of 'em don't have happy endings like this... Don't you forget to count your blessings.

Count your blessings.

Yes, perhaps she should do just that.

Meir studied a picture taped to the wall in Avner's classroom. "Who's Yosef?"

"One of my students," Avner answered, smiling.

Meir whistled. "He's really an artist."

"Yes, he is. Meir, I'm counting on your help this week. The

library's a mess, and I need you to straighten it out. Think you can handle that?"

"Sure I can. I think."

"I'm right here if you need me." Avner pulled out a textbook catalog and immersed himself in it until the bell rang shrilly. Avner jumped. School was out, and in the unusual quiet, he hadn't anticipated the noise. He stretched and made his way to the now-vacant teachers' room. In a few weeks he might miss the chit-chat, but for now he was enjoying the solitude. He sat down with a coffee and let his thoughts run free in the stillness.

He felt rather buoyant. It was a strange feeling for a man whose son just broke off a promising *shidduch* at the last minute and whose mother-in-law was in the hospital following a stroke. On top of that, he'd spoken to Shimon's *shadchan* last week and she had, not unexpectedly, upbraided him. He'd apologized and explained as much as was needed for both Shimon's and Ilana's sakes, without going into unnecessary detail. He acknowledged the correctness of everything she said, but held firm in the notion that another date or two was not going to do the trick. And after the initial, awkward hello, he hadn't felt any of the usual fear.

Fear? Of what?

"Hello, Avner."

Startled, Avner looked up sharply, jerking the hand that held the coffee cup in the process. Gedaliah had entered the teachers' room together with another man.

"Sorry, didn't mean to surprise you," Gedaliah said.

"No problem." He swiped at a spot of coffee that had landed on his sleeve.

"Here's someone I'd like you to meet. Avner Lehrfeld, Zev Gordon."

Avner gave Zev the once-over as he shook his hand. Zev was red-haired, clean-shaven, lean—and young. He wore a freshly starched shirt and a pair of glasses in the latest style.

"Zev is going to be our new seventh-grade *rebbi*."

Avner's hand fell to his side. He wouldn't have been more surprised if Gedaliah had said Zev was going be a new seventh-grade student.

"This will be his first year teaching. Zev has a lot of enthusiasm and fresh ideas," Gedaliah continued. "I'd like you to take him under your wing."

"Of course," Avner stammered. "I'd be delighted."

Gedaliah smiled. "I'll leave you two to get acquainted, then. Avner, Zev wants to see what kind of illustrated texts are available."

"Sure. I was just going over catalogs."

"Please come back to my office when you're done, Zev."

"I will. Thank you, Rabbi Newman."

Gedaliah nodded and left.

"Rabbi Newman tells me you're the tutor here."

"That's right. Come on, let's go to my room." He led the way.

"This is really cute," Zev said as they entered.

Avner paused only for a second. "I like it. Have a seat and I'll show you what we have and what we might order."

"Great, thanks."

Avner slid over a catalog. "These are *menukad*, these are illustrated."

A light shone in Zev's eyes as he pored over the text. "This is *exactly* what I'm looking for. Can we get one of each for every student?"

Avner smiled. "I think you might have to settle for one of each as reference, or maybe a few copies to share among the boys. We can't ask the parents to spring for these."

"We can't?" He paused. "Well, then, the school can buy them."

"The budget for textbooks isn't big enough for thirty of each book, either."

Zev's eyes dimmed.

"We can call the publisher and ask if we're allowed to copy a limited number of pages," Avner suggested.

Zev's brow furrowed and he studied his fingernails.

Avner's gaze drifted behind Zev's head and landed on the picture Yosef had drawn. "I have an idea," he said. "One of my students is quite an artist. He drew that picture of the *bigdei kehunah* right behind you."

Zev turned his head. "Cute."

Avner forced his shoulders to relax. "He's going to be in your class next year. Anything you want illustrated, I bet Yosef could do it for you. I can work with him, make sure he understands the material." He smiled. "It would help you, and it'd be great for him."

"That's... nice of you. But, you know, a *rebbi* has to be professional. Besides, I don't believe in playing favorites." Zev stood. "Well, thanks for your help."

"You're welcome," Avner mumbled as he watched Zev's retreat. The door clicked shut behind him.

And in Avner's mind, another door clicked shut, leaving him with a sudden feeling of longing—and remorse.

"Are you comfortable now?" Tova asked.

"I'm fine," Aidel said. "Really, Tova, you can go home. You've been sitting with me for over two hours already. This isn't a hospital, it's a rehab center, and you're going to have to get used to me being here by myself."

Yerucham grunted.

"Ma, I can sleep in that chair just as well as I did in the hospital," Tova said, pointing.

Meir bounced up and down on the chair. "This chair is much better than the one in the hospital. I wouldn't mind sleeping in it."

"Stop bouncing, Meir," Tova said.

Aidel waved her good hand. "Feh. No one needs to sleep here anymore, it's getting silly. And no more worrying about my food, either. The whole place is *glatt*, and I'm told it's pretty good, too."

"We still have some time," Avner said. "Would you like to get some fresh air?"

"I had plenty of fresh air on the way here, thank you."

There was a knock on the open door, and a petite woman with bright eyes and frizzy black hair entered. "Good afternoon."

A chorus of good afternoons answered.

"I'm Esti, the physical therapist." She smiled at Aidel. "You must be Mrs. Lewin."

"Yes."

Tova spoke up. "I'm Tova Lehrfeld, her daughter. And this is my father, my husband, and my son Meir."

"Well, it's nice to meet all of you." Esti pulled up a chair close to Aidel. "I'm looking forward to working with you. Do you feel all right? Are you in any pain?"

"I'm fine, thank you."

"Glad to hear it." Her smile was genuine. "Can you tell me a little about yourself?"

"Myself the person, or myself the patient?" It was said lightly, but Tova heard the frustration in her tone.

Apparently, so did Esti. "It's not simple, is it? *Nisht pashut.*"

Yerucham leaned forward, and Aidel's eyes twinkled. "Do you speak Yiddish?" she asked.

"Just enough to understand what my mother didn't want me to understand."

Aidel laughed.

"Mrs. Lewin, I've read your chart, but can you tell me in your own words why you're here?"

"I had a stroke," Aidel answered.

"Can you tell me what happened?"

Aidel told over the events since the previous Wednesday, with Tova adding an occasional detail. When she finished, she sat back, fatigued. Her speech was slow but clear, though the more she spoke, the more pronounced her lisp became.

Esti took a few notes but mostly just listened. When Aidel finished, she asked, "What are your goals?"

"To get out of here as soon as I can."

"And after that?"

She stole a peek at Yerucham. "I need to get well so I can take care of my husband," she said weakly.

"And what, specifically, do you need to do in order to take care of him?"

Tova's fingers gripped the seat of her chair. Esti was sweet, but it seemed there was some iron underneath the surface. "Esti, my mother's exhausted. Perhaps you can continue this conversation tomorrow."

"Okay, sure," Esti said easily.

Tova's hands relaxed.

"All I want to do today is get you standing, Mrs. Lewin. Then I'll go and we can continue tomorrow."

Tova stood. "If my mother is too tired to talk, she's certainly too tired to stand."

Esti paused and looked around the room, studying each person in turn. Finally, she smiled and said, "Okay, Mrs. Lehrfeld, I see your point. We'll try again tomorrow afternoon. I'll be here around three."

Tova smiled, but the smile didn't reach her eyes. "Fine, then, so will I."

Tova cringed as she walked through the empty frame where the front door used to be. "I can't believe this is going to stay like this."

"Just for a couple of days," Avner said.

"But Mordechai is coming *tonight*."

"Tova, remember—"

Tova put a hand out. "I know, I know. If Mordechai is put off by it, he's not worth regretting." She sighed. "I didn't expect it all to be finished and cleaned up in one day, but this..."

"He won't get to see it close up, anyway. Mr. Andrews is going to nail the doorway shut with a board before he leaves for the day. So Mordechai will be coming in through the back door."

"Straight through my half-disassembled kitchen," Tova mumbled. "We'd better get that message passed along to him. Meir, please tell Brachie we're home."

Meir ran his hand along the exposed door frame.

"Don't touch that," Tova warned. "There could be a live wire in there."

"Not with the breaker off," Avner said.

Tova rolled her eyes. "Don't remind me. I suppose we'll have to host Mordechai by candlelight."

Avner grinned. "That would certainly give them something to talk about when they leave."

"It certainly would. I guess we'll sit in the dining room instead."

"It can't be helped."

"When is the electrician coming?" Tova drew open the curtains

"Not till the day after tomorrow."

"The day after tomorrow! That's ridiculous. If he can't come today, can't he at least come tomorrow?"

"Mr. Andrews says the guy he works with is busy until Wednesday."

Tova marched into the kitchen. "So let him find someone else." She threw open a drawer.

Avner followed. "Tova, this is electrical wiring we're talking about. We don't just want it done fast, we want it done right."

"But—"

Avner stopped in the kitchen doorway, his face grim. "We've had two close brushes with fire, Tova. You want to take any more chances?"

"No, of course not. I'm sorry, Avner, you're right." She dropped into a chair and murmured, "Sometimes, I think I lose track of what's important."

Avner sat down across from her. His voice was soft, gentle. "We all do sometimes."

Tova sighed. "We have a different problem," she said, her voice strained. "How can I be here when Brachie gets home, and stay with my mother?"

Avner waited.

"I don't want my father to stay there either. He needs his rest."

Avner hesitated. "What about taking your mother at face value, that she really doesn't need someone to stay with her?"

Tova looked at him, and he held her gaze.

She looked away, then rested her head in her hands. And still his words hung in the air.

Finally, Tova said, "I guess... if my mother says she's fine by herself, then maybe... she's really fine by herself."

A strange feeling washed over Avner, as if he was sitting in half darkness and half light. They sat that way together for some time, the silence melting into a comfortable rhythm.

Brachie's voice startled them both. "What do you think?"

They saw her at the same time.

"You look stunning," Tova answered.

"Thanks," Brachie said shyly. "While you were out Chava Miriam came and did my hair for me."

"And you're wearing makeup. You look..." Avner tilted his head to one side. "You look beautiful." He smiled. "Not to mention about three years older."

"Thanks, Tatty. I did the makeup myself."

Tova stood and put a hand on Brachie's arm. "When did you learn how to do that?"

"In sem. You really like it?"

"I really do," Tova answered. "It's subtle, but it brings out the sparkle in your eyes."

"Wait till you see it with my outfit." She ran upstairs.

Avner ran a hand through his hair. "Remember how you said you were feeling old?"

Tova laughed, and took out an onion and a cutting board. "I remember."

Brachie soon came downstairs, ready and anxious. She was too nervous to sit down to dinner; besides, what if she dropped food on herself, or something got stuck between her teeth? The most Tova could convince her to eat was a handful of seedless grapes and a glass of Dr. Pepper. While Tova, Avner, and Meir ate in the kitchen, Brachie wandered between the dining room table and the closest mirror. Avner felt sorry for her; with the circuit breaker shut off, she didn't even have the luxury of pacing the living room.

Truthfully, he was rather nervous himself. After propping up the pantry door to block the view of its topsy-turvy interior, he tried to open a *sefer*, but after reading and rereading the same line six times gave it up. Tova, at least, kept her hands busy shining the kitchen counters, then finding imaginary specs to wipe yet again.

As eight-thirty approached, Meir was told to make himself scarce and strongly cautioned not to peek from the top of the stairs. Avner sat down next to Brachie.

"How are you doing?" he asked.

"Okay. Just nervous."

"It'll pass. Just be yourself."

"What if I can't think of anything to say?"

"Then ask him something about himself."

"We had classes on dating."

Avner raised his eyebrows.

"I'm just scared that I'll run out of easy questions, and a first date isn't supposed to get too serious."

"It's good to know all the dos and don'ts, but also remember there are no ironclad rules. Trust yourself, Brachie."

"Yeah," Brachie sighed. "Anyway, if it gets too quiet, it's his job to make conversation."

Avner's stomach tightened. In a few minutes, *he'd* be the one forced to make conversation. He'd never been very comfortable with small talk. Avner's ear was trained on the back door.

"Avner!" Tova hissed from the kitchen. "He's here!"

Brachie flew upstairs.

Avner hurried to the door. Tova passed him in a blur heading in the opposite direction.

Avner swallowed and opened the door. Mordechai was quite tall. He wore his hat at a slight angle, his dark hair peeking out in front. "Hello, please come in. I hope you found the house okay. The number must be hard to read in the dark."

"No problem, I'm familiar with this part of Brooklyn." He smiled. "Besides, most of Flatbush has a certain logic to it, and once you figure out the one-way streets, it's simple."

"Follow me, please, we can sit in the dining room." Avner led the way, feeling far less uncomfortable than he'd anticipated.

Tova greeted him and hurried to add, "I'm sorry about your having to use the back door."

Mordechai sat in the chair indicated by Avner. His lip curled up slightly as he spoke. "Mrs. Kaplan explained to me about your renovations. I totally understand. My grandfather lived with us for three years, and he had special needs, too."

Avner looked at Tova, and she looked back with a smile only he saw.

"So," Avner said, "what are you learning?"

16

LATER THAT EVENING, TOVA was at the kitchen door before
Brachie rapped out two knocks. "Avner," she called out as she
turned the lock, "Brachie's home!"

She pulled Brachie inside. "Nu, how was it? Did you have a
good time?"

Brachie put down her purse just as Avner joined them. "I
had a *great* time. He's *really* nice."

Tova cringed at the word "nice."

"I was nervous as anything, I could barely talk. But he was
so calm, so... comfortable, that I was able to relax."

"What did you talk about?" Tova asked.

"Mostly about me. I mean, he asked me lots of questions. I
told him about sem, about high school, about Bubby being in
the hospital."

"Sounds like you covered a lot of ground," Avner said.

"Yeah, the time flew. I definitely want to go out with him
again."

"What's he like?" Tova asked.

"He's fun to be with. He finds lots of things amusing and

made some interesting comments about them."

"Such as?" Avner asked.

"Well, when we were heading back home, he came around and opened the passenger door first. He held up the remote in his hand and said, 'Really, it works fine, but this way I know you'll tell the *shadchan* that I'm a gentleman.' It was cute."

Avner smiled. "I'm glad you had a good time."

Tova brought Brachie a drink. Brachie's smile faltered, and her hands were a little shaky as she lifted the glass to her lips.

Avner's brow furrowed. "Are you worried about something?"

Brachie gave a nervous giggle. "It's just that... I feel like I finished an exam and I'm desperate to know how I did."

"Well, there's one way to find out," Avner said. "We call the *shadchan*."

"Already?" Tova asked. "We can't call now, it'll look like she's too eager."

"She likes him, she wants to go out with him a second time, what's wrong if she looks eager?"

Tova frowned. "It's a matter of appearances."

"I don't understand," Avner said.

"I'll explain," Tova answered. Then she suddenly pressed her lips together and stared at Brachie. "What do you think, Brachie?"

Brachie swallowed. "Whatever you think is best, Mommy." When Tova didn't respond she added, "But I'm really *plotzing* to know what he thought."

"He's not even home yet. Chances are his parents won't call until tomorrow."

"I know," Brachie said, "but can it hurt to try? I don't care if they know I'm eager to see him again." She looked at Avner. "Right?"

"I don't see why not," Avner agreed.

"Fine. I'll go call the *shadchan*."

Avner's eyebrows shot up. "Right now?"

"Right now." Tova reached for the phone and headed out of the room.

"I want to hear what she says," Brachie pleaded.

"I'll tell you everything after I hang up."

Avner stayed with Brachie and attempted to distract her, but her mind was upstairs with Tova.

She was back in a few minutes. "She hasn't heard back from him and doesn't expect to until tomorrow."

"What did you tell her?"

"I told her you had a nice time and want to go out again."

"Oh."

Tova yawned. "And now, Brachie, I'm going to sleep, it's been a very long day."

"Goodnight, Brachie," Avner said.

Brachie closed her eyes and relived the past few hours. She was still at the kitchen table when Shimon walked in. He saw her and stopped short.

Brachie blushed.

"How'd it go?"

"I had a good time. I don't know yet what he thought, I guess I'll find out tomorrow."

"Where'd you go?"

"A lounge."

"Which one?"

"I don't even know," she shrugged. "I was too nervous to notice where I was."

Shimon smiled. "I know that feeling."

"You do? I thought the girl was always the nervous one."

"I don't think it has anything to do with being a girl." Shimon slipped into a chair opposite Brachie. "Most people get nervous on dates. Especially first dates."

"Were you nervous when you went out with Ilana the first time?"

"Oy, was I ever!"

"When did you get over that?"

He gave a self-conscious smile. "Uh, never. Even on our last date, it took me at least ten minutes until I could look her in the eye."

Brachie's jaw dropped open. "Is that why she broke it off? Because you were too shy?"

"She didn't break it off. I did."

Brachie's eyes widened, then she crossed her arms. "Nobody tells me anything."

Shimon stared at the table.

"Wow, you totally surprised me. From the way you were moping around I just assumed she was the one who called it off."

"I wish. I feel terrible. Besides," he said with a rueful grin, "I think calling her afterwards to apologize was harder than anything I've ever done before." He reached for a napkin and began rolling it between his hands. "But I've been speaking with the *mashgiach*, and I think I know where I went wrong."

Brachie's eyes invited him to continue.

"Every time I went out with Ilana, I went out with her twice—once when I was actually with her, and a second time later, in my mind, when I was home. When I was with her, after I got past my initial discomfort, I had a nice time. I liked her and enjoyed her company. But when I replayed it, it was like I was looking through a lens, watching myself say the wrong things, do the wrong things. And the lens didn't just focus on me, it focused on her, too. I'd see things that at first I thought were okay, but afterwards... I don't know. Being scared of making a mistake kept me uptight. The *mashgiach* says it also kept me from being real. It's almost as if I was playing a part. I didn't get to know her, and didn't let her get to know me."

"But she liked you well enough to get engaged."

"Maybe I did a good acting job."

"Or maybe she saw the real you and liked you just the way you are."

Shimon chewed his lip.

"Do you think Mordechai could have been nervous also? He didn't talk much about himself." Brachie played with her necklace. "But it's kind of a shame. I don't really feel like I got to know him."

"That's what second dates are for. Just ask him questions, things he'd be interested in."

"I know," she sighed, "but somehow it always got turned back to me."

"So then when you tell him things, see how he reacts."

Brachie was thoughtful. "I see what you mean. I'll do that. If, that is, he wants to go out again. How am I going to sleep tonight not knowing?"

"That's a tough one. I don't think I slept for weeks." He stood. "*Hatzlachah.*"

"Good night, Shimon. And thanks."

Tova checked her watch as she navigated the still-unfamiliar hallways of the rehab center. It was just past two; that would give her time to see how her mother was doing before Esti showed up.

Tova didn't like the way Esti had pushed her mother to stand right away, when she had barely settled in. Tova understood Aidel's needs better than anyone, and she needed to be there to protect her from being pushed around by a salaried worker who probably needed to show quick progress in her reports.

As Tova entered Aidel's room, the greeting died on her lips.

Aidel was standing.

Esti was supporting her under her left arm. "See if you can bear just a little more weight on your left side. That's good." She spied Tova. "Oh hello, Mrs. Lehrfeld, look what your mom is up to this afternoon."

Aidel's face was chalky and her lips were set in a thin line.

Yerucham looked on silently, his brow furrowed.

"Okay, we're going to finish up now," Esti chirped. "Let's just get you over to that chair right next to your husband so you can sit down."

Tova dropped her bag on the floor and raced to the chair. "I'll bring it closer."

"No, that's all right," Esti said, "your mom's doing great."

Yerucham waved Tova away.

Tova stopped and wrung her hands.

Aidel inched forward, with Esti supporting her. "You're doing fabulous. Only another two steps. We're almost there."

Tova held her breath.

An eternity passed until Esti helped Aidel sink down into the chair. "You did it!" she exclaimed. "Look how far you walked!"

Yerucham smiled, relief etched into his features.

Aidel nodded, too spent to respond.

Esti made some notes in her file. "You did great work today, Mrs. Lewin. You just rest there for a while, and when you feel up to it, someone can help you back into your bed. Call the desk if you need to." She turned to Tova. "Your mom is a real trouper."

Tova's eyes smoldered. "May I speak to you outside, please?"

"Sure. 'Bye, Mrs. Lewin, Mr. Lewin. I'll see you tomorrow."

"Good-bye," Yerucham answered. "Thank you."

"Did you want to ask me something?" Esti said when they were alone.

Tova attempted to keep her voice level. "You are pushing my mother very hard."

Esti nodded. "Yes, I am pushing her. Did you see how well she did?"

"I don't call that 'doing well.' Did you see her face? It was white. She looked like she was about to faint."

"Mrs. Lehrfeld, I understand your concern. I assure you I wouldn't push your mother past what I feel she's able to handle."

"But you don't even know her!" Tova's voice was rising. "You just come in here and give orders that she has to follow whether she's up to it or not. Look at how you left her, stuck in that chair. How's she supposed to get back into bed?"

"You'll help her, or your father will. It was not an accident that I left her in the chair, it was intentional. With help, she is capable of getting back into bed. And if she'll stay in the chair a little longer, that's even better."

"You just met her yesterday, and the second time you see her you think you understand her limitations!"

"Actually," Esti said, "this is our third meeting. I had another opening this morning, so we had our second session together then."

"You said you'd be here today at three. I purposely came early so I'd be here for your session. What are you trying to pull?"

"Your father was present for both sessions, Mrs. Lehrfeld, and I am not trying to *pull* anything. You're welcome to be here for the sessions, as long as you don't interfere."

Tova's eyes narrowed into thin slits. "And what exactly do you mean by that? Are you saying that my presence here is an *interference*?" Tova demanded.

Esti took a step back. "I didn't mean that, Mrs. Lehrfeld. I just meant that if you have something you want to discuss with me, I think we should do so where your mother can't hear. I have a certain program I'm trying to follow—"

"Yes, it's obvious that you have an agenda."

A small sigh escaped Esti's lips.

"I mean," Tova said, lowering her voice, "it's clear that you are following a program. I'm only asking you to stop making my mother work according to a set schedule. She's not herself.

She's going through a very difficult time right now."

Esti stared at Tova but said nothing.

Tova forced a smile. "You don't know my mother. She's a real fighter. Believe me, if she felt up to pushing herself right now, she would."

"Thank you for your input," Esti said stiffly. "I'm late for my next patient, would you excuse me please."

"Of course." Tova watched her go, a strange prickling feeling creeping up her arms. She trudged back toward Aidel's room. She hadn't meant to, but she had obviously offended Esti. But her mother's feelings were more important than Esti's!

Tova blew out a breath. Not for the first time she wished she had Avner's diplomacy. She told him as much as they huddled together in the kitchen while Brachie got ready for her second date the following week. "I've been there for most of their sessions. I don't know how to get through to Esti. She pushes Ma too hard."

"Is your mother complaining?"

"No, of course not. But during the time Ma works with Esti, her mood always takes a turn for the worse, and then I have to step in and ask Esti to slow it down, or even to stop for the day. Esti always smiles and agrees to pick up next time where they left off." Tova sighed. "I've tried several times to explain that if she would only demand a little less, Ma's mood would improve, and then she'd make much more progress."

"And how did Esti react to that suggestion?"

Tova frowned. "She thanked me and gave me one of her standard smiles."

Avner stirred his iced tea and took a small sip.

"The thing is," Tova continued, "my mother really seems to like Esti, even more than the speech and occupational therapists working with her. Otherwise, I might just complain to the administration."

"Yes, it's probably wisest not to say anything. Having new people all the time can't be good for her, either."

"You're right."

"Why not take a back seat and let Esti operate the way she's used to?"

Tova straightened the napkin holder in the center of the table. "I wish you could see her in action. Then you could judge for yourself."

Meir came in holding the cordless phone. "Here, Ma, it's for you."

Tova took the phone.

"This is Na'ama Rubin..."

Tova covered the mouthpiece and whispered, "It's Na'ama Rubin." She shooed them out with her other hand. "I'm sorry, Na'ama, what were you saying?"

"I said I'm sorry it took so long to get back to you. I was waiting for a final answer from the other side."

"I understand," Tova said.

"Yes. Well, you see..." She cleared her throat. "It seems the family heard something."

Tova gripped the phone. "What can they have possibly heard? We have nothing to hide!"

"It's just a rumor, and they couldn't get anyone to confirm it." She paused. "But they also couldn't get anyone to deny it, so they asked me to—"

"What rumor? What are you talking about?"

"Nothing major, someone heard a rumor that one of your boys had a broken engagement. Since no one seems to know anything about it, they can't know that it's not true, and they want to know—"

"It's not true," Tova interrupted again. "None of my boys was engaged."

"Are you sure?"

"What do you mean, *am I sure*?" Tova retorted. She took a deep breath and forced herself to speak calmly. "Na'ama, of course I'm sure. I would know if one of my boys had gotten engaged, wouldn't I?"

"I suppose. I mean, yes. It's just that... well, they heard something very definite. They didn't say who they heard it from, of course, but someone, a neighbor, was quite sure there was a broken engagement. If they knew for sure it wasn't Yoni, I'm sure this wouldn't be an issue."

Tova sat down hard. "I don't know what they heard, or who they heard it from." Suddenly Shaindy Ungar's face swam before her eyes. Shaindy had been there when she and Brachie were in the department store, when the word "*l'chaim*" had just slipped out of her mouth. "Let me clear up the rumor."

"Please do!"

"I have another son in *shidduchim*. He was dating someone quite seriously, but they did *not* get engaged. Obviously, someone took things totally out of context."

"I'm so glad you cleared this up," Na'ama breathed. "The Solomons kept hitting a dead end with this. Now that you explained, I'm sure there will be no problem." She seemed satisfied and hung up with assurances that she'd call back within a day.

Tova, though, was less than satisfied. She sat immersed in thought. Finally, she made up her mind and burst out of the kitchen in search of Avner. He wasn't on the first floor, so Tova climbed the stairs. She heard Brachie on the phone.

"No, Chava Miriam couldn't come do my hair this time. But don't worry, it looks good." She giggled. "Very funny, Rena. I'm just about to put on my makeup."

Tova reached Brachie's room. "Brachie," she said.

"Yeah, it's like a bronze color." She giggled again, then looked up at Tova. "I gotta go. I'll call you later."

Fleetingly, Tova wondered how appropriate—or wise—it was for Brachie to be discussing Mordechai with Rena. Who knew what problems her input could cause? "Brachie, where's Tatty?"

"He said something about driving Meir somewhere."

Tova sighed, then returned to the kitchen and scrubbed her soup pot until her reflection scowled back at her. She pounced on Avner as soon as he came home.

"So that's what was taking the Solomons so long," Avner said. "I was beginning to wonder. Well, if that's really all that was holding the *shidduch* up, I imagine we'll hear back from them soon."

"Na'ama Rubin said tomorrow." Tova adjusted the kitchen chairs. "But Avner, the whole thing is so upsetting!"

"What's upsetting? I think the Solomons did the right thing by taking the direct approach and having the *shadchan* ask us straight out."

"No, no, that's fine. It's the rumor itself that's eating me." She started pacing. "Shimon is a good boy, he's just a little unsure of himself. If he *had* broken an engagement, would that suddenly make him second-rate?"

Avner's brow contracted, his lips pursed. "Tova, you know how I feel, there's no such thing as a second-rate Jew. There are just people more suited to each other and less suited to each other." He relaxed his features. "But maybe now's not the best time for philosophy. What you're asking is if a broken engagement puts Shimon into a different category."

Tova nodded.

"Let's put it this way." Avner crossed his legs. "If we got a call for a *shidduch* for Brachie with a *bachur* who'd been engaged already, would you agree to it?"

Tova's mouth opened and closed. What would she say? No, there's no reason to look for trouble? Or yes, if he had a good reason? What, then, would be considered a "good reason"?

Avner seemed to read her thoughts. "Things are always so simple when we see them through our own eyes, aren't they?" His glance fell on the pantry door. It was detached from the frame, which had been widened, and was merely propped up against it. "It's like this little room..." He fell silent.

"What's like this little room?" Tova prompted.

Avner shook his head, as if dragging himself out of his thoughts. "All these years, this room has been a pantry, and all of a sudden we're turning it into a bedroom. Look, all the shelves are down, and there's a mark over there where a window will be. To an outsider, it's just a messy pile of dust and rubble."

Tova was tempted to say that it seemed the same way to an insider, but she held her tongue.

"We see the bigger picture, though. We know there's good reason for the mess." He rubbed his hand along the wood. "Doors are useful to keep up appearances, and to maintain privacy. But they do keep people from seeing the whole story."

Tova looked sideways at Avner. "Anyway, Na'ama Rubin should be calling back tomorrow. Meanwhile, we have Brachie to deal with."

Deal with Brachie they certainly did. Her outfit, her hair, her makeup—all were inspected and reinspected, under various lights and before various mirrors. Tova, while not as anxious as before their initial introduction to Mordechai, attempted to cover up as much of the construction mess as she could. At least this time they were able to greet him through the front door.

After they waved good-bye to Brachie and Mordechai, the waiting began. Avner was able to open a *sefer* and learn, but Tova couldn't settle down. Finally she took out her sewing basket and reinforced the buttons on Meir's shirts. When that was done she moved on to Avner's, then Shimon's, Brachie's and her own. She put the basket away and wandered around, finding herself in front of the linen closet. She opened the door and began refolding sheets.

The linens wore sharp creases, the towels stood at attention in perfect columns, and still Brachie hadn't come home.

It was after midnight when the door creaked open. Tova looked up sharply as Brachie entered, and Avner was startled on the sofa where he'd been dozing.

Brachie said nothing as she drifted inside and lay down her purse. Her eyes had a faraway look in them.

Tova's stomach somersaulted. She'd seen that look before. It was the look Shimon wore after his sixth date, right before he'd decided he was ready to get engaged.

17

TOVA SET THE TIMER and pulled off a pair of green oven mitts. "I'm nervous, Avner."

Avner looked at his watch. "It's too late to back out now. Penina might be on her way there already. I still don't understand why you felt this meeting was necessary."

"Lots of people meet the girl before their son goes out with her. A mother's intuition is worth a lot."

"You didn't do this with Ilana," Avner pointed out.

Tova untied her apron. "That's right; I didn't. And look how that turned out."

Avner shook his head. "Yoni is not Shimon."

"True. But still I've learned my lesson."

Brachie joined them in the kitchen. "You look nice, Mommy."

"Thank you. I was thinking that I should've worn something a little more formal."

"No, that blouse is just right."

Tova smoothed down her collar. "What will we talk about?"

Brachie laughed. "Now you sound like me!"

"Tova, you're supposed to be looking Penina over, not the

other way around. What are you worried about?"

"She'll be just as curious about me as I am about her. First impressions are so important."

"But you have nothing to be concerned about; you look great," Brachie said.

"And you always know what to say to people," Avner added.

"Thank you both." She smiled. "I'll be fine. Brachie, remember to shut off the fire when the timer goes off. I'm ready, Avner."

He dropped her off at the small hotel ten minutes early. Tova took a seat with a good view of the entranceway and held her breath each time someone entered alone. After several wrong guesses, she spotted her—a single girl with a small purse, her head turning this way and that. Her reddish-brown hair was carefully pulled back into a pony, but with the impression that it only wanted to escape. As she drew nearer, Tova could see her bright green eyes and creamy skin dotted with freckles.

Tova stood and nodded, a smile set on her face.

Penina noticed her and changed course. "Mrs. Lehrfeld?"

"It's nice to meet you," Tova said.

"Thanks, you too."

"It's so warm out today, what will you drink?"

"Do you think they have Diet Dr. Pepper?"

Tova hid a smile. "We can ask."

They were soon settled with drinks, and Tova began awkwardly. "I hear you just came home from seminary."

"Yes. It was amazing. I can't believe I learned so much in just one year." A wistful smile stole over her features. "And I can't believe it's over."

"My daughter Brachie says the same thing. She raves about Yerushalayim."

"Yerushalayim is special. Some people complain that it's become so modernized, so urban, it's like any other city, but I don't agree. If your antennas are focused on what's important, you realize that it's imbued with *kedushah*. I'm really looking forward to going back." Penina's eyes lit up, and in that instant, Tova could see that she was sincere—and that Yoni would find her very interesting.

"Did you form a special relationship with anyone in particular?" Tova asked. Then she realized how rehearsed that sounded and told herself to just relax and be herself.

"Yes, our *eim bayis*. She's a wonderful person and an incredible mother. I started doing *chesed* by her, and then we became close and I found myself there more and more."

Tova smiled her encouragement.

"I really admire the way she manages everything. I learned a lot from her about being happy with what you have."

Tova was impressed with the young lady before her. "Have you settled on what you'll be doing now that you're back?"

"Not completely, but I'm thinking about medical billing and coding. Have you heard of it? It's an up-and-coming field for *frum* girls."

Tova's fingers tingled. "Yes, in fact we looked into it and my Brachie is going to do that program. I think it's a wonderful idea."

"It looks great," Penina agreed, "but I'm not totally sure yet."

"What's your hesitation?"

"I'm just not sure it's practical for me." She looked directly into Tova's eyes. "I have to find out if it's something that I could also do in Eretz Yisrael."

Avner knocked on the door. "Zeidy? It's time for *minchah*. Are you coming?" He paused, then slowly opened the door. The room was empty. He went downstairs, put on his hat, and called Meir to join him.

"It's hot," Meir said as they stepped outside.

Avner nodded. "Looks like rain." They walked halfway up

the block, only to meet Shimon and Yerucham coming from the opposite direction.

"Good Shabbos," Shimon said. "I didn't want Zeidy to walk in the rain, so we went to an earlier *minchah*."

Avner peered upwards. "Wish I'd thought of that. We'll see you back home."

Meir put his hand out. "I think I felt a drop."

They quickened their pace. The shul was fairly empty, as it often was during the summer months; it seemed that almost everyone was up in the mountains. A sudden clap of thunder sounded, and heavy rain soon followed. When they'd finished davening, Meir looked out the window of the shul vestibule and said, "We'll get soaked on the way home."

Avner looked at his watch. "We have time before *shulosh seudos*. You want to go back inside the *beis midrash* and learn something with me?"

"Okay." He didn't move. "Tatty, can I ask you something?"

"Sure."

"Does Zeidy like me?"

Avner's chin popped up. "Of course he does. He loves you. Why do you ask?"

"It's just that lately, I feel like... I don't know, like I'm bothering him.

Avner kept his face carefully neutral. "What makes you say that?"

"He makes these strange faces at me, like he's angry.

"The faces aren't directed at you, Meir. Zeidy's just not himself."

"But he's fine around Shimon. As soon as Shimon walks into the room, Zeidy smiles and seems all happy again. It's just me." He looked away.

Avner put his hand on Meir's shoulder. "It's not you at all."

Meir's mouth pulled to the side.

"It's hard for Zeidy to be out of his own house, and he's... well, he just hasn't been in a good mood since Bubby had her stroke. For some reason, when Shimon's around, he feels better."

"Why?"

"I have no idea. In fact," he smiled, "neither does Shimon."

"But Shimon's only home at night, and on Shabbos. The rest of the time..."

"I know. Hopefully, when Bubby moves in, Zeidy's mood will improve. Meanwhile, just remember that you're not doing anything wrong, and Zeidy loves you as much as ever." He thought for a minute, then added, "When Bubby does come, she may not be totally herself, either. We have to be understanding until things get back to normal."

"I guess." He paused then said, "I saw Bubby's new walker. It's really cool. There's a seat that flips down so she can rest. I can't wait to go for walks outside with her."

"That'll be nice. But remember she's still using a wheelchair."

"So I'll push her outside."

Avner noticed that the rain had slowed to a drizzle. "I think we should go before it starts pouring again."

During *shalosh seudos*, Avner watched Yerucham carefully. It did seem as if he was giving Meir the cold shoulder. He wished he'd noticed it himself. Even though he was preoccupied by everything else going on in the family, Meir's present happiness was no less important than the others' future happiness. Still, besides noticing, what could he do?

"Zeidy, you want to play Scrabble with me?" Shimon asked after Havdalah.

Avner stopped short. Only yesterday, Tova had told him about an article she'd just read on the aging population in the *frum* world. The author had mentioned that playing word games was a healthy mental exercise. Had Shimon read that as well?

He stared at Shimon. This was a new side of him that he'd

seen blossoming lately—not only responding to others' needs but actually anticipating them.

"No, thank you," Yerucham said. "I'm too tired."

The phone rang.

"I'll get it," Avner said, seeing Tova at the sink. "*Gut voch*, Tatty."

Avner looked at his watch in surprise. Yoni never called this soon after Shabbos. "How are you, son? Any special reason you're calling?"

"I just wanted to make sure Mommy knows I'm not coming home tomorrow night. My *mashgiach* says it's better if I go and come back from here, even though it's my first date."

"Okay, I'll break it to her gently."

Tova's head whipped around.

"You have everything you need?" Avner asked.

"Sure. I kept my suit clean, I have a nice tie, brushed my hat, I'm all set."

"And money?"

"Yeah, I'm fine. I'll call you when I get back, okay?"

"Please do. We'll be waiting up to hear from you."

Tova shut the water and dried her hands. "You'll break *what* to me gently?"

"Just that Yoni's not coming home tomorrow."

"But—"

Avner steered Tova out of the kitchen and into the living room. "He can leave from yeshivah and go straight back there afterwards. No need for him to lose any time learning."

Tova frowned. "I don't like this plan. Yoni should come home, he should be comfortable and have our support. This is a major milestone in his life."

"Agreed, it's a big step. But he's not Shimon, and he's not Brachie, either. Yoni doesn't need to be fussed over."

"I know, I just feel like I want to be a part of it." Tova absently ran her hand along the arm of the sofa.

Avner studied her. "What else is bothering you?"

Tova dropped down onto the sofa. "Eretz Yisrael, Avner? If I'd known that before I met Penina, I never would've agreed to this *shidduch*."

"Lots of young couples go for a year or two. It doesn't mean they'll end up there permanently."

"I know," she sighed, "and lots of girls say they want to go back and don't. But Yoni's just the type to be drawn back there. He never did feel that his one year there was enough."

Avner sat. "So why did you agree?"

"Because I honestly think she's a good match for Yoni. She's intelligent and sincere and... well, I like her." Tova stood. "Let's forget it for now, okay? We'll cross that bridge if and when we come to it."

Avner smiled. "I couldn't agree more."

The next day's errands were a helpful distraction for Tova. Toward evening, the phone rang and soon after Tova appeared, shaking her head but with a wide smile. "You're not going to believe this."

"Try me," Avner smiled.

"That was a *shadchan*."

"Which one, Brachie's or Yoni's?

"Shimon's."

Avner's smile dropped. "Shimon's *shadchan*? You mean Mrs. Krieger? That can't be good." His mind was racing. "Do the Moskowitzes want Shimon to reconsider? Is Ilana still upset?"

"No, sorry, I didn't mean Mrs. Krieger. This is someone else, with a new suggestion for Shimon."

Avner sat bolt upright. "You can't be serious."

"I told you that you wouldn't believe me," she chuckled.

"What did you tell her?"

"That we'd look into it and get back to her."

Avner stood suddenly. "Tova, this is not the right time for another *shidduch*."

Tova set her hands on her hips. "Avner, I don't understand you. I want Brachie to wait, you say there's no reason to wait if the right one comes along. I want Yoni to wait, you say he's mature enough to get married. And now I want Shimon to plunge right back into *shidduchim*, and you say no!"

Avner ran a hand through his hair while Tova went on.

"I know things are crazy now. Brachie, Yoni, my mother... everything. But Avner, this is perfect! When you fall off a bicycle, you have to get right back on."

Without realizing it, Avner's head moved back and forth.

"Don't you see?" Tova continued. "The Solomons nearly said no because of a rumor about Shimon's near-engagement. If that gets back to Shimon, it'll make him even more insecure. He can go out with this girl—who sounds perfect for him, by the way—and even if it doesn't work out, it'll put him back in the right mindset."

Avner dropped back down onto the couch.

Tova tapped her foot.

Avner held his head in his hands.

"Well don't just sit there, *say* something."

For a fleeting moment, Avner was tempted to remind her of what she'd said the other day—that she sometimes lost track of what's important. But he held back, knowing that he probably wouldn't change her mind about Shimon, and he'd likely hurt her in the process.

He sat up straight. "We have our hands full, don't you think? Put half your *shidduch* energies into Brachie, and save the other half for Yoni."

"As if my energies can be neatly divided into two. You might as well say we should wait until my mother is back on her feet, since I'm not able to divide myself into so many pieces."

"I didn't say that. I'm not saying *you* can't handle this, I'm saying that Shimon can't."

"Well, he'll just have to learn how to handle it. I'm sure he's grown a lot from what happened with Ilana."

"Has he?" Avner asked quietly.

"Yes." Tova crossed her arms. "He must have. I'm sure he wouldn't make the same mistake twice."

"Which mistake?"

"To rush into things."

"You call seven dates rushing into things?"

Tova's arms fell to her sides, then she perched on the end of the easy chair. "I don't mean that. I mean..."

"Yes?"

"I mean... he would know not to give a girl the wrong impression, to say he's ready when he's not."

"And how many more dates do you think he would have needed to be truly ready?"

Tova brushed her hands along her skirt. "I don't know. Who can answer such a question now?"

Avner only nodded. Who, indeed!

"Haven't you seen how Shimon's changed?" Tova challenged. "He's been taking such good care of my father."

"Agreed," Avner said in a measured tone. "It's a step in the right direction. But it's only a first step. Shimon has some more growing up to do before he's ready to date again. Before he's ready to get married!"

"But Avner, he's already twenty five, how long—"

"Tova, I'm sorry. I'm just going to have to veto this one. Call it intuition."

Tova opened her mouth to speak but Avner was quicker.

"However, I'll make a deal with you. No dating for three months, and after that we can renegotiate."

"That's some deal." She sat stiff and unmoving.

"Tova," Avner said, and waited until he held her eyes in his. "Please, Tova, I'm asking you to trust me on this. You know there are very few things I take such a strong stand on. Shimon needs more time."

Tova grimaced and looked away. After a long pause, she turned back to him. "I don't agree with you. I think it's a mistake to make Shimon wait."

Avner's stomach tightened.

"But," Tova continued, "since you obviously feel so strongly about it, we can wait another three months as you suggest."

Avner felt air fill his lungs, and he realized he'd been holding his breath.

"I'll tell the *shadchan* that Shimon is not available right now." She looked at her watch. "I'll call her back tomorrow." Tova sat back in the chair, a heavy silence hanging between them. Suddenly, she chuckled.

Avner tilted his head to the side. "Is something funny?"

"I just realized how much more time we've been spending together lately."

Avner smiled, gratified by Tova's willingness to move on. "Yes," he said, "we don't seem to run out of interesting topics."

The evening stretched out as they waited for Yoni to call. When he finally did, Tova quickly switched the call to speaker.

"She's very smart," Yoni said, "and we had some nice conversation."

"And?" Tova prompted.

"And I'd be willing to see her again."

Tova motioned for Avner to say something.

"Is there anything you'd like us to find out more about before you meet her again?" Avner asked, more to please Tova than because he thought Yoni would take him up on it.

"No, I'll just meet her again if she agrees, and we'll see how it goes." He yawned. "It's late. I'll call you tomorrow to hear what Mrs. Rubin has to say from Penina."

Avner wished Yoni a good night, and Tova stood there, staring at the phone. "That's it? That's all he has to say?"

"He's right," Avner teased, "it is late."

Tova shook her head, a reluctant half-smile escaping.

"That's pretty much all anyone can expect after a first date. Especially a first, first date."

Tova threw up her hands in mock surrender. "Okay, okay. Maybe you'd prefer if I leave the boys' *shidduchim* up to you completely."

Avner looked up sharply. Tova's playful smile showed she wasn't serious, but he believed that there is always a kernel of truth nestled inside every joke. "No thanks, I'm glad you met Penina. A mother's instincts are always so important."

Tova raised an eyebrow, but a soft smile stole over her face.

Brachie held one hand on the door knob. "'Bye, Mommy. I might be a little longer than usual. I'm going to wait for Simone."

"Okay, but don't let her talk you into anything strange. Just a regular haircut. Do you have enough money?"

"Yes."

Tova watched her go, then turned to find the contractor standing and waiting for her. "Mr. Andrews, can I help you with something?"

"Yes. Remember that blackened connection I showed you for the porch light?"

As if she could forget. "Of course."

"It seems that some of the wiring in this house is very old, and the electrician thinks it's a good idea to check certain areas."

"Why?"

"To make sure there are no more frayed wires anywhere."

"What are the chances of that?"

"He won't know until he has a look, but do you want to take the chance?"

Tova tapped her foot. "What does this entail?"

"Would you like to talk to him yourself?"

"No, no, just tell me what he's going to do to my house."

Mr. Andrews pointed to different areas on the wall as he spoke. "Here, here, and here, he'll need to open up the wall. If he finds any problems, he can rip out those sections."

Tova winced.

"When he's finished rewiring, I'll plaster and paint."

A flurry of thoughts blew through Tova's mind. "How long will all of this take?"

"I can't say," Mr. Andrews shrugged. "It depends on what he finds. I'll let you know as soon as I have the specifics. I just wanted your okay to begin work."

"Let me just discuss it with my husband first."

"Sure thing. I'm leaving now for the day, anyway. We can talk tomorrow."

Tomorrow...

Brachie was seeing Mordechai tomorrow. What if she got engaged soon? How would she host a *l'chaim*? Or even meet his parents? They'd rushed to get the pantry done first, so that her mother could move in as soon as she was ready to leave rehab. She sighed, wondering why lately it always seemed that she was going from one emergency to the next.

Tova dragged herself back to the kitchen and dropped down into a chair. She wanted the contractor and the electrician to pack up their things and leave. She wanted her house back. She wanted her *life* back—her life before Shimon met Ilana, before her mother had a stroke, before things were so... different, so challenging.

She stopped herself. Since when was she afraid of challenge?

Tova sat forward, resting her head in her hands. No, she wasn't afraid of challenge, of climbing mountains; the fear lay in the newness of the scenery.

Without knowing what she was doing, Tova eased herself over to the erstwhile pantry and opened the door. With its soft beige tones and subtle pastel accents, a framed embroidery on the wall and crisp new curtains at the small window, it was no longer a pantry—it was a bedroom, small but beautifully finished. As soon as the bed arrived, her mother could move in.

Slowly, almost reverently, Tova closed the door. This truly was a strange place for a bedroom. Yet she smiled, comfortable with her conviction that they were doing the right thing.

Brachie came running in, breathless. "Mommy, you'll never guess what happened."

"Brachie! What happened to your haircut?"

Brachie shook her head and waved her hands. "Simone had three people waiting for her. She said she'll take me in another hour."

"It would've been better to make an appointment," Tova pointed out.

"Mommy, guess who I saw?"

Tova shrugged. "I can't guess. Who'd you see?"

"Suri!"

"Who's Suri?"

"Suri *Moskowitz*."

"Who... oh, you mean Ilana's sister? Was it uncomfortable for you?"

"I didn't have a chance to feel uncomfortable. As soon as I saw her, she told me the news."

Tova braced herself.

"Ilana is engaged!"

18

THE FRONT DOOR OPENED and closed. It had to be Shimon. "I'll do it," Tova said.

Avner looked surprised. "If you like."

"No, you do it," Tova said quickly. "I don't have the heart."

They walked into the living room just in time to hear Brachie blurt out, "Did you hear? Ilana's engaged! I heard it directly from her sister Suri."

Tova and Avner both turned to look at Brachie, their faces matched bookends.

"Oh, was I not supposed to say anything?"

"Engaged?" Shimon's eyes widened and his mouth hung open. "To who?"

"Yissachar Baumgarten. You know him?"

"Baumgarten! We were *chavrusas*." He turned his hat around in his hands. "I saw him just the other day. He's engaged to Ilana? I just can't believe it!"

Brachie laughed. "I know, that's how I felt when my friend Blimi got engaged."

Shimon was rooted to the spot, his hands nearly crushing

the front brim of his hat.

Brachie plopped herself down on the sofa.

"Uh, Brachie," Tova said, "would you mind going upstairs and seeing if Meir has money for his trip tomorrow?"

"Right now?"

"We'd like to talk to Shimon alone," Avner said.

Understanding dawned. "Oh. Okay."

Tova eased the hat out of Shimon's hands. "Come, let's all sit down."

Shimon obeyed Tova as if in a trance. "I can't see them together," he said.

Tova and Avner listened quietly.

"I mean, she's gentle and quiet, and he's the total opposite. He has a comment about everything, and this big, deep laugh."

"You know what they say," Tova said, "opposites attract."

Shimon's eyes focused on her. "But I'm nothing like that. I'm more like her, quiet and shy. How could she be looking for strong and loud?"

Avner said, "Personality isn't necessarily something you look for. It's something you decide whether you're comfortable with it or not."

"Just like you have many types of friends," Tova said. "You can get along with different kinds of people."

As they spoke, Shimon's eyes darkened and his shoulders slumped. "Yeah, but there are always some guys you click better with. Shy is fine for a girl, but a guy has to be outgoing. Tough."

"That's not true," Avner said. "Ilana had no problem with your being quiet. It was probably something she liked about you."

"Or something she was willing to compromise on."

Tova shook her head.

"It just wasn't *bashert*," Avner said. "We can see that clearly, especially now that Ilana's engaged."

"Yeah," Shimon said bitterly, "engaged to my old *chavrusa*."

Aidel released her walker and collapsed onto a chair.

"Mrs. Lewin, you did great!" Esti cheered. "You walked half-way across the room!"

Aidel returned a tired smile.

"I know you're leaving here today, but if there's anything I can do for you, or if you have any questions, call me."

"Thank you."

"And promise me you'll call when you're walking on your own."

"I'll call," Aidel promised. "Dance at your wedding."

Esti laughed. "As soon as I figure out who I'm marrying."

"Think of someone," Aidel said, tapping her temple.

"Good-bye, Mrs. Lewin. It's truly been a pleasure." She turned to Tova. "Good-bye, Mrs. Lehrfeld."

"Thanks for, uh, everything."

Yerucham and Avner entered the room.

"Here are all the papers. That's it, you're free to go."

Yerucham held the walker steady while Tova helped Aidel up. "Maybe you want to rest for a few minutes first, Ma."

Aidel shook her head. "Feel better already. Rest later."

Tova ran her tongue over her teeth. Her mother could say she was feeling better, but she was still speaking in half sentences—a clear indication that she was wiped out.

Aidel must have seen her deliberation. "Want to go *home*." The words sounded harsh, and everyone stared. A weak smile appeared on her face. "Got to move forward."

Tova could not refuse.

Tired as she was, Aidel insisted on saying good-bye and thanking everyone who had helped her there during her stay. Getting her into the car was a new, trying experience, and Tova was afraid that her mother would simply collapse from the strain. She should not have allowed Esti to insist on that last session right before she was due to leave. But that was

Esti—single-minded and stubborn.

Aidel's face was white as they drove home. They half-carried her into her room. Tova had hoped her mother would be delighted with her new sleeping quarters, but her eyes were closed before her shoes were off.

Tova stood over Aidel, love and warmth bubbling up inside her, along with so much gratitude. And a powerful feeling of freedom.

Aidel had been released, but it was Tova who felt like a bird let out of its cage. Finally, she was on her home turf. She'd be the one to establish her mother's schedule, provide good meals, and pamper her the way only a loving daughter could. And if an overzealous therapist overstepped her bounds, Tova would simply replace her—before she could get a grip on Aidel's emotions.

Tova turned off the water. Had she heard noise coming from the pantry—that is, from her mother's room? She dried her hands on a towel and stepped toward the door.

"Yerucham!"

Tova opened the door.

Aidel grasped the light blanket like a toddler clutching her beloved teddy bear after a nightmare, her eyes revealing the same wild panic.

"Ma, are you okay? What happened?"

Aidel's eyes slowly came into focus. "Tova," she breathed and lay back down. "Tova."

Tova's heart hammered in her chest. "Ma, what is it?"

"Where am I?" Her eyes darted around the small room.

"You're home. In my home, I mean. This is your new room."

"How'd I get here?"

"Avner drove us. From rehab." She swallowed hard. "Don't you remember?"

"We left, I remember. But this room—no."

"You were exhausted and half asleep."

Aidel nodded.

"Do you want to get up? Or can I bring you something?"

"Help me up, please. I want to see this room you wasted all that money on."

Tova rushed to help Aidel, hiding the tears which came unbidden. "Should I bring your walker?"

"Bring Tatty."

Tova was loath to leave her mother alone. "Tatty," she called from the doorway, "Ma's up!"

There was no answer.

"I'll be right back." Tova sprinted through the living room and up the stairs. Yerucham was nowhere to be seen. She raced back to Aidel. "Tatty must have gone to *maariv*," she said breathlessly.

"Who's home?"

"I am," Tova smiled.

Aidel made a curt motion with her hand. "Besides you."

"No one. Tatty and Avner, and I guess Meir, must all be at *maariv*. Brachie should be home soon."

"I'm going back to sleep."

"But Ma, you haven't eaten anything all day!"

"I ate lunch."

"That was hours ago! Let me bring you something. How about a bowl of vegetable soup?"

"No. I'm going back to sleep."

"A glass of orange juice?" Tova attempted.

Aidel paused, then said, "Fine." Suddenly she smiled. "Thank you, *sheifeleh*."

Tova brought Aidel the juice and watched her drink it, sip by sip.

"Now I'm going back to sleep." Aidel inched herself back down.

"I'm right here in the kitchen if you need me. When you get up, you'll see that your room is right here next to the kitchen, and I'm right outside..." Her words trailed off as Aidel once more closed her eyes.

Tova stood there over her mother. She was alone and not alone. The house was unusually still, the silence around her broken only by her mother's rhythmic breathing. She let her tears fall, unchecked.

At length, Tova sat herself down at the kitchen table, head resting on her arms. She must have dozed off, since she thought she heard Shimon's voice, and the next thing she knew, Avner was standing over her.

"Tova," he said gently, "Yoni's on the phone. I can talk to him myself, but I know you'll want to speak to him." He held out a cordless phone.

"Yoni?" Tova rubbed her eyes. "Tell him to call tomorrow when he comes home from his date with Penina."

"That's tonight, he's on the phone now after his date."

She was instantly alert.

"I'll put it on speaker," Avner said. "Go on, Yoni, we're both listening."

"Thanks. Well, she's a great girl," Yoni said, "and I enjoyed myself. But she's not for me."

"That's a pretty quick decision, don't you think?" Tova said.

Avner motioned to Tova to wait. "What makes you so sure?"

"For one thing, she's a real intellectual."

"I thought you wanted an intelligent girl," Tova said.

"Intelligent, yes, but not so intellectual. Penina can quote Rambam and Malbim from memory. A great accomplishment, just not what I'm looking for."

"And what's another thing?" Avner asked.

"She has freckles."

"What?" Tova cried.

"Just kidding, Ma, sorry. In some ways she's mature, but in other ways, she still has some growing up to do."

Tova rolled her eyes. At twenty-two, Yoni was the self-acclaimed authority on maturity.

Unprompted, Yoni continued, "Like her ongoing debate about career, family, and where she wants to live. She's got conflicting priorities, and I think it'll take her some time to work them out."

"I hear," Avner said. "You want us to call Mrs. Rubin? Or you want to think about it some more?"

"Of course he wants to think about it more!"

"Yeah, let me sleep on it. I'm pretty sure, but I'll make a final decision tomorrow."

They said good night, and Tova looked at Avner helplessly.

Avner smiled. "Well at least I didn't have to pump him for information."

"Tova," a voice called.

Tova jumped up. "Ma!" She opened her mother's door.

In the light that spilled past her from the kitchen, Tova saw that Aidel's eyes were closed; she must have called out in her sleep. Tova closed the door gently.

"Go on, Tova," Avner said, "go upstairs. Your mother will buzz you on the intercom if she needs you."

Tova spun around. She hadn't shown her mother how to use the buzzer—or even told her that one existed. How could she go upstairs and leave her mother all alone? "Avner, I think we have a problem. I can't believe I forgot to tell her about the intercom. I can't leave my mother alone downstairs."

"She probably won't need you," Avner said.

"But she slept most of the day. She's bound to get up, and she's not strong enough to call out." Tova yawned. "I'll have to sleep down here."

"Shimon can sleep on a mattress in the kitchen."

Tova shook her head. "It's me Ma needs, not Shimon. *I'm* sleeping here. Pull in the easy chair, if you don't mind. I'm used to sleeping sitting up."

Avner frowned. He thought Tova had been mellowing a little lately, letting other people share in the added responsibilities.

"Please, Avner, I can't keep my eyes open. Would you mind bringing me the chair?"

Avner sighed and did as Tova asked, wishing her a good night.

The morning brought brilliant, clear skies, but Tova's face was clouded. "Ma didn't sleep well," she confided. "It's a good thing I was down here."

"I'm sure she'll adjust. And under your loving care, she'll be up and around in no time."

"Thank you," Tova smiled. "I think I should sleep down here for a few days, though, till I'm sure she's sleeping better."

Avner held back his opinion, accepting the bag lunch Tova handed him. When he got to the yeshivah, there was a note from the principal waiting for him on his table, asking him to stop by the office. Avner made himself a cup of coffee and brought it along. "Good morning, Gedaliah."

"Hello, Avner. Please have a seat." Gedaliah placed out a folder in front of him. "How's your mother-in-law?"

"She moved in with us yesterday. Hopefully, my hours should be a little more regular now."

Gedaliah waved his words aside. "You know you have leeway, especially in the summer."

"I appreciate it."

Gedaliah inclined his head, then tapped the folder. "This," he said, "is Zev's year plan."

Avner nodded, keeping his face neutral.

"You remember, Zev Gordon, the new seventh-grade *rebbi* I introduced you to?"

Avner's answer was guarded. "Yes, of course I remember. Seems like...a very nice guy." He laced his fingers together.

"I want to know what you think of it."

Avner accepted the folder. "I'll look it over and get back to you."

"Would you mind doing it now? I have to make some decisions based on it, and I'd rather not put it off." Gedaliah stood. "I have to go meet with the janitor. I'll be back in around ten minutes. Enjoy your coffee."

Avner was taken aback. He knew that Gedaliah valued his input—and Gedaliah knew that Avner would carefully formulate an opinion before offering it. Yet now he was being asked for an instant evaluation. Avner flipped open the folder and immediately understood. Zev's plans for reaching his stated goals read like a product catalog. Following were additional plans that would involve reorganizing half the school. Avner let out a low whistle. No wonder Gedaliah thought he could make a quick assessment.

Gedaliah was back. "Well?"

"Ambitious."

"And?"

Avner shrugged.

"Avner, don't try to be political. He's a new teacher, he needs guidance. He seems to rely heavily on... *things*. I want your opinion as to how much of this, if anything, I should accommodate."

Avner rubbed his beard. "Let me ask you something. Why did you hire him?"

"My choices were very limited, as you know."

Avner looked sharply at Gedaliah, but his face bore no ill will.

"I interviewed several candidates with far less personality, though perhaps with more classroom experience. I appreciate his grasp of the learning process, of the way a boy's mind assimilates information. The rest I was hoping he would pick up as he went along." He leaned forward. "When I said I wanted you to take him under your wing, I was quite serious."

Avner thought for a moment before speaking. "I see."

"Back to my question. How much of this should I go along with, and how much should I tell him, No, this is how we do things here, adapt?"

"Some of this can work, like the projector and some other equipment. I suppose I can sift through this month by month. I think we should tackle it together, Zev and I, so that he feels like he's part of the decision-making process, and I'm not the big bad wolf breathing down his neck."

"I'm sorry to burden you with this, Avner. Use your discretion, I trust you completely." Gedaliah sat up straighter. "Zev is going up to the country later on today. I hope you don't mind—I told him you'd have some time for him before he leaves."

Avner wasn't sure if he should be flattered or annoyed.

Back in his own room, Avner flipped open the folder again. Helping Zev was going to be an ongoing project, time-consuming and emotionally draining. It would have been easier to just teach the class himself.

He swatted that thought away as one would a mosquito. He had other reasons for rejecting the offer to teach the class. He wasn't afraid of work, he was afraid of...

What, exactly, was he afraid of?

He sat there for some time with the question hanging, until his mind began to drift. He closed his eyes and envisioned each of the people in his intimate family circle. He pondered how every change in one person's life affected the others in the circle. Like turning the sections of a Rubik's Cube—it wasn't enough to just get one side all the same color, you had to keep an eye on all six sides at once. Yerucham's presence was clearly affecting Meir and Shimon in very different ways, and Aidel's appearance would change the dynamics yet again. He didn't know where it would take Tova or Brachie, either. As for himself...

I just want everyone to get along.

The thought was sudden, intrusive. An uncomfortable feeling settled in his chest. As a warm, personable tutor, in his little room with no distractions, he had no discipline problems— unlike a classroom teacher, who doesn't have the luxury of focusing on the needs of every child at every moment, can't create a tailor-made curriculum for each one, can't shut out unwanted distractions. As a tutor, when a child came in with a conflict, *he* was the peacemaker; the problem-solver, not the problem.

He shifted in his seat. He had repeatedly told Gedaliah—and Tova, for that matter—that he was happy where he was because he was making a difference. He'd have to ask himself how much of that was true, and how much was an excuse to get out of standing up in front of a classroom.

His eyes fell on the folder. He'd have to sort through those thoughts and feelings. For now, he would settle on sorting out Zev's year plan.

"I don't know if I can take another upside-down day," Tova said. "I can't understand why Ma is sleeping all day and up at night."

"Something got thrown off in the move. Maybe tomorrow you can try to keep her busy and awake more," Avner suggested.

"I'll have to. She's starting some of her therapies on Sunday. I'm glad I didn't have the therapists come right away, it would have been pointless."

Avner nodded.

Tova rubbed her eyes. "I'm up during the day dealing with regular household things, I'm up till late waiting for children to finish their *shidduch* dates, and then I'm up at night with my mother. It's like having a newborn." She clamped a hand over her mouth and threw a fretful look over her shoulder. "Oh,

Avner, I didn't mean to complain. It's a privilege to have my parents here, and I'm so grateful that the children are being thought of for *shidduchim*."

He smiled. "I know you weren't complaining, it's just exhaustion speaking."

The front door closed quietly, but they both heard the click as the lock turned.

"Speaking of children coming home," Avner said.

"Sorry I'm so late," Brachie said, entering the kitchen. She sat down and opened her mouth to speak, then changed her mind and went to the refrigerator. She stood by the open door without moving.

"Can I get you something?" Tova asked.

Brachie abandoned the fridge and sat. "I wanted some Dr. Pepper, but we don't have any."

"It's right there, I'll get it." Tova poured Brachie a glassful, but she made no move for it.

Tova licked her lips.

Avner crossed and uncrossed his legs.

Brachie stared at the table, then finally broke out in a huge grin and said, "Mordechai is everything I'm looking for."

Tova's glow mirrored Brachie's.

"He's smart and wants to learn as long as he can. He's fun to be with and appreciates my sense of humor but is serious about the important things."

Avner tensed, waiting for the "and."

Brachie folded her hands.

No one spoke.

Avner threw a brief glance at Tova, who seemed just as confused as he felt.

"Is that all you wanted to say?" Avner asked.

"Yes. I mean, no, I'd like to marry him."

At that moment, Avner understood the difference between

a son getting engaged and a daughter. His Brachie, his little girl—married?

He stared at her, seeing a starry-eyed teenager, with utopian visions swimming in front of her. At the same time, he saw the set of her jaw which showed him she'd given this some thought.

"Brachie," Avner said softly, "you know this is the first boy you've dated. Maybe you just have nothing to compare him to."

"I have Shimon, and I have Yoni." She smiled. "And I have you. He'll fit right in to our family, Tatty. Didn't you like him?"

"Yes, I really did like him when we met."

"So did I." Tova tried to smile, but Avner could see that her eyes were wet.

"Do you know how he feels?"

"He asked me about where I'd want to live, what I see myself doing in five years..." She laughed. "He even made a comment about eating *gebrokts* on Pesach."

Avner's attention was riveted. "Did he say anything, or hint anything, about getting engaged?"

"Not in those words, and that's why I'm not sure if he feels ready. I mean, it *is* only three dates. But he did hint that he might ask his parents to call the *shadchan* when he gets home, even though it's so late."

"That really does sound promising," Tova whispered. "Brachie I—"

The phone rang.

As one, they fell silent. The phone rang twice more before anyone could move—and then everyone jumped.

"It's got to be Mrs. Kaplan!" Brachie squealed.

"I guess you should take it." Avner reached for the phone and handed it to Tova.

Tova steadied herself. After quick apologies for the late hour, Masha Kaplan explained that Mordechai insisted she call right away and assured her they'd still be up.

"Brachie said you might call," the smile evident in her voice.

"Are you sitting all together, then?"

"Yes, we are."

"Perhaps this would be better in private," Masha suggested.

Her voice was steady, but not upbeat the way Tova expected. A knot formed in her throat. "Hold on, please."

Brachie glowed, the stars in her eyes shining more by the minute, but Avner's face betrayed his concern.

Tova forced a smile. "I'm going into the other room a minute, okay?"

A voice called out weakly, "Tova."

Her mother. She spun around.

"Can you call her back?" Avner whispered.

Tova covered the mouthpiece. "This could take time, and it's so late already."

"Tova," the voice repeated.

She froze, gripped by indecision. Her mother, her daughter... "You'll have to take it," she held it out to Avner.

Avner blinked at the phone, then accepted it. "I'll go upstairs," he told Brachie as Tova slipped into Aidel's room.

"What is it, Ma?"

"I have a cramp in my leg."

"Which leg?"

"Left, the calf."

"I'll massage it out for you." She sat at the edge of the bed, trying to ease Aidel's pain, while her mind was in agonies. What did Masha need to say in private? Tova's thoughts hovered like a helicopter, stirring up all the corners of her mind, as she tried to root out the possibilities. She landed on finance; Mordechai's parents must want to meet before things progressed further. A refreshing breeze blew through her mind.

"You're pressing too hard," Aidel said.

"Sorry. Is this okay?"

Perhaps this would be better in private. No, there was some-thing in her voice, something that did not herald good news. But perhaps she only wanted to ask a question, clear something up, like Mrs. Rubin had about Yoni.

If only *she* were on the phone now, instead of Avner! But she had to be here with her mother; no one else could take her place.

And who could take the place of a mother for such an impor-tant phone call?

A father. An intelligent, resourceful, loving father. She might be aching with curiosity, but Avner was perfectly capable of dealing with whatever issue had come up.

Tova's hand began to ache. She stopped massaging and looked at her mother. She had no idea how long she'd been sit-ting there, but Aidel was fast asleep. Tova slipped out of the room.

Brachie was still there, the Dr. Pepper untouched and that serene look not leaving her face.

"I'll go see what this is all about," Tova said.

Brachie gave no indication that she'd heard her mother.

Tova climbed the stairs and found Avner sitting with the phone lifeless next to him.

He raised his eyes to her.

"Well?" she burst out.

Avner squared his shoulders. "It's over. Mordechai doesn't think Brachie's the right girl."

The words hit her like a physical blow, and her hand landed on her stomach. "Why not?"

"He's looking for someone a little more... settled."

Tova grimaced. "What's that supposed to mean?"

"I think he means mature."

"Oh, come on." Tova crossed her arms. "People settle down after they get married. That was just an excuse."

"I'm not so sure," Avner said. "I remember Yoni said pretty

much the same thing about Penina."

She rolled her eyes. "Yes, Yoni, the expert on maturity."

"You have to admit, in a lot of ways, Brachie is not terribly mature. She has only one foot in the adult world."

"I know she's immature! That's why, if you recall, I didn't want her dating in the first place."

"So why do you mind so much now?"

Tova tried to keep the aggravation she was feeling out of her voice. "Because now, Brachie has found the person she thinks is right for her. Why should she be rejected for nothing?"

"But if he's really not the right one—"

"Maybe he's wrong!" Tova cried. "Maybe he's being too shortsighted. What does he expect from a girl who just came home from seminary?"

Avner shrugged. "Maybe he should look for someone a little older."

Tova's eyes narrowed. "Did you tell her that Mordechai should give it another try?"

"I told her that Brachie feels strongly that this can work, and that perhaps Mordechai would reconsider."

"And?"

"She said, 'I know my nephew. He's given this a lot of thought.'"

"That's ridiculous," Tova snapped. "He just brought her home a few minutes ago, how could he have given it a lot of thought?"

"My guess is he was wavering, and this date was going to decide for him. And it did."

"Your guess?" She put her hands on her hips. "What else did she actually say?"

"Not much."

"Did you ask for more specifics? See if there was something he wasn't sure about, something we could clear up for him?"

"I didn't grill her." Avner's tone was growing defensive.

"I didn't say you should have grilled her, I just think you could have gotten a little more information out of her."

"She sounded pretty definite, and I didn't see the point."

"The point is to see if they could make it work. They only went out three times. If she feels so strongly, there's no harm in him giving her another chance. You heard Brachie, she's ready to say yes."

Avner stood. "Brachie's yes is not worth very much if the other party says no."

Tova stared.

Avner met her gaze and held it.

Tova was the first to look away. "In other words," she said slowly, her voice softening, "you think there's nothing to talk about."

Avner's voice matched hers. "The message was loud and clear."

Tova ran a hand across her eyes. "Avner, how could Brachie have read this so wrong? She's going to be crushed."

"I was just thinking about that, right before you came upstairs. From what Brachie said, I got the impression that they were talking about their long-term plans together. But then I thought back to her words and realized my mistake. She said he asked her about where *she* wants to live—not where would *they* live. He asked what *she* sees herself doing down the road, not where would *they* be."

Tova let his words sink in. "When you put it that way, it makes more sense."

Avner nodded. "Because she really likes him, she interpreted his words in a way he never intended them to be understood."

Tova sighed. "So now what?"

"Now we go downstairs and break the news to her."

19

"I CAN'T BELIEVE IT'S over," Brachie moaned. She was hanging upside down off her bed, pressing the phone to her ear. "Your mom called last night to tell us."

"I know, Brachie," Rena sympathized.

"He's *such* a great guy. I mean, he even laughs at my dumb jokes. He's a happy person, y'know what I mean?"

"Sure I do."

"Things were going so well! What happened? Did I do the wrong thing? Say something strange?"

"Don't torture yourself with questions. It just isn't *bashert*."

"But I *am* torturing myself. Rena, your mother must have told you something. Why'd he say no all of a sudden?"

"My mother didn't say a word, honest. And anyway, you know how these things are. I'm sure the next boy will come along soon enough, and you'll forget all about Mordechai."

"I don't know."

"My sister's been dating for three years already. Believe me, she doesn't think about all the what-ifs."

"Maybe that's because she never found the person she

thought was so right for her." Brachie picked at a cuticle. "I just don't get it."

Rena was silent.

"You still there?"

"Sure. I just, um..." Her voice trailed off.

"What?"

"Nothing. Listen, my sister needs the phone now. I'll talk to you after Shabbos, okay?"

Brachie flipped over and bolted upright. "Rena, don't do this to me! I need your help."

"Can't you see that this is a little... strange? Mordechai is my cousin, my mother was the *shadchan*, and my best friend is pumping me for information I don't have!"

"I am not *pumping* you. I just want a little sympathy."

"You can have all the sympathy you want. But every other word you say is 'why'! I don't have the answers you need, and it's really unfair of you to put me in this position. Besides, Mordechai is—" she stopped short.

"Is what?" Brachie begged. "See, you do have information you're not telling me!"

"I didn't mean that. I mean..." She heaved a deep sigh. "My sister needs the phone now. I'll call you later, 'kay? 'Bye."

Brachie stared at the phone in her hand which had suddenly gone dead.

Instead of a warm, sympathetic conversation, she was left with an annoying, angry tone—the phone's, and her friend's.

"You want to sit in the dining room, Ma?" Tova asked. "Or maybe the living room would be better, there's more space in the middle. We could move the coffee table over, and—"

"Tovaleh, we'll ask the therapist what she thinks is best."

"Okay, Ma." Tova looked at her watch. "She's late."

"What's her name?" Aidel asked.

"I don't know. First they assigned you a man, and I told them you'd be uncomfortable, and they had to make some calls. In the end they told me they'd work it out, gave me a choice of times, and told me she'd be here, whoever *she* is."

"Fine."

"I hope there wasn't some misunderstanding," Tova frowned. "They promised me this time slot." She sighed loudly. "I should've insisted on a name and number to call."

The doorbell rang. "I'll bring her in to you," Tova said. She walked to the front door, a smile at the ready.

"Hello, Mrs. Lehrfeld."

Tova stared. It couldn't be. I just couldn't be.

She found her tongue. "Esti! What are you... what a surprise! How did you... I mean, what—"

"I'm the physical therapist assigned to your mother," Esti said, with her trademark smile firmly in place.

This had to be a joke—a bad joke. She'd finally gotten her mother away from Esti's iron grip, and here she was, standing on her doorstep!

"May I come in?" Esti asked politely.

Tova's brain screamed, "No!" but she moved out of Esti's way and said, "Of course." She stared without saying anything further.

"How is your mother?" Esti asked.

"She's been disoriented," Tova answered too sharply. "Up a lot at night, sleeping on and off during the day. She's been weak, too. I think she needs a little more time taking it easy until her strength is back to what it was at the rehab center."

"I understand, it's been an adjustment. But don't worry, she'll pull through it."

Struggling to regain her composure, Tova asked, "How long have you been doing home visits? I thought you worked only for the center."

"Oh, no, I've been doing home visits for a few years now. Since I started at the center I had to cut down some, but I didn't want to give it up entirely. I feel that in the home environment, a patient can work more directly on the most crucial skills."

"Such as?"

"She has to be able to manage in her home environment. That means navigating first with, and then without, her walker. And it means progressing as quickly as possible to resuming her former tasks, such as cooking."

"I see," Tova managed.

"Part of that falls under the category of occupational therapy, part physical therapy. I'm going to have a talk with your mother about setting goals, and setting up a program to keep her moving. She'll be up and around in no time."

Tova felt the muscles in her neck tighten. "Esti, I want you to promise me that you won't push my mother too hard."

"Too hard?" Esti smiled. "I know your mother well, and I would never push her past what I think she's capable of."

Tova frowned. Esti had said the same thing with the utmost confidence after she'd met Aidel only once or twice.

"Can you take me to your mother now? I want to get started. I have another patient after this."

Tova grudgingly led the way.

When she saw Esti, Aidel's face lit up. "Esti!" she exclaimed. "What are you doing here?"

"Surprise! I'm your home care physical therapist."

Aidel wagged her finger at Esti. "You didn't say a word!"

"I just found out myself on Friday."

"It's wonderful to see you!"

"You can do better than that," Esti teased. "I want you to walk over here and give me a hug."

Aidel struggled to push herself out of her chair.

"Here, Ma, let me help you." Tova rushed over to Aidel.

"Mrs. Lehrfeld, I think—"

"There you go, Ma. Easy does it. You don't want to overdo it on your first day."

"Thank you," Esti said. "I'll take it from here."

"Fine," Tova agreed with a thin smile. "I'll just sit down over there and watch."

Shimon straightened his tie for the fourth time as he paced the living room.

Avner turned a page in his sefer.

"Okay," Shimon announced, "that's it. I'm going."

Avner stood and put a hand on Shimon's shoulder. "You sure you'll be okay at the *vort*?"

"Yeah, fine," he answered, his voice cracking. He stood there for another moment before grasping the knob and walking outside. A blast of hot air startled him, and he hesitated before heading out.

Ilana Moskowitz and Yissachar Baumgarten, engaged. Ilana and Yissachar. This was crazy, totally crazy. It was hard enough dealing with the fact that Ilana was engaged. But that she was engaged to his former *chavrusa*?

His steps quickened. He'd really enjoyed Ilana's company, liked the way she let him finish his thoughts without interrupting, the way she thanked the man who'd brought them a drink. Maybe he'd made a mistake. Maybe he should have spoken to his *mashgiach* more before making a decision. Maybe he should have dealt with his doubts and admitted that they were just his own insecurities, not faults in Ilana. His father had hinted as much, but it was only after he'd called it off that he'd been able to hear it. If he'd only held on just a little longer, maybe he'd be the one who was engaged.

But no, it was *bashert*. Someone else couldn't get the girl intended for him.

On the other hand, he'd heard of people "passing up" their *bashert*. What if he'd done that?

Shimon stopped, his breath coming fast. These were thorny philosophical issues. Since Ilana was now engaged, he had to just accept the fact that it wasn't meant to be.

He spotted the house and slowed down, hoping his turmoil wasn't obvious.

Last time he'd been here, Mr. Moskowitz had patted him on the shoulder and told him he was looking forward to seeing him again, and Mrs. Moskowitz had given him a smile of encouragement. He'd never been quite comfortable in their presence, but now he felt like an outcast—a self-made outcast.

And here he was, standing in front of this too-familiar house, with its too-familiar lawn and porch. The crooked seven at the end of the address greeted him like an old friend, but he felt like a traitor.

He wasn't afraid of running into Ilana; she'd be safely ensconced in the den where the women were sure to be. But what would he say to Ilana's father? And how could he face Yissachar, not knowing if he was aware of their near-engagement? Shimon shook his head. Who was he kidding? Whether or not Yissachar knew, it was going to be a real challenge to look him in the eye and wish him a heartfelt mazel tov.

Shimon stared at the house, willing himself to go inside. A couple passed him, the man turning around to see if he was a familiar face.

You can't just stand here. Pull yourself together and go!

Shimon wiped the sweat from his forehead, adjusted his hat, and walked up the stairs. He screwed his face into a smile, wondering how long he'd be able to keep it there.

The crowd was thick, and movement slow. Shimon inched his way inside, terrified that at any moment, he would be seen by Mr. Moskowitz.

Instead, he was accosted by Leibish, another fellow from his yeshivah.

"Hey, Shimon, what's doing? They're dropping like flies, eh? Maybe one of us will be next."

"Yeah," Shimon said, "maybe."

"No, really," Leibish insisted. "This isn't only good news for Yissachar, it's also good news for guys like us. Yissachar's the kind of guy that won't rest until all of his *chevrah* is married. Believe me, a few weeks after the *chasunah*, he'll sit down with his *kallah* and figure out which of her friends would be good for which of his friends. I wouldn't mind being next."

Shimon's eyes darted around. "Sounds good."

A third *bachur* joined them. "*Shalom aleichem*," he said, putting his hand out to Leibish.

"*Aleichem shalom*," Leibish returned. "Do you guys know each other? Shimon Lehrfeld, this is Nachum Gavin."

The two nodded shyly at each other. "Nachum's my neighbor. Learns in that new place, what's it called? Toras Yitzchak?"

"Toras Yaakov," Nachum said. "It's not so new anymore, it's just that I've only been there for one *zman*."

He told Shimon, "You know his *chavrusa*, Gadi Kahn."

"Sure I do," Shimon agreed.

"Actually," Nachum said, "Gadi's leaving the yeshivah. Feels he needs a bigger place, more *bachurim*."

Shimon raised an eyebrow.

"Toras Yaakov is a small place," Nachum said, almost defensively. "The *rosh yeshivah* keeps it that way. He believes in getting to know every single *bachur* personally. Gadi wants more variety." He shrugged. "I know a lot of guys feel that way, but I..." he trailed off. "Never mind."

"Go on," Shimon encouraged him, intrigued. "Where's the yeshivah, out of town?"

"No, local." He smiled. "I know, it's not your typical,

thriving New York *beis midrash*. But it's a place for real serious guys who just want a more personal connection to the *rosh*, or to the *mashgiach*. Most of them are a little older, you know, guys who've done the regular yeshivahs and are ready for something different."

Leibish thumped Shimon's back. "Hey, Shimon will be your new *chavrusa*." He laughed at his own joke. "Too bad you're so settled where you are."

"Yes," Shimon said thoughtfully, "I've been there for three years."

"Hey, there's Bodner," Leibish said. "I'm gonna go say hi. Come with me, Nachum. See you later, Shimon." He walked away, pulling Nachum along.

Shimon watched them retreat. *Very settled.* At the moment, he was feeling anything but settled.

The noise in the room grew louder and then dropped significantly. He supposed a group of people had just left. Shimon said hello to a few more people, then spotted Yissachar. Fortunately, Mr. Moskowitz was nowhere in sight. Shimon's feet wanted to run in the opposite direction, but he propelled himself forward. Yissachar had just finished speaking to someone, when he turned in Shimon's direction.

"Mazel tov!" Shimon said. He pumped Yissachar's hand.

Yissachar threw his arm around Shimon.

They let go and stood facing each other.

Shimon felt a wad of cotton trapping his tongue. And then he looked into Yissachar's eyes and saw intense joy shooting outward. In an instant, his agitation was overshadowed by happiness for his friend. "This is great," he said, beginning to mean it. "I'm so happy for you. When's the *chasunah*? I'm really looking forward to being there."

"Sometime in August, we didn't settle on the date yet, but you'll be one of the first to know."

"I'll be there, count on it."

"You better be. Ilana's a great girl, and this is such an amazing family. I can't believe how lucky I am!"

"You deserve it," Shimon said.

"Mazel tov!" A pair of *bachurim* stepped between them, and Yissachar turned his attention to them.

Shimon moved away. Now that he'd seen Yissachar, he was desperate to leave before anyone in the family recognized him. The crowd was growing once more, and he maneuvered around two young boys and a man holding a plate piled high enough to wobble dangerously. There was only one more person between him and the door.

"Excuse me," Shimon said, trying to get past him.

The man turned around.

Shimon paled.

"Hello, Shimon," Mr. Moskowitz said.

"Uh, Mr. Moskowitz," Shimon stammered.

Mr. Moskowitz nodded and stepped aside.

Shimon looked away and took one step forward, then balled his fists and stopped himself. "Mazel tov," he said, not quite meeting Mr. Moskowitz's eyes. "Yissachar was my *chavrusa*. He's... he's a really terrific guy."

"Thank you," Mr. Moskowitz said quietly.

Shimon set his jaw and forced his head up. Looking directly into his eyes, he said, "I mean that. He's very modest, so maybe Ilana doesn't know about all the ways he helps people. He's one of a kind. I'm really happy for him. And..." He swallowed hard. "And I'm sorry about, uh..."

Mr. Moskowitz smiled. "Thank you, Shimon. You see it's all for the best. We certainly don't hold any grudge, neither does Ilana."

They parted, Shimon's thoughts whirling around like a hurricane.

Before the *vort*, his anxiety had been so intense that he'd debated staying home. His sense of rightness—and the fear that his absence would raise some uncomfortable questions—compelled him to go. But never, never had he expected to be walking out this front door with such... lightness, such closure.

He was forgiven, he was happy for his friend, and he was proud of himself. He adjusted his hat, threw back his shoulders, and went home.

20

YERUCHAM STARED AT THE kitchen table, his thumb and forefinger rubbing against each other.

"Good morning, Tatty," Tova said. "Were you waiting for me? I'm sorry, I hadn't realized you were back from shul."

"It's not the same."

Tova stared. "What's not the same?"

"Doing it late. The *yahrzeit seudah*. It's not the same."

"I know, Tatty, but you said Kaddish on the right day, and—"

"It's not the same."

"But you were the one who said we should have it anyway, even if—"

"I'm waiting for Mommy to wake up." He looked at her bedroom door.

Tova hesitated, then switched gears along with him. "She was just waiting for this from the laundry." She held up a lightweight sweater. "Can I get you something first?"

"No, thank you. I'm waiting for Mommy."

"Okay," Tova said, and knocked on Aidel's door. At her "come in," she opened it and stepped inside. "Here we go," she said, handing Aidel the sweater.

"Thank you. Excuse me, please, I heard Tatty's voice." She pushed her walker toward the door.

Tova pressed herself against the wall to let her mother pass. She entered in time to see their warm smiles as they said good morning.

"You're home early," Aidel said.

"Some young fellow in a rush at the *amud*," Yerucham said.

"A cup of tea?" Aidel suggested.

"Yes, please."

"I'll get it," Tova chirped.

"Thank you, *sheifeleh*, I'll get it," Aidel said.

Tova's eyes widened. "Ma, how will you carry it and push the walker?"

"It's only a few steps, I can manage. I practiced a few times with Esti."

"But not with something hot! Wouldn't it be simpler—"

"No. I can do it."

Tova swallowed. "I'll just put up the kettle, then."

The edges of Aidel's mouth pointed down. "Tova, Tatty wants tea, and *I* am going to make it for him."

Tova turned away.

Leaning on her walker, Aidel made her way over to the stove. She reached out and grabbed the kettle, then held it in her hand as she grasped the walker. Her movements were slow and jerky.

Tova looked on in silence as Aidel filled the kettle. She added only enough water for one cup, then made her way back over to the stove. The kettle banged down on the stovetop so hard that a few drops sloshed out of the spout. She turned on the fire, then collapsed into a chair.

Yerucham had been watching Aidel intently, a smile creeping up his face.

Tova looked from one to the other. "How about breakfast? Some crackers with cheese?"

"That sounds fine," Yerucham said.

Aidel nodded.

Tova set the table, slipping neatly folded napkins under each fork. She sliced some vegetables and arranged them on a plate.

The kettle whistled. Instinctively, Tova turned off the fire.

Aidel pushed herself up out of the chair. Tova bit her lip as she watched her mother stand and then laboriously make a cup of tea. She held her breath as Aidel leaned on the walker, clutching the steaming cup.

When she placed it in front of Yerucham, he said a simple, "Thank you," but the smile never left his face.

The next few weeks elicited the same internal tug of war, Tova's dedication to providing every comfort battling her need to step back and let her mother do things. On this particular morning, the struggle involved a different conflict. While her fingers skimmed over the yogurts in her neighborhood grocery store's refrigerator case, her mind was focused on two words—Gitty Schechter, the next girl Na'ama Rubin suggested for Yoni. Na'ama had called just before she'd left home. She'd told her all about Gitty's family, schooling, present employment, and personality. But she didn't seem to know her age.

"Excuse me." A woman reached over Tova, pulling out a strawberry yogurt.

Tova picked up two coffee yogurts and set them down in her basket. The sooner she finished her shopping, the sooner she could return home and see if Na'ama had called back. She stepped into the express lane, then went outside to join Aidel and Brachie, who were waiting for her on a bench.

"Did you rest up?" she asked her mother. "Ready to head back?"

"Yes, I bought a round-trip ticket," Aidel said. Brachie chuckled.

As they walked home, Tova fell behind, her thoughts wandering. She saw them stop, then Brachie pulled down the seat on Aidel's walker. Tova quickened her pace and heard Brachie say, "Maybe we should've taken a shorter walk."

"No," Aidel panted. She was somewhat pale, but the color was quickly returning to her face.

"Are you okay, Ma?"

"Fine. Stop hovering, please, I'm enjoying my walk with Brachie."

As much as she tried to be inured to her mother's uncharacteristic—and often harsh—comments, they still stung each time anew. But she said nothing. Aidel was so focused on regaining her independence, she couldn't see that pushing herself too hard made her surly. Then she'd be forced to slow down, and the independence she was seeking would be pushed further out of reach.

Aidel and Brachie started off again.

"It's at least a block more than we did yesterday," she heard Brachie say.

"I have to push myself," Aidel responded. "Every day, just a little more than the day before."

"Isn't it exhausting?"

"Yes. But it's worse to be stuck in one place."

"Stuck?" She looked at Aidel's legs. "Oh, you don't mean actually stuck, you mean... *stuck*."

"Yes," Aidel said, glancing over her shoulder at Tova. "Stuck."

Tova sighed.

"Crisp linen white," Avner said, reading the small print on a paint chip.

"I think I like antique white better," Tova said.

Avner compared the two chips. "They look pretty much the same to me."

"And then there's this one, swan white. It's just a touch more yellow than the others." She held the three colors next to each other. "Which one?"

"Honestly, whichever one you pick is fine with me."

Tova's lip curled up on one side. "You mean you have no patience for choosing paint for the living room walls."

"I mean I trust that whatever you pick will be beautiful." He grinned. "And I can think of one or two things I'd rather do than agonize over paint chips."

Tova tossed them down on the coffee table. "All right. Let's talk about Yoni again, and whether or not we should pursue this *shidduch* with Gitty Schechter."

"I changed my mind. Let me see those paint chips again." He snatched them off the table and pretended to scrutinize them.

Tova laughed. "Okay, okay, so I've been driving you a little crazy about this."

"I do understand why this rubs you the wrong way."

"Since when does a *shadchan* not know a girl's age? She has to be hiding something. I figure it this way: Yoni is twenty-two. Penina, the first girl Na'ama Rubin set him up with, is eighteen, fresh out of sem. She knows that suits Yoni, because he wants a girl who's not so far away from seminary that she's lost her enthusiasm."

"Yoni said that?" Avner's chin popped up.

"He didn't say it in so many words, but that was the implication."

Avner shrugged.

"Now, Gitty must be a year or two out of sem, and Na'ama Rubin is trying to hide that. She must be twenty, maybe even twenty-one."

"And if she is? What's wrong with that?"

"What's wrong is that she's trying to hide it. And if she's hiding that, what else doesn't she want us to know?"

"I can't imagine that she's purposely misleading you about anything. To be on the safe side, we'll make careful inquiries. Take our time with the references, and get references from those references. We'll just tell Mrs. Rubin that we won't be able to make a fast decision.

"And another thing," Tova barreled on. "How well can she know Yoni if she sets him up with two girls who are completely different from one another?"

"Who says they're completely different?"

Tova ticked off points on her fingers. "Penina was a top student from a top seminary, Gitty was just average and didn't even go to seminary. Penina is career oriented, and Gitty is a preschool teacher. Penina is outgoing and charismatic, and Gitty is—"

"You haven't met Gitty, so you don't know what she's like," Avner pointed out.

"Na'ama Rubin says she's on the quiet side."

"You said she's also a deep thinker and has an innate *tzeniyus*. Sounds like less sparkle, more substance."

"Then we go back to where we started—the fact that we're missing the most basic piece of information."

"And don't forget the freckles," Avner joked.

Tova smiled. "No, I haven't forgotten. You're merciless, making jokes while I'm all wound up."

Avner shuffled the paint chips. "I'm sorry, Tova, a twenty-year-old girl doesn't qualify as 'older.' "

"Well if you say it like that, of course it sounds ridiculous. I'm not saying she's an 'older girl.' I was just comparing her to the first girl Yoni went out with, that's all. Three years is significant at this stage of life."

"Let me ask you something. If everything else was good—*hashkafah*, goals, personalities—would you turn her down because she's twenty-one? Or even twenty-two?"

Tova ran her tongue over her teeth. "No. But I would like a straight answer."

Avner reached over for the cordless and tossed it to Tova. "Here, let's get one."

"She said she'd call me back, I..." She stopped. "Okay."

The conversation was brief, consisting, on Tova's side, mostly of *mm-hmms* and *I see's*, but her jaw drew forward and her eyes blazed. She hung up and stared at Avner. "She's not twenty, and she's not twenty-one. She's—"

Shimon walked in suddenly, with another *bachur* in tow. "Hi Mommy, Hi Tatty. This is Nachum Gavin, a new friend of mine."

Avner stood and put out his hand to Shimon's friend.

Shimon said, "Nachum and I met at, uh, Yissachar's *vort*."

Avner's face was blank.

"You remember, Tatty, the *vort* I went to a few weeks ago."

Understanding dawned. "Yes, of course I remember."

Tova went into the kitchen to bring drinks, and Shimon invited Nachum to sit. "We've learned together a few times. Nachum learns in Toras Yaakov. Ever hear of it?" His face was eager.

Avner rubbed his beard. "Toras Yaakov... I think Rabbi Newman mentioned a son there." He asked Nachum, "Is there a Newman there?"

"Baruch Newman?"

"Yes, that's him. His father is the principal in the school where I work."

Tova came back with drinks and some sliced chocolate cake. "Please, help yourself." A polite smile was on her face, but her eyes flashed desperate signals at Avner.

"Help yourselves. I hope you'll excuse us, we were just

finishing up something. It was nice to meet you." With a nod of his head, he followed Tova into the kitchen.

With a calmness she thought herself incapable of only five minutes earlier, Tova said, "Avner, forget about this *shidduch*. Just forget it."

Avner raised an eyebrow.

"This girl that Na'ama Rubin wants to set Yoni up with—this Gitty Schechter—she's twenty-five! Twenty-*five*!"

With an ironic smile, Avner said, "That bad?"

"Go on, joke about it. Does she think Yoni is desperate?"

Avner ran a hand through his hair, then walked to the counter and stood there for several minutes.

Tova remained standing also, waiting in anxious silence until Avner finally turned around.

"Seems like all we do lately is make difficult decisions. We toss around the latest quandary, then one of us gives in. This is one issue I don't think we'll ever see eye to eye on. I haven't the slightest objection to Yoni going out with a girl several years older than him. On the contrary, I think there are pointed advantages to it."

He took a breath and continued before Tova could interject. "On the other hand, I know you feel equally strong that it's a bad idea. We could debate the point. I can tell you that it's a prejudice—perhaps a community-wide one—and you can make counterarguments... But I don't see the point. I know how you feel, you know how I feel. Now I'm going to leave the decision to you. I will make peace with whatever you decide."

Tova took a tiny step backwards.

"I mean that. Your feelings are very important, and even if I don't agree with your logic, I'll respect your decision."

A quick, happy flutter in her stomach gave way to a sudden heaviness in her limbs. She tried to shake it off, but failed. "I'm not sure I... There's something about talking it out that makes me..." Her voice trailed off.

Avner tilted his head and raised his eyebrows.

Tova rubbed her arm, then wandered over to the table. She straightened the napkin holder and brushed off a speck of dirt. She sat, eyes down, finger tapping the table. Finally, she looked up at Avner. She cleared her throat, but her voice was still shaky. "The problem is, I really do feel strongly about this. But at the same time, I have so much respect for your opinion, I just can't ignore it."

Avner sat across from her. "So what do you want to do?" he asked softly.

Tova bit her lip and blew out a breath. "Would it be completely crazy if we... if we just ask Yoni what he thinks?"

Avner's eyes brightened. "Crazy?" A lopsided grin settled on his face. "I don't think it's crazy at all."

"I'll keep looking on this side, can you check out those?" Yoni pointed to the opposite wall.

"Sure," Avner said. He strolled over to the huge tie display. There were ties of every color imaginable—and some unimaginable. Wide, narrow, striped, floral, dollar signs, Mickey Mouse... who wore these ties, anyway?

"You like this one?" Yoni asked over his shoulder, holding out a conservative blue stripe.

Avner drew close and fingered the silk. "Classy. But one second, what's *in* now, wide or narrow?"

Yoni chuckled. "Narrow. A good thing, since wide always makes me look like Dumbo."

"It's nice, but not very different from the last three you showed me. Come to think of it, it's very similar to the one you wore last Shabbos."

"I guess you're right." He threw Avner a sheepish grin.

"Really, Yoni, after three dates, you think she's paying that much attention to your tie?"

"I don't know her well enough to answer that. But I do know that she's a details person." He lowered his voice. "And I also know myself well enough to think that this might really be going somewhere, and I'm not taking any chances."

Avner nodded, his satisfaction dulled by a twinge of guilt. The whole *shidduch* process with Yoni was an exciting, intriguing part of being a father, compared to the tightrope walk he performed every time he turned to Shimon's page in this book.

"You know," Yoni broke into Avner's thoughts, "this *shidduch* thing really makes you think. You want to put on your best face. But on the other hand, you don't want to pretend to be something you're not." He held up the tie. "Appearances do count. But since what's behind it counts even more, you have to figure out how to present yourself and understand the other person at the same time."

Avner smiled.

Yoni tried on the tie. "You're right, Tatty, it's exactly like the one I have at home. Nice to know I'm consistent." He folded the tie neatly and put it back in its tiny cubby. "If things continue like this, I'm thinking that maybe we should ask Mrs. Rubin to set up the meetings closer together."

"Just because it's *bein hazmanim* doesn't mean you have to cram all your dates into these three weeks. Momentum is good, and you don't want to have to plow through half an hour of shyness every time. But it's also good to have some time in between dates to think, to analyze your feelings. There's no rush."

"I'm not rushing," Yoni said easily. "It's just that my time is so much freer now, I might as well use it. I don't want to miss any part of the new *zman*. You know how it is, Tatty, a new *zman* is always so... exciting, so fresh. Makes you want to dive into the *beis midrash* and stay as long as you can before you have to surface. Especially Elul *zman*."

"I know exactly what you mean."

"Besides, I need to work out my roommates, set up my *chavrusas*, you know, get settled in."

"I thought you already had most of that worked out."

"Some. But there are always guys who aren't sure of what they're doing till the *zman* actually starts, some new guys come in, some guys switch yeshivahs."

"I hear."

"And some," Yoni continued, "get engaged..."

Aidel shifted her weight in the chair. "It's a shame Meir can't be here tonight for the *yahrzeit seudah*."

"He should come home from camp," Yerucham grunted.

"He's still got another week," Brachie said, pouring herself a drink. "Anybody want some Dr. Pepper?"

"So let him come home a week early," Yerucham replied.

"It's good for him to finish out the summer with the other boys," Tova said.

Yerucham gave another grunt.

"Besides," Aidel said, "we never have children at the *seudah*. We always have babysitters for the little kids. Ahuva Feingold's been doing it for what, three years already?"

"Meir is almost bar mitzvah. He's a good boy, doesn't run around wild like other boys."

"Next year he'll come," Tova soothed, "and he'll even count as part of the *minyan*. Won't that be special, to have all our boys part of the *minyan*?"

Aidel shuffled over the stove and stirred the meatballs. "They're almost defrosted," she reported, dropping back into a chair.

"Ma, you've done enough. I'm going to start chopping onions."

"Thank you, *sheifeleh*," Aidel answered, "but I'm going to

make the soup without anyone's help."

"But Ma—"

"Mommy is making the soup," Yerucham said in that tone Tova knew so well.

"I appreciate everything you're doing, Tovaleh. When I need help, I'll ask for it. I'm much stronger now."

Tova bit back a reply. Yes, her mother was stronger. If she would just pace herself more—

"Besides," Aidel continued, "some of the cooking was done before my stroke. Such *hashgachah pratis!*"

Tova pulled out a cutting board. "I'll start on the salad."

"I'll do it," Brachie said.

Tova paused. Brachie's help was the last thing she needed right now. But looking at her eager expression, she considered that cucumbers couldn't be burned, smashed, or undercooked. "Great idea." She whipped out a stockpot and two onions. "Whenever you're ready, Ma, it's all set up for you here."

Aidel frowned. "I am perfectly capable of taking two onions out of a drawer."

Yerucham's fingers played against each other.

Aidel turned her attention to him. "Did you buy the schnapps?"

"Yes. Does everyone know we're doing it here this year? And that the program will be the same even though the *seudah* is late?"

"Yes."

"Everyone? The whole family? And Rabbi Hess?"

The whole family. The whole family consisted of three children—Tova and her two brothers—and a third cousin.

"Everyone was told," Aidel assured him.

"Did you invite the Webbers?"

Aidel looked at Tova.

"Tatty, we agreed we'd have a smaller crowd this year,

remember? Family but no neighbors."

Yerucham's eyebrows drew together. "You mean *you* agreed."

"I just wanted it to be a little easier on Ma. All the noise—"

"How noisy can another couple be?" he growled.

"It's not just one couple," Tova said. "It's another four or five couples."

"Call them," Yerucham commanded.

"What, now? Last minute?"

"Yes, now. Right now." He stood, glowering. "Did you forget that we need a *minyan*?"

"But we're having the Feingold boys from next door for dessert, and Mr. Dresner—"

"We'll call them," Aidel interrupted. "Of course we'll call them."

Yerucham's face turned a dangerous crimson. "There are some things that cannot change." He stormed out.

Tova looked helplessly at Aidel.

"You know how Tatty gets about the *yahrzeit*. And I know it's not a real *yahrzeit seudah*. I'm so sorry to burden you with all this." Her hands shook.

Tova swallowed a lump in her throat. "You're never a burden, Ma."

Aidel's sigh filled the kitchen.

Yerucham closed the *sefer* he was holding. "And that is exactly the kind of man my father, *zecher tzaddik liverachah*, was, the kind of men my brothers would have become." His voice choked with emotion. "And my sisters..." his voice was barely a whisper. He nodded at Hershel, his oldest son, to take over.

Hershel stood and read out the names of Yerucham's entire family, all presumed to have been killed on the same day.

Avner knew how important this reading was to Yerucham. In the weeks leading up to the *yahrzeit*, Yerucham would go over the names the way one counts gold pieces. At the *seudah*, his forehead was turned into a roadmap of creases as he listened with intense concentration, and as each name was recited, he winced, an arrow piecing him every time anew.

Though the proceedings were much the same as always, there was a tense undercurrent accompanying this year's gathering which unfolded after the guests had gone and the immediate family sat together in the living room.

"You really look terrific, Ma," Yanky said for the fourth time.

"Thank you," Aidel said. "*Baruch Hashem*, I'm getting stronger every day."

"I bet you can't wait to go back home."

"I am certainly looking forward to being able to do everything on my own again." Aidel smiled at Tova. "But I'll miss being here, too. Tova is spoiling me rotten and is the most wonderful daughter anyone could ask for. Plus I'm getting to spend so much time with Brachie, and soon Meir will be back too."

"Does Tova let you wheel your walker on the carpet?" Hershel joked.

Tova's eyes darkened.

"By now I mostly use it outside, and besides, soon I hope to be done with it for good."

Yanky took a look at Tova's face and whipped out some photos. "Look, Tova, this is Tuvia with his new haircut." He pulled out another. "And this is Simsy. Tell me she doesn't look just like Brachie did at that age."

Tova squinted. "I see a slight resemblance in the eyes."

"A slight resemblance!" He shoved another photo at her. "Look at this one."

"Yes, I see it a little more here."

"Simsy," Yerucham muttered. "She has a beautiful *Yiddishe* name, and they call her Simsy."

Yanky threw an arm around Yerucham and squeezed. "Tatty,

may she be a *tzaddeikes* like your sister Sima."

"And as beautiful," Aidel added.

Yerucham's gaze rested on each of his children in turn and softened by degrees. "Amen," he said.

"Now," Aidel said, "I want to hear all about this new business development of yours."

"Yanky and I just signed on a new client," Hershel said.

"A big client," Hershel amended. "It means longer hours for both of us for a while, but if all goes well, it could mean an expansion."

"And if *that* goes well, it could mean we can hire more staff."

"We want to merge our two jobs into one and delegate the rest of the responsibilities."

"And then we can take turns sitting in the *beis midrash*."

Amused, Avner's head ping-ponged back and forth. Despite the five-year gap between the two brothers, they seemed more like twins.

Tova's serious expression encompassed them both. "I thought you two had plans to move back to New York once this business could run independently."

"We thought that would work," Hershel said, "but it's just not realistic."

"We need to be on site."

"But the children," Tova said, "they—"

"There are excellent schools for both the boys and the girls," Yanky responded.

"But what about having a bubby and a zeidy?" Tova asked. "You're so far away..."

"Well, we always come in the summer to visit," Hershel said.

"You didn't this summer," Tova commented dryly.

Yanky sat forward. "You know very well why we didn't this summer." He glanced at Aidel.

"The same way we always find babysitters for the kids

during the *yahrzeit seudah*, we could have found babysitters again, and you could've spent some time with Ma."

Yanky shifted uncomfortably.

"In fact," Tova said with a pointed look, "it was all the more reason to come. Even if only *one* of you could have been here at a time."

"We're here now, that's what counts," Hershel said, trying to steer the conversation to safer ground.

Avner watched Tova closely. Since Aidel's stroke, Tova had never said a word against her brothers. Still, he sensed her resentment at their not having come at all, even though she was the one who had insisted there was no need. And on top of that, now they were making light of it.

Tova's jaw was set. Her index finger tapped the table steadily, then grew still as she inhaled deeply and allowed her features to relax. "You're right, what counts now is that we're all here, together. Isn't that right, Tatty?"

Yerucham seemed to relax into his chair. "Yes," he said, "it is."

"You did a really nice job with... everything." Hershel said, waving vaguely around him.

She caught Avner's eye, and a wry grin stole across Tova's face. "Thank you," she said simply.

Later, after everyone had gone, he found her in the kitchen sorting silverware and asked her about that grin. "You looked like the cat that had swallowed the canary. What was that all about?"

The same grin appeared instantly on her face, but this time she let it blossom into a full-fledge smile. "I'll tell you, but..." Her voice trailed off, and she grew suddenly self-conscious. "You have to promise not to laugh."

"You know me better than that!"

"Yes, I do." She removed a towel from a drawer, avoiding eye contact. "When Hershel tried to gloss over the fact that he hadn't once made the trip out here to see Ma, I wanted to demand, 'Where were you those first few anxious days? What about those weeks in the hospital, and all that time afterwards in rehab?' I wanted to shout, 'Where were you two?' The words were on the tip of my tongue."

It was not a difficult scene to picture. "So what stopped you?"

Tova hesitated, then said, "You did."

Avner's mouth twisted and he shook his head in puzzlement. "What?"

"You stopped me. Just as the words were about to leave my mouth, I caught sight of you and thought, if I were Avner, how would I react?"

He cocked his head to the side, never more interested in what she was saying.

"It all passed through my head in a flash. You would smile and let it go. You would know, for yourself, that you were right, and you wouldn't try to rub it in their faces. You'd let Hershel deal with his guilty feelings on his own, without punctuating them with comments and insinuations."

Avner's lips parted.

Tova continued, "Do you remember the conversation we had about Gitty? About her age, I mean."

"Vividly."

Tova seized a few forks and began to rub vigorously. "After that conversation, I realized two things."

"Yes?" he encouraged.

"One, I realized how much I trust your opinion. How much I need it to balance out my own strong opinions." She darted a quick glance at Avner. "And two, I realized that... I admire the way you respect *other* people's opinions."

He tried to force his tongue to move.

While he was always lambasting himself for not speaking more forcefully, for keeping the strength of his convictions to himself, here Tova was declaring that it was something she *admired*! And not only that, it was what made his take on things all the more valuable to her!

Avner grabbed the back of a chair.

In the silence, Tova stopped rubbing and peered up at him. "You're not laughing?"

He saw her anxious face and found his voice. "I'm not laughing, Tova. I would never—could never—laugh at you." A pool of delight bubbled up within him, and he felt suddenly carefree and light. "No, scratch that. I *am* laughing. Laughing and smiling and dancing. That was the nicest thing you could possibly have said to me."

21

MEIR STOOD WITH HIS friend on the porch.

"How come you didn't call me earlier?" Yehuda asked. "We could've had a catch."

"Gimme a break, I just got home today."

Yehuda shrugged. "Did you know we're getting a new kid in our class?"

"Yeah, I heard in camp. You guys are lucky. The last time we got a new kid was in third grade."

Yehuda tossed a ball up into the air, then let it drop neatly back into his baseball glove. "I dunno, I kind of like knowing who everyone is. With a new kid, it could change everything."

"I like when things change," countered Meir. "Keeps it interesting." He threw a look over his shoulder at the house. "Most things, anyway."

"Well, we'll find out soon enough. Yeshivah starts right after Labor Day."

"It's not fair. My brothers still have *bein hazmanim.*"

"Mine, too."

"You wanna come inside for a drink?"

"Nah, I gotta get home. See you tomorrow."

Meir waved good-bye and bounced into the kitchen. He yanked open the refrigerator and poured himself a glass of lemonade.

Yerucham strode in after him. "I would like some, please."

"Oh sure, Zeidy." He put the first glass on the table, then poured himself another and made for the door.

"We missed you at the *yahrzeit seudah*," Yerucham said, sitting down.

Meir froze. It wasn't *his* fault he wasn't at the *seudah*. Did his grandfather want him to apologize for something he had no control over?

Yerucham stared.

"I'm sorry, I was in camp."

"I know, *tatteleh*." He made a loud, slow *shehakol*, then an awkward pause followed. Yerucham sipped his lemonade. It seemed like he wanted to say more but didn't. Finally, he said, "Now that you are home, maybe you want your room back. I'm sorry that I'm taking up your space. Your bed."

"That's okay, Zeidy, really. I'm fine in Shimon's room."

"But now that Yoni's back, you're sleeping on the floor."

"I'm on a mattress, on top of the carpet. It's comfortable."

Yerucham's face revealed his skepticism.

"Besides, I like being there with Yoni. The whole year, he's away in yeshivah, and this way I get to spend more time with him."

Yerucham hesitated.

"Really!" Meir said, his smile growing, inside and out.

"Okay, *tatteleh*. If you say so." He put his glass down. "Listen, Bubby didn't take her second walk yet today. Do you want to come along with us? We can stop at the candy store. I'll buy you a Milk Munch."

Meir peered at Yerucham. It was like he had been wearing

a mask, and all of a sudden, someone came and pulled it off. "Sure," Meir said, "I'd really like that."

Shimon wiped his forehead and bounded up the porch steps. "Hi Mommy. Why are you sitting out here?"

"Bubby's cooking dinner. It was easier for me to be outside than to stay there and not help."

"Oh." He followed Tova's glance and tucked in his shirt.

"How was your day?" Tova asked after a moment.

"Really great. I'm so glad I let Nachum talk me into this *kiruv* camp. We went to Flushing Meadows Park in Queens and made a barbeque."

Tova squinted. "You look a little sunburned."

"Since today was the last day, we had a whole good-bye thing. Some of these kids are..." He shook his head. "This is the first time most of them ever opened a *siddur*. Some of them never saw the *alef-beis* before. It was incredible to watch them." He paused. "To be a part of it, I mean. To make a difference."

Tova's eyes invited him to continue.

"They looked up to me, you know? I was some kind of role model. Some of them asked for my number, they want to keep in touch."

"That's sweet."

"I'm trying to figure out how I can do this more often."

"How can you? Summer's over."

"I know. They have activities sometimes, *shabbatonim*, some stuff during the week."

"Hmm. Your schedule doesn't have much leeway."

Shimon's eyebrows drew in briefly. "I've been giving it some thought." He sat down. "I've been talking to Nachum, and —"

The front door opened. "Mommy," Meir said, "you have a phone call. Here." He handed her the cordless and disappeared.

"Hello? Oh, Zelda, always a pleasure to hear from you... I

know, but none of those suggestions were quite right. But we always appreciate your thinking of her... Another suggestion, sure, I'd love to—" She shot a quick glance at Shimon. "He's not... Let me talk in private, just a moment please." She excused herself, leaving Shimon wondering.

He didn't sit long, preferring the coolness of the house to the sticky August air. He found Brachie inside, poring over a heavily filled page and scribbling an occasional check mark in the margin.

"That looks like last year's sem list."

"I wish," Brachie said. "This is my schedule of classes, plus a book list."

"When do you start?"

"Too soon." She rested her cheek in her hand.

"Not looking forward?"

"Don't know."

Shimon hesitated, then sat down across from her.

Brachie tapped her lip with the pen. "What happened with Yoni?"

"Yoni?"

Brachie rolled her eyes. "Oh, come on. He was dating someone. He was barely home the first half of *bein hazmanim*, now he's suddenly around again. Did they break it off?"

Shimon rubbed a hand across his upper lip. "He didn't tell you anything?"

"No."

"If he didn't tell you..."

Her eyes darkened.

Shimon rubbed his chin. "All he said was that things are slowing down. Something about Gitty wanting time to think things through."

"To you, she's Gitty. But me? No one even told me he was dating."

"Were you upset when I didn't tell you I was in middle of a *shidduch*?"

"Yeah. Especially with Ilana, when it got serious. Lucky I didn't hear it from the neighbors first."

"That's just it, there was nothing to hear."

Brachie pursed her lips and Shimon tried again.

"Forget me a minute, think about Ilana! What if I'd found out something terrible about her and broke it off? I wouldn't be able to tell you that."

Her eyes widened. "Is that what happened?"

"No! I'm just saying people need privacy."

"Privacy from me."

"From anyone! I wouldn't have the guts to date if I thought a girl was discussing me with everyone."

"But talking helps you think it through."

"So schmooze it over, but no names, or at least no last names. Your brother and uncle and cousin don't need to know."

Brachie looked up sharply. Then her brow furrowed and she said slowly, "I think you have a point."

"I do?"

"Mordechai is my best friend's cousin. When I talked to her about him, she closed up, and till now I couldn't figure out why."

"So that's why you've been moping around for weeks?"

"I guess. Honestly, I think I'm kind of... stuck." She sighed. "I really liked Mordechai. I thought it would work out. I still think about it sometimes. Maybe we're really meant for each other."

"I think it's normal to feel that way."

Brachie raised her eyes to him.

"I felt that way with Ilana. I know, I'm the one who called it off, but still, there were so many things I really liked about her. I kept asking myself if I made a mistake."

"And?"

"After I got used to the idea of her being engaged, I realized that just because it's not *bashert* doesn't mean those great things about her don't exist."

Brachie was thoughtful.

"All those great qualities of hers are going to make her a great wife—for Yissachar. I'm not looking for another Ilana, I'm looking for someone who will be the right fit for me. I have a feeling that when the right one comes along, I'll know it." He paused. "And so will you."

"Well, the suggestions aren't exactly pouring in."

Shimon tried to hide a smile.

Brachie pounced. "What? You know something! Out with it!"

"Let's just say... I think you may be hearing about something soon. I heard Mommy on the phone, and—" He colored.

"Nu?"

"I shouldn't have said that." He saw her face, and his stomach twisted. "Maybe it's not about you. She just said that she always appreciates when people think of you. Then she said she'd love to hear something, and she got up and went away."

Brachie's eyes sparkled. "You think it's for me?"

"Who else could it be for?"

"You."

Shimon blinked. "Me? Can't be." But he remembered the way she looked at him before she'd left the room, and her words, *He's not...* "You know, maybe you're right."

Brachie grinned broadly as Shimon continued. "Then again, maybe you're not..."

Brachie threw her purse down and trudged up to her room. She kicked off her shoes and tossed her notebook on the desk. Then she lay down and let the quiet wash over her.

After a whole summer off, going back to a full schedule of classes was exhausting. It was also rather depressing. Instead of soaking up Chumash, Navi, and *hashkafah*, she was sitting through biology, physiology, and medical terminology. She was ology'ed-out.

Brachie hesitated, then reached for the phone and punched in some numbers. "Rena, we need to talk."

"Okay." Her voice was cautious.

"I want to apologize for being so dumb. I shouldn't have tried to pump you for information about Mordechai. I probably shouldn't have spoken to you at all about him, since he's your cousin and everything. I thought that since you knew him, you could really understand what I was saying."

"I'm sorry, too. I should've kept my nose out of it. I was just excited, thinking maybe you two would end up getting married, and then we'd be cousins."

"I know. And I realize that after we went out a few times, you did try to steer the talk away from him. It's just that we share all the important stuff..."

"Brachs, we still can, I'm here for you. I think maybe you're still upset about what happened with Mordechai, and if you want to share your feelings, I really want to listen."

Brachie twirled a strand of hair around her finger. Did she still want to talk about Mordechai? She did. But not with Rena. Her mother was the person she needed for that. "No, but thank you," she said.

"Oh," Rena said in a small voice.

"But I really want to tell you about school. I miss Rebbetzin Berlinger! These classes I'm taking are, like, an hour long..."

Avner sat at his desk with a pile of manila folders, neatly printing his students' names on the tabs. A quick knock sounded on the door before it opened, and the principal entered. "Avner, we have a problem."

This opening was so unlike Gedaliah. It would normally take a hurricane to ruffle his feathers.

"It's Zev. You know, Zev Gordon, the new seventh-grade *rebbi*."

He did not need a reminder as to who Zev Gordon was. "What's the problem?"

"Have you spoken to him at all?"

"Not yet. I wanted him to get his feet wet first. I was also hoping he'd approach me, so he'd be the one asking for help and wouldn't feel like I'm trying to boss him around."

"Believe me, his feet are wet. He's up to his neck and is about to drown." Gedaliah sat down hard. "I haven't expected much in the way of actual learning. But the boys are walking all over him."

"How so?"

"I just passed his room. The noise was so loud I'm surprised the teacher next door could be heard, even with the door closed." He pulled at his collar. "It's been like that all week, but now it's really gotten out of hand."

Avner leaned over and flipped on his air conditioner. "Have you talked to him?"

"Of course, several times. Went over some basic teaching techniques. When I ask him what's been going on, he smiles and says everything's under control. When I mention the noise, he says every teacher knows that kids this age are rowdy. I get nowhere with him."

"Have you considered observing him?"

"I did observe, but only once. You know how it is. When you observe, you get to see the *rebbi*'s style, but not much else. The second I walk in, the room is utterly silent."

Avner smiled. "You're too good at commanding respect."

Gedaliah didn't return the smile. "Will you talk to him? See if he'll talk to you, he's sure not talking to me."

"Sure, if you think it will help."

"It certainly can't hurt any, and I can't think of what else to try at this point. I'm all out of ideas."

"Can it wait until recess?"

Gedaliah frowned. "I suppose it must. Calling him out of class to talk wouldn't work. After you speak to him, find me, wherever I am."

"I will," Avner assured him.

When the bell rang, Avner stacked the folders into a neat pile and straightened his desk. As he reached out to open the door, it opened by itself.

Zev's face was inches in front of his own.

Avner stepped back.

"I'm having a problem," Zev said immediately. "Do you have a minute?"

Relief spread through his limbs. His advice would stand a greater chance of being heeded now that it was sought after. "Of course, have a seat."

Zev pulled out a chair.

"What's the problem?" Avner asked.

"The problem," Zev said, "is Rabbi Newman."

Avner kept his face neutral, though his shock was complete. "Rabbi Newman is the problem," he repeated.

"That's right," Zev said.

"Why don't you tell me what problem we're talking about, and let's see what we can do."

"You saw my lesson plans."

"Of course, I went through them with you." *For you* would have been more accurate.

"I mean the revised version, the one that I handed in."

Avner hesitated. He wasn't sure if Gedaliah wanted Zev to know that he'd seen it. "I see a lot of the *rebbis'* lesson plans. Rabbi Newman likes me to have a picture of what's happening in the yeshivah."

"Well, I had to take out a lot of my more innovative ideas.

And Rabbi Newman wants me to stick exactly to the lesson plans I gave in, line by line."

"Go on."

"But at the same time, he keeps lecturing me on reaching the boys. 'We teach students, not material.'" He leaned forward. "You see the problem? He wants me to do exactly what I've planned, without taking into account that it only works on paper, not in real time."

Avner sat back. "Can you give me a clearer picture? What's happening in the classroom?"

"We open a *sefer*, I call on someone to read, and before he's said three words, a couple of kids in the back start making noise."

"And then?"

"Oh, I've tried a few different things, but they don't work. And the reason they don't work is because Rabbi Newman is tying my hands behind my back."

"In what way?"

Zev shot out of his chair and began pacing the small room. "These are teenagers, or preteens. Before they'll be willing to listen to me, they have to like me. I need to go outside and play ball with them, be their friend, be one of them. I have to be cool. What's so cool about standing up in front of a classroom and... speaking?"

He threw himself back into his chair. "Rabbi Newman says that the parents won't appreciate hearing their kids were playing ball instead of learning. I get that, I really do. Especially not the first week of school. But there are other ways I could win the kids over. Like some of those ideas I had in my original plan. You nixed most of them because of technical reasons." He threw a disgusted look at Avner. "Or money."

Avner ran a hand through his hair.

Zev leaned forward. "You see the problem?" he repeated.

Avner saw the problem in bold, vivid colors.

"I know myself," Zev continued, "I'm a real people person. I've been head counselor in a camp for years, and the boys love me. They *love* me. Doesn't matter if it's a sports activity, in the lunchroom, or a *shiur*. They hang on my every word."

Avner could easily picture Zev winning boys over with his enthusiasm, not to mention a charm which he had often sensed Zev possessed—although it was presently hidden behind a mask of aggravation.

"How can I make the principal understand?"

"Seventh grade is not an easy grade to teach," Avner said, aiming for a tone that was sympathetic, not condescending. "It's always hard to balance teaching material and reaching students."

"Especially when you're not given any options for reaching them."

"Let's talk about those options."

"There *are* no options," Zev insisted. "Rabbi Newman is saying, just get up in front of that class and *make* them learn."

An image flitted through Avner's mind of his own seventh-grade *rebbi*, pointing to a Gemara with one hand, clutching a tissue to wipe the sweat from his forehead with the other. This was in December. "You know, I think about that sometimes. How do you suppose *rebbis* motivated their students, say, twenty years ago?"

"Times have changed. We both know that today's kids are very distractible. No one had to turn somersaults back then to get their attention."

"Very true," Avner said with a nod. "On the other hand, a professional, in *any* profession, has to be able to work within the framework he's given. A CPA who joins an accounting firm can ask for a computer program that does most of the work for him. But if his firm doesn't have computers, he needs to take out his calculator."

Zev rolled his eyes. "In this case, he'd need to take out his abacus. I asked for very simple materials. When you said no, I didn't complain, though I really can't understand how a yeshivah of this caliber can do without them. Now all I'm asking for is the tools to win the boys over, so that even when the lessons get stale, they have that feeling to fall back on."

Avner's mouth felt dry. "Some *rebbis* feel that with proper preparation, they can make the lessons come alive without all the bells and whistles."

"They're kidding themselves. Today, you need bells, whistles, and MP3s. There's no other way." He stood. "Will you please explain my position to Rabbi Newman?"

"Oh, yes." Avner licked his lips. "I certainly will."

"Look at those," Aidel pointed. "They're called impatiens."

Meir bent over and brought his face close to the flowers. "Who gives flowers their funny names, anyway?"

"Most of them come from Latin, I think."

"Latin? I know enough languages already. English, Yiddish, and Hebrew are plenty."

Aidel chuckled.

"I think we should turn back now, Bubby. We walked a block past where we went yesterday. Mommy said we shouldn't go too far. "

"I know, but I'm feeling wonderful, and this breeze is delightful." She adjusted her sunglasses. "I'd like to go one more block."

"Okay, Bubby."

"How is yeshivah? It must be hard to sit in class for so long after the summer."

"Yeah. But it's nice to be back with my friends, and I have a really good *rebbi* this year."

They reached the end of the block and turned around, sometimes talking, sometimes simply relishing the cool breeze.

A short distance before they reached home, Aidel stopped

and firmly said, "Meir, I want to try the last stretch on my own, without the walker."

Meir's eyes opened wide. "Can you do that?"

"I practiced walking on the sidewalk today with Esti."

"But it's bumpy. Besides, Mommy said—"

She patted Meir's shoulder. "You just hold my walker. Sit in the little seat if you like." Aidel let go and took slow, small steps. Her right leg dragged, but she didn't stop until she stood in front of the house.

"Bubby, that was great!"

Panting, Aidel motioned for Meir to bring the walker. He ran with it and opened the seat for her.

"Are you okay? Should I call Mommy?"

Aidel wagged her finger. When she recovered, she said, "I'm fine, just out of breath. Wait with me, then I want you to call Zeidy. I want to show him."

Meir watched a passing car, then his neighbor's dog as it sauntered down the street. He turned his gaze to his grandmother. "You really want to walk without that thing, don't you."

"Yes, Meir, I really do."

He looked down at her placid face. "Don't you ever feel like giving up?"

She pursed her lips. "No."

"But it's hard work. You have to learn something you've known how to do almost your whole life."

"I do get discouraged, sometimes, but I won't give up."

A boy whizzed by on a bicycle.

"You know how to ride one of those, don't you?" Aidel asked.

"Sure."

"How did you learn?"

"I just learned." He shrugged. "I mean, I got on, and Tatty helped me, or Shimon or Yoni, and I just started pedaling."

"Did you get it the first time?"

"No, it took a few days, maybe longer; I don't remember. I think at first it was hard to keep my balance."

"Did you ever fall?"

"Lots of times."

"Did you get hurt?"

Meir's eyes looked into the distance. "Yeah. Once I scraped my knee really bad."

"So why did you keep trying?"

"Because I really wanted to ride a bike." He smiled. "I get what you're saying, Bubby. It's hard work, and sometimes it doesn't go the way you want. But if you want it badly enough, you make yourself keep doing it."

"Exactly. Now then, I'm ready. Can you please call Zeidy? I want to show off."

"No problem." Meir jogged up the steps and went inside, leaving the front door open. He came back with Yerucham trailing him.

"You wanted to show me something?" Yerucham asked.

"Watch this," she said. She stood up and straightened the seat, then began to walk unaided.

"What are you doing?" he shouted. "Aidel, be careful!"

Aidel smiled and took another two steps.

"Don't worry, Zeidy," Meir said. "She practiced first."

Tova joined them on the porch. "What happened, Tatty?" She saw Aidel. "Ma, what are you doing? Where's your walker?"

Aidel ignored her as she had Yerucham, but Tova didn't stand on the porch ogling. She hopped down the stairs. "Ma, you're not ready for this." She grabbed the walker and rolled it to Aidel. "Please, Ma, grab the handles. You don't have to lean on them, just hold them in case."

Too tired to respond, Aidel shook her head with stiff, jerky motions, and kept walking until she reached the ramp. She waved at Tova and pointed to her walker.

"Bubby wants you to bring her the walker," Meir said.

"I know what Bubby wants," Tova muttered, pushing it toward her mother.

Aidel flipped down the seat and sank down onto the small cushion.

Yerucham stepped slowly down the stairs and stood by her side. "You did it," he said quietly.

She threw him a tired smile.

"Let's get you inside," Tova said. "You look as pale as the sidewalk."

"Soon," Aidel gasped. "Myself."

Tova crossed her arms and drummed her fingers on her sleeve. "Meir, go inside and bring Bubby some cold water."

"Feh." Aidel waved her hand. "No water. Time."

Meir's eyes bounced from Aidel to Tova, who gave a little shrug.

All eyes were on Aidel as her breathing slowed. "Ready," she said at last. "Ramp."

Meir thought Aidel should rest a few more minutes, but he kept his mouth closed.

Tova's hand was under Aidel's arm as she stood.

"Myself," Aidel repeated, her smile gone.

With obvious reluctance, Tova let go but hovered by her side.

Aidel pushed her walker forward. When they got to the foot of the ramp, the walker jerked suddenly, and Aidel collapsed, right into Tova's arms.

Avner marched into the office and saw that the principal's door was closed. "Mrs. Strauss, is Rabbi Newman in?"

"No."

Avner rubbed his chin. "Please tell him I'd like speak to him before he leaves for the day."

Mrs. Strauss glanced at her watch. "That's a long way off, there's plenty of time."

"I'll be in the teachers' room, then the library, maybe the book room. Hmm. Maybe it's better if I come back. Please tell him it's in reference to what we discussed earlier, and that it's... rather important."

Avner tried to put Zev Gordon out of his mind. He went directly to the teachers' room in the hopes of encountering a like-minded colleague to restore his faith in the teaching profession. Instead, he walked straight into a circle of *rebbis*, with Zev Gordon right in the middle. He tried to duck out before he was seen.

"Hey, Avner," Zev greeted him loudly. "I was just telling everyone about my idea for an end-of-year PowerPoint presentation."

Avner pasted on a smile. "An end-of-year presentation? Well, you certainly think ahead."

"Have to. We need photos from every *rebbi*, every month. Think about what a smash it'll be at the end of the year."

Avner looked around. "What does everyone think?"

Kalman was, as usual, the first to speak up. "Great idea, my boys will love it. I'll have them bring cameras to school."

"That's against school policy," Yitzchak reminded him. "And I, for one, think it's a good policy."

"You do?" Zev's surprise could not be more evident.

"Electronics are distracting. And they create competition."

"And they get lost," Chaim said.

"True," Shmuel agreed. "But for my eighth-graders, it'll be an amazing memento."

"It won't cause competition," Zev said with his usual assurance. "Nowadays, everyone has a digital camera. In camp this summer, there wasn't a single boy who didn't have his own."

"Maybe the families who can afford sleep-away camp can afford to give each kid a digital camera," Chaim said. "I can think of three of my students right off who I'm sure don't have a camera. Not them, not their parents."

"You should've seen the end-of-summer presentation," Zev said. "We couldn't have done it without the kids snapping pictures all summer."

Yitzchak shook his head. "Just what I need. Kids busy with their cameras instead of their *chumashim*."

"That wouldn't happen if you use it as a tool, instead of banning it so the kids have to hide what they're doing."

"Bell's about to ring," Shmuel said, "I'd better get back."

"Don't wait for me today," Chaim told him. "I'm not going straight home."

The *rebbis* dispersed, and Avner followed them.

Zev's voice stopped him in the doorway. "What do you think

of the idea?" he asked Avner.

Avner turned around and came back into the room. "I would have to give it some more thought, consider the advantages and disadvantages of such a move."

"What's your gut feeling?" Zev pressed.

"My gut feeling is that I would weigh the two sides..." he look pointedly at Zev, "and then confer with someone with more experience than myself."

Zev laughed. "Okay, you think about it as much as you like. I'm going to sell the idea to the other *rebbis*, and then I'm going to present it to Rabbi Newman."

Avner tread carefully. "Perhaps you should discuss it with Rabbi Newman first, before you try to convince anyone of anything. That way, if he doesn't allow it—"

"I gotta go, or the boys'll be wrestling in the aisles by the time I get there. See you later." He strode out.

Avner blew out a breath and sat down hard. Zev Gordon was a disaster waiting to happen. Not only was he losing his own class, causing who knew what kind of damage now and in the future, he was going to sow unrest among the entire staff. Rabbi Oberlander's defection had been a blow to the school; Avner feared that Zev Gordon would destroy all sense of unity and undermine the principal's authority.

Avner stood. There was no sense in putting off his talk with Gedaliah. He turned toward the office with a determined step, but his pace gradually slowed. How much was he allowed— or required—to say? Such questions had come up in the past, and had been discussed with Avner's rav. Though his natural inclination was to make peace between all parties concerned, he knew that his duty lay in finding a solution to the problem at hand. And in order to find that solution, he would have to explain the problem in far greater detail than he cared to.

Avner felt queasy. On top of the revulsion he felt for what

he was about to do, he was drowning in guilt. Over and over, Gedaliah had begged him to take the job as *rebbi*. His refusal was what caused this whole mess in the first place.

He reached the office, and Mrs. Strauss looked up. "Rabbi Newman is in now. He said you should go right in."

"Thank you." Avner squared his shoulders and strode inside.

Gedaliah's face was a combination of curiosity and dread.

Avner sat down, his back not touching the chair. "I think we have a problem on our hands."

"I know we do. That's why I asked for your help."

Avner took a deep breath and plunged in. "Zev is very charismatic. I believe that's what made him so successful as a head counselor and learning *rebbi* in camp. You yourself said that that's one of the main reasons you hired him, despite his inexperience."

"Correct."

"Zev feels that we are not letting him do his job. You, by not letting him be a 'friend' to the boys, me, by not giving him all the gadgets he feels he needs. Between us both, he feels we are, in his words, tying his hands behind his back."

"I don't understand. His revised lesson plan is solid. If he just sticks to that, he should be okay."

"I'm afraid he submitted that lesson plan under duress. He understood that we needed some solid plans on paper, so he put them down. But he didn't let go of his ideas of how to fulfill those plans. He believes that the only way to get the students to learn is to make them have fun."

"But—"

"I know," Avner smiled, "we're not anti-fun, we just think there are other ways to make learning enjoyable besides video presentations. I told him as much."

"And?"

Avner sighed. "He didn't hear me. He wants *me* to convince

you that there's a problem, and that it's not him, it's us."

Gedaliah sighed heavily. He removed his glasses, plucked a tissue, and slowly cleaned them. Then he looked at Avner. "What's going to be?"

Tova staggered under Aidel's weight.

Yerucham stepped forward and added his support while Meir looked on, his mouth open in shock.

"Call Hatzolah!" Tova shouted.

Meir flew up the stairs and inside.

"I can't just hold her like this," Tova cried, "what should I do?"

Yerucham's face was frozen in terror.

"We have to lay her down." She looked around frantically. "Tatty, can you help?"

"Yes," he croaked.

"Here, on the grass."

Together, they lay Aidel down.

Meir appeared on the porch. "I called Hatzolah," he said.

Aidel's eyes fluttered open.

"Ma, are you okay? Ma!"

"Why aren't they here yet!" Yerucham barked.

A siren screamed in the distance, coming closer and closer.

Aidel's eyes opened and darted around.

"Ma? What happened? How are you feeling?"

Aidel didn't answer.

The siren drew near. All eyes followed the car with the flashing red light as it approached.

An EMT hopped out of the car. "What happened?"

"My mother collapsed."

"Excuse me," he stepped in front of Meir, "I need you to move back."

Three teenage boys had gathered on the sidewalk. Another man joined them, followed by a woman not far off.

"Can we take her inside?" Tova asked.

"First let's see what's happening. Did she hit anything when she fell?"

"No. I was standing right next to her and caught her."

"Do you have some pillows? I'd like to raise her head."

"Meir!" Tova snapped.

Meir ran back into the house.

"What's your mother's name?"

"Aidel Lewin. She had a stroke recently." Her voice broke.

"Mrs. Lewin, what day is today?"

"Tuesday."

"Smile for me."

Aidel stared.

"Can you smile for me, Mrs. Lewin? Or just show me your teeth."

Aidel bared her teeth.

Another EMT trotted up to them.

"Can you raise your arms?"

Tova held her breath. Slowly, both of Aidel's arms lifted into the air. Almost immediately, they began to fall.

"Can you hold them up for me?" Aidel closed her eyes and held her arms up.

"That's terrific." He looked up at the second EMT. "Hi, Ari. Recent stroke history."

Ari started taking her vital signs.

"Now squeeze my hands. That's right. Ari, call for a bus."

Meir was back, and they slipped two pillows under Aidel's head. A light was shined in her eyes, an oxygen mask strapped to her face.

"How do you feel now?" the EMT asked.

"Tired. Just tired."

"Can you remember what happened right before you fainted?"

"Yes. I was walking. With my walker." She took a few deep

breaths. "I hit the ramp. Couldn't hold on. I don't know what happened."

Ari examined her arm and looked at the first EMT. "Look at this."

He looked. "Mrs. Lewin, did you drink anything today?"

"Not thirsty."

Tova wrung her hands. "I offered her a drink earlier. She didn't want it."

The ambulance pulled up, drawing a few more spectators. Two paramedics dashed over to Aidel. They quickly consulted with the EMTs, started an IV, and put Aidel inside the ambulance.

As one, Tova and Yerucham made for the back door. Their eyes locked.

Yerucham stepped back. "You go."

Tova nodded and climbed inside. "Call Avner," were her parting words before the doors slammed closed. Eyeing the IV line snaking up from Aidel's arm, Tova took her mother's other hand and closed her eyes. Tehillim flowed from her mouth, from her soul, accompanied by her own words as they tumbled out.

"When we get to the hospital," Aidel said slowly, "I want you to go outside and wait for Tatty. Tell him everything's fine."

"I'll just stay with you a bit," Tova responded. "It'll take a little while till Tatty gets there. Don't worry about a thing."

"Please stop patronizing me. You can stay with me until they take me inside for whatever tests they want me alone for. Then I insist you go wait for Tatty."

Tova made no answer. This ambulance ride was very different from the last one, when half of Aidel's face was frozen. Now Aidel seemed quite herself, and Tova's feelings zigzagged from fear to hope.

The ambulance stopped, and Tova followed Aidel into the emergency room. This time, she knew where she was going. Her understanding of the whole process checked her anxiety, and she was able to observe more than she had the last time. She was now able to discern an ordered pattern to the procedures.

As her mother had instructed, at the first opportunity Tova left to look for Yerucham, leaving her under the care of a very sweet nurse. She found him, sitting next to Meir in the waiting room.

"Meir! What are you doing here?"

"Zeidy asked me to come. He didn't want to be alone."

"Where's Tatty?"

"He must be in shul, his phone's off."

"How'd you get here?"

"Taxi."

Tova turned to her father and paused. Eyes unblinking, Yerucham looked like a wounded sparrow. "Ma looks good," she said. "They just took her now to do a CT scan. Remember, like last time?"

"Did she have another stroke?" Yerucham squawked.

"They're checking that out right now."

"Take me to her."

"I'll take you outside the room where they're doing the test. We're not allowed inside."

He stood, and Meir followed.

"Stay here," Tova ordered.

"I'm almost thirteen, maybe I'm allowed to come."

"Just stay. If Tatty comes, you'll tell him where we are."

"But Tatty doesn't even know—"

A man bumped into Meir. "Excuse me. I'm sorry." He held a screaming toddler and was wholly focused on reaching the desk as soon as possible.

"Let's go," Yerucham said, heading for the doors leading inside.

"But—" Meir attempted.

"Just tell Tatty."

*   *   *

"I don't see a lot of choices here," Gedaliah said, replacing his glasses on his nose. "Whether we make Zev toe the line or give him more leeway, it seems to me like a lose-lose situation."

Avner spelled it out. "Scenario one. We let Zev do it his way, give him what he asks for—books, audiovisual equipment, anything we feel we can give him within acceptable bounds for the yeshivah. He may or may not be able to make the kids listen to him. If he does, they may learn something this year, but I don't relish the impact it will have on them, or the rest of the school, for the long term."

"And if he doesn't succeed doing it his way?"

"If he doesn't succeed, the kids will walk all over him and they'll waste the year."

Gedaliah made a face. "Waste seventh grade, a really crucial year. I should've listened to you and moved Rebbi Fast up to seventh."

"Scenario two. We try to fit a square peg into a round hole, make him toe the line, as you put it. If he manages, we've made a teacher out of him. If he doesn't, the kids walk all over him."

Gedaliah drummed his fingers on the desk. "Scenario three. He quits or I fire him."

"Actually, I see his quitting as a possible consequence of both scenario one and scenario two."

"Even if he gets what he wants?"

"It pains me to say this, but I'm not sure he can make it. As long as he believes he needs to be their buddy, he doesn't stand a good chance of commanding their respect."

A ghost of a smile flitted across Gedaliah's face. "That's my line."

"Well I'm toeing it," Avner quipped, then he grew serious again. "I don't think we're going to be able to satisfy him. He may be willing to stick it out, or he may not. He feels cheated, like we're supposed to be this great yeshivah, and instead we're these old-fashioned, anti-progressive fuddy-duddies."

Gedaliah leaned back in his chair and closed his eyes. "I made a serious mistake, Avner. I'm scared that the students will be the ones to pay the price. I don't see a happy ending to this." He sat forward. "Do you? Do you see any way out of this hole I dug?"

Avner swallowed. "Actually, I do. I've been giving it a lot of thought, and—" Avner felt a buzz on his chest. Unaccustomed to the feeling, it took him a few seconds to realize the source: the cell phone in his jacket pocket. He looked at the number and frowned. "Hello?... Meir, slow down. She's where?" His heart beat fast. "I see. Okay, I'm on my way." He slid the phone back into his jacket. "I'm sorry, Gedaliah, I have an emergency."

Tova led Yerucham through the halls and into the elevator. "Left," she pointed as they exited. They stopped outside the room where she'd left Aidel. "Ma's inside. We have to wait here, we might as well sit down."

Eyes downcast, Yerucham followed and lowered himself into the hard plastic seat.

Tova sat with him until she felt a familiar pressure ballooning inside, then she began to pace. The movement gave vent to the mounting tension and allowed her thoughts to coalesce. Her mother's face seemed symmetrical, her hands steady and even, her speech normal. Surely, this wasn't another stroke. Yet who was to say that a second stroke would result in the same symptoms as before? If a blood clot lodged itself elsewhere in the brain, who knows how it would affect her?

She yearned for Avner's calming presence. Never before had she felt a need for a cell phone, but the inability to contact him at this crucial time was maddening.

It wouldn't be long now. As soon as Meir got ahold of him, he'd drop everything and rush to the hospital. Then she remembered: Meir didn't have a cell phone, nor change for a pay phone; there was no way he could call Avner. Perhaps that was what he'd been trying to tell her. Well, there was nothing she could do about it now. Meir would have to sit out there and occupy himself, and sooner or later Avner would come home to an empty house and wonder. Or maybe Brachie would beat him home and panic.

Tova checked her watch. What was taking so long? She sat down again next to her father. "You okay, Tatty?"

"What's taking so long?" he grunted.

"I'm not sure."

"Go find out."

Tova scanned the corridor. A few scattered patients, some doctors who were obviously unconnected with her mother, a woman holding a bouquet of flowers. She glanced at her father, his features chiseled from stone.

"Tatty..."

A door opened, and a doctor beckoned her. "You can come in now."

Yerucham came suddenly to life, and the two of them went inside.

"Aidel," Yerucham whispered.

"Don't worry, I'm fine," she smiled.

Tova bit her lip. Her mother had said the same thing after her first stroke.

The doctor smiled. "The scans looks fine."

Tova felt as if her heart had just begun beating.

"Your mother simply got dehydrated. We're going to pump another pint of saline into her, then she can go."

Dehydrated. Her mother was only dehydrated. All the worry, all the tension—it was entirely preventable. Her lips pressed into a thin line.

Yerucham broke out in a glorious smile.

"We're going to wheel you back..." The doctor's voice faded in Tova's ears as her muscles went limp. This whole event seemed like a dream—but at least it hadn't become a nightmare. She forced herself to pay attention and get instructions. As soon as the doctor had finished, she left her parents together and hurried outside to find Meir.

He was slouched over two adjoining seats.

"Bubby's fine," Tova smiled. "She got dehydrated. I must call home and speak to Tatty and Brachie. They're probably worried sick not knowing where we are."

"I spoke to Tatty, he's on his way."

"You had money for a pay phone?"

"No, I asked someone to borrow their cell phone."

"Oh." In her worry, she hadn't thought of the obvious. "That was a good idea. Bubby's got to stay here a little longer, then they're letting her come home."

"I reached Tatty on his cell phone. He was still at the yeshivah, said he had some kind of problem he stayed late to deal with. So he's coming straight from there. I didn't speak to Brachie. She's probably wondering where everyone is."

"Yes. Or Shimon, if he's home by now."

"Yeah, or Yoni."

Tova rubbed her eyes. "Oy. I forgot it's still *bein hazmanim*. When Bubby fell, everything else flew straight out of my head."

"I have my MetroCard. If you want, I can go home now and let everyone know that Bubby's okay."

Tova's eyes lit up. "That's a wonderful idea. Thank you."

"No problem. See you at home." He gave a little wave and made for the exit.

Tova watched his retreating back. Why hadn't she ever noticed before how resourceful Meir was?

As she retraced her steps, she pictured her three oldest children finding themselves at home without an adult present, without dinner, and without knowing where anyone was. She laughed softly. There would be *three* adults present, and between them, no one would starve. She wouldn't be surprised to find dinner waiting for *her*. Even if it turned out to be tuna and a plate of sliced vegetables.

Not long after, Avner found them.

"Ma's fine," Tova said quickly.

"*Baruch Hashem!*"

"She was dehydrated," she said with an arch look. "I'll tell you the whole story afterwards."

"I'm so relieved, I can't tell you how worried I was on my way over."

"I'm sure you were."

"Despite the happy ending, I'm sure it wasn't easy for you. I'm sorry I wasn't here when you needed me."

Tova turned curious eyes on Avner. "Meir said you were still in yeshivah, that there was some kind of problem. What happened?"

Avner hesitated. "Maybe now's not the best time."

"No, but once we get home, who knows if we'll have even five minutes. I can leave my parents for a few minutes."

An uncertain smile teased Avner's features. "I'd like that."

They walked until they found a quiet hallway. Avner stopped but didn't speak.

"Well?" Tova prompted. "What's the problem?"

Avner leaned on the wall. "The problem," he began, "is actually part of the solution. It's like this..."

The morning was pleasantly cool, and Avner left the car home. As he walked to yeshivah, he relished the feeling of his feet hitting the sidewalk, each step a tiny jolt of energy coursing through his body, bolstering his nerves. He'd spoken to Tova; he'd made up his mind. He had prepared something to say, and he was going to say it.

Avner's fingers tingled. He marched straight into the office. Shoulders back, he greeted Mrs. Strauss. "Is Rabbi Newman in yet?"

"He's here, but he's not in his office at the moment. You might try the teachers' room."

Gedaliah often made it a point to mingle with the *rebbis* before the day began, but Avner would rather not run into Zev just then. Instead, he climbed the stairs and turned into his own room, waited for the first bell, then checked the office again.

"I'm sorry, Rabbi Lehrfeld, you missed Rabbi Newman, he stepped out again. Should I tell him you're looking for him?"

"That's all right, I'll come back later."

Avner prowled the corridors, circling the building until he found himself back in his own room. He opened his briefcase, slid out a file, and picked up a pen. He stared at the folder for half a minute, then closed it. He'd never be able to concentrate now, who was he kidding?

He stood and made his way to the teachers' room. He knew he'd find it empty, but the process of boiling water and stirring his coffee would keep his hands busy, if not his mind. Avner sipped slowly, reading the notices on the bulletin board, some of them memos from himself.

It was strange, seeing his signature there, carrying such authority. But it was a quiet authority, expanding ripples caused not by the splash of a pebble being tossed in from above, but by the unseen kiss of a fish from below the surface.

Avner tossed his cup in the garbage and went once more in search of Gedaliah. This time he found him in his office, sitting behind his desk and speaking on the phone.

He nodded at Avner and motioned for him to take a seat. "I understand... Yes, that can be difficult... I hear. I suggest that he try to sit through the morning."

Avner closed the door behind him and sat across from the principal.

"If he can't, let him come to me personally... You're welcome." Before the phone was out of his hands, he said, "I've been waiting for you to drop by, you left me in terrible suspense yesterday. On two fronts."

"Sorry about that," Avner said. "My mother-in-law was rushed to the hospital. She's fine, *baruch Hashem*, and she's back home. I wanted to call you at home, but—"

"No apology necessary, I'm glad she's okay. Now, if you'll please put me out of my misery..."

Avner took a deep breath. "We both know that there's a certain... something you need in order to teach the upper grades. I believe Zev has that something."

Gedaliah steepled his fingers. "I agree."

"Given time, he really could become a first-rate *rebbi*."

"I wouldn't have hired him if I thought otherwise."

"Well, if he gives us that time, I will do my best to help him," Avner pledged. "At this point, I've done as much as I can. Now it's up to you to decide which of his demands—his real demands, not what he politely committed to paper—you can honor, and which you absolutely can't. Keeping in mind, of course, that the more leeway he has, the better the chance that he'll stay."

Gedaliah leaned over and extracted a folder from his briefcase. He opened it and passed it to Avner. "Last night, I did just that. I went through this with a fine-tooth comb. Four times. This is what I can give him," he tapped his index finger on a paper, then turned the page, "and this is what I can't."

Avner picked up the paper and read it through. "He's not going to like this."

Gedaliah rested one elbow on his desk and placed his forehead in his palm. "I know." He looked up and threw his hand out. "But I can't sacrifice the entire yeshivah to accommodate

the rest of his demands. I can't change who we are, the direction
we're headed, even for one year. It could trickle down, it could
have permanent ramifications."

"Agreed."

"On the other hand, what are my choices?" He stared at
Avner.

Avner's stomach flip-flopped.

The silence grew between them.

Gedaliah leaned forward. "Well, what's this idea of yours?"

Avner sat up straight. "My idea is that we take your list and
present it to Zev. If he's willing to persevere, then he and I will
work together. He sees me as more of a colleague, less of an
authority figure than you."

"Mm-hmm. And if he's not willing to work with you?"

"Then we replace him."

Gedaliah threw his hands up. "With who?"

Avner's cheeks colored slightly. "With me."

THE DOORBELL RANG. TOVA smoothed out her shirt and forced her features to relax. She opened the door.

"Good morning, Mrs. Lehrfeld. How's your mom today?"

"Good morning, Esti. That's just what I wanted to talk to you about."

Esti's brow creased as she followed Tova inside the house. "Isn't she feeling better? I assumed since you told me to come she had recuperated from the dehydration..."

"Oh, yes, she's feeling much better, *baruch Hashem*." She pointed to the couch. "Please, have a seat for a minute."

They sat across from each other.

"We're all very happy with the progress my mother is making, and we're all grateful to you. My mother has really taken to you, and it's obvious you care about her."

Esti waited.

"From the beginning, I've felt that you push my mother just a little too hard. You don't stop when she's tired, or even when she's in pain. You just keep pushing."

"As I've told you before, I never push your mother past what

I feel she's capable of."

"You say that, but you set the bar very high. Your goals are nearly impossible."

"The goals are hers. I help her reach them."

"Those goals are ones you cajole her into."

"Cajole?" Esti's politic smile appeared as if on cue. "We spend a small part of every session talking. Reviewing what she's accomplished, and mapping out where she wants to go. If by cajoling you mean discussing the value in attaining the next goal, reaching the next step on the road to independence, then I accept the word. I cajole. But I do not coerce."

Tova swatted her hand. "Semantics. You push too hard."

"Mrs. Lehrfeld, you began by saying you are pleased with your mother's progress."

A pause, then, "I am. But you could accomplish the same thing without putting her in danger."

Esti's head drew backwards, her eyes wide. "Danger? What are you talking about?"

"My mother collapsed. Fainted."

"From dehydration."

"Yes. And do you know why she got dehydrated? Because she was outside on a hot day, pushing herself past her limit. She walked another block, and another, probably with your voice ringing in her ears, pushing her."

"Cheering her on, you mean."

Tova shook her head.

"Look, your mother made a mistake, and unfortunately she ended up in the hospital because of it. But it's a mistake any-one can make. A professional athlete, thinking he's invincible. A kid, too engrossed in playing ball to come inside and take a drink. A mother, too busy cooking for Shabbos to stop and sip some water. Dehydration is not terribly uncommon. Now that it's happened once, your mother will be on guard not to let it happen again." A small smile escaped. "And I'm sure you'll be vigilant as well."

Tova's voice was shaky. "She could've gotten seriously injured when she fell. Broken something, or hit her head. It was a miracle that I caught her. We can't take such chances! You think slowing down will ultimately delay her progress? I think she'll have more strength and will get better even faster. The way things are, you have her so over-focused on moving forward that she never stops to think about whether or not what she's doing is good for her. She just forges ahead, no matter what."

"Mrs. Lehrfeld, you and I have the same ultimate goal. The motivation is hers. She is determined to regain full function. My job is to facilitate that."

"Well, I'm also determined to help her regain full function. But this unrealistic pace you set! She follows your lead, she *trusts* you. *You* are the one putting her in danger, taking unnecessary chances. No one thinks this whole process is going to be easy, but you are making her work too hard."

Esti thought for a long moment before answering. "Physical therapy is about getting your body to do what it should be doing but, for some reason, can't. It *is* hard work. But if you have a goal, that work gets put into perspective. Think about a baby, learning to walk. He knows what he wants to do, and he'll try over and over again, falling down dozens—maybe even hundreds—of times, until he masters it."

Tova was losing patience with this conversation, with Esti's whole approach. "You probably do a lot of work with children and babies, and I'm sure you're right about them. But I don't see how that's relevant here."

"Actually, I used to work with babies, but now I specialize in geriatric PT. I see a remarkable likeness between the two populations. The difference is, with young children, people see the need to push past the child's comfort zone. With adults, people suddenly develop a resistance to being pushed."

Tova gazed at her thoughtfully.

"You have children, surely you can understand this. Sometimes, the biggest favor we can do for our kids is to push them past what they feel they can do. It's a little uncomfortable, but it helps them grow. Like a mother watching that baby learn to walk. The baby wants to walk and is willing to take chances. But if the mother is afraid he'll fall, she won't let him try." She looked Tova squarely in the eyes. "Would any mother hold her own child back?"

Tova's breath caught, and a thousand defenses died on her lips.

Long after Esti had gone, her words reverberated in Tova's mind.

The biggest favor we can do for our kids is to push them past what they feel they can do. It's a little uncomfortable, but it helps them grow.

It helps them grow.

There was no denying it: Esti was right. Aidel's progress was a direct result of her inner motivation, coupled with Esti's constant encouragement. Her mother wanted to progress; she had a goal in mind, she pushed herself, she succeeded. Step after painful step, never giving up, always looking for the next mountain to climb.

And Tova had been placing rocks in her mother's way.

It was a painful realization. Still more painful were Esti's final words. *Would any mother hold her own child back?*

Tova sighed deeply. Not only had she encouraged dependence, she hadn't even recognized it well enough to call it by that name. She had been weaving a life together with her family. But instead of carefully guiding the threads as the design unfolded, she had been holding on to them, pulling too tight.

Yet strangely enough, even without this awareness, the family dynamics had been changing. She'd been more involved in her mother's care, less involved with her children. Some people resented that shift when it was thrust upon them; for her, it was a gift—both unlooked-for and unseen.

The front door slammed. Tova dried her hands and went to the living room.

"Hi, Mommy," Meir said. "I'm going to the store with Yoni." He ran upstairs and was already back down when Avner entered, followed by Yoni and Shimon.

"You ready?" Yoni asked Meir.

"Yup."

"We'll be back soon," Yoni said. "I promised Meir a pack of gum."

"Meir's getting the royal treatment," Tova said after they left.

"What else are big brothers for?" Shimon put away his hat. "Is now a good time to talk to both of you?"

Tova looked at Avner.

"Sure," Avner said, "what about?"

"Um, can we sit down?"

Tova sat down on the sofa and Shimon followed. Avner sat in the easy chair, the three of them forming a neat triangle.

"Do you remember meeting Nachum Gavin?"

Avner nodded.

"Yes," Tova said, "while we were looking at paint chips."

"Like I told Tatty, he learns in Toras Yaakov, where Rabbi Newman's son learns. I learned a few *sedarim* there."

"During *bein hazmanim!*" Avner asked. "It must be nearly empty."

"Some now, some before the end of the *zman*." He smiled. "And actually, it's not so empty. Anyway, I've been doing a lot of thinking... and starting in Elul, I want to learn there full time."

Tova's hands grazed the cushions as she leaned forward.

Avner looked no less surprised. "You want to switch yeshivahs? Why?"

"I thought you were happy where you are," Tova said.

"I am. I mean, the learning is fine. But I want a place where the *rosh yeshivah* will notice if I come or not, and ask me what's doing—all the time, not just once in a while."

"And that's the kind of *rosh yeshivah* he is?"

Shimon grew animated. "Yes. I've schmoozed with him a few times. He's... well, he's a tremendous *talmid chacham*, and he understands people."

Tova and Avner shared astonished expressions.

"The yeshivah is very small, with a real emphasis on personal growth." Shimon's voice grew quiet. "I feel like... like I need a *rebbi*. I think it's something I've been missing." He looked up anxiously.

"Well, you caught me a little off guard," Avner said. "But I know Rabbi Newman speaks highly of the place. You have your mind made up?"

"Pretty much." He looked from Tova to Avner.

"I can see you've given this a lot of thought." Tova leaned back. "I'm fine with whatever you and Tatty decide."

Avner threw her a curious glance.

"Any reason you can think of that this wouldn't be a good move?" Shimon asked.

"No," Avner answered after a short pause. "Mommy's right, it sounds like you've given it a lot of thought."

Shimon's smile was a mixture of shyness and delight.

"What are your plans for the last day of *bein hazmanim*?" Avner asked.

"Nothing special. My hat needs a good steaming."

Tova stood. "If you two will excuse me, I'm going to make sure all my *talmidei chachamim* have their shirts ironed in time."

"Thanks, Mommy."

Tova left them to continue the conversation. She had only gone through two shirts when her parents returned from their walk. She heard Yerucham say, "I'll bring you a drink."

Tova switched off the iron and went into the kitchen. "Can I get you something, Tatty?"

"Mommy needs a drink. She's lying down in her room."

Tova poured a glass of cold water and brought it to Aidel, who was propped up on pillows.

"I'm fine," Aidel said automatically. "Just tired from my walk, I need to rest for a few minutes."

"Okay."

Aidel eyed Tova and accepted the water.

Tova hesitated. "Ma, can we talk for a few minutes?"

"I told you, I'm fine, I didn't overexert myself."

Tova swallowed a sudden lump in her throat. "It's not that. I want to ask you something."

"Yes?"

"I mean I want to tell you something."

She put down her water. "Go ahead, then."

"I just wanted to... to apologize."

Aidel's eyes popped open wide. "Apologize? For what?"

"For being overprotective. For making decisions for you." Her voice caught.

"Come here, sit down." Aidel sat up slowly and made room on her bed.

Tova's words came quickly. "I was only trying to help. I didn't realize that I was suffocating you."

Aidel smiled. "You aren't suffocating me, Tovaleh."

"But I've been doing everything for you, even though—"

"Nonsense. You've been taking excellent care of me, and no one could do it better. You've earned the right to be a little over-protective, and when I felt I could take over a task from you, I wasn't shy about saying so, was I?"

"Well, no."

"So there is nothing to apologize for."

Tova drank in Aidel's words.

"If anyone needs space, it's Brachie. She's the one you're overprotecting." She patted Tova's shoulder then sank back down onto her bed. "I'm sorry, Tovaleh, I'm exhausted after my walk. Tell Tatty to wake me in half an hour."

Tova left, closing the door behind her. She knew her mother was right about Brachie—she had just drawn the same conclusion herself—but her mother's words rankled.

She went back to her iron and pulled out one of Yoni's weekday shirts. She began with the collar, her thoughts gently wafting out and up with the rising steam. Her mother's personality had developed a few rough spots since the stroke. She hoped they would smooth out over time.

Still, even perfectly ironed shirts still had a few wrinkles, somewhere.

On Shabbos afternoon, Brachie half-sat, half-lay on the couch, nose deep inside a book.

Meir lounged in the easy chair, munching potato chips and staring out the window. "I can't believe this rain."

Brachie turned a page.

"I mean, I'm glad the heat wave finally broke, but this is crazy. How am I gonna go to *minchah* like this?"

Yoni came down the stairs with Shimon on his heels. A peal of thunder tore through the air, and he gave a low whistle. "Wow, that's some storm."

"Good thing Zeidy went to an early *minchah*," Shimon said.

"Yeah," Yoni agreed. "I'm going to wait it out and catch a later *minyan*."

"Me, too," Meir said.

Brachie looked up from her book. "Can you guys please keep it down? I'm at the most exciting part!"

Yoni looked at the cover. "Oh, you mean the part where they

find out that Ariella is really adopted?"

"Yoni! How could you?" Brachie cried. "You've totally ruined it for me!"

Yoni chuckled. "I'm just kidding. She's not adopted, she's really her sister's twin but her parents never told her her true age."

Brachie's eyes popped open.

"Kidding, kidding. I don't know how it turns out, I'm making this up."

Shimon laughed. "Since when do you read that kind of stuff?"

"Now *you're* kidding, right? I wouldn't read that stuff if I was tied to a chair for a week and someone waved it in front of my face. Teenage girl fiction? Yuck."

"Well, you seem to know enough about it," Brachie teased. "Maybe you're a closet reader."

"I happened to have discussed that book with—" he stopped short. "Someone was telling me about the book, that's all. It was a purely philosophical conversation."

Brachie sniggered. "Philosophical conversation," she muttered. "Right."

"Excuse me." Yoni reached behind Brachie and pulled out a throw pillow. He paced out three steps, turned, and aimed the pillow at Brachie's head.

It hit the book and knocked it to the ground. "Hey! I borrowed that book." She picked it up and inspected it. "You're lucky you didn't damage it."

"Soooo sorry," Yoni grinned, moving farther back.

"Sorry, my foot." Brachie grabbed another pillow and threw it hard at Yoni. She missed by several inches.

"Well, now we're even," Yoni laughed.

Brachie laughed, too, and grabbed another pillow. "No, but now we will be!"

It hit him in the arm. "Oh, yeah? Meir, toss me that one," he pointed to the one on the floor.

"No fair," Brachie cried, throwing her hands over her head. "Two against one."

Shimon unobtrusively picked up the last pillow and lobbed it suddenly at Meir. "Make that two against two."

In seconds, they were all grabbing for pillows and flinging them at each other, sometimes hitting their targets, sometimes not. The laughter grew amidst shouts of "Got you!" and "Duck!"

"Look out, Brachie, I've got him cornered!" Shimon whooped.

Meir dashed behind the easy chair, potato chips flying in every direction as the pillow bounced off the top of his head.

Brachie squealed with delight.

"That's it," Yoni said, "no more mercy." He lunged for two pillows and shouted, "Quick, Meir, grab those two."

Meir scurried on the floor and picked up one pillow and snatched the remaining one from Brachie, who was laughing too hard to protest.

"On the count of three, Meir, we launch an all-out attack. Ready? One, two—" He never finished.

Tova appeared at the bottom of the stairs, arms akimbo and mouth agape. Her eyes narrowed, then her lips pressed into two fine lines. "What, exactly, is going on here?"

Still panting, Yoni looked around, seeing things now through his mother's eyes. Shirts untucked, hair rumpled, couch cushions scattered about, potato chip crumbs dotting the carpet. It looked more like the aftermath of a five-year-old's birthday party than a newly refinished living room.

Shimon bit his lip. "Sorry, Mommy, did we wake you?"

"Yes, you did," Tova said in clipped tones. "I'm surprised you didn't wake Zeidy with the ruckus you children were making."

Brachie picked up a pillow and held it in front of her.

Meir tried to straighten one of the cushions with his knee.

"Well?" Tova demanded.

"We just got a little carried away," Yoni said.

"We'll clean it all up," Brachie said.

Yoni studied his siblings' faces, then met Tova's eyes and braced himself for the list of instructions that was surely going to follow.

Tova's mouth twitched. "You really..." She stopped and shook her head. "I haven't..." Slowly, the corners of her mouth turned up into a small smile. "Yes," she said, her voice light. "I'm sure you *will* clean it up. Together. I'll leave it to you to turn this room right side up before *shalosh seudos*. I'm going upstairs. Call me when it's safe." She turned and climbed the stairs, a soft chuckle escaping.

Yoni blinked at her retreating back, then turned his eyes to Shimon, who returned an equally baffled look.

"Come on, you guys," Brachie said. "It looks like a big mess but it's just a few couch pillows."

"You forgot about the potato chip crumbs," Meir said.

"You work on those," Brachie said, "and you two straighten up."

"Are you the supervisor?" Yoni joked.

"No, I'm going to set up *shalosh seudos*. And when you're done here, you can come help me."

Yoni picked up a pillow and brushed away some crumbs.

"Yes," Shimon said, "let's surprise Mommy."

"She sure surprised me," Meir mumbled.

Brachie smoothed out her hair. "She did take that awfully well."

Yoni clutched the pillow as his eyes wandered up the stairs after Tova. Yes, she certainly had.

Avner waited outside the classroom, fidgeting with the folder in his hand. He checked his watch. Maybe he should wait for Zev in the teachers' room, make it a more casual meeting.

No. He had to meet this—to meet Zev—head on. Zev had to know that there were rules he had to play by.

The bell rang, and Avner's stomach tightened.

The boys tramped out. Zev remained at his desk, rubbing his temples.

"Hello, Zev."

Zev sat up. "Oh, hello Avner. What can I do for you?"

"I spoke to Rabbi Newman like you asked, and I thought we could go over some things."

A smug smile brightened the younger man's face. "Did you explain my position to Rabbi Newman?"

"May I?" Avner indicated a chair.

"Sure."

The chair was slightly too small for Avner's frame, and his knees poked up uncomfortably.

"Let's see what you've got." He reached for the folder.

Avner gripped it tighter. "In a minute."

Zev's hand fell, as did his expression. "I only have a short break. Can we just get down to business?"

"I am. I discussed your requests with Rabbi Newman. He went through your original lesson plan again carefully. Very carefully. He believes in you, and wants you to succeed. As such, he is going to give you everything you asked for—"

"Yes!" he pumped his fist into the air.

"Within reason."

"Oh, please. Everything I asked for is reasonable."

"From your point of view, I can certainly see that. Nevertheless, there are certain practices that are not, shall we say, in the spirit of the yeshivah." He held out a paper.

Zev scanned the paper and threw it down. "This school has a reputation as a top-notch place. I am seriously disappointed."

"I understand your feelings. You had certain expectations

that are not being met."

"Exactly. Sorry, Avner, this isn't good enough."

"I'm afraid it'll have to be."

Zev's young face was deeply creased by a frown. "Whose side are you on, anyway?"

"I'm not taking sides. I'm trying to help the two of you work this out."

"I don't see anything to work out. If I can't do it my way, I can't do it at all."

"Meaning?"

"Meaning he'll have to find a new seventh-grade *rebbi*." He waited.

"I understand. I told Rabbi Newman quite clearly that you would probably not be willing to work under these circumstances."

Zev's smile escaped from behind his sober look. "And?"

"And if that is your final decision, he'll respect it." Avner slipped the paper back into the folder. "Rabbi Newman should be in his office; you can tell him yourself." Avner stood and moved toward the door.

"Avner!"

Avner slowly turned around. "Yes?"

"I... Well, I mean, I..." He loosened his tie. "I can't just quit on him like that. It... It wouldn't be fair."

"I agree. Not to him, or your students. Would you like to give some notice?"

"Yes. I mean no." He stood behind his desk, gripping his chair. "I'm not being fair, am I? I can't just... quit. Besides, the year just started. I'm sure things will get better."

Avner inclined his head. "I admire your attitude."

He left the room and made straight for his own little classroom. His legs quivered as if he'd just run a marathon, and he sat in front of the air conditioner, breathing in the coolness.

He replayed the scene in his mind, a potpourri of emotions filling his chest: thankfulness, satisfaction, and above all, disbelief. Of the many outcomes he'd envisioned as a result of their tête-à-tête, Zev agreeing to their demands was the most favorable and the least likely. He had a sudden urge to do as Zev had done, and pump his fist into the air with a "yes!"

Avner smiled, anticipating Gedaliah's reaction. He should march right over to his office and share the good news.

Instead, he sat, his euphoria mellowing into... what?

He closed his eyes and tried to understand. He felt a heaviness descend on his limbs, a nauseous feeling in his stomach. He had braved Zev—braved his own demons—and he felt... let down. Disappointed.

With stark clarity, he realized that he'd been hoping that Zev would turn him down, would quit on the spot, leaving Avner to fill the vacancy. Avner knew he was a good teacher. No, he was a great teacher. Yes, there would be challenges, new situations he'd never dealt with, but he was ready to face them. Now, he wouldn't get the chance. He would work with Zev, guide him and mold him and help him in every way. And Zev would become, in time, a fantastic educator. He had all the raw ingredients. After a year—or more likely, several years—of investing time and energy into Zev, Avner would remain the same: a quiet, helpful part of the scenery.

Avner shook himself away from these thoughts. It was just as well. He'd probably make a mediocre classroom teacher, anyway. Teaching over twenty kids could not compare to teaching two or three. And discipline? He shuddered. Having one-on-one talks to work out problems, smooth ruffled feathers, or learn from mistakes wouldn't regularly be a viable option.

Bidding farewell to a last, wistful, secret wish, he reached across the table and grabbed a pen. Clicking the ink into position, he flipped open a file and got back to work.

24

THE FRONT DOOR BANGED closed and Brachie joined Tova in the kitchen. "Hi, Mommy. Did Yoni leave his jacket here? It's draped over one of the dining room chairs."

"He didn't leave it, he came home today."

Brachie raised an eyebrow. "Any special reason?"

"He just... needed to come home for something."

"You mean he has a date with Gitty."

Tova didn't respond.

"He usually leaves from yeshivah, why the sudden change?"

Tova shrugged in what she hoped was a casual gesture. "Maybe he wanted to talk to us in person."

Brachie smirked and left the room.

How much had Yoni told Brachie? Tova wondered. Or maybe he'd asked her advice? No, Brachie was the last person Yoni would consult. She knew nothing about dating, she was so naïve, so immature...

And she, Tova, was keeping her that way. A small sigh escaped.

Brachie returned to the kitchen to find Tova still sitting in the same place. "Is everything okay?"

"Yes."

"So why are you just sitting here?"

Tova looked around in confusion. "I don't know," she confessed. "I was just... thinking."

Brachie looked at her strangely.

"How was school?"

"Boring."

"Boring?"

"Yeah. We have a class called—get this—the Laws of Insurance."

"Are all your classes so boring?"

"Not all. Disease Classification is pretty interesting. Some others, too. But I can't say it's a thrill to go." Brachie sat. "I'm starving, what's for dinner?"

"Chicken, I'll serve you."

"Know who I met today? Breindy Wolfson. She's doing the same program as me, but she's been sick. I told her I'd go over my notes with her."

"That's thoughtful of you." Tova placed a plate before Brachie.

"Thanks."

Tova sat down again. "Can I ask you something?"

"Sure."

"Are you sorry you're in this program?"

Brachie's fork froze in midair. "What?"

"Now that you understand what kind of work this is, maybe you regret taking medical billing and coding."

The fork clinked against her plate.

"Well, do you?"

"Some of the classes make me want to put my head down and sleep. But this stuff's just preparation. The job itself sounds pretty interesting. Once I learn all this background material, I think I'll like it."

"More than being a *sheitel macher*?"

"Forget that. I've never been good with hair. Plus standing on my feet all day, making conversation when I'm not in the mood, smiling at women who drive me crazy because one hair's out of place..." She speared a string bean. "Do we have any Dr. Pepper? We were out yesterday."

Tova moved to stand, but Brachie jumped up. "I'll get it, I just wanted to know if we had any."

"It's on the door of the fridge."

Brachie poured herself a glass. "Now can I ask you something?"

"Of course."

"Why are you asking me all these questions?"

Tova smiled self-consciously. "I was just thinking that, well, maybe I was too pushy about you taking this program, and I was worried that... that you did it because I wanted you to, not because you really wanted it."

Brachie looked down.

"Be honest," Tova said.

"Well... yeah, I didn't take the course for me."

"You didn't?" It came out as a whisper.

"No. I did it for you."

Tova flinched. "You... did it for me?"

"Well, you thought it was a good idea," Brachie said.

Tova felt as if she'd swallowed two aspirins without water.

"But I had the whole summer to think it over, plus the time I've spent so far in class. I'm *glad* you pushed me."

The aspirin began to dissolve. "You are?"

"Yeah. You know, I was thinking like a kid—what's fastest, not what's best."

"And medical billing and coding is... *best*?"

"I'm sure it will be. I just have to get through the dull stuff, be patient and all that. But like I said, the work itself sounds pretty interesting once I start doing it."

"Can you be patient for two years?"

"I have *shiurim* some nights, and I'm learning how to cook, and I get to spend lots of time with Bubby and Zeidy... So, yeah, I'm fine."

Tova's eyes brightened.

"I was just telling Rena yesterday," Brachie continued, "the time is flying."

Tova reached out to straighten Brachie's placemat, then pulled her hands back. "Are you and Rena back on speaking terms?"

"We were never *not* speaking, but we're back to normal."

"I'm glad." Tova wandered over to the *milchig* sink and began scrubbing. Her thoughts bounced around inside her like a rubber ball, and she was unaware that Brachie was still speaking until she was ready to leave.

"...with Breindy. See you later."

Tova looked up to watch Brachie's retreating back. She put down the sponge and stepped over to the *fleishig* side. Only after she began scrubbing did she realize that Brachie had washed her own dish.

Avner pulled up to the curb, shut the engine, and peered at his house through the streaked window. Yoni would be there by now. He said had something he wanted to tell them.

There was little doubt as to what Yoni was going to say. He was ready to hear it, but was Tova?

Instead of going up the stairs as he usually did, Avner ascended the ramp, running his hand along the railing. The paint was bright and intact, just as it was along the porch and inside the living room as well. So new, so... unlived in. He was almost looking forward to the first mark on the wall.

He found Tova in the dining room, adjusting the tablecloth so that its lines ran perfectly parallel to the table.

"Hi. Where's Yoni?" he asked.

"Upstairs. He said I should call him when you get home." Her hands smoothed out the fabric.

Avner waited.

"He's ready, isn't he," Tova said quietly.

"Looks like it."

Tova's hands dropped to her sides. "I'm having second thoughts."

"A bit late for that now, isn't it?"

"They're not engaged yet."

"No, but it looks like they will be before long."

Tova walked around the table, moving each chair a fraction of an inch. "I have a sinking feeling about this whole thing."

Avner's brow furrowed. "Intuition?"

"That's just it, I don't know if it's intuition or just... cold feet."

"What does your heart tell you?"

A smile, almost too brief to be seen, flitted across her face. "That Gitty's a wonderful girl and she'll take good care of Yoni."

"But...?"

"She's too old for him."

"We agreed it's just a prejudice and that Yoni could decide."

"I know. I can't seem to move past that prejudice, even though it's not logical."

"So fake it."

"Excuse me?"

"Fake it. Tell yourself—and anyone else who will raise an eyebrow when they hear—that it doesn't matter."

"You want me to pretend something I don't feel?"

Avner walked around the table until he was standing right in front of her. "I want you to show on the outside what you really *do* feel on the inside."

"But inside I'm torn!"

"That's only your insecurity speaking." He looked into her

eyes. "Am I right?"

Tova met his gaze then looked away. At length, she said. "Yes." She ran a finger across the top of the chair, then suddenly laid her hand down flat across the top. "Right. Time to move on."

Anver was surprised. Not with Tova, that she'd come to that conclusion, but with himself—that he'd expected her to do so.

None of them were quite what they were just a few months ago, were they?

Except him. He was exactly what he was before: a tutor.

Tova must have seen his expression change. "What's the matter?"

"Nothing, I..." His voice trailed off. He was being unfair—to one of them, at least. "The seventh-grade *rebbi* decided to keep his job. I'm staying the tutor."

"That must have been hard to swallow. Rabbi Newman told you today?"

"Actually, I found out a few days ago."

Tova's eyes narrowed, her head angled to the side.

"I was taking my own advice, putting on the outside what I feel on the inside." He attempted a smile. "The students are better off with him. He's young and dynamic, and it's unsettling for them to get a new *rebbi* after the year's started."

"Are you disappointed?"

"I want what's best for the students." He looked at his watch. "Let's call Yoni."

Tova hesitated only for a second. "Okay."

Yoni entered the room, his confident stride and contented grin sweeping away the cobwebs of Avner's discomfort. He looked from Avner to Tova. "I guess you know what I want to talk to you about."

Avner snuck a peek at Tova. Her fingers wrapped themselves around each other, but her smile was genuine. "We have some idea..."

*　　　*　　　*

As he walked down the stairs, Yoni eyed Meir who lay sprawled out on the couch, a book resting on his chest.

"Not such a good book?" Yoni asked.

"It's a great book. I was just thinking," Meir said.

"About what?"

"Lots of things."

"Mmm. Hey, you want to take a walk with me? It's really nice outside."

"Sure." Meir jumped up and put on his shoes.

Yoni led the way down the avenue and then toward a quiet, tree-lined street. "See? Much nicer than sitting inside."

"Okay, Yoni, what gives?"

Yoni laughed.

"Really. You're never home during the week, and you were also home this Shabbos."

Yoni smiled self-consciously. "I'm not quite sure how to tell you this."

Meir stopped short. "Don't tell me you're going away again. I can't believe Mommy's letting you go back to learn in Eretz Yisrael!"

Yoni shook his head. "I'm not going back. Well, not right now, anyway."

"So what is it?"

Yoni started walking again. "I may be going away, though."

"Where?" Meir demanded.

"Not far." He saw Meir's face. "Okay, okay. The deal is that I'm getting engaged."

Meir spun and grabbed Yoni's arm. "When?"

"Tomorrow night."

His eyes widened. "Where are you going to live?"

"We're going to start out in Brooklyn somewhere."

"And after that?"

"We'll see."

Abruptly, Meir let go of Yoni. "Mazel tov."

"Hey, I'm still just a phone call away. Besides, you'll come to us for Shabbos and we'll get to spend more time together than we do now."

Meir looked up at Yoni. "I guess. But it'll be different."

"Yes, it will. But so will you. In a few months, you'll be bar mitzvah, and after that you'll be starting a new yeshivah. Changes happen to us, and around us, all the time. You gotta roll with it."

"Like Tatty does."

Yoni smiled. "Yes. Like Tatty." He thought for a minute and added, "And like Mommy."

Meir was bouncing a superball on the kitchen floor. Tova sailed past him, a full laundry basket perched on her hip.

The phone rang. "Please answer that," she said from halfway down the stairs. "Tell whoever it is that I'll call them back in five minutes." She simply had to finish the laundry today. Tomorrow they would be busy with Yoni and his future in-laws—

She dropped the basket. Yoni's in-laws. Her *mechutanim*. An excited shudder ran up her spine. This wasn't the way she'd imagined things would be—her second child getting married before the first, and to an older girl!—but her anticipation was growing stronger than her dread.

Tova sorted through the piles quickly and tossed in a shirt load, then pulled out the darks from the dryer. When she got to one of Yoni's pajama shirts, a wave of anxiety rolled over her once more. How could she let Yoni get engaged to this... stranger? This girl he barely knew? That *she* knew even less?

What would it be like for Tova not to be washing his clothes, folding his socks? The thought made her smile. Gitty would probably be bringing her laundry over to her mother's house for a while.

"Who was on the phone?" Tova asked, back in the kitchen.

"Someone named Nava Rubin."

Tova spun around. "Na'ama Rubin?"

"Could be. Yeah, I think so."

"Did she say anything?"

"Just that she called."

"That's it?"

"You should call her back. Tonight, she said."

Tova abandoned the laundry basket on the floor and dashed upstairs. "Hi, Na'ama?"

"No, you want to speak to my mother?"

"Yes, please."

Tova smoothed out her blouse.

"Hello?"

"Hi, Na'ama, this is Tova. I got a message that you called."

"Oh, thanks for calling back. I— No, Rivkie, I need the phone now. Sorry, Tova. The baby woke up, and his crying woke up two of the others. Things are a little loud here right now."

Tova forced the words out. "Should I call you back later?"

"No, it's fine. I really need to speak to you today, and I'm going out later. I spoke to— Oh, hold on a second."

A knock sounded in her ear as the phone was obviously put down somewhere. Tova's fingers rapped impatiently on the dresser. The crying abated.

"Sorry. I settled them now, so we should be able to talk for a few minutes." She gave a little cough. "Right. Okay. So, the reason I called you is that— No, Rivkie, let her crawl, it's fine. Sorry. The reason I called you is, well... This is going to sound a little funny. Or maybe it'll come as a bit of a shock, after you've already met the Schechters." She paused, as if waiting for a response.

Tova held the phone in an iron grip, every second an eternity.

"It just that— Rivkie, I can't talk with the baby pulling at

the phone cord like that. Can you please move her over there?
Thanks. Now, as I was saying, this may sound very strange,
after you've met the Schechters, and after everything Yoni must
have told you. It's only—"

Suddenly, the phone went dead.

Tova froze. She stared at the phone, her knuckles white.
Trying to shake off the heaviness in her arms, she fumbled to
hit redial.

The line was busy.

She tried the number again. And again.

Perhaps Na'ama was trying to call *her* back. She threw the
phone down on the bed and stood by the dresser, her index finger hammering away on its polished surface.

Her face was pinched, her shoulders cramped. Gitty must
have given it more thought and decided that Yoni wasn't for her.
Or maybe the Schechters didn't like her and Avner; something
must have rubbed them the wrong way.

After another agonizing minute, she grabbed the phone and
once more hit redial. After half a ring, the phone was answered.

"Tova, I'm so sorry, my baby pulled out the phone cord, and
I had to fiddle with it to make it work again. I was just about to
call you back."

With great effort, Tova made a polite comment and waited.

"I know you met Gitty's parents already, so I hope this
doesn't come as a surprise."

This was it. She was about to say the *shidduch* was off.

"Really, they could have called you directly, but, well, I guess
they were feeling a little awkward, so they asked me to do it,
and I said I would. I hope you don't mind."

Tova pulled at her neckline, struggling to take a full breath.

"The Schechters want to meet with you again. They want to
work out a better date for the wedding. Gitty's older sister is due
the end of November, and..."

Tova sank down onto her bed, barely hearing what Na'ama was saying. They didn't want to call it off, just reschedule. *They just wanted to reschedule!*

Tova tried to concentrate. After they hung up, she relived the waterfall of emotions that had cascaded over her during the past few minutes. Fear had converged into eddies of panic, coming up against islands of logic and coolly swirling around them, finally emptying out into a pool of relief.

Yes, that was what she felt—relief. And the force of her feelings pushed aside every last misgiving about Yoni marrying Gitty. She wasn't just resigned to their marriage; she was truly delighted.

Avner's eyes twinkled back at him as he looked in the mirror and straightened his tie. Strains of "Did you check if the flowers were delivered?" and "I can't find my Shabbos shoes" reached his ears, assuring him that the family was nearing the final stages of readiness.

He picked up his hat, examined it, then reached for a hat brush. After one stroke, his cell phone rang. He frowned, debated, checked the number. He debated again, put down the hat and brush, then picked up the phone.

"Hey, Avner, it's Zev."

"Hello, Zev."

"I saw the note up in school today."

He waited.

"Mazel tov."

"Thank you very much. I hope I'll be seeing you at the *vort* later."

"Actually, no, I can't make it. Something else came up."

Avner's mouth twitched. "I understand. Well, it was nice of you to call—"

"Well I guess I want to explain. I'm sure Rabbi Newman and

some of the other *rebbis* will be there."

"I'm sure." Avner ran his fingers along the horsehair bristles.

"And it would be a little awkward for me."

Avner put the phone down on the dresser and hit speaker. "Why awkward?" He reached for his hat again.

"Well, you know, because I'm not working there anymore."

Avner lunged for the phone, dropping the hat on the dresser. "What are you talking about?"

"Oh, didn't you hear?"

Avner pulled his tie loose and jammed the phone against his left ear. "I left early today. You know, for the *vort*."

"Oh. Well, I quit."

Avner ran a hand over his eyes. "You quit? Just like that?"

"Yeah. I found a different job."

Avner could almost see the smug smile roll across Zev's face.

"There was a sudden opening in a big *kiruv* organization where I interviewed last year. They called me, I accepted. I'm starting tomorrow. There, my talents will be appreciated."

"But how can you do that? Leave just like that, without a replacement, with no notice?"

"You can sub for a few days till Rabbi Newman finds someone new. I'm sure you can handle that."

Avner's spine snapped erect. "I'm sure I can."

"Anyway, I just called to say mazel tov. I'm sure you're pretty busy, I'll see you around."

"Yes, I guess so."

"Oh, and thanks."

Avner blinked at the phone in his hand. Gently, afraid that it would shatter, he eased the phone down onto the dresser.

He stared at it, suspended in time.

Until he began to feel a pull toward the mirror. It beckoned him, and he felt almost guilty as he heeded its call.

He looked at himself, fascinated, as his eyes narrowed and a small, intense smile stretched across his face.

Tova let her eyes sweep the room. With a tingle of pleasure, she surveyed the scene: Gitty, whispering something in her little sister's ear that set her running off with delight; Aidel, pouring herself a drink, her walker nowhere in sight; Brachie, being introduced to Gitty's Aunt from Chicago.

This *shidduch* had been easy. Well, it had been easy once she'd agreed to let Yoni and Gitty go out. As far as the couple themselves was concerned, there were no hesitations, no agonizing doubts, no what-ifs. Gitty had slowed things down a bit along the way, but like Yoni said, that was not hedging, that was simply a demonstration of Gitty's maturity.

And now here she was, standing at Yoni's *vort*, grateful and buoyant. Tova's eyes swept the room, mentally thanking every single person who came and dropped another pearl in her basket of *simchah*.

Her complacent feelings were suddenly halted by the one person whom she dreaded seeing.

Esti.

The hum of the party dulled into an incoherent buzz as their last conversation echoed in her mind, an unintended admonition. She had avoided Esti since that moment, not wanting her to realize that she'd struck a nerve. Tova was utterly, painfully humiliated.

Tova shrank into herself as Esti made her way inside the room and held her breath as Esti homed in on Aidel. She stood frozen, watching in silent dismay as Aidel introduced Esti to Gitty and her mother.

Her heart beat fast as Esti's head swiveled around the room. She drew a sharp intake of breath as Esti's eyes found their target.

A smile lit up Esti's face. She made one last comment and kissed Aidel's cheek. She was on her way over.

Tova swallowed hard and willed herself to stand straight.

"Mazel tov," Esti said, extending a hand.

"Thank you," Tova said, her voice as stiff as her handshake.

"After all you've been through lately, it's so nice to have a *simchah* in the family. Your mother speaks highly of Gitty."

"Yes."

The buzz of the room seemed to grow, mocking the silence between them.

"Well, mazel tov again." Esti nodded and stepped away.

"Wait."

Esti stopped. "Yes?"

"I... I wanted to thank you."

Esti's chin inched up by degrees.

"My mother has made remarkable progress."

"Your mother is a remarkable woman."

Tova flushed. "And you have been the driving force behind her. She could never have gotten so far without you. Certainly not so quickly."

The smile Tova knew so well spread across Esti's face. "It's your mother who did all the work."

"You're too modest. You are... the most dedicated therapist I know. You are skilled and focused and encouraging."

"And pushy."

Tova had to smile. "I'm sorry for getting in your way. I can't thank you enough."

"You don't have to. I'm going to stick with your mother until she chases me out on both feet and with two hands."

"I'm glad."

Esti fixed a steady gaze on Tova. "Thank you, Mrs. Lehrfeld."

"Thank you, Esti."

They parted. Suddenly released from the invisible ropes binding her, Tova felt lighthearted.

She saw Brachie slip into the kitchen and joined her.

"Hi, Mommy. It's some crowd, isn't it? This is *so* much fun!"

Another voice answered. "I think so, too."

"Shimon, you scared me," Brachie said. "What are you doing in here?"

"I could ask you the same question."

"I hid a bottle of Dr. Pepper in the fridge for myself."

"Typical."

Brachie poured herself a cupful.

Shimon put out his hand. "Aren't you going to offer me any?"

"You always drink Sprite."

"Maybe it's time for a change."

Brachie sniggered. "Sure thing." She poured a second cup. "For Gitty," she explained. "I'm trying to convert her."

Shimon shook his head at her retreating back, then turned to Tova. "Yoni asked me to find some more potato chips for Gitty's little brother. Any clue where they'd be hiding?"

Tova pointed. "Have a look in that corner."

"Thanks." Shimon poked through a few bags, unearthed the potato chips, and poured some into a bowl.

Tova watched him carefully. "You look happy."

"Yeah, I am."

"You're really okay with this whole thing? You *are* three years older than Yoni."

Shimon grinned. "So's Gitty."

Tova laughed.

"I wouldn't mind Brachie getting engaged before me, either."

She shot Shimon a curious look.

"Yeah, she told me about the guy Mrs. Fogel is setting her up with. She wanted some advice."

Tova gave a slight shrug. "It's different for a girl to get married younger. Yoni's your younger brother."

"I mean it, Mommy, I'm thrilled for Yoni. I wasn't really ready to get married till now."

"And now you think you are?"

"Yeah, I do."

A round of "*Siman Tov*" broke out from the living room.

"I better bring those chips. They'll probably be starting with the speeches soon."

"Okay. Just tell me, how's Zeidy?"

"He's having a great time. Yoni insists on introducing him to every single person in the room."

"That's wonderful."

"How's Bubby?" Shimon asked. "When she came in, she looked almost her old self again."

"She's fine. Go on, don't keep Gitty's little brother waiting."

Tova lingered in the kitchen another moment, pondering Shimon's words. Her mother may not exactly be back to her old self—perhaps she never would be—but she was her new self. And that was just fine.